Deep Trouble

MARY CONNEALY

BARBOUR
PUBLISHING

Other Books by Mary Connealy

Cowboy Christmas (a prequel to *Deep Trouble*)

Sophie's Daughters series:

Doctor in Petticoats
Wrangler in Petticoats
Sharpshooter in Petticoats

Lassoed in Texas series:

Petticoat Ranch
Calico Canyon
Gingham Mountain

Montana Marriages series:

Montana Rose
The Husband Tree
Wildflower Bride

Nosy in Nebraska (a cozy mystery collection)

Cover design: Lookout Design, Inc.

For more information about Mary Connealy, please access the author's website at the following Internet address: www.maryconnealy.com.

Published by Barbour Publishing, Inc., P.O. Box 719, Uhrichsville, OH 44683, www.barbourbooks.com

Our mission is to publish and distribute inspirational products offering exceptional value and biblical encouragement to the masses.

 Member of the
Evangelical Christian
Publishers Association

Printed in the United States of America.

Dedication/Acknowledgments

This book is dedicated to my new grandson. He'll be here by the time this book comes out, but this dedication has to be turned in NOW. His parents are sure he's a boy. So I'm being brave and claiming that truth months before it's been made official. Welcome to the family little one. This grandmother business is fantastic.

And I would like to acknowledge three books I referred to often while writing *Deep Trouble*, beyond my own research and one long-ago visit of my own to the Grand Canyon. The first is *Hiking Grand Canyon National Park, a Falcon Guide*. I went over and over and over the maps and trails in this book trying to figure out where my heroes could have found a lost village and descended into the canyon. *The True North Series: Your Guide to the Grand Canyon-A Different Perspective* by Tom Vail, Michael Oard, Dennis Bokovoy, and John Hergenrather—this book is full of the most dazzling pictures of the canyon along with many fundamental facts accompanied by scripture. *The Man Who Walked Through Time* by Colin Fletcher is one man's impressions of the canyon as he walked through it.

These books helped me immensely. I tried to do justice to the Grand Canyon, even though the more I researched it, the more I realized I could only do my best and fall short of its true majesty.

And I'd like to thank fellow author Sandra Leesmith. She lives near the Grand Canyon and gave me a few details that really made the book come alive. Thank you, Sandra.

One

May 1881

Where's the gold?"

Shannon Dysart staggered back in the face of her guide's fury then squared her shoulders. Showing weakness to Lobo Cutter was a mistake. Hiring him was a mistake. Leaving St. Louis was a mistake.

"Mr. Cutter, I employed you to help me find an ancient city. We've done that. It's spectacular. Imagine the research—"

"A city of *gold*." Cutter stormed right up to Shannon's face. The spurs on his boots made an ugly metallic ring with every step. "Them was your own words when you asked me to sign aboard this trip into the West."

Shannon stepped back again, and her foot slipped into nothingness. She glanced back at the dead drop behind her.

Cutter's fists clenched and moved too close to the Colt six-shooter in his holster. He was a brute of a man, brought along mainly to handle the pack animals. But once they'd found this place, he'd worked as hard as any of the six people in their expedition searching these ruins.

But he'd finally faced the same fact Shannon just had—after three days of searching this ancient cliff city: there was no gold.

"I wasn't searching for this city to make myself rich, Mr. Cutter. My father's research was—"

"Your *father* was an old fool. Everyone in the West has heard the stories of Delusional Dysart."

Everyone in the West? Shannon flinched. She hadn't realized that. Everyone in the world of ancient studies, yes, had come to reject her father's work. Professor Delmer Dysart. The Delmer had been twisted into Delusional. Everyone in the three universities that had fired him sneered at his theories. But everyone in the West, too? What had her father done to be so infamous? It was the rejection and outright mockery by the other scholars of ancient history that drove Shannon to retrace her father's footsteps and prove him right.

The rest of the world was enamored of ancient Greece and the ruins of Rome, but her father had believed America had its own ancient wonders. Chief among them the Seven Cities of Gold. He'd devoted his life to searching for the lost kingdom of Quivera. But these abandoned cliff dwellings were fascinating. A find of great importance. No gold, true, but still of scientific merit.

"Where are we going next?" Cutter stepped closer and jabbed Shannon in the chest with a beefy finger. She had no room left to back away. He looked savage, more animal than man. His teeth were bared.

No man had ever put hands on her before, and her heart pounded with fear even as she fought to remain calm and use reason on this unreasonable man.

Her father's maps, what was left of them, were hidden in a pocket she'd sewn into the lining of her riding skirt. Shannon had been painfully careful never to let any of this group see where she hid them.

"I want to stay here longer, Mr. Cutter." Shannon could take notes for weeks, and just this place alone would help her gain respect in the field of ancient studies. But her father's name would be even more deeply blighted because he hadn't brought out news of this place. Instead, he'd ignored it and gone on searching for gold. "We've got all summer to travel on. These ruins are beautiful. There's no gold, but—"

Cutter grabbed the front of her gingham blouse with one hand and her hair with the other. "Shut up."

Shannon saw her dark braid gripped like it was a leash in his massive hands and was so shocked she couldn't even cry out in fear. She was an academic like her father. She'd spent her life studying books and artifacts. This expedition was her first attempt at finding old ruins. And it was certainly her first time to be threatened and abused by an uncivilized brute.

"We go now." He lifted her to her tiptoes. "I know you've got another map. Hand it over."

"Stop this right now." Shannon's temper erupted. "I am paying you—"

Cutter, with Shannon's blouse clutched in one hand, shoved her backward. She felt the ground crumble under one foot and grabbed at the man's ugly fist.

"The map. Where is it?"

Keeping control of her maps was something Shannon was fanatic about, but she was also a bit paranoid, which might make all the difference now. She wouldn't give up too easily. "No, they're mine."

Another shove and her feet went out from under her. She dangled over the edge of the cliff dwelling. His grip was the only thing keeping her from plunging to her death.

A frantic look around the cave showed the avid greed in the faces of the others, including two women she'd brought along for propriety's sake. They'd seemed so helpful and honorable, excited even, as they'd searched the cliff dwellings for the last three days.

Until they'd reached this last cave and found only more rock.

The people with her were all on Cutter's side. She'd hired the man on a recommendation from someone she respected at the university. Cutter was known for tracking in the West. He'd offered to find a crew, including women, so all would be proper. Including her, six of them had made this journey. Now all of her traveling companions practically licked their lips as Cutter tried to shake loose a secret that led to a city of gold.

"The map. Now. Or I let go then search your dead body." He shook her so hard her head whipped back and forth. She was strangling, and a rending sound told her the fabric Cutter had a grip on wasn't going to hold.

A compulsive glance down was dizzying. They were on the highest level of the cliff houses. A ladder was the only way up. Cutter was showing her there were two ways down.

"I'll give it to you. Please, pull me back."

Cutter yanked her back to solid ground then threw her down at his feet. Her head struck rock, light burst behind her eyes, and the air was battered out of her lungs. Gasping and disoriented, she could only scoot away, on her back, as one of the women knelt beside her and dug deep in Shannon's pockets.

"No!" Shannon shoved at the woman's hands. Ginger. With tight curls of hair and crooked teeth that hadn't looked ugly until just now. "Get away from me."

Ginger backhanded her across the face, and her head cracked against stone again. Her vision blurred.

Cutter went to her knapsack that she always kept at hand.

"Go down and search her bedroll," Cutter ordered.

Shannon felt warm liquid run over her lips and reached up to find her nose bleeding. Ginger frisked Shannon with crude, rough hands and glared as if she wanted an excuse to strike again.

Pressing her wrist to her nose to staunch the flow of blood, Shannon let the woman's hands roam over her. What choice did she have? She could only pray Ginger wasn't smart enough to suspect Shannon's tricks.

The two other men in the expedition scrambled down the ladder, the rungs creaking. Shannon wondered how old that ladder was. They'd found it lying on one of the lower levels of the cliff houses and had used it, but very carefully. It was missing every other rung at least, and the wood was brittle from age. There were no trees close by to build another.

They'd found handholds to climb to the lower caves, but when those had revealed no gold, the upper levels had taunted them. This morning they'd risked using that ladder and climbed up here to search and find. . .nothing.

Shannon had talked of research and history and truth, and these ruins were magnificent. But when she'd risked her neck to climb that old ladder and found only more rock and dirt, she'd admitted in her heart that she'd wanted the gold, too.

"I've got something." Ginger pulled a map out of Shannon's pocket triumphantly. She unfolded it with reckless speed.

"Be careful of that." Shannon sat up and reached for it.

Ginger shoved Shannon flat on her back. With a harsh laugh Shannon had never heard from the woman before, Ginger rose to her feet and turned to the other woman in the expedition.

Lurene was a quiet woman, dark haired and hardworking. Of all of them, Lurene had been the friendliest. But none showed on her face now. Only cruelty and sharp intelligence as she reached for the battered map Shannon had found among her father's effects. "Just take her whole saddlebag," Lurene ordered. Yes, the woman *ordered* Cutter. When had Lurene started giving orders? Lurene studied the papers Ginger had found.

"You'll never understand that map without my help. My father encoded it."

"I've been watching you." A smile revealed a row of wolfish teeth that looked sharp enough to rip someone's throat out. "I've figured out the code you're using."

Shannon's stomach twisted as Lurene took one short stride to be right at her side. "We don't need you anymore, Miss Dysart."

Shannon got her elbows braced, waiting for the next shove.

With a soft *whoosh* of metal on leather, Lurene produced a razor-sharp knife.

A moan of pure terror escaped Shannon's clenched jaw.

"Don't kill her." Cutter came up beside Lurene.

"We have to. I don't want her alive. If she gets to a town, she can call in a marshal, and we'll all have a price on our heads."

"I've got a better idea." Cutter's smile chilled Shannon's blood to ice.

Lurene looked away from Shannon. "We've got no choice."

"Sure we do. A choice that's a lot more fun than slitting her throat."

Shannon swallowed hard. She was very fond of her throat. And considering the cruelty of these people, what could Cutter have in mind that was more. . .fun?

"We leave her here." Cutter laughed.

"She might be able to walk out. We can't risk it."

"No, I don't mean *here*." Cutter made a grand gesture at the rugged wasteland around the cliff village. Then he pointed at his feet. "I mean *here*."

A smile broke out on Lurene's face that showed those canine teeth again. "And take the ladder."

Their smug satisfaction doubled the pace of Shannon's terrified pulse.

"No, please! You can't!" They'd been here three days. They'd worked hard trying to reach the treacherous upper caves without that ladder. They'd found it too sheer, completely lacking in footholds. Then they'd found the ancient ladder, nearly buried in generations of accumulated desert sand. The very existence of the ladder showed that the folks who built these dwellings had needed them to get to this top row of homes.

She regretted crying out instantly. It only made these outlaws happier that she was frightened.

"After you." Cutter tugged his hat low on his brow. His words sounded grand and gentlemanly. Instead, they were obscene considering what they planned for her.

Ginger headed down. Lurene was right after her.

Cutter turned to Shannon, and his look was pure evil.

She had a heart-sickening moment to realize she was here, alone with him. Defenseless. Bleeding. Trapped.

Then he laughed and left her.

Alone with no water. No food. No way down.

She saw the top of the ladder wobble, and even knowing it was futile, she threw herself at it and caught it, stopping it from falling away. She looked down at Cutter, and the man looked up.

He let go of the ladder with a smile on his face, and for a second she thought maybe he'd changed his mind. Maybe he'd give her a fighting chance to walk out of here.

Instead, he pulled his gun and aimed straight at. . .the ladder. Aiming off to the side, he blew one rung away, then a second and a third. His bullets ricocheted and hit the cave.

Screaming, Shannon hung on doggedly to her only chance for escape. Then the side of the ladder in her right hand snapped. Shards of wood cut her hand, and she cried out again to the sound of Cutter's laughter. She pulled her hand back to find she held a foot-long section of wood. Useless.

Then the shooting changed, aimed straight for the roof of her cave.

Shannon felt a bullet hit just inches from her head and shatter a rock that gouged into her skin. She rolled for the back of the cave, screaming in terror.

Two

Gabriel Lasley heard gunfire. Next screaming. He spurred his horse and raced toward the trouble with a prayer on his lips.

It sounded miles away, but he couldn't be sure. Sound carried forever in the desert. Canyon walls echoed, and soon enough the sound seemed to come from all directions.

But Gabe had spent years riding with the cavalry, and he knew the land.

The gunfire died away.

The screaming cut off.

The thunder of his horse's hooves and the wind rushing past his ears were the only sounds. But he knew right where the screaming and gunfire had come from. Or he hoped he knew.

Investigating would send him on a long run in the wrong direction—away from the nearest town and a badly needed drink of water. But a woman screaming, out here where there weren't any women, well, Gabe couldn't see he had much choice. Her screams, long faded to silence, were still in his head, begging for help.

He slowed as he drew near the spot where he was sure the

trouble had come from. Caution. He saw tracks and followed them to what looked like a dry spring bed up a rugged hill. The tracks were fresh. Whatever had happened here had to be the source of the gunfire and screams. It also was clearly over.

He slipped the tie-down loose on his Colt and followed the tracks with the care of a man who'd ridden for the cavalry for nearly a decade. He was too late to stop whatever had happened, but maybe not too late to dig a grave and see the dead given some respect, see if there were families to contact.

He got to the top of the narrow arroyo and pulled his horse to a dead stop. He was looking at something he couldn't believe.

A mountain carved up into—homes?

Shaking his head, he looked closer, trying to make the structure in front of his eyes something created by nature. But it wasn't. These were man-made. The lowest levels had structure to them. Rockwork that formed walls. There were depressions in the rocks above the structures. Cave openings, multiple levels of them. He counted four layers, one above the other, of what had to be dwellings of some kind. And now abandoned.

Gabe had never heard of this. He was just passing through the area now, but he'd ridden with the cavalry in Texas and the Southwest for years. How could this have gone undiscovered? And who had found it now and died?

Fascinated, Gabe walked his horse into this lost valley, then swung down and tied the gelding to one of a thousand mesquite bushes. The wind whistled through the hills and canyons. It was the only sound, and that moaning wind told him no one else was here.

Those tracks cut in the dust were the only sign that humans had ever passed through here. Seven horses in, seven out. Judging by the tracks, he'd say two pack horses, maybe three. So five people had come in here. How many had ridden out?

He tried to remember exactly where that sound had come from, and it wasn't hard to figure out. He could see where people had stood, horses, supplies. A camp had been set up here and had only been torn down a few minutes ago. A chill sliced up his spine in the Arizona heat as he realized he'd barely missed whoever left this place. The folks doing all the shooting.

But who had done the screaming?

He stared at the wonder before him and studied the sign and terrain with no idea what to do next. There was nothing. No one.

The place was eerie, as if whoever had lived here before still watched, testing those who came. He heard wind whistling like a specter, calling to him from the unnatural caves high overhead.

Where had the people gone who had done such work, created such a home? Who would work this hard then leave? Had they died? Had they abandoned all their labor? Had they been killed? And if so, where were those who had done the killing?

His eyes went up four levels of stone homes. Gabe felt a quick chill of fear. No human hand created this. And yet what were the other possibilities? He was left with the sense that it was ancient and utterly empty of life.

"Help me."

He jumped, drew his gun, and whirled around toward where the riders had left. Heart slamming, he looked left and right. Blinked and gasped for air and saw. . .no one.

There was no one anywhere. Could the place be haunted? He didn't believe in such things, but—

That cry echoed and bounced until Gabe was surrounded by it.

"Help me, please."

This time it was stronger, and even with the echo, Gabe whirled back and looked up and up and up.

A woman.

Gabe almost screamed.

Her face was soaked in blood, one arm flung over the edge of the cliff as she lay on her belly, looking down.

He probably would have screamed if he hadn't choked on spit when he drew in an involuntary breath. While he coughed, he fought to get a grip on his nerves. Spooks and haints were something he'd heard of plenty growing up in the Blue Ridge Mountains of Tennessee. Lots of superstition in those mountains. But his ma raised them Christian and wasn't given to such nonsense. Still—

"I'm trapped. They left me." Her voice was weak, but it carried on the quiet of the canyon. This was no ghost. Except could ghosts fly? Because that's the only way Gabe could see that she'd gotten up there.

The coughing ended and, with a *whoosh* of relief, his head cleared and he knew there was a woman up there. A real woman. A living human being, definitely in terrible distress.

She was so high overhead, her face streaked in bright red blood, dark hair spilling down over the edge of the cliff. He had no notion of what she looked like, only her voice and long hair told him she was female.

"Ma'am?" Gabe had no idea what to say or do.

"Help me, please." Each word shook as if she gathered every ounce of her energy to keep talking. "Help me get down."

"I'll help you." His voice didn't exactly work. He tried again, loud enough so she could hear him. "I'll help you."

"Promise you won't leave me." She sounded on the verge of pure panic.

Gabe couldn't say he blamed her. "I'm not going to leave you. I promise."

"Thank you." Her voice broke, and he heard a muffled sob. "I need you to get me down."

"How?" It wasn't fair to ask a trapped, bleeding woman how to save herself.

"I don't know."

Not fair at all.

Three

❀

Shannon was calm and brave and ready to help.

And she intended to tell her rescuer that just as soon as she could quit crying.

She rolled onto her back and rested her aching head on the unforgiving rock. But she couldn't stand to just collapse and cry her eyes out. Besides, her ears were full of salt water.

Also, she was afraid she'd imagined that man. What if he vanished while she was lying here trying to stop crying and bleeding?

Goaded by panic, she gathered her strength, sat up, and turned so she could look down and down and down. The world circled sickeningly. For a moment she thought she might cast up her breakfast.

The man hadn't vanished. He still stood there, looking baffled and dismayed.

She couldn't say she blamed him, but if he wasn't happy now, just wait till she retched on him.

"How'd you get up there?" He plunked his hands on his hips

and studied the wall in front of him. He looked almost annoyed. Like he blamed *her* for this situation.

Something her mother would do.

Well, she could get him part of the way up. She'd break the news about the last twenty or thirty feet when he was close enough to hear without her raising her voice. Yelling made her head hurt.

"You can get close by going up there." She pointed to a spot to his right that was rough enough for hand- and footholds. "Then if you go down there"—she pointed past a row of cave dwellings to his far left—"you can—"

"Okay. Hang on," he interrupted her and headed for the right side. "Let me get up on this side first."

She wasn't sure how to break it to him that the last level was un-climbable. Her head was swimming, her thoughts were scattered, and her eyes were a little blurred—whether from injuries or tears or terror, she just couldn't say.

He did seem to be real though. Not vanishing. Not a mirage or a figment. It was vastly encouraging really.

He made short work of scrambling up the first level. "Now, where next?"

"You have to walk along that ledge." With a shudder, Shannon thought of that narrow, crumbling ledge. "And climb up to the next level on the left side."

He started along a ledge that wasn't more than six inches wide, though he could have stepped off the ledge into the structures built on that level. About two steps in he turned to face the wall and slid along on his tiptoes. "How did you say you got up there again?" He was so close to the wall his voice was muffled against rock.

She leaned out and wobbled on the ledge. Pulling back, she rolled onto her stomach and poked her head out. The height was still dizzying, but with no risk of falling, she could handle it. Besides, she felt a lot better lying down.

He inched along until he came to the first opening. On the

lower levels there were definite walls built with stone, a very clear structure. "What is this place?" His voice echoed because he was speaking into the opening.

She leaned farther out to see him cross the open space cautiously. "I've had a very bad day."

She almost started crying again. Really, where did she begin? And besides, since she'd kept a very big secret from the expedition members, she was in the habit of not talking. "I came here with a group. . .exploring." Searching for gold. . .exploring, they were kind of the same.

"I saw sign of riders heading out. Six of them?"

"Six when we came in. Only five rode away. They turned on me and left me here and stole my horse and all my supplies." Shannon heard her voice rising as her panic built. She quit talking before it all turned into hysteria.

He reached the left side and began climbing without asking for more direction until he was only two levels below her. He looked around then up at her, and she pointed back to the right.

This ledge was even narrower, and the structures there were more rugged and partially collapsed, making it easy for people to convince themselves it was just a jumble of rocks. If they didn't want to believe their eyes. But the lower level forced one to accept that a human hand had erected this strange home.

She thought she heard grumbling as he inched along, but he was clinging to the rocks, and that deadened the sound some so she couldn't be sure.

"Who built these?" He was getting closer. She could hear him easily now.

"I don't know. They are long deserted from what I can tell. Very ancient, I think. A lot of the stone is crumbled away to dust." Including any natural place to climb to her level from the lower one he was just now reaching.

He stepped across a wide spot where the ledge was completely caved off, and just as he shifted his weight, a bit more of it crumbled away. But he made it and started climbing again until he was only one level below her. He looked up, and she saw his brow soaked with sweat and a tight expression on his face, possibly caused by his recognizing he had a very good chance of falling to his death at any moment.

She knew how he felt.

He squared his shoulders and firmed his jaw and gave her an encouraging nod. "Where next?"

"I don't know." And that was the absolute truth.

His brow arched so high it disappeared into his Stetson. "Then how'd you get up there?"

"I had a ladder. The people who stranded me here shot it to pieces."

The man looked around his feet.

Shannon leaned out farther to try and see the damage. Her head went foggy and she teetered—yes, even lying flat on her stomach—and almost fell the rest of the way forward. A gasp brought his head up.

"How badly are you hurt?"

"I'm fine."

"Uh, miss, your face is all bloody."

Shannon looked down at her hands and saw blood. "I had a nosebleed."

"That doesn't explain all of it, I don't think. I heard gunfire."

"Ricocheting bullets. I—I don't think—" She scanned her body, assessed her aches and pains, and didn't feel shot. "I wasn't struck by one, but—" She did seem to remember being hit. "I think maybe some rocks went wild when the bullets struck. They may have hit me." Getting hit by rocks, getting shot—none of it was the least bit pleasant. It took more energy than she had to tell him more.

She did take a moment to wonder just how bad she looked.

A woman liked to make a good first impression, and she seriously doubted she was accomplishing that.

"Let me think. I've got a lasso on my horse. I could throw it to you, and you could tie it off."

Shannon looked around the utterly empty cave. "There's nothing to tie it to."

"Okay, okay. . .uh. . .what's your name? I'm Gabe."

"Shannon." She barely had the energy to say that out loud. In fact, she didn't have the energy to say much more of anything. "Don't leave."

"I won't."

"Promise me, swear to me on your mother's life, you won't leave."

"My ma's dead, but I won't leave. You have my word, I'll stay, and we'll figure out a way to get you down from there."

She just barely had the strength to roll away from the ledge.

"Shannon?"

It was like someone was talking to her in a dream.

"Shannon, answer me."

For just a second she thought it was Bucky calling her. Poor Bucky. He'd told her not to come.

"Shannon!"

As things stood right now, Shannon had to admit the man was probably right. She wouldn't mind being back in her mother's elegant drawing room right now.

"Shannon, are you all right?"

She tried to figure out when she'd agreed to let her fiancé come along on this trip. And why he was shouting at her so loudly. And while she pondered that, she stared at the roof of her cave and wondered why it was going inexplicably black.

She could be dying up there for all he knew. But how to reach her? Gabe closed his eyes and prayed for inspiration.

Rebuild the ladder?

Pieces of it were scattered on this narrow ledge, more pieces had fallen all the way to the canyon floor. There was one fairly long section with a few broken rungs clinging to it. Maybe he could do it.

Had it been a still, small voice suggesting that? Since it was an idea very unlikely to work, Gabe didn't think so.

Was there another way to the top of this cliff? He had a long rope on his horse. Could he get above her and lower a noose? He leaned back to look up and up and up. It was too high for his rope to be of any use. Besides, he didn't see any way up there.

Praying quietly, he scooted along the ledge and stepped into the cave opening nearest him. Nothing. Not one rough spot or heavy rock of any kind. If her cave was like this one, she was absolutely correct in saying there was nothing to tie on to.

Gabe poked his head out the cave opening and looked down on his horse, standing tied to the mesquite bush. He had an idea. He had to climb all the way back down, which was fairly terrifying considering the ledges were only slightly sturdier than the hardtack biscuits he had in his saddlebags.

And Shannon had to help. A lot. Since she was bleeding and unconscious, that was a real weak spot in a real weak plan.

While he was down there, he'd look at those ladder fragments and see what he could do. There were no trees of any size to use to build a new ladder. How far might he have to ride to find such? And then he had no ax to cut down even a small tree. Hacking one down with his knife was possible, probably, though it might take days of hard work. Still, he'd do that if he had to.

Leave her up there alone while he rode away? She might well lose her mind if he did.

Gabe could almost hear his ma nagging him to quit dallying and get that girl down from there. With a quirk of a smile, Gabe knew his ma would also want him to marry her. His ma pretty much wanted him to marry any unattached female he came across when he was living at home. His ma believed people were supposed to go through life two by two, for sure.

He'd joined the cavalry instead, eager to be out on his own. And he'd never gone home again. And his ma had died a hard death with no family at her side.

Swear to me on your mother's life.

He'd done worse than that. He'd left his mother to die alone at the hands of villains. It appeared evil people had harmed this woman, too. But she wasn't alone anymore. He wasn't going to let her end up like his ma.

His smile shrank, and he stepped carefully out of the cave to make his way back down to the ground.

Shannon's eyes blinked open, and she looked at rock. Nothing but rock. No golden city to be seen anywhere. She lay bleeding, one hand covering her face, terrified at her aloneness. The moan of the desert wind hummed into the cave.

How had she come to this? Shannon Dysart. Daughter of Delmer Dysart, nicknamed Delusional Dysart. The academic world knew him as the professor who'd lost his mind and his reputation over an obsession with gold. Shannon knew him as an honest man who died in her arms, haunted by an expedition he'd barely survived.

Her father had emerged from the West, the sole survivor of harsh deserts, wild Indians, and a brutally hard land. She'd known his expedition was late returning. Long overdue. In direct defiance of her mother, she'd gone hunting.

His group had been large and well known—funded with her family's money. It had made him easy to track until he vanished into the Arizona desert. She'd headed for his last known location.

Within days of her arrival in West Texas, Father had been found, barely lucid, near death, and very much alone.

Her gentle-spirited father had been crawling when a train had passed him and a compassionate engineer had broken the rules and stopped the train to pick him up in the middle of nowhere. Her father had known little more than his name, but it was enough for Shannon to hear he'd been found and rush to his side.

Shannon's mother, bitterly tired of her husband's neglect as he pursued his passion for researching America's distant past—especially fables about the kingdom of Quivera, a hidden city built of pure gold—had refused to come west. Giselle Dysart was years beyond feeling anything but bitter resentment for her gold-obsessed husband.

But Shannon had been there, and she'd cared and listened. Her father had pressed on her notes from the journey. He'd lived for several days, but his words about treasure were taken as rantings by anyone who'd come near them in the dusty Texas town.

Shannon had known better, and she'd taken his words to heart. She'd returned to her mother in St. Louis then burned away two years searching for the key to understanding the intricately secretive maps her father had drawn.

Last winter she'd finally broken his code. She understood what he wrote. Her father truly had found Cibola and Quivera, the two most renowned of the legendary Seven Cities of Gold.

She'd approached a university hoping to find historians who would share her father's dreams, and found only mockery. Her father had tried and failed too many times.

Determined to go alone to restore her father's name, she'd defied her high society mother, who wanted Shannon to settle down and marry an acceptable man and let Delusional Dysart rest in peace. Shannon couldn't betray her father by letting him stand as a madman. She'd used her last dime to fund this expedition for Cibola and Quivera, cities of gold.

She'd searched and found only death.

"Shannon, are you there?"

Was this death then? Come calling?

"Shannon!"

Something whipped past the edge of her vision, and she turned her head but saw nothing. She had a flicker of memory. Bucky had been shouting at her. Odd, Bucky was a sweet-natured, easygoing man. Not one for yelling overly.

"Shannon, wake up!" Whoever it was shouted until Shannon wondered that grit didn't cascade down off the ceiling.

"Yes." As she said it, Bucky faded from her foggy mind and another face sporting a heavy moustache took his place. "Yes, I'm here."

Rolling over, her stomach threatened to rebel. She fought the sickness, stretched out to look over the edge of her cave opening, and got hit in the face by a rope. It settled around her head, and she was well and truly lassoed.

He saw her and dropped as if his knees gave out. Her rescuer was near a cave opening on the level below her. "You're awake." He grabbed the lip of that cave and struggled to stay on the narrow ledge. "Thank You, dear Lord God. I've been so worried." Like he'd knelt to pray. Or maybe he'd collapsed, and since he was on his knees anyway, he included a prayer. He swiped his wrist across his face, almost like he was wiping away tears, but the setting sun cast him in shadows, so she wasn't sure. Then his shoulders squared and he stood, looked up, and smiled. "Sorry for roping you."

She was so happy he was there she'd have let him lasso her and slap a red-hot branding iron on her backside. "That's okay. Gabe, right?"

"Yep. I didn't hurt you, did I?" He made a small grimace. "Yet."

That sounded ominous. Which made her ask, "Have you figured out a way to get me out of here?"

"Maybe?" He sounded like he was apologizing. It all boded

very poorly. "I'll need your help."

That would be her pleasure. "What do you want me to do?" She pulled the lasso off her head.

"Don't drop it!"

She hung on tight. It felt as if she were connected to the world again. She couldn't help the lift in her spirits, though she still didn't see what he wanted her to do. "There's nothing to tie this to up here." Her chin wobbled, but she fought the urge to cry. She'd wasted enough time and salt water on that.

"I know. You said. And I looked in a cave down here and didn't see a thing that would work."

"So, what do you have in mind?" Her fingers curled around the rope so hard her knuckles turned white.

"Uh, well, I'm open to other ideas." He grimaced again.

"Such as?" Shannon was open to ideas as well.

"I thought maybe you'd have them." He gave such a tiny shrug from where he stood about twenty feet below her that she wouldn't have noticed it if she hadn't been riveted on the man.

Thinking, thinking, thinking.

She'd always done well in school, and this situation she'd gotten into notwithstanding, she'd always considered herself intelligent. "Nothing comes to mind."

"For me neither." His dark eyes almost seemed to beg for forgiveness. "Except one thing."

Dark hair hung from beneath his hat. He seemed very tall, too, though honestly it was a little hard to judge from her position. He had a droopy moustache and broad shoulders, and she found him almost stunningly attractive for the shallowest of all possible reasons—he was here. She'd have thought a warthog was cute.

"So what do you want me to do?" she asked.

"I want you to slip that noose around your waist and snug it tight."

"And pull you up?" She shook her head. "What would be the

point of that? I doubt I'm strong enough to hold it while you climb, and besides, if we were successful, then we'd both be up here together. Our problems wouldn't be solved at all."

So far a cute warthog might also be a bit more help.

"No, I don't want you to pull me up." That small flinch again. Hard to tell what his expression really meant. His mouth was covered by the moustache; his face was tilted almost straight up to be able to see her. Maybe she was misinterpreting it. Maybe he wasn't flinching and grimacing. Maybe it was just because she was so overwrought that she thought Gabe had something unpleasant to say.

"What do you want then?" She slipped the noose around her waist while she waited for an answer.

She noticed that he was standing on a ridiculously narrow ledge. He began moving to the far side. When he was well off to her side, he took a few seconds to pull on leather gloves then wrapped the rope around his own waist and around his wrists several times. He looked up, and though he was farther away, he was at more of an angle so his face wasn't quite so tilted. She could see him quite well. That was definitely another grimace.

"I want you to jump."

ᚠour

———————— ❧ ————————

Gabe wished there was a better way to word his plan.

"You want me to what?" Shannon had obviously recovered somewhat from whatever had happened to her. Recovered enough to be horrified at his idea. He was a little horrified himself. "Are you out of your mind?"

Gabe had been rehearsing this. Not because he wanted to convince her, but because he was trying to convince himself. "It'll be like swinging. I'm off to the side, and you'll fall at first, a little."

"A little? Fall a little? At first? I will *plummet* straight down to the earth like a stone. . .only more easily killed." She paused as if waiting for him to show signs of intelligence, then added, "It's called gravity."

"But then you'll reach the end of the rope, and you'll swing. Since I'm off to the side, see?" He held up the rope as if to show her where he was. As if her eyes weren't already locked on him in horror. "It won't have the impact of just jumping straight down with a noose around you."

"It's called being hung. It's a method of execution."

"Now, Shannon. That'd only be true if the noose was around your neck. Your belly is a lot tougher than your neck."

"You hope."

He did hope. "It stands to reason. They don't hang horse thieves from the *belly* until they're dead after all."

"How long was I unconscious?"

Gabe didn't have a watch, but it had taken him awhile to crawl down, fiddle with the ladder pieces, give up, get his rope, and climb back. The sun had lowered past the rock wall they were standing on. The caves were facing east, and the whole canyon was filling with shadows. "Not long."

"Obviously not, if this is the only plan you had time to come up with."

"Shannon, c'mon." Gabe froze. That tone of voice. He hadn't heard it for a long time. It was his "little brother" voice. Many of his big brothers would call it whining. He paused for a second to apologize silently to his brother Abe, whose home Gabe was heading to before he'd heard Shannon's screaming.

He was gonna be late. Not that he minded. Whenever he was near any of his six big brothers, he immediately began feeling about ten years old. He caught himself acting like a kid, too.

Deepening the tone, he said, "I haven't been able to think of another way to get you down. It's this or nothing."

"What's wrong with your voice?"

Gabe glared at her. "Don't change the subject. Come up with a better plan or jump."

"My belly isn't all that tough. Not today certainly. And it feels a little queasy besides." Partly from her abusive day, partly from Gabe's plan.

"Got the collywobbles, huh?"

"The what?" Shannon had a second to wonder if this was another part of Gabe's plan to save her. "Collywobbles?"

28

"It's what my ma called it when our food wouldn't stay in our belly."

"Oh, collywobbles. I've never heard it called such before."

"The rope around your stomach won't help, I'm afraid."

Shannon was afraid, too. Very, very afraid. "We have to think of something else."

"Okay." Gabe could swear he heard a clock ticking in the silence. He'd been thinking until he'd about worn a hole in his skull. "I looked at the ladder. It's broken off too short."

Women liked to talk. His big brothers, all six of them married, had told him that. So, if Shannon wanted to talk around all sides of this problem, he was okay with it. There was no real hurry for her to get down. It wasn't like she was starving to death or anything.

"I haven't eaten or had a drink of water since breakfast, Gabe."

Maybe she *was* starving. But on the good side of that, maybe starving would help convince her to jump.

"There's one somewhat long piece of ladder. If I brought it up, I might be able to reach you with it if I stood straight below you. If I could get it braced against my shoulder and the wall, you could shimmy down it."

"Shimmy? What's that?"

"Well, it's something my ma called it when we'd sort of wiggle around. I reckon it just means you wrap your arms and legs around the piece of wood and sorta slide down."

"Collywobbles? Shimmy? Where exactly are you from, Gabe?"

"I'm from Tennessee originally. We can talk about that later. If you do shimmy, you. . .uh. . .you might get splinters."

"If my legs are wrapped around the wood, those splinters might end up in. . .in. . .in. . .unfortunate places."

"Well, honestly, Shannon, there aren't any *good* places to get splinters."

"Some places are better than others if I want your help pulling them out."

So true.

"Then if I can keep the long, narrow board from tipping while you—uh—"

"Shimmy." She repeated the word so it sounded like the voice of doom.

"Yep, until you get all the way down."

"And you're going to keep it from tipping?"

"Try to." Gabe did his best to sound confident.

"Tipping, like. . .backward? Tipping off the cliff backward?" Shannon's voice seemed higher than he remembered. Panic most likely. But maybe she had a higher range when she was fully conscious. If she got any more conscious, at this rate, she'd sound like a train whistle.

"It might go sideways instead of backward."

"And that's better because—"

"We might be able to control the fall. You'd be against the rock wall and land on that ledge over there." He saw her look to his right at the four-inch ledge. The crumbling four-inch ledge.

"Hmmm."

"And then if the board doesn't break—"

"The board from the ladder that's probably hundreds if not thousands of years old that was shot full of bullet holes a few hours ago and shattered into near toothpicks—all but that one long, jagged-edged, splinter-riddled piece?" Shannon jabbed a rather unsteady index finger at the ladder fragment far, far, far below.

"Yep, that board. If it doesn't break, and you don't go backward, and you don't fall off, and I don't drop it—"

"I'll end up alive and well and stuck so full of splinters in unmentionable places that a porcupine will want to marry me and take me home to his place in the woods."

"Which is why I thought you should just jump."

"I'll just jump." Shannon swung her legs over the edge of the cave, looked down and down and down, and swung her legs right back.

"So, Gabe, tell me a little bit about yourself."

"Like if I've got a good grip, strong arms, a healthy back?"

"No, I'd just like to get to know you better. Where did you grow up?"

Gabe grinned up at her, now lying on her belly with only her poor, blood-streaked face showing.

She'd rubbed the worse of it off—though Gabe doubted she even knew her face was bloody. She'd probably knocked it off without intending to because her face itched. From the blood. The blood she didn't know about. But she still looked really, really awful. Cute but awful.

"Quit stalling."

A moan of distress was her only response before her head disappeared and her feet reappeared. She sat on the ledge again.

He gave her one last warning. "Check the rope around your waist."

Gabe checked his. If he did this exactly right, her weight wouldn't pull him off this ledge and drag him a hundred feet down to land on top of her and crush what was left of her into the stone floor of the canyon.

And also kill him. That was a real weak spot in his plan. One of about ten.

Shannon tugged somewhat frantically on the rope as if she hoped it'd come loose. It didn't. Gabe knew his way around knots.

"The rope's good." She didn't sound all that happy about it.

Gabe didn't knot his end around his own waist. He wanted to be able to let it out and pull it in. And he *didn't* want to be dragged off the ledge. Which seemed a little selfish, but if she did fall—he swallowed hard—he couldn't rush down to help if he plunged to his death, now could he? "Okay. Good. Get ready to jump on the count of three. One. . ."

"Why three? Why not ten?"

"We're doing three." Gabe looked up to meet her terrified eyes. "Two. . ."

She gripped the edge of the cave as if she planned to dive straight out.

"Wait!" He gripped the rope in case she thought he'd said three.

She didn't come close to accidentally jumping.

Gabe had a sneaking suspicion it wasn't going to be all that easy to get her to take the big leap. Couldn't say he blamed her. "I think I should climb in this cave instead of being on the ledge. There's less chance of me dropping you if I've got a more solid place to stand."

"Dropping me? You're worried about dropping me?" That train whistle was definitely coming closer.

"No, I'm just, uh. . .I had a little time to think and decided this would be a way to be extra careful."

"Is there any chance in the world that you could come up with a better plan than this if you had a little *more* time to think?"

Gabe scooted into the cave. It was high enough inside for him to stand up, barely, once he ducked through the opening. Once in, he poked his head back out. "Now, the reason I told you to wait was—"

"You mean besides needing to go into the cave."

"I thought of that after I said wait."

"I don't mind giving you more time. You're thinking up stuff right and left."

"The reason I told you to wait was because I didn't like the way you were going to jump."

"There's a right and wrong way to cast myself off a cliff?"

Gabe sure hoped so. "Instead of diving or even jumping straight out, how about you flip over on your belly so your legs hang down, then scoot out and hang from your hands. Keep your body flat against the cliff. Use the cliff to slow you down. Yes, you'll still fall, but see if you can kind of slide down. I'll reel in the rope as fast as I can to take up the slack. The less distance you fall and the slower you fall, the less you'll jerk on the rope. It won't hurt you as much."

"Except for the part where I grind my face into the side of the rock the whole way down."

"Yep, except for that part." Gabe wondered if they hadn't ought to forget the whole thing and try again in the morning when they were both rested. He could send up some water on the rope. A biscuit. Maybe in his dreams something better would come to him.

"Pull your head back in the cave."

"What?" Gabe was already planning where to put his bedroll. They both definitely needed to sleep on this.

"Pull your head back. I'm going to scoot over the edge of this cave. Then I'm going to do my very best to hang from my arms. That should take some distance out of my fall, right?"

"If you're five and a half feet tall."

"That's about right." Shannon seemed to want to talk.

Gabe didn't blame her. "And your arms add two more feet to the length of your body."

"I've been told my arms are very slender, but I don't think they're particularly long."

"Let's go with two feet. You should hang down about seven and a half feet closer on a twenty-foot drop. So you'll be dropping. . ." Gabe reflected that he should have paid a little closer attention to arithmetic in school. But who could predict a situation like this?

"Twelve and a half feet instead of twenty." Shannon the genius had it right close to hand. Of course if she was real smart, she wouldn't be up in that cave, now would she?

"That seems better than twenty, doesn't it?"

"Couldn't hurt." She sounded like it really could hurt. Very badly.

"So swing around."

"After you pull your head in."

"Why? I want to be ready when you fall. I need to watch you."

"When I do my dangling and hanging and falling, my. . . my. . .unmentionables and possibly even my. . .limbs may be temporarily revealed. It wouldn't be at all proper for you to see them."

"How'd you say you got stuck up there again?" Gabe hadn't grown up around girls except for his ma. And he'd headed for the cavalry as soon as he was old enough. All men there, all the time. He didn't much understand what went on in a woman's head. "It seems a whole passel of improper things had to happen to get you stuck up there. I can't imagine how a glimpse of a petticoat can even begin to bother you at this point."

"And yet it does."

Gabe stared.

She stared back. Waiting.

He pulled his head in the cave. "Okay!" He yelled mostly to be clearly heard but partly because he was pretty scared for her and yelling helped a little. "Are you ready?" He sat down and braced his legs against the ground and gripped the rope with both hands.

He heard some muttering and scratching around out there. She was definitely doing something. "I'm ready."

Gabe could hear the mail train pulling into Durango in her voice.

"One. . ."

"I'm going to do it this time."

He'd believe that when he saw it. "Two. . ."

"I'm ready. I mean it."

Gabe braced himself just in case she went through with this madness. "Three!"

He heard her come sliding down. He dragged hand over hand

on the rope. Within seconds it was taut. . .and. . .it never jerked. He made sure his grip was secure then poked his head out.

She was standing on the ledge just as if she'd flown down there and landed like a red-tailed hawk. Her arms were lifted over her head and spread wide, flat against the cliff. Her face was turned away from him. Her toes were semisolid on a narrow ledge. The rope was a firm line between them. Her. . .petticoats and limbs were. . .

Gabe jerked his head back fast. "So, you made it." It seemed stupid not to look at her. But he'd give her a minute to address various issues of decency.

She shrieked. He leaned forward to see the ledge crumble under her feet. He pulled at the rope desperately and she fell, but instead of plunging down two more levels of cliff houses to the canyon floor, she swung. His plan exactly. Now there she dangled like a plump spider spinning a web.

Lowering her quickly, he said, "Grab hold of the next ledge. I'll hang on until you get a firm foothold."

The rope swayed as she hung from her tough belly. Finally, with his doing his best to manipulate the rope without leaning out too far and being pulled down after her, she caught a cave door and pulled herself to the ledge and stood.

He looked down. She looked up.

"Your turn to jump, Gabe."

He smiled. "I don't think so, Shannon." Hanging on tight, paying the rope out the least amount possible, he used footholds to make his way carefully down to her.

They stood, facing each other, grinning like idiots.

"Let's go on down." It took him a few seconds to even think of it. "I don't like it up here very much."

"Me neither."

They inched their way across the front of this row of caves without his letting go of the harness he had tied on her. Carefully they finally reached solid ground.

She turned to him. Her face was scratched from the fall. Her nose was dotted with dried blood. Her hair was as wild as a wolverine in a feeding frenzy. She was the most beautiful thing he'd ever seen.

And he realized he hadn't seen anything yet when she launched herself into his arms.

Five

Shannon held on, knowing it was crazy. "Thank you."

Knowing he was a stranger. "Thank you so much."

But he was solid and his feet were on solid ground. "Thank you."

So were hers. "Thank you, thank you, thank you, thank you, thank you."

She needed him to know she appreciated it. "Thank you, thank you, thank you."

"You're welcome. It's all right. You're safe."

His arms came around her so naturally she could have cried. It might not even be a bad thing to cry. It might help wash her face.

It went on way too long before she gathered her composure enough to let go of her death grip. Life grip was really a better way to describe it.

She raised her eyes to look into his and saw such kindness. "Hi. I'm Shannon Dysart."

"I'm Gabe Lasley." He lifted one hand and touched her chin. There was a little dent in it, and Gabe looked at that dent for what seemed a bit too long. "Uhhh. . .how did you say you got up there again? And how did you come to be stranded? And what are you doing out here in the wilderness? And why are you—"

"I need to excuse myself for just a minute, Gabe."

Gabe's brow furrowed.

She knew the man had waited a long time to question her, but she really did need a moment of privacy.

He must have figured out what she meant, because his face went bright red.

"Okay. I'll go. . .check my horse." He turned away and almost dragged her off her feet.

Shannon realized she was, in fact, still lassoed. She started fighting with the noose, which was handy. Now she didn't have to see him blush.

Gabe noticed the rope wrapped around his own waist.

If ever a couple could say they had the ties that bind, it would be Gabe and her.

He unwound his side of the rope. They both got free about the same time. Then he rushed over to his horse, a pretty chestnut that was standing only feet away, in no way needing to be checked. Gabe firmly turned his back.

Shannon raced for a moment of necessary privacy. She returned and faced his black-as-midnight eyes. "I'll tell you everything. But we need to be on our way to town."

"It's too late tonight. We'd be riding in the dark inside an hour. Not safe."

"Well, we can't stay out here."

"We have to. There's no choice."

Shannon really didn't want to go to fussing at the man moments after he'd saved her life, but she had no other course of action. "I can't spend the night with a man out here. It wouldn't be proper."

Gabe arched a brow until it disappeared into his Stetson. As if to uncover that arch, he pulled his Stetson off his head and scowled at her while he gripped the brim with both hands and held it to his chest. "I would never do anything to shame you, Shannon. In fact, I think it's insulting that you'd say we can't stay together."

"But we *can't* stay together."

"I am a Christian man, Shannon Dysart. I would never dishonor a woman. I wouldn't harm you. In fact, if you will think back long and hard to. . .oh, about *five minutes ago*. . .you will realize I would do whatever is necessary to protect you, or any woman, from harm." Gabe frowned until the downward curve of his mouth was a match for his moustache.

Shannon wasn't handling this well, but it had been a long day. She was clean out of tact. "I apologize, Gabe. It's not that staying out here. . . What I mean is. . .I. . .I trust you. I'm not saying you'd. . .you'd. . ." She fell silent as a shocking parade of improper things trampled through her exhausted brain— throwing herself into his arms foremost among them.

"Let's get you something to eat. Then I'll build a fire and we can bed down. . .uh. . .I mean. . .get to bed. . .That is we can. . .can. . . *settle in*." Gabe was strangling his hat.

And the poor hat hadn't done a thing. Neither had Gabe, except save Shannon from a slow, painful death by inches from thirst and hunger.

And here she stood insulting him. "It's not that anything sinful would go on, Gabe. I do trust you. It's that people would *think* it had."

He turned and stalked toward his horse.

Shannon watched him go, wondering just what a woman was to do in such a situation. She couldn't quite wish he'd never come along. "We'll have to use the caves for sleeping." She looked up the wall. The lowest one was a ways up. Horrible, dark, nasty place. With a shiver of dread, she tore her eyes away from a hole in the rock that was now deeply shaded as the sun went lower. She felt her throat swelling shut with terror at the thought of poor Gabe having to sleep in that cave.

"All right, if that satisfies your fears about what people would say." Gabe pulled the leather off his horse and began unpacking his saddlebags. "Or I'll ride off a piece so everything is good and proper. I don't want you to be shamed by my presence."

Shannon almost started crying at the thought of his riding off.

He crouched down and began snapping a mesquite bush into kindling. He wheeled on the toes of his boots and glared at her. "But if it's improper to be out here, because of what people will say, then when we ride into town together, the same people who are *not* here to see the truth are going to look at us and believe whatever they want."

"A man and woman traveling alone together like this is shameful unless they're—" Shannon wasn't about to say it.

"Married."

And she wished he wouldn't have either.

"I saw a spring nearby." Gabe got a small fire going.

The comforting crackle of wood and the soothing aroma of wood smoke eased some of the crazy out of her. "That's probably why whoever lived here picked this spot."

Pushing a few larger sticks into the fire, Gabe said, "I'll go get water and we'll eat. Then we'll do whatever it is you decide we need to do so the people that aren't here won't be scandalized."

He stood and would have walked away if she hadn't grabbed his arm. "*What?*"

The man could surely growl.

"Thank you. You saved me today." Shannon had all she could do not to hurl herself into his arms again. "I'm sorry about this. I do trust you, and you're absolutely right that in the end people will just have to believe what they wish. Besides, so what if we go riding in late tonight or early tomorrow? For all they know, we could have been riding around together for weeks."

"And if they wish to believe something terrible, then what?"

"Then I'll go on my way with a bit of shame attached to my name and never see these people again."

Gabe's jaw tensed as he looked at her. Shannon realized his eyes weren't pure black but such a deep brown that it was hard to see where the center of his eye quit and the color began.

Silence stretched between them. Shannon felt caught by his gaze, unable to break free.

Finally, he spoke so quietly she almost thought the words came from inside her own head. "What were you doing up in that cave, Shannon?"

"I'll tell you everything. I promise. But first I would desperately love a drink of water." Which was nothing less than the truth. Desperate thirst definitely described it.

"It probably wouldn't hurt for you to wash the blood off your face either."

She'd forgotten how she must look. Following him to the spring, she did her best to clean up. The blood was dried in her hair and behind her ears. It was awful. She was grateful for the absence of a looking glass to tell her the horrible truth.

After she was done, she drank her fill of the cold spring then went back to the camp where Gabe was pulling provisions from his saddlebags. She wasn't that eager to tell Gabe everything. She thought he might decide, especially considering the utter lack of gold in this city they'd just found, that he had someone on his hands who might easily be named Delusional Dysart.

"You did a good job. You look a sight better without the blood." Gabe studied her as if he was trying to probe her brain for the information inside.

He handed her some beef jerky and hard biscuits, and Shannon got very busy eating her supper.

"Okay, time's up. What are you doing here?" Gabe leaned back on the cliff wall, cradling his tin cup and stretching his feet out toward the crackling fire. Dusk was settling into dark, and the desert air was cooling rapidly.

Shannon felt almost fully human. She'd given it a lot of thought, and she had a good idea. Considering the last idea one of them had come up with was her jumping off a cliff, she didn't think this was so bad. "I'm searching for a city made of gold."

Crickets chirped in the background. A coyote howled. The wind gusted but not enough to disturb their sheltered fire.

Too bad. A tornado would be a nice distraction about now. She just hoped Gabe wasn't tempted to slip away in the dark.

"Ummm. . .so. . .having any luck?"

Shannon was tempted to hit him. "My father read every document he could that referred to a group of bishops that escaped from Madrid—"

"Madrid, New Mexico? I've been through there. A little coal mining town. Don't remember any bishops, although there might have been a house of worship. Maybe a Catholic—"

"Madrid, *Spain*." She wanted to add a knock on the head to get him to stop interrupting. Her great idea, about getting Gabe to help her on the next leg of her journey, was starting to feel not so great.

"Oh, Spain. Sure. Heard of it. They speak Mexican there, right? Go on."

Shaking her head, Shannon continued. "A battle was coming, threatening Madrid, and these seven bishops were reported to have loaded up a king's ransom in gold. They fled. Some say across the ocean."

"This year? They just got here?" Gabe looked up at the cliff as if willing to search for the bishops.

"No, the battle that caused them to run happened in 1150."

"Eleven fifty?" Gabe pulled his hat off his head and tossed it aside, as if maybe he had a headache and was considering blaming it on an overly tight Stetson. "That's about—" She saw his lips moving and his hands. He was counting on his fingers.

Shannon couldn't help counting along.

"Seven hundred years ago?" He faced her, a skeptic if ever she saw one. "Didn't the pilgrims land at Plymouth Rock in 1492? I learned that in school. The first folks from across the ocean to come to America?"

"You want to hear this story or not?"

There was an extended pause. He must really not want to hear it. Fine, she didn't want to tell it either.

"I just don't get how a bunch of Catholic priests—"

"Bishops."

"Who must have been dead for quite a while now—" Gabe's dark eyes flickered in the firelight. Almost like he was mocking her. Exactly like he was mocking her.

"Probably six hundred and fifty years at least."

"Got you stuck up on that cliff." He was definitely mocking her.

Shannon forged on. "The story goes that they made their escape across the ocean to America. With shiploads of gold and jewels, they settled in the West. But they told no one."

"That part's true for sure."

She needed a stick to whack him if she was going to get through this.

"Stories emerged—"

"Emerged from where if they told no one?"

Shannon spoke through clenched teeth. "About cities built with gold."

"Uh. . .did they take enough gold to build whole cities or did they find some of it once they got here? How many ships does it take to carry enough gold to build a city? Was it solid gold or just—"

"Shut up and listen."

"Go on." Gabe threw another stick on the fire.

"So have you heard of Coronado?"

"It's in California. On the ocean. One time I took a ship to—"

"*Gabe!*"

"What?"

"It's a *man*. I mean *he's* a man. Francisco Coronado is a man who came from Spain searching for the cities of gold."

"The ones that came over hundreds of years before the Pilgrims, on all those big ships, and didn't tell anybody, right?"

Well, at least he was listening—she'd give him that. "Coronado thought they'd landed in South America, so he traveled all over down there. When he didn't find the cities, he came up north, searching for the gold. He never found it."

"Because it wasn't there?"

"Because he was looking in the wrong place." Shannon felt a shiver run up her spine. "It's true. My father followed all the clues he found in ancient writings. He devoted his life to studying the cities of gold." She paused, hardly able to believe it herself, but she had to convince him if she wanted any chance for success. "He found them."

It was very dark except for the crackling fire. And even that was dying down.

She heard Gabe more than saw him lean closer. The fire might even have revealed a gleam in his eye. Was it the same thing that had overcome her expedition so that they robbed her and left her for dead? Greed? Gold fever? A thirst for wealth?

She wanted to shout at him. Beat on him. Tell him he was failing her. Tell him he was supposed to be better than the people who had hurt her.

"Is this rock pile one of them?"

Tell him he was a sarcastic idiot.

"I've got the notes he left and the words he spoke. I used what he told me to break the code of his maps and writing, and now I've discovered what he found."

Gabe sighed so long and deep he sounded like the wind blowing past their meager shelter.

"This place was one of the destinations. I knew it was special, and because of that, I hoped it was one of the golden cities. But Father talked of treasure, and he was a history scholar. He would consider these caves a treasure. Now that I've seen it, I understand why Father was so fascinated. But there was another place he told me to go. Another destination on the map."

"I've wandered the West a lot, Shannon." He sounded very kind, which probably meant he pitied her. Thought she was delusional. "There aren't any cities of gold. I'm really sorry, but there just aren't."

"Did you know this place was here?"

"No."

"Well, then why couldn't there be another city somewhere? The bishops would have taken pains to hide because they'd run away with so much wealth."

"How many ships did you say they took? Because it'd take a lot of ships to carry enough gold to build even a real small town—"

She cut him off, "They'd build the city in a hidden canyon, on a mountaintop, or in a secluded valley sheltered by a vast woodland. Why not?"

"Okay, I suppose a city could be hidden out here somewhere. Doubt it."

"Well, I don't."

"But that still doesn't explain why you were stuck up in that cave."

"The people I hired to travel with me stole my maps and left me stranded."

"Oh." Gabe nodded. "Guess that explains it. You should've said that about two hours ago. Saved some time."

45

"And I'll prove I'm right about the lost city of gold just as soon as I can get back to a town where I can buy a horse, hire more people to scout the land for me, and head for the next place on the map."

"Hire more help? Didn't you say it was your hired help who stranded you in that cave?"

There was no possible way to deny it. "Yes. Three men and two women were with my expedition."

"And you're going to trust yourself to hire more? 'Cuz no offense 'r nuthin'..."

"Why am I suddenly bracing myself to be deeply offended?"

"But you're not that good at picking hands."

Shannon wanted to slug him, but now wasn't the time or place. "Yes, I picked poorly that once."

"Real poorly. Awful." Gabe shuddered.

Right here in front of her was an utterly trustworthy man. Gabe. "What do you do for a living?"

"Why don't you go home?" He ignored her question, but that might be because he was busy telling her how to live her life. "Where did you say you came from?"

"My mother lives in St. Louis. But that's not my home anymore. She's very unhappy with me for taking this journey."

"Sounds like a wise woman."

"No, she's not! She's a wealthy snob who has looked down on my father and his work for years." Gabe had finally said something she couldn't just brush aside. "She's more interested in her high society connections and the cut of her overpriced gowns than she is in her own husband or her daughter. I will *not* go happily on my way while my father's life's work is subjected to scorn. My father died trying to bring education to people. His colleagues think he had gold fever, but he was not searching for gold. He was searching for knowledge. He wanted to find the history of this country. He wanted to prove America had inhabitants and old ruins just like ancient Greece. He asked me to find this place, and if I can't prove he found it, then he died for nothing! He left me for nothing!"

Gabe was silent, thank the good Lord.

It would be like him to comment in some stupid way right now that would not help at all.

"Your father did leave you something. He loved you. He left you knowing that. No parent can do better for a child than to let her know she is loved."

That actually helped a little. It would help even more if Shannon could be sure her father cared more for her than he did for gold. "He did love me." Shannon wondered if saying it out loud made it true. "In the end my mother no longer believed that, but I did. She said all he cared about was gold, but he was already rich. Why would he need more money?"

"Instead, he wanted respect."

"Yes."

"Honor from other teachers at his college."

"Professors, not teachers."

"He wanted to put his name on a discovery for the ages, like Christopher Columbus discovering America or Lewis and Clark mapping the West."

"Yes, that's all he wanted."

"So he didn't leave you for gold."

"Absolutely not."

"He left you for pride."

"Yes, that's exactly—" Shannon stopped herself. "What?"

"I'm very sorry about your pa dying, Shannon, before he could find what it was he was searching for. If you're planning to spend your whole life searching for a lost city of gold, do everyone a favor and don't get married and have a husband and children to abandon."

Shannon's throat felt swollen, and she couldn't speak.

"Let's get to sleep."

Gabe's suggestion distracted her so she didn't start crying. She gathered her self-control and responded in a hoarse voice. "Yes, it's been a long day. A terrible day." She looked at him, sitting almost shoulder to shoulder with her, the glowing embers casting his face in a red light.

Earlier today he'd saved her life. Just now, he'd broken her heart.

Or maybe Gabe just shined a light so she could see that her father had broken her heart.

"Be careful climbing up there." He gave her a pat that was supposed to be encouraging. "Those ledges aren't safe."

"Me? I'm not sleeping in that cave. *You're* sleeping in that cave." That distracted her even further from her hurt. She preferred to be distracted.

"No, you're going up. I need to stay down here."

"Why?"

There was a moment of silence. "Because it's the man's job to. . .to. . ."

"To make the woman scale the cliff while he stays safely on the ground?"

"Is that a trick question?"

"Fine, whatever you say. I'll sleep in that spooky, dark, empty, possibly haunted cave."

"I don't believe in ghosts, so it's not haunted. The rest is sure enough right."

She thought maybe she heard a squelched laugh.

"Humph." She turned with all the dignity she possessed, which at this point was almost none, and took two firm steps toward the cliff.

"And I'll stay down here with the rattlesnakes, scorpions, and cougars." Gabe's voice followed her. "And I'll be ready in case the five armed outlaws who left you to die a lingering death of hunger and thirst come back."

When he put it like that, maybe being down here wasn't a big improvement over the cave.

"I need to be down here between you and danger, Shannon. Surely you can see that."

"I know." She should stay down here with him. Two of them to face down five armed outlaws. But she knew they wouldn't come back; she hoped very much they were busy following her map, which wouldn't make enough sense to ever inform them that they hadn't gotten everything they were looking for. That thought reminded Shannon that she'd never fully shared her great idea with Gabe.

She turned back to him. Her two steps had actually brought her face-to-face with him. The fire crackled, and the night breeze blew cold. She felt that wimpy sense of being rescued again.

To drive back the terror of the nonexistent ghosts who did *not* haunt that cave, Shannon threw herself into his arms again. Surely a woman ought to be able to rescue herself. She thought of that high cave where she'd been left to die slowly and knew she'd lived only because of Gabe. "Thank you."

His arms came around her, and they were so strong. He had literally held her with those arms on this side of the pearly gates.

"Thank you, thank you, thank you."

The embrace went on for far too long. It kept the cold of the night at bay.

Shannon dreaded leaving him. She wasn't sure she could. So, when her head cleared enough to think, she stepped out of his arms—not very far out, but it was the best she could do—and decided to delay bedtime for a few more minutes. "What did you say you do for a living again, Gabe?"

"I'm a rancher."

That meant he was very busy. "Are we on your land?"

"Nope, my ranch is up north, near Ranger Bluffs, in Wyoming."

"Why aren't you there?" Perhaps he *was* a man with some spare time.

Shrugging, Gabe looked down at his boots as if they were fascinating. "I've been traveling. I've just started up ranching and only had a few head of cattle. I turned them over to a neighbor because I wanted to see my brothers before I settled in, half a country away from most of 'em. I figured to spend the summer with my brother in New Mexico. And see a couple of others in Texas. I thought to spend the winter with one or the other of 'em."

Definitely some spare time. She ran her hand down her thigh to feel the slightly thickened spot in her skirt where she concealed her remaining maps. They'd taken her notes and the maps that had led them to these cliff dwellings, but they didn't have the one that led to the next city. The one that was going to be made of gold. "Thank you for saving me today, Gabe."

"You're welcome. No decent man would've done nuthin' else. Good night, Shannon. I'm glad I came riding along when I did."

"So am I." She opened her mouth to ask him, beg him to help her. And found she couldn't do it, not when he'd just held her so close. She couldn't bear another dose of his sarcasm. "Good night, Gabe."

Six

"This isn't the right map." Lurene Lester jerked her head up from reading the papers they'd taken from that fool of a woman this afternoon. She lurched to her feet and whirled to face Ginger. "You told me you searched her."

"I did." Ginger reached for the papers Lurene held.

Lobo got there first, grabbed the papers out of Ginger's hand, and shoved her aside with one of his massive hands. "You're saying we don't have the map?"

"What difference does it make?" Darrel Lloyd kicked at the dirt between the fire and where he'd lolled since they'd finished setting up camp. "You saw what she led us to today. Dirt and rock. The next map is gonna lead to the same kinda place if it leads anywhere at all."

Lurene had all she could handle not to wrap her fingers around the man's dirty neck. "That map she had led us to those caves today. It wasn't gold, but you can see it was deserted. Whoever lived there had strange ways. I can believe they carried gold into that secretive place and kept it hidden. Those people took it with

51

them when they moved on. The next step on her map was gonna lead us somewhere. Maybe to where those folks went who built the caves."

"Their new home and their gold." Ginger rubbed her hands together.

Lurene liked to see the greed on the woman's face. It kept her in line.

"Lobo, you've lived in this area for years. You ever seen anything like those caves before?"

"Nope." Lobo looked up from the papers. "This don't mean nothin' to me. This is all squiggly lines and initials."

"A code." Lurene poured herself more coffee and wished everyone would shut up so she could think, but she didn't really need to think. There was only one thing they could do. "We've got to go back."

"To those caves?" Darrel shifted and turned away from the fire to stare into the night. "I didn't like that place. It felt haunted."

Lurene hadn't liked it a bit either. She didn't admit that, because what would be the point? "I'm going back. If you searched her thoroughly, Ginger. . ."

"I did." Ginger jumped to her feet and started pacing. She always had trouble being still. Her red hair, wild frizzing curls, flashed in the fire when she came close then turned dull when she walked into the darkness. *All the motion oughta keep the rattlesnakes away.* And if it didn't, they'd get Ginger first.

"Then she must have stashed it somewhere," Lobo said.

"Wait a minute. Did anyone check her saddlebags?" Lurene whirled to face the bags, still hanging from the back of Darrel's saddle, where it had been thrown when they'd bedded down for the night.

"I never saw her take nuthin' out of there except food and clothes," Darrel said. "And I was watchin' for when that map would show up in her hands. She'd usually go off alone then come back.

She didn't take her saddlebags with her. Figured it was in a pocket."

"Let's see if she's got anything else in there." Lurene strode to the bags and flipped one open. "Supplies," she muttered as she pulled the contents out, tossing things aside. She reached the bottom of the bag and almost gave up. Then her hand hit a ridge in the bottom that had her poking her head down to look. She ran her fingers along that ridge and realized it wasn't the bottom. It was a flat leather folder almost the exact width and length of the saddlebag. She pulled it out. "It's heavy."

Fumbling it, it spilled and rained gold. The metallic clinking and the flash in the firelight drew the rest of her companions like that gold was a bright light in the darkness.

And they were a swarm of bugs.

"Lots of money," Ginger said, dropping to her knees to claw at the coins. "Fifty- and twenty-dollar gold pieces."

Cutter knocked her hand aside. "We split this even. Five ways."

Lurene didn't feel much like sharing the coins, and she thought, not for the first time, that she didn't want to share any city of gold either. She wondered who she'd pick to die first. She looked to make sure the wallet was empty and saw a paper. *The map maybe?* Her heart pounded as she pulled it out. "What's this?"

She unfolded it and saw a name she recognized, John Jacob Astor. The words were printed an inch high in fancy swirling letters across the top of the sheet of paper. Below that, a letter began:

Dear Shannon,

Lurene didn't read the letter. That would take some doing. Reading wasn't her strong suit. So she slid her eyes down and saw it was signed:

Affectionately,
Your Cousin John Astor

Below the signature, it read in slightly smaller but no less elegant script than on the top, John Jacob Astor IV.

"John Jacob Astor is her cousin?" Lurene raised her eyes. Everyone in the West had heard of the people who owned most of the land under New York City.

Those words were printed on the paper, engraved just like the top. As if this man was so rich and important he hired others to print up lots of sheets of paper like this. No doubt his time was occupied spending his millions.

Lurene looked at Cutter then shifted her gaze to look at Randy. She could tell the kid was thinking.

"I'll count the money out by the fire. All of us watching." Lurene could get it back out of their saddlebags later. . .when they were dead. "Watch me pick it up so you'll know I'm not holding out on you."

Cutter jerked his chin in agreement. Randy watched her as if she were holding a shooting iron aimed right at his heart.

She sat down by the fire with her shirt turned into a pouch to hold the coins. She made neat piles in front of her. When she was done counting, there was over five hundred dollars. "We each get a hundred dollars, with about fifty dollars more in small coins."

Lurene looked up at the starving hunger in her band of outlaws. Lurene had never had a hundred dollars in her hand at once, let alone five hundred. She could live for two years if she was careful on a hundred. Forever on five.

But the money wasn't what really hit her. "She's rich. Did any of you pick up on Shannon Dysart being rich?"

Cutter shrugged. "She didn't flash a lot of money around. She didn't buy a high-stepping horse or wear silk clothes. She offered me fair pay but no fortune. And she could've paid more, too." His displeasure was clear, though it was laughable considering the way they'd treated Shannon. They'd been worth a whole lot less than she'd paid.

"If she's really rich," Randy said, holding his share of the coins so the fire sparkled on them, "we ought to go get her out of that cave. She talked about her pa enough that we know he's dead, but she's probably got other people, folks who'd pay to get her back."

Ransom.

Lurene could feel the rain of money showering her clean right now. "And I know she's got another map. She'd let me look at it sometimes and talk to me about it, how she'd broken the code. She never told me *how* she'd broken it, but I watched her work on the map that led us to those caves, and I figured out what she was doing. But I never saw her carrying it during the day. She'd set the next day's course. Then, when she got up the next morning, we'd let her lead the way. I figured it to be in her satchel, but maybe, once we got to those caves, she hid it, buried it, or stuck it behind some rocks. We've got to go back there and get it from her."

"She won't tell us where she hid it. Not after what we done to her." Randy Lloyd was a quiet one. Not as given to talk as his big brother, Darrel. But he was always thinking. Lurene knew it about the man because she saw in him the same thing she saw in herself. A planner. Someone who thought everything through before he acted. But Randy struck Lurene as none too bright. So all his thinking probably wouldn't lead to much.

"She *will* tell us if she wants to come down from that cave."

"But she won't believe we're gonna let her live. Why would she?" Randy met Lurene's eyes. Not belligerent. He seemed to really want to know what she had planned.

"We'll let her down, and then we'll get the truth out of her."

"How?"

"Most women have their limits." Lurene laughed when she thought of it. She'd had men push her past her limits many times. But these days there wasn't much Lurene wouldn't accept. Shannon, though, she'd be easy to scare.

"I think we can hunt around until we find what'll shake the

truth loose from Miss Rich Lady Dysart." Lurene liked having a chance to hurt the city girl who thought she could buy loyalty with cash money. The little woman had been a fool from the start, and there was no reason to doubt she'd die a fool. It had suited Lurene to leave the woman to die alone. But if fancy Miss Shannon wanted to speed things up, Lurene would be glad to help.

"We'll tell her about the ransom and make her believe we have to return her alive to collect," Ginger said. "And while we wait for her folks back east to pay up, we'll hunt for gold."

"I don't know much about kidnapping," Randy said. "But it's a sure bet that we'll have a better chance of finding gold from Shannon's family than we will from her stupid map."

Lurene didn't want to admit that.

"I know one thing," Cutter said. "I talked only with her in St. Louis. She didn't have some fancy crowd around her, smoothing out the details. She set out on this journey on her own. Probably against her family's wishes."

"You think they won't pay 'cuz of that?" Ginger asked.

"No." Cutter smirked. "I think they'll expect trouble because of that. They'll half expect she'll end up needing to be rescued. And paying a bunch of money won't be a big surprise. Those rich folks like to buy their way out of everything. I think all five of us can come out of this rich, with or without a city of gold."

"I like the sound of that real well." Ginger smiled a hungry smile.

"And we need to stick together," Cutter added. "It'll get real complicated picking up the money and keeping her hidden. It'll take all five of us to run this kidnapping right."

Lurene wasn't sure if Cutter was subtly telling her to give up on her idea of thinning out the number of hands reaching into the pot. She hadn't told him she was planning it, but Cutter was a sharp one. He'd know what she had on her mind. Or was he trying to give the Lloyd brothers a good reason to stick with them and not get greedy?

"It's too dark to ride tonight." Cutter had set the pace after they'd finished with the caves, putting as many miles between them and their crime as he could. They'd ridden through rough land, up and down narrow trails. There was no way to retrace their steps in the dark.

"Shouldn't we try and get back there?" Ginger asked. "How bad was she hurt when you left her? No chance'a her dying is there?"

"She'll live." Lurene had a cold idea that she was fond of. "I wonder what her family would pay for a dead body?"

"Well, it don't matter, because we won't ask them to pay for a dead body," Randy said. "We'll ask them to pay for her alive, even if she ain't."

A shiver of pleasure raced down Lurene's spine. She really couldn't help liking how Randy's mind worked.

"Let her spend a cold night in that cave. It'll make her more agreeable tomorrow. Let's turn in and get an early start." Cutter shoved the worthless papers Shannon had given them at Ginger as she walked close to him, then went to his bedroll and turned his back to the fire.

A dangerous man, Lobo Cutter. Of them all, Lobo was the one who worried Lurene the most. She could handle the rest of them, right down to putting a knife between their ribs. But Lobo was a savvy, trail-hardened outlaw, and he'd be a hard man to best. If she let any of them live, it might be Lobo, just because taking him on might cost her too much. Anyway, Cutter had gotten her into this and taken her off the streets. So she owed him. And she'd pay, until it didn't suit her anymore.

A quick look at Randy Lloyd reminded her not to underestimate him. He was proving to be smart, and she could use that in a kidnapping. It was a little different than anything she'd tried before.

Shivering in the cold night air of the desert, she crawled into her bedroll and almost asked Cutter to share hers. It wouldn't be the first time. Cutter had been one of her regulars back in St. Louis. They'd played it quiet about their past for Shannon's sake. And now Lurene wasn't sure she wanted Ginger and the Lloyd brothers to know of her connection to Cutter. It might arouse suspicion, especially in Randy, if he figured them for a team. After all, it aroused *her* suspicion thinking of the Lloyd brothers backing each other.

For now, she'd sleep alone in her cold bed. It reminded her too much of her cold nights on the streets back east. She wanted a whiskey to help her forget the ugliness of the life she'd been reduced to. Enough gold and she could put that life far in her past.

Shannon Dysart was the key to cash money and a city of gold.

Lurene thought that if she had a whole city full, it might be enough to make her feel safe and clean.

"If you want her, you're going to have to go get her," Giselle Dysart said as she fanned her gently tilted-up nose.

Buckstone "Bucky" Chatillon Shaw *did* want Shannon Dysart. But did he want her bad enough to go get her?

It was a long, hard trip, and honestly Bucky was used to comfortable living. But the idea had some allure. He'd been raised on the trapping and scouting stories handed down from his great uncle, Henri Chatillon. Living a rugged life in the unsettled West was a childhood dream of his. But honestly, those dreams were best enjoyed in a soft bed in a warm room with plenty of food ready to be prepared by a skilled cook and delivered by an efficient maid.

But more than he didn't want to go get Shannon, he didn't want her mother, Giselle, nagging him anymore, nor his own mother, nor his father, nor any one of six living grandparents. The only one who wouldn't have nagged was Shannon's father, and since the man was both a lunatic and dead, it hardly mattered how Delusional Dysart would have acted.

So, he'd better go get her. With a sigh he accepted the inevitable. He was taking a trip west. He tried to look on the bright side. Maybe it would be fun. Maybe his childhood dream would become the adventure of a lifetime.

And maybe he'd end up with an Apache tomahawk embedded in his skull. He didn't know much about Apaches, but what he did know. . .was all bad.

However it ended up, it had to start somewhere, and Shannon was his and had been since birth. Their marriage would join four of the most powerful families in St. Louis—the Chatillons, the Astors, the Shaws, and the Campbells. His marriage to Shannon Dysart would be the stuff dynasties were built on. He played around with the image of himself as governor and liked it well enough. And to be governor, he needed a wife. Shannon.

It was past time for action. He'd waited long enough for Shannon to give up her dreams and marry him. It pulled Bucky up short to think the woman he planned to marry needed to be hunted down to do her duty. Add to that, she had to give up the great goal of her life, her own dream, to do it. That didn't make this the love match of the century.

"You're right, Mrs. Dysart." Bucky felt almost certain that Giselle Dysart was wrong, wrong, wrong. "I let Shannon go on this journey because I believed she needed to retrace her father's steps before she could settle down. But we haven't heard from her in too long. She may be in trouble."

"She hired competent help." Giselle waved a hand as if Shannon being out of contact for nearly a month now didn't concern her in the least.

Bucky suspected that was exactly the case. What concerned Giselle was her own comfort, her own wants being catered to quickly and without the burden of hearing about any problems.

Giselle wanted this dynasty. Though she'd done her best to wash her hands of her unfortunate marriage to a peasant, she always acted as if her husband carried a bad smell. She wanted better for Shannon, and Giselle wanted to secure her own place slightly higher in St. Louis society. Having the Astors as relatives of course made her unassailable, however tenuous the connection, but Giselle always wanted more.

She was the perfect vision of beauty. Her blond hair was pulled high on her head so the elegant curve of her neck showed and the defiant tilt of her chin was emphasized. Her carefully pampered skin glowed in the gaslight. Giselle sat on a fragile-looking chair, cooling herself with a delicate fan.

Bucky's mother sat beside Giselle. The two were a vision of wealth and culture. Which didn't really hide the fact that they were as stubborn as Missouri mules. Unlike Giselle, Bucky's mother was dark—Bucky took after her with his brown hair, but his eyes were blue like his father's. Both women were slender as reeds, dressed in silk and coifed to perfection. And both of them rarely lifted a finger.

With his hands clasped behind his back, Bucky stood before them as they dictated his life. He understood perfectly why Shannon had run off to the West. He chose to see her as escaping from her overbearing mother rather than from him. And yes, he might as well admit he could be lying to himself.

But her escape meant nothing, because it was only temporary, and therefore, it was no escape at all. Shannon was stuck with him, and it was time she accepted it.

Stuck with him? Give up her dreams? It was the love story of every woman's dreams.

He pictured himself on one knee, holding her hand.

Shannon, I'm sorely afraid we're stuck with each other. Would you please give up your dreams and marry me? And can we do it before our parents drive us crazy?

Bucky almost buried his face in his hands. He made a fervent promise to himself to spend all his spare time thinking of a better way to propose. The truth was obviously out of the question.

"I should have married her and gone along on her trip." He hadn't asked her, and as obsessed as she'd been about her father's ridiculously garbled last words and arcane map, he didn't think she'd have paid him much mind if he had.

"You should have married her and insisted she give up on this rubbish," Mother said as she straightened the ruffles along the rounded collar of her dress.

"But I didn't." It occurred to Bucky that if he left right now for the Wild West, he wouldn't have to talk to any of Shannon's or his family for a long, long time. That alone recommended the idea. "Now it's time to rectify the situation."

He envied Shannon her absence. Yet another thing he could leave out of his marriage proposal.

"If I'm to strike out in the wilderness, I'll need to hire a few people to go along with me." A shiver of pleasure surprised him. Why, he was looking forward to the trip.

"I took care of it," Mother said.

Bucky kept the scowl off his face through years of practice, but his heart was definitely scowling. "Thank you, Mother."

"I've bought you a train ticket as far west as Shannon's last known location." Giselle fluttered her fan and gave Bucky a smile that almost chilled his blood into ice. A big part of why he'd always wanted to marry Shannon was to save her from this scary woman. "I've had someone checking on her routinely throughout this venture."

"You have?"

"Yes, of course."

"But she had a terrible time hiring someone to accompany her. If you hired someone to follow her, why didn't you just hire someone to go with her?"

"She'd have seen that as my giving her my blessing. I couldn't do that."

"Certainly not." Bucky's mother sniffed. "Such nonsense, Giselle. Why didn't you put a stop to it?"

"It was her father's fault. Dreadful man. Such a mistake to marry him." Giselle shrugged her dead husband off with a mere lift of her shoulders and her snooty nose. "And she has complete control over her inheritance from my father. What was my Grandpapa Shaw thinking?"

"He was too much influenced by Chatillon and his fur trading stories. Henri always was a law unto himself. So often men are. No reasoning with them."

It was not the least bit fair that Bucky stood here taking orders from these two old hens while they lamented unreasonable men. He had a flicker of rebellion and for once enjoyed it rather than feared it.

"So this person you've got following her. . ." Bucky needed them to get back on the topic of Shannon. "Why don't we just telegraph him and find out where she is?"

"Well, he isn't actually with her of course. She set off into the wilderness, and my inquiry agent stayed behind in the nearest suitable town."

"What town? I think Durango, Colorado, is the last I've heard from her." Bucky had tried to find it on a map, but with no luck. A train did pass through there, though, so Bucky could go to Durango, in Colorado, home of mountains and perhaps a buffalo or a mountain lion or a grizzly bear. Or an Apache.

He decided to pack his rifle. There would be reasonable comfort since his family owned their own train car. They owned a fair share of several trains, too.

"My agent said Durango isn't a town fit to live in. He hired someone to inform him when she returned, and then he traveled on to Denver."

Nodding his head silently, Bucky found himself rehearsing testimony.

But your honor, the man was supposed to protect, or at least follow, my fiancée. Instead, because Durango was too rustic, he went to Denver to await word. Simple human decency forced me to kill the worthless worm with my bare hands.

He suspected the judge would acquit him instantly.

"When am I to meet these people you've hired to accompany me, Mother?"

His mother said, "Ring for the butler, please. Ebersol has the details."

Mother hired the butler; the butler hired the men who would accompany him. Giselle hired an inquiry agent; that agent hired someone to do his job. Bucky yanked on the bell pull with far more force than was necessary. He gripped his hands behind his back.

"Would you mind terribly telling Ebersol to send in a tray of tea, dear?" Mother asked. "Then discuss this business outside. Giselle and I have to consult with my secretary about sending invitations to this fall's rout. I don't believe you'll be back from fetching Shannon home in time to attend. Pity.

With a stiff smile he left the room, having another stiff talk with the judge. This one about matricide. And—and matri-in-law-icide. Was that a word? Because it certainly should be.

With a grim smile, Bucky knew he'd be acquitted again, with the judge's thanks for making the world a less pretentious place.

It wasn't the first time that Bucky had felt a passion to marry Shannon just to get both of them away from these two shrews. His father had already purchased the lovely home here in St. Louis where they'd live. His mother's father was already dropping a quiet word here and there about Bucky's political ambitions.

Hopefully, Grandfather would drop a word in Bucky's ears soon, so he'd know what those ambitions were exactly. Giselle and

Mother were planning the wedding, the social event of at least the decade.

He was quite sure they'd already ordered Shannon's dress. He really did have to get on with rounding up his bride.

Bucky wondered if Shannon would be interested in moving permanently to Durango. . .or maybe Denver.

Seven

Gabe watched Shannon climb down the wall with such agility she might well have been part mountain goat.

Except with dark hair. And petticoats. And she smelled real good.

Shannon wasn't really much like a mountain goat at all.

Her hair was in a tight braid, not smooth and nice. He doubted she had a comb handy. But she'd done her best and looked tidy. Her eyes, a warm brown, much lighter than his, snapped with energy as she approached the fire in the chill morning air and gave him a bright smile. It was only when she got close that Gabe realized all of it was fake. The energy, the smile, the mountain goat imitation—all of it phony as all get out. Once she was close, he saw the dark circles under her eyes. "Good morning, Gabe."

"Did you get much sleep?" He'd hated that she'd been in that cold, spooky cave alone overnight. And he'd nearly frozen down here by the fire. How much could she have slept?

"Enough."

Which meant not nearly enough.

"My headache is nearly gone."

Which meant it wasn't gone.

"I feel altogether better able to cope with things."

She looked ready to keel over.

He didn't bother to mention any of his impressions because they had to move out whether she felt good or not. "Okay, let's eat quick, and I'll take you into the nearest town. I can give you enough money to take the stage to the nearest train, and I'll make sure you have enough to buy a ticket home to St. Louis."

Gabe had thought it through carefully. He could afford this, and she was helpless. Giving her money to solve her problems was the exact right thing to do. It felt generous and wise and heroic. He waited for her to thank him. Maybe hug him again. He was especially waiting for that.

"Nonsense. I'm not going home."

His smile faded. "Why not?" Then he was sorry he asked, because why ask a question if you don't want to know the answer?

"You said last night you're free for the rest of the summer, right?" She squared her shoulders and turned that pretty, phony smile even brighter. It didn't look even close to natural.

"Not free exactly. My family is expecting me sooner or later. I didn't tell 'em exactly when I'd show up, but—"

"I don't have any money with me, but I have funds available to me back home. I think you should help me find the next city. The one that's *really* made of gold."

Gabe wished so hard he could believe her. He'd like to find a city of gold. Who wouldn't? But Gabe had lived with reality just a little too long. He'd lived in the Blue Ridge Mountains growing up, and they got by just barely if Pa and Ma and his six brothers and he worked hard every day. They lived on food from their garden, milk from their cow, eggs from their chickens, and all the meat they could hunt. Then he'd joined the cavalry, and army life almost ground a man up and left him for dust. There was no time for dreaming of cities of gold.

He'd even been to a mining town. It was a blight on the face of the earth. Greed and filth. Brutal work, and if a gold strike did turn up, it had to be dug out of the ground with hours and days and weeks of backbreaking labor. Then a man had to fight to hold on to it with knives and guns and ruthless strength.

It came down to Gabe being a realist. "Shannon, I know you want to prove that your father's work was worthwhile, but—"

"You're not doing anything anyway, Gabe." Her smile vanished, and she grabbed the front of his shirt in both hands. Her desperation was actually a nice change from the phony smile. "Why not come with me? We can find someone to travel along. An older woman maybe who's interested in heading west. Maybe a husband and wife. Then the trip would be. . .proper for us. Together. You can hunt for food. We don't have to spend a lot of money to travel. We'll live off the land while we follow my map to the next stopping point. Those folks took my money, but I have more. I could pay you enough to buy a nice herd, get your ranch off to a solid start."

It was quite a speech. "You been practicing that for long?"

With a sheepish shrug, Shannon nodded. "Most of the night."

Which might explain why she looked as if she'd gotten next to no sleep. "No. I'm not going on your treasure hunt, Shannon. The closest town east is—"

"You might as well take me to the closest town west." Shannon crossed her arms and turned into the very picture of beautiful stubborn womanhood. "Because I'm heading west."

"Now, there's no sense getting riled."

Her eyes could just as well have been flaming arrows shot from an Apache's bow. "I'm not riled."

She didn't *sound* riled. She sounded calm. Insanely calm. "There's nothing to the west for a hundred miles. You—"

"I'm going west, Gabe." She cut him off. "I'm afraid, and I wish very much you'd come along because I have no way to care for myself, but if you won't come, then please point me in the direction of the nearest town. We can part company now. I appreciate all you've done—"

"You know good and well"—Gabe ripped his Stetson off his head—"that I can't just ride off and leave you in the wilderness."

"Certainly you can. I'd prefer the nearest town a bit southwest if you please, because that's the direction I'm going. I'll be walking of course—"

"I'll take you!" Like he had any choice, short of tossing her over his saddle and dragging her onto a train heading east. He wondered if the other passengers would support him if he shackled her to her seat. Abusing women was a mighty serious business, so he might have his hands full keeping her on the train until it chugged out of the station. But probably, if they listened to his reasons, they'd side with him and keep the little idiot on board.

Her stubbornness just melted clean away. "Thank you."

"You're *not* welcome."

"Did you have somewhere you intended to go?"

"I told you I was drifting. I'm on my way to my brothers', and there's no hurry, but that's beside the point. My plans are none of your concern."

"Because you don't have any?" Shannon gave him a smile that seemed to soothe the grizzly in him.

"That's right. But I'm not going on the whole treasure hunt. I'm dropping you off at the first place I can and leaving you."

Her smile faded, and her chin came up in a defiant little tilt. "That suits me just fine."

"Go fill this pot with water so we can get some coffee on."

"Yes, Gabe." Shannon whirled and rushed for the spring.

"And hurry up. This place feels haunted. I hate it."

"I hate this place." Randy used to be so quiet. Lurene sure wished he'd go back to it. But he seemed to feel comfortable voicing his unwanted opinions.

Lurene didn't admit it, but she hated this place, too. They rode into that eerie canyon and looked at those homes built into rock, rising high on the wall. Her eyes went straight to the highest one, and suddenly she realized they had no way to get up there and shake the truth out of that woman.

"Hey, Shannon Dysart." Her shout echoed off the canyon wall until it sounded as if a hundred people were calling for Shannon to come out. "We're back."

There was no response.

"She can't have died yet. I wonder if we can still collect ransom if she's dead. I ain't never tried kidnapping before." On that ugly comment, Ginger rode her horse forward at a fast clip, as if she weren't afraid of ghosts one whit.

Lurene followed, and she heard the men fall in line. They rode up to the base of the cliffs, and the five of them stared up, trying to figure out what in the world to do.

"It don't make sense that she'd be dead." Lobo looked sideways at Lurene.

"Nope. And it don't make sense that she'd ignore us. She's got to know by now that she'll never get down without help. Maybe she's scared, but it'll come to her soon enough that she needs us."

"We've been half the day riding back here." Randy swung down off his horse and tied it. "I'm gonna get a fire goin' and cook these rabbits I shot. I'm hungry."

Because it would keep him busy, Lurene didn't stop him, assuming she could have.

"If we climb up there and I—" Lurene looked at Lobo, measuring his height. "If I stand on your shoulders, I can—"

"Nope, not enough. You'll be a good four feet short."

They both turned to look at Ginger who wasn't all that tall.

Randy lit a match to the fire. "Why don't you just use a ladder?"

"Because we shot the ladder to pieces." Lurene wanted to do the same to Randy.

"Not *that* ladder, the one out in the brush." He nodded his head toward a section of the canyon floor that looked impenetrable with mesquite. "It's old, but it's in decent shape, at least as good as the one we used."

"Yep, let's use that one." Lurene spent her life being calm. She'd learned she could outthink most anybody, and she'd learned to keep that to herself, especially around men. Her hardfisted pa taught her men didn't like being bested by women, not even their own daughters. She decided then and there that she'd like very much to calmly cut out Randy's liver. She'd deny herself that pleasure only until after they'd found the gold. "Can you show us where it is, Randy?"

"Reckon I can." Randy looked her right in the eye, and Lurene had the sudden sense that he knew exactly what she was thinking. And she thought for the first time he might be as hard to kill as Cutter. And if Randy stuck with his brother, then both of them might be hard to get rid of without sharing the gold.

Lurene didn't like any part of it.

Getting slowly to his feet from where he crouched by his pile of broken twigs, Randy walked carefully, skirting the mesquite with their reaching, scratching branches, and vanished into what looked like a solid wall of scrub brush. The brush was high enough that she couldn't even see the top of his head, but minutes later he came out carrying a ladder that looked almost as rickety as the one they'd used yesterday.

"Let's get up there and have it out with her." Lurene remembered their struggle of yesterday to get the ladder to that top level.

"You go on. You don't need anyone else up there." Randy laid the ladder on the ground and turned back to the fire. "And I don't have much of a belly for watching you threaten a woman until she tells where to find something that doesn't exist. Were it up to me, we'd worry about ransoming her and forget a buncha gold no more true at the end of her next map than it was at the end of this one." Randy looked pointedly at the dull, dusty rock. No one could deny that Shannon's first map had led them to this worthless stretch of ground. "Whatever you do to her, leave her alive." Randy went back to his fire, turning his back to them as if he had no fear of a bullet crashing into his spine.

Darrel stood on past Randy, though, facing Lurene and the others. Though Darrel was slow of thought, he was watchful. And Randy clearly trusted him.

The whole thing gave Lurene reason to worry. She looked at Lobo. "Ready to fight with that ladder?"

"Ready. We won't use it until that last climb. No sense straining it more than we have to."

Lurene nodded and stepped back while Lobo went to work.

<hr>

"Can't we ride any faster than this?" Shannon had promised she wouldn't ask that question again, but it slipped out, about once every mile.

"No, we can't." Gabe shifted as though he was irritated. "The horse is carrying a double load."

Shannon was riding behind Gabe, holding on with strength born in fear. She'd never done much riding in St. Louis since her family had a carriage. She'd thought she was learning the way of it, though they'd come a long way on the train before turning to horseback. But this wasn't exactly riding. It was more clinging for dear life. And clinging to a strong, warm man, who shifted his weight and turned to look at her once in a while.

She found holding Gabe very disturbing. Nothing like hanging on tight to the cold, solid saddle horn. She wanted it to be over badly. "He seems like a big strong horse. How far did you say it is to town?"

"We're gonna push hard all day, and we'll spend the night with a family of Navajos who run a herd of sheep and have a small settlement near a waterhole. I spent the night there just yesterday." There was an extended moment of silence. "No, two days ago."

Gabe shrugged, and Shannon clung.

"As for a town, Tuba City is to the east. To the west, well, I've never been all that far west of here, not this far north. I'll ask Doba Kinlichee."

"Doba what?"

"That's the father of the family of Navajos. Doba Kinlichee. They're the first place east of here I know of. I was coming from that direction because I've been out to see my brother in California, so I stayed with them."

"I thought you said you'd never been west." Shannon bristled. He was making excuses not to help her.

"I've never been straight west. There's nothing that way because of the Grand Canyon. I came from the southwest." Gabe twisted around to look at her. "Is that where you want to go?" He sounded almost like he'd consider coming with her if that was her goal.

Shannon saw no sense in burdening him with the truth. "I'd have to check my map."

"I was heading to see another brother in New Mexico. My oldest brother, Abe. He's got kids almost grown. It's a long ride to the waterhole where Doba lives with his wife and kids. Doba's mother and some aunts and uncles are there, too. Lots of family. It's a welcoming place."

"They live alone a long day's ride from the nearest city?"

"Their family has lived around this waterhole in the high desert since long before there were any cities."

"And they're Navajo? Indians? Are they dangerous?" She clung a little tighter to him. It was no hardship.

"They're good people. Friendly to me. I don't know 'em except for the night I stayed there, but I trust 'em."

"What will they think of us riding in like this—together and unmarried."

"I think it will be fine unless Hank Ford is there."

"He's the judgmental type?"

"It's kind of his job."

"To call people to task as sinners?"

"He's Parson Ford, a missionary to the Navajo. There is a parson who lives at the settlement with his family, and they're kind, friendly people. But Parson Ford is...well...he's big into fire and brimstone, or so Doba said."

"A little fire and brimstone never hurt anyone." Shannon had heard a few revival preachers, and she enjoyed them.

"Hearing about it, sure. But honestly, Shannon, a little fire and brimstone never hurt anyone? I don't think you can say that."

"True."

"Parson Crenshaw does live at the settlement with Doba and his kin, but Parson Ford is a traveling missionary. He's gone for long stretches of time. Doba talked about the parson like he was one to set the devil running for cover."

"I wish he'd been with me yesterday when my expedition members left me to die alone. The devil was in that."

"From what I heard, Parson Ford would have terrified them until they ran away."

Shannon thought of the way Lobo had dangled her over the ledge, the ruthless way Ginger had shoved her and enjoyed hurting her, the way the Lloyd brothers had gone down that ladder without a thought of the fate they were leaving Shannon to, and the cold in Lurene's eyes—the one member of her party she'd felt a friendship with. The good parson would have had his work cut out for him.

As the day stretched longer, Gabe's temper shortened.

The horse sidled around a jumble of rocks in the barely existent trail.

Shannon gasped and grabbed a tighter hold on Gabe. "Stop it."

Leaning forward, hanging on tight, Shannon poked her head around Gabe's broad shoulder. "Stop what?"

"You're strangling me."

Shannon thought that over for a second. "You're a good one to talk. You didn't spend a part of yesterday swinging from a noose."

"It wasn't a noose."

"I was the one swinging. It felt like a noose."

Gabe growled.

"Hey, it was my belly. I'll judge if I got hanged. . .hung. . . anyway, it was a noose."

"It doesn't count as a *hanging* if it's around your belly."

"Does, too."

"Does not."

"And anyway, what does that have to do with me being afraid of falling off the horse and hanging on tight to *your* belly?"

Gabe growled.

"That's no answer."

"Shut up and ride, woman."

"You know, some things about you are very heroic, Gabe."

"Well, thank you." Gabe turned to meet her eyes, a bit less crotchety—for a second.

"And some things, not so much."

Gabe growled.

The sun glared down, but they had stretches of shade when they'd ride through thick stands of pine. They passed barren stretches with beautiful red rock rearing up out of the ground, and Shannon saw trails wind up into higher ground, dotted with quaking aspens.

Gabe didn't head for the high ground. He unhooked his canteen from his saddle horn and handed it back to her without turning. "Drink light." The man grew increasingly gruff and taciturn as the day wore on.

Shannon's thirst started to gnaw. She wanted to take long gulps out of the canteen but knew she didn't dare. "Can't we ride up there and search for water where those aspen grow?" She pointed at what looked like a fairly lush spot on the mountain they were riding past.

"No."

She felt lucky for that grunted answer. "Why not?"

"Done with that canteen?"

Fighting the urge to drain the water, Shannon took a sip so small it barely wet her throat then handed it back. She noticed, as best she could from behind him, that Gabe drank little more than she did. She squeezed him to get his attention. "Why not? Those trees can't grow without water can they?"

"Stop that."

"Stop what?"

"Holding on so tight."

Shannon frowned at his back. "I really don't feel all that safe back here. I need to hang on."

There was a long moment of tense silence. Shannon loosened her hold, but still she was riding on a tall horse. She needed *something* to hang on to. Besides, he hadn't answered her question.

"So why can't we hunt water?"

"I don't want to climb a mountain and spend an hour searching for water we can do without. We're already going to be getting to Doba's late in the day."

"That makes sense. Why didn't you just say that in the first place?"

Since she was hanging on, she thought she actually heard his insides growl as if he were a wolf getting ready to pounce.

"Say something." She jostled him a bit with her arms to get him to answer.

"Time for a break." Gabe rode his horse toward a mountain that was rising up on their left. A clump of aspens offered a bit of shade.

"Hang on to the cantle."

"What's that?"

"The back edge of the saddle that you're sitting so close to. Too close to. Right up against. Hard up against."

Shannon let go of him with one arm and touched the back of the saddle seat. "Cantle. Okay." She brushed her hand against Gabe when she gripped it. There was really no avoiding the contact.

"I'll get off first." Gabe almost threw himself off the horse and practically kicked her in the head. . .bad enough with his boot, but the spurs would've really hurt. Then he turned and dragged her down. Holding her waist in his hands, when her toes finally touched the ground, she expected, considering his mood, for him to plunk her down and stalk away grumbling. Instead, he held on. "You really want to know why I'm not talking to you?"

"Yes, I really do." She suspected suddenly, based on the fire in his eyes, that no, she really didn't.

Their gazes met as he forgot to let go. His strong hands flexed at her waist, and Shannon got the impression that there was something deep in Gabe's eyes that she needed to see. Had to see. She inched closer.

He was still in his state of forgetfulness apparently.

They stood, Gabe looking as hard at her as she was at him, and suddenly, slowly, as if he wasn't even trying to stop himself, Gabe very deliberately leaned forward.

"This is why," he spoke against her lips, and then he kissed her.

It felt right to slide her arms up his broad chest and wrap them around his neck. She'd been holding him all morning. He was familiar and heroic and kind—except for the one-word answers and the grunting.

The kiss ended long before she was ready. Gabe eased back just inches. "All your talk last night of what's proper?"

Shannon vaguely remembered that. . .while she lay awake alone in that cold, definitely-not-haunted-but-only-because-there-was-no-such-thing-as-ghosts cave. "Yes."

"This is why we shouldn't be alone together for long stretches of time." He kissed her again, and her toes weren't even touching the ground. Gabe was holding on tight, but for a fact, she felt like she was floating and it had nothing to do with his grip and everything to do with his lips.

"Does this happen *every* time a man and woman are not chaperoned?" In truth she'd never had such happen to her before. But then she'd never spent any real time in the company of a man, and certainly not alone. Not even with poor Bucky, whom her mother was determined she marry.

"Not every time. But it can. Especially when a woman is as beautiful as you." He lowered his head again and tightened his arms, and Shannon was lost.

What time passed, passed without notice. Finally, Gabe pulled away and reached up to unfasten her arms from his neck. "We've had a long enough break. We have to go on to the Kinlichee hogan."

"Now?"

"Oh yes. Right now. Right this very instant before things get out of hand and I end up hunting down Parson Ford.

"The one you said might insist we get. . .married?"

"Yep, that's the one." He rested his forehead against hers, and she wanted another kiss, just one more. One more moment that was not at all proper.

She sneaked and got herself one. And Gabe sneaked, too. A couple of times.

"What would you hunt him up for?" Just because her thoughts had gone to one idea didn't mean his had.

"To do some. . .insisting of my own."

Eight

Gabe pushed his poor gelding as hard as he dared. But he couldn't run away from himself.

Shannon kept a snug hold on his waist all afternoon, and that meant he couldn't run away from her either.

He knew, in the most reasonable part of his mind, that he couldn't be falling in love with Shannon. Just because her arms around him made him light-headed with pleasure, and he wanted to kiss her senseless, and he felt an almost uncontrollable need to protect her, and he kept picturing her standing in front of the potbellied stove in his house back in Wyoming, and he wanted to take her to meet his brothers, and he could imagine what their children might look like. Just because of that, it did *not* mean he was falling in love with her.

A man couldn't fall in love with a woman he barely knew. Add to that, he'd never been around many women. Really only Annette back in Wyoming. And seeing as how she was married to another man, that hadn't worked out all that well.

What with a house full of brothers and a cavalry full of

soldiers, there'd been no women to tempt him. He might well fall in love with any woman he ever spent ten minutes with. How could he know?

Add to that, a lot of what he did know about this particular woman wasn't reassuring. She was bent on hunting all over the western lands for gold, of all stupid, hard-to-find things. Most gold hunters would make more money driving a stagecoach. Work less, too. And sure as shootin' live better.

Even worse than digging for gold, she had some half-witted notion that she'd find a city built out of the stuff. And she hadn't even shown him the map. If he agreed to ride along with her, he didn't even know where he was going.

West.

That was all she'd really said.

West.

Like that wasn't vague.

It figured a city of gold that had never been found would likely be in a real hard-to-find place, like the middle of the Sonora Desert or the top of some snowcapped mountain. Both of those were west—kind of.

But even knowing she was probably a lunatic, Gabe had never felt anything sweeter than Shannon's arms around him. He thought of Annette back in Ranger Bluff, and how he'd connected with her instantly.

A sister. He tried to convince himself of that. A sister. He'd felt *brotherly* feelings for her. Why not? He'd never had a sister. That could be how a man felt about his sister.

And she'd already been as good as spoken for when Gabe had finally gotten close enough to her to know how sweet she was. Up until then, he'd thought she was a likely culprit in the death of his ma. No romantic notions there.

But he'd felt for Annette much of what he was feeling for Shannon, and there was no one to stake a claim on Shannon. Less than no one. The woman was in desperate need of someone to protect her, love her, feed her, care for her, talk some sense into her.

They were riding alone, and Gabe had kept his mouth shut mainly out of a rock-solid fear of what would come out if he spoke. But now he realized he was wasting time. If he didn't know her, then he'd just missed out on a huge chance to change that.

He opened his mouth to start getting to know this pretty woman with the tough belly and the very warm, tight arms.

A herd of sheep charged out of a stand of mesquite and spooked his horse.

Before the chestnut was done rearing and Gabe had it back under control, Shannon was hanging from the side of his saddle, her legs dangling, still clinging like a burr to his waist.

He looked down, smiled at her ashen face, grabbed her, and pulled her back, in front this time, onto his lap. He liked having her there, and he was done talking himself out of it. She needed him. And he certainly needed her. "Shannon, will you—"

"Sorry. Crazy *dibeh*. Crazy sheep."

Gabe's attention was torn from Shannon to a young woman who came bounding up out of that same scrub brush. He'd noticed her at the settlement yesterday. . .or the day before. Whenever he'd been there. She was the daughter of the parson. What was her name? Gabe fumbled around for it and finally remembered. "Emmy." That was it. "I'm Gabriel Lasley. Remember me?"

The girl was a beauty. Dark hair pulled back in a single braid. Her skin tanned by long hours in the desert sun. Eyes an unusual shade of bright, strong blue. What he'd noticed though was the mischief in her expression. After five minutes in her presence, he caught the close supervision of her overprotective mother and the indulgence of her sentimental father. She also had lived with the Navajo so long she knew their language and their life. She was a wild one. She smiled at Shannon with teeth so white they glowed in her tawny skin. "You've rounded up a lady to travel with in a single day, Mr. Lasley?"

"Well, it's been quite a day."

Emmy laughed and looked at Shannon. "I'm Emmy Crenshaw. My father is the parson at the Kinlichee settlement."

"I'm Shannon Dysart." Shannon rested her head against Gabe's chest as if only his strength were holding her up. Her brown hair had come out of its untidy braid thanks to the long day and the recent brush with catastrophe. Her face was streaked with dirt, she acted like riding a horse was one long brush with death, and she'd been awhile between baths.

By comparison, Emmy was tidy and clean and comfortable in her skin. And her smile was all for Gabe.

"Yes, Emmy. We'll see you after you catch your crazy sheep."

The girl laughed and hurried after the flock.

"You mentioned Parson Crenshaw had a family, but you didn't mention a young, beautiful daughter."

"I didn't mention any of 'em. He's got a passel of young'uns."

Shannon glared at him for no reason Gabe could imagine.

Gabe rode on into a green oasis in the middle of land that up until now had sprouted more rock than grass. The first thing he saw was a line of heavily loaded mules, obviously ready to depart Doba's settlement. Gabe had left here just one day ago. He furrowed his brow. Not one day, two days? He wasn't sure.

This team must have come in from the south, from Flagstaff, after he'd headed east. There were boxes and bags all over the ground, and the now much more lightly loaded mules would probably head. . .where? Somewhere with a telegraph office hopefully— which Gabe could make use of to explain the delay to his brother.

Gabe had come to Flagstaff from California on the Beale Wagon Road. Lieutenant Ned Beale had laid it out using his famous Camel Corp. The camel experiment had finally been abandoned, and many of the camels were set loose in the wild. Gabe had seen a pair of them himself during his cavalry days. All he knew about camels was that they had a reputation as mean-natured critters who'd charge a passing horse, so the cavalry riders had learned to stay clear of them.

"I need to talk to that mule handler over there. I should send a message to my brother Abe telling him I'll be late."

Shannon nodded.

"You want to let your ma know where you are?"

Her head stopped moving as if she'd been frozen solid. Shannon's chin trembled then lifted just a bit. "Mother has washed her hands of me, I'm afraid."

"Surely it's not that bad." Gabe couldn't resist touching that little dent in her chin. Which drew Shannon's wide-eyed attention to him. "You could at least send a few words letting her know you're all right."

With a little shrug, Shannon said quietly, "I don't have the price of a telegraph message, Gabe."

"I do." He smiled at her struggle with pride. He'd figured out she wasn't used to being penniless, and she had no talent or inclination for begging or borrowing. "Go ahead and send her a message. It might make things a mite easier when you get back east." If she got back east. Gabe was thinking about keeping her.

"I—well—all right." Shannon frowned. "Thank you, Gabe. I appreciate your generosity."

"Glad I can help." He rode to the man in the lead of the line of ten sturdy mules.

"Where're you heading?" Gabe saw the sharp intelligence in the homely face of the mule skinner.

The man rode a buckskin mare and was checking the ropes on his string of mules. He took overly long studying the way Shannon hugged up next to Gabe. Then he scratched his whiskered face and spit a brown stream of tobacco on the ground. "Ridin' straight through to Tuba City."

"Can I send a message for you to wire to my brother, and

another from Shannon here to her ma?"

"I reckon I could get a couple of wires off." The man was as lanky as his mules and smelled about as good. But Gabe knew the kind of man who rode a hard trail like this. He was trusted with packages and money, and no dishonest man could make a living at it. If a mule skinner gave his word, he'd keep it.

"Obliged." Gabe reached out a hand. "Gabe Lasley."

The man shook.

"And this is Shannon Dysart."

"Not your wife?"

"No." Gabe wouldn't lie, but it occurred to him that he and Shannon should have discussed just what to say.

The mule skinner scowled over Gabe's answer but didn't comment.

Gabe fumbled in his shirt pocket for a piece of paper and a pencil he kept there. He jotted a few words to his brother Abe, telling him where he'd gotten turned aside and not to expect him anytime soon. Shannon got a few seconds with the pencil and paper, too. They handed the notes over along with enough money to send the wires, and the mule train headed out.

Gabe watched them go, still holding Shannon. He was about to dismount just as a heavily accented voice drew his attention.

"Back so soon, my friend?" Doba Kinlichee greeted Gabe with a smile. Gabe wouldn't exactly call the man a friend since they'd only met the once, but he was certainly friendly. It didn't hurt that he had possession of the best waterhole in the area. People came by. Doba was friendly. People paid for food and a place to sleep while they got a drink, watered their horses, and filled their canteens.

Doba held the horse's reins while Gabe swung down with Shannon still cradled against him, her arms around his neck. He was reluctant to lose the feel of her, even though she'd been driving him loco all day. "Thanks. We'd like to stay the night."

"You and your. . .wife? You didn't mention you were married when you came through before." Doba smiled as if he had done the matchmaking. His face was weathered. His eyes black as a raven. He wore a soft leather jerkin over a faded red shirt. His pants had fringe down the outside of the legs, and he wore a battered black hat with an eagle feather dangling from the beaded band.

"We have an empty hogan you can—"

"No, she's not my wife." Gabe thought again they should have come up with a clear explanation. He stood Shannon on her feet and wished he'd done that a bit earlier.

Doba's smile faltered. "You travel with your—sister?"

Gabe shared a long look with Shannon. "No. I just found her stranded and brought her in."

"Just today?"

Gabe wasn't a bit good at lying. He waited for Shannon to take over and do the talking.

The silence stretched far too long. Gabe finally said, "Well, yesterday. She was traveling—"

"You and an unmarried woman traveled together for days, Gabriel?"

Gabe noticed movement to his side and turned to see a squat, gray-haired man striding toward him. Wearing a parson's collar. "What is this, Doba?" The man stopped in front of Gabe, standing shoulder to shoulder with his very outraged Navajo friend.

A couple who made the parson look like a youngster were bolder than the other residents of Doba's little community. They walked up behind the parson.

"Parson Ford, is it?" Shannon swallowed audibly. "Hello. We are looking for a place to stay."

The parson cut Shannon off with one cauterizing look then swung his eyes to Gabe. The brimstone in the parson's eyes reminded Gabe of where he *didn't* want to end up for all eternity.

Behind the parson's back, Gabe saw the bustling settlement where Doba lived. A dozen or so hogans were scattered in the pretty mountain valley, near a pond fed by a flowing spring. Children were watching them with open curiosity. The adults were more subtle, but Gabe knew they were paying attention.

He didn't see a sign of the more kindly Parson Crenshaw, though he saw a half dozen stair-step children who didn't look Navajo, diverted from their play with Doba's family by Gabe and Shannon.

"Gabriel," Doba said mournfully, "we talked yesterday. You told me you were a man of faith."

"And now, today, you ride in with a young woman in your company," the older man said. "We have children here. We can't have an unmarried couple traveling together."

The parson's eyes snapped with a bit of temper. "Hosteen Tsosi, I'll handle this. He's right, Gabe. You have ruined this young woman. And I clearly saw that there was an affection between you. This can't be allowed. You will stand before me and do the right thing, or I will—"

"Now, Parson, nothing improper happened between us." Gabe wasn't about to tell the man of God the details, because Gabe was fairly sure that some of what had gone on with Shannon would not fit the man's definition of the word *proper*. "I found her. I needed to bring her to safety, didn't I? You wouldn't have had me just ride away and leave her—"

"So you couldn't have gotten here in what remained of the day? You rode in from the east. The distance isn't so far between us and Tuba City. You could have gotten to one of these places even if you got a late start. Why did you keep her company over night?"

"It was late when I found her."

"You found her late at night?" Hosteen Tsosi's face was cut with lines that spoke of a lifetime of deep disapproval.

"Well, no, Mr. . . .uh. . .Tsosi. . .it was late afternoon. But the sun was already setting by the time we got things straightened away enough to travel."

"The sun was setting in the afternoon? In the late spring in Arizona?"

"We were in a canyon. The rock walls were to the west. I suppose if we'd ridden out of the canyon we'd have had some daylight left."

"But you know nothing of canyons and shadows cast from the west?" The parson adjusted his collar, most likely to let off some steam.

"Well yes, I know about it. I served in the cavalry in the Southwest for a while."

"But still you're afraid of the dark?" Hosteen tilted his chin and had the regal look of a Navajo holy man. His long black braids, streaked with gray, practically quivered with indignation.

"No, she just needed to rest and recover from the trouble she'd been in." And now she was in more trouble. Gabe could see in the holy man an unhappy frown, and even more in Hosteen's fiery eyes.

"So, you spent the night together?" The parson wove his fingers together across his chest.

"Yes, parson." Shannon decided to do some talking. Well, it was about time she spoke up. "But we only slept."

"You admit you slept together." Hosteen jumped on that. The woman beside him gasped and covered her mouth, her wrinkled eyes wide with shock.

Hosteen rested his hand on her shoulder. "Be strong, Mother Hozho."

"No, we didn't *sleep* together!" Shannon sounded scandalized.

"So you stayed *awake* together then?" The parson sounded even more so.

"Yes! Wait, no."

"Which is it, miss?"

"It's—" She swallowed so hard Gabe heard it. "Neither."

"I don't believe *neither* is a choice." Hosteen looked sideways at the elderly woman with him. Both shook their heads and looked back at Shannon.

"You were either asleep or awake." The parson slapped his hands together behind his back and scowled. "And you were by your own admission together."

"It's just that I wasn't up to travel." Shannon laced her fingers together. But Gabe thought the way she did it looked like she was begging the parson and his friends to believe her. Gabe thought begging was an idea with merit.

"But you were up to sleeping. . .and not sleeping."

"Our time together was perfectly innocent, Parson," Shannon insisted.

Mother Hozho made a sound that was amazingly rude.

"So nothing sinful passed between you? Two attractive young people alone overnight? Two young people that I saw with my own eyes were holding each other very close?"

Gabe should've put her down right away for sure.

"Well. . ." Shannon swallowed, if anything, even *more* loudly and caught Gabe's arm with both hands as if to keep from falling over. "Nothing. . .much."

Gabe thought under the circumstances she should have kept her hands off of him, but he couldn't just knock her down, now could he? So he let her hang on.

"Nothing *much*?" The parson's voice rose an octave. Gabe knew about octaves because of his mother and her love of playing the piano. The parson was hitting very close to a high C. "Explain this *nothing much* to me."

"I have young children here, Mr. Lasley." Doba decided he needed to get involved with the conversation.

Thank you very much, Doba.

"Is Parson Crenshaw here?" Gabe asked. He sounded like a merciful man.

"He and his wife are visiting a sick woman a few miles to the north," Doba said.

"Our whole community saw you ride in here with her in your arms." Hosteen's mouth curved down so it was nearly lost in the layers of wrinkles.

"Impressionable young children, Gabriel." Doba shook his head.

Gabe never got called Gabriel except when he was in trouble. By his ma. But it was looking like he was indeed in trouble right now. He decided to interrupt before he found himself married to the woman and then shot just for good measure. "We couldn't travel, Parson. Shannon needed a chance to recover."

"She was injured?" The parson's brimstone eyes fastened on a very healthy-looking Shannon.

"Sh–she—yes."

"I see no injuries."

"Well, she had a nosebleed—" Gabe pulled her closer. He'd been protecting her ever since they'd met. He wasn't about to stop now.

"I have one of those on occasion," Doba said. "I hold my nose for a few moments then I continue to work."

The nosebleed sounded like a poor excuse even to Gabe. He was sure the parson agreed. "And besides, she'd been through a lot, and she was very upset."

"I was very, very upset," Shannon interjected.

Gabe considered adding just a few more *verys*. It was worth a try.

"You can't even keep your hands off of her now, in front of me and Mr. Kinlichee and his family."

Gabe moved to let go of her, but he was sorely afraid she might collapse.

"I would say, Miss—what was your name again?" Parson Ford straightened the coat of his black parson's garb with a few quick, indignant tugs. "All I remember is that it isn't Lasley."

Gabe heard Shannon hesitate as if she thought the man, once armed with her name, was going straight to Shannon's mother to tell of her sins.

"It's Dysart. Shannon Dysart."

"Well, Shannon Dysart," the parson spoke as if he were handing down an eleventh commandment that he'd just received straight from a wrathful God, "I'd say that your upset has just begun."

"When did you say your brother was gonna show up?" Tyra Morgan looked a long time at Abraham Lasley.

She would be well satisfied if Gabe turned out to be half the man his big brother was. Gabe didn't look like Abraham. She'd seen Gabe a few years back, and he'd been dark haired and dark eyed, not fair like his brother. Abraham often said the six older brothers, of which he was the oldest, were the image of their pa, but Gabe took after their mother. He'd made a point of saying it to Gabe, too. An old family tradition of teasing.

But whether he resembled his big brothers or not, Gabe was tall and strong and quiet. In that way he was Abraham all over again.

Her sister had been happily married to Abraham since before Tyra was old enough to remember. Adam, their oldest son, was seventeen in a few months, and her nephew had been Tyra's playmate from her earliest memory.

Tyra had wondered about Abe's baby brother many times. She'd met most of Abraham's family, named in alphabetical order as if their mother were afraid she'd forget what order they were born—Abraham, Bartholomew, Canaan, Darius, Ephraim,

Felix, and Gabriel, the baby of the family, just as Tyra was the baby of her big family.

Tyra's pa was slowing down, and would welcome help around the ranch with an eye toward Gabe taking over and running the place when he died. Abraham had assured her that this was all fine with Gabe, but Tyra was the youngest in her family, and she knew how big brothers and sisters could plan a person's life.

"He should have been here days ago, but Gabe isn't always the most dependable." Abe shook his head in affectionate disparagement. "Still just a big kid."

"He rode with the cavalry for years, Abe." Madeline poured steaming coffee into Abraham's cup and took a second to run one hand into her husband's dark hair. "If he was a kid when he went in, you can be sure he grew up fast."

Abraham tilted his head back and smiled a private smile at Maddy, Tyra's big sister.

Tyra wanted like crazy to marry Gabe. It had been a fond wish of her childhood that she'd marry her big sister's husband. It hadn't taken much growing up before she'd figured out why that couldn't happen. Over the years as the brothers had stopped in, Tyra had cast her eye at each of them, but of course, she was always too young. But lately she'd done some growing up and she'd turned her fertile imagination to Abe's baby brother. The only one of the seven left single.

She'd even met him about five years ago, before she'd turned into a woman. Gabe had ridden through scouting for the cavalry, and she'd let her dreams run wild. Gabe had treated her like a little child.

It was infuriating that he couldn't have waited two years to ride through. At thirteen it had been hopeless. By the time she was fifteen she could have caught his attention. She was eighteen now, and Abe, her pa, and she agreed Gabe ought to marry her and ranch with Pa. The man didn't have a chance.

"And he's been in California visiting your brother?"

"Yep, Bartholomew and Darius live in the southern part of California. Gabriel just up and handed his stock over to a neighbor and spent the last year roaming."

"Wait a minute." Tyra shook her head so hard she whipped herself in the face with her single, long dark braid. "I thought you told me you and your brothers all ganged up on him and wrote a whole buncha letters begging him to come and see you before he settled down for good."

"We did. We hadn't seen him for a long time. He went through Nebraska to visit Ephraim, and then he went on east to where Canaan farms in the Blue Ridge Mountains. Felix lives in East Texas. He headed to California and was going to end up here before he headed home. I haven't seen much of him. I moved west when the boy was thirteen, and the only time I've seen him since was when he came through with the cavalry. Then he only stayed a couple of days. But Ma always sent her letters, and we'd pass them along to each other. So we stayed in touch that way until Ma died."

When Gabe had been here, it had been long enough for Tyra to get ideas. "So if you begged him to do it and he did it, why do you sound like he did something wrong?"

"No man abandons his ranch like that."

"Then why'd you ask him to?" Tyra wanted to fight on Gabe's behalf. He'd thank her when he finally got here.

"Figured maybe he couldn't handle his own place. I told my brothers about Maddy having such a pretty little sister. Your pa needed help on his place. Gabe's gotten too old to still be wandering. We'll introduce him to you, show him the ranch, and get him settled for good."

"What about his ranch in Wyoming?"

Abe shrugged. "What about it? Let someone else have it."

Tyra wanted Gabe, but she wanted to knock Abe over the

head with a stout branch, too. "He's not gonna thank you for planning his life, Abe."

It didn't miss Tyra's notice that they were planning hers along with Gabe's. But since their plans suited her right down to the ground, she didn't kick up a fuss about herself. She could have her dream husband and never have to leave home.

"Sure he will, once he sees how pretty you are, Tyra, honey." Maddy patted her on the shoulder.

Looking into Maddy's blue eyes, the exact same color as Tyra's, she knew she was being treated like a child. Tyra was a tough woman. Born and raised on some mighty hard land in southern New Mexico. But she'd be the baby of the family until the day she died.

She did want Gabe though. So she postponed fighting to be treated like an adult. She'd do the fighting after she was a married woman. Then she and Gabe'd stand shoulder to shoulder and tell all their bossy family to leave them alone.

Except for her pa. He needed help, but as long as he was drawing breath, he'd always be in charge of the Morgan spread. The Rocking M was his. He had shed his blood for that land. Tyra had three older brothers who had struck out on their own after they realized Pa was too stubborn to move aside and let one of his sons be a real partner. But now Pa was aching in his joints and he got tired a lot faster. He'd lost a lot of his love of the ranch when Ma had died. She was buried in a quiet grave along with two little sisters. Pa was ready to let a son-in-law in, Tyra just knew it.

She sure hoped that suited Gabe okay, because her heart was set on it.

"So when is he supposed to come then?" Tyra tapped her toe impatiently as she sat at the kitchen table in Abraham and Maddy's cozy cabin, quiet now with their four sons in school.

Abe grinned. "Why don't you and Maddy come to town with

me? I'll take the wagon in to pick up the young'uns. It's the last day, so we won't make 'em walk this once. I told Gabe to write if'n he got delayed. If there's a letter or a wire, we'll know when he's showing up."

Tyra smiled. "I'll run home and see if Pa needs any supplies, but I'll be back in plenty of time to ride along to town."

"She's gone!" Lurene stared, shook her head and stared, started down the ladder, stopped, climbed back up, and stared some more. Because she couldn't stop herself, she climbed the rest of the way into the cave and ran her hands all around the walls. There was no back door into the heart of the mountain. No secret tunnel. No big rock with Shannon hiding behind it. No sign that a giant bald eagle had landed and carried her off. No amount of staring would make a woman appear in this small space.

"She can't be gone." Cutter shouted at her as if yelling would make a woman who wasn't there suddenly become visible. "Are you sure that was the right cave?"

There were three of these high-up caves, and their group had searched each of them in turn with Miss It's-Not-about-Gold-It's-About-Education Dysart. Lurene knew she had the right cave, but she wanted to deny it, too.

Lurene's eyes fastened on blood, dried black on the stone floor. Shannon had only bled in one cave.

Shaking her head, trying to make her jumbled thoughts come into order, finally, Lurene forced herself to climb back down the ladder. "I saw blood, Lobo." The ladder shrieked like a tormented soul. Lurene carefully stepped down each rung. The ones that were there anyway—about every third rung was missing. When she reached the narrow ledge the ladder was resting on, she heaved a sigh of relief, then got mad and turned to Cutter.

"How could she have gotten down from there?" Cutter was

the only one who'd come up this far with her.

These ledges were just looking for a good reason to crumble away. Lurene glared at Cutter to get him moving. "Go on up if you want to hunt around, but the cave is about ten feet square. I'm sure I didn't miss a woman lying up there."

Cutter glared at that worthless excuse for a ladder, obviously almost crazed to check for himself. "Where could she have gone?"

Lurene looked at the ledge they were standing on. It was more gone than there. But was it worse than it had been earlier? More broken away? Hard to tell.

"She must have. . ." Lurene shrugged as she looked at the ledge and the one below and the one below that, ending in the hard stone of the canyon floor. "Jumped?"

Lurene and Cutter exchanged a doubtful look.

"What's going on, Lurene?" Ginger and the Lloyd brothers had stayed down. There was no use in them all coming up.

"Just a minute!" Lurene wanted to hurt someone, and right now Ginger seemed like a good choice. Good thing the woman was beyond her reach.

"Okay, she's gone." Cutter's voice was at least gratifying. He believed she wasn't so stupid he had to risk his life to check on the woman himself. "Impossible as it sounds, she got down somehow."

"You're the one with the bright idea to leave her here." Lurene glared at him.

"Yep, I know. We shoulda put a bullet in her. I won't make that mistake again."

"A'course if she had a bullet in her, she wouldn't be able to tell us where she hid that map, would she? So we'd be even more out of luck than we are now."

"I know how to read a trail. If she got down without dying, then she had to get out of this canyon." Cutter looked at the other high caves. "No way to get from one to the other. No sense climbing up there."

Cutter's eyes practically burned through stone they were so fiery hot with rage. "The only way is down. On a lower level, like this one, there are other caves she could hide in, rocks on the canyon floor she could be hiding behind. Let's go find her."

Cutter and Lurene took the time to look in every cave on that level. Then Cutter, still furious, stepped aside to let Lurene pass him and descend using the precarious handholds. It wasn't the first time Lurene had to force herself to turn her back on him.

They painstakingly checked the caves on the other levels. As they searched, the others were snarling and snapping at her and Cutter.

Once on the ground, she strode to the others. "She's not there." Lurene saw no reason to break it to them gently.

"Not there?" Ginger roared and glared up at the cave. "She has to be there."

"Are you sure there isn't a back corner of the cave?" Darrel gazed up at the cliff as if ready to climb the rocks and check himself.

"We were all in it a couple days ago. We were hunting for *hidden gold*." Lurene was annoyed with herself for answering. "I think we all checked pretty carefully." Let the idiot go up there if he doubted her ability to see with her own two eyes. "You know there wasn't a back room in that place."

She was particularly aware of Randy's sharp eyes as he looked up. He made no comment. Immediately he began scanning the ground.

Lurene joined him. "She'd never have survived a fall."

Randy looked up again. "Apparently she did."

And Lurene felt as stupid as Ginger and Darrel were, which made her mad.

"Everyone quit moving. You're wrecking any sign she left." Cutter was like a wolf trying to catch a scent.

"A little late for that." Randy stopped moving but continued to scour the ground with his eyes, then looked back overhead. "Somehow she. . ." He fell silent, thinking.

For some reason, it made Lurene nervous when Randy was thinking. She wanted to join the pack of angry wolves snarling when she should be sniffing around.

"If she jumped—" Randy kept his eyes on the cliff side with its four levels.

"She'd be dead," Ginger cut him off.

"If." Randy began again. "She." His voice became more forceful. "Jumped." He glared at Ginger until she closed her mouth. "She could have landed on the ledge. Slid down on her belly and caught the ledge somehow. That's what I'd have done if I was desperate. If it was live or die. That's what anyone would have done, though I'm surprised she got desperate as fast as she did. Most people would be a day working up the nerve, sitting around caterwauling and hoping for a miracle."

"So she's a woman of action," Cutter said. "I never figured her for one. She seemed like the type to curl up and die. I shouldn't have left her alive."

"Except we need her alive because we need the map," Lurene reminded them all. "So it's a good thing she's alive. If she hid it, cached it somewhere, then picked it up and headed out with it."

"Where?" Randy wasn't asking a stupid question; he was thinking out loud."

Cutter jabbed a beefy finger at the ground, back in the direction they'd just ridden in. "Those aren't our tracks."

Lurene was no tracker, so she couldn't begin to tell one horse from another. But she knew Cutter was good.

"One horse came in and rode back out. Hard to tell on the rocky ground, but it looks to me like a rider carrying a heavier load leaving than coming."

"Someone found her." Lurene remembered the screaming and shooting. Good chance that anyone within ten miles would have heard it and come to check. "This is Navajo country."

"Pony's shod." Cutter shook his head. "That don't always mean nuthin'. Navajos are purely tame Indians these days. They'll sometimes shoe a horse or buy or steal a horse with shoes."

Lurene looked back at the gap they'd ridden through. "Let's see which way she went." Then Lurene had a notion that cheered her considerably.

"What?" Randy asked. He was watching her mighty close to have seen that she'd had a comforting thought.

"We were worried about finding the map, figuring she hid it somewhere."

"Yep, so what?" Ginger headed for her horse. Never a thought in her head.

"Well, it'd've been hard to get her to talk. We hoped she'd tell us what we wanted to know in return for us taking her down out of that cave, but she'd've known we meant her to die. It might've been hard to get the truth out of her."

"Sure." Cutter was watching Lurene now, too.

"But now she'll have taken it from wherever she stashed it and have it back where it's easy for us to find. We don't have to worry about getting her to talk."

"And that means"—Randy smirked—"we don't have to be overly careful about how we treat her when we find her."

"Except for the kidnapping." Lurene rubbed her hand over her mouth as she pondered. "We need her alive for that."

"Why?" Ginger asked. "You know we have to kill her after what we done to her. The law'll be on us if we let her live."

"We've just got to convince the folks that'll pay for her that she's alive. If we send them a—" A smiled bloomed on Lurene's face.

"What?" Randy asked.

Lurene almost liked the kid. He was showing her a little respect.

"One of her maps. We'll prove we have her by sending a messenger with one of the maps and a note telling them to leave the money somewhere if they ever want to see her alive again. We'll have to think it out, figure a place for them to drop the money that we can get to it and get away."

"Why wouldn't they just think we'd stolen the maps from her?" Ginger shook her wild red hair. "I wouldn't pay on such flimsy evidence."

But Ginger wouldn't pay ransom to save anyone but herself. So Lurene wasn't so sure she was right. "For now, I think we need to catch her, take her alive. Make her write a note in her own hand. That oughta prove we have her."

"We can take her, get that map away from her, and drag her along on this treasure hunt. We might find what she's looking for. But whether we do or not, we'll have her to get the money out of John Jacob Astor." Cutter smiled. "I heard someone call him the richest man in America. And I've heard it's a big family. All of 'em are rich. The way I see it, we've got something the Astor family wants. I like the sound of that."

Ginger laughed with cold pleasure.

Lurene couldn't help laughing right along.

Nine

⎯⎯⎯⎯⎯⎯⎯⎯ ❧ ⎯⎯⎯⎯⎯⎯⎯⎯

Shannon stepped out of the Kinlichees' hogan on her wedding day, not one bit the joyful, blushing bride. Rather, she felt like a coyote with her leg in a trap, and she was gnawing everywhere she could think of, but she still wasn't getting loose.

Kai Kinlichee had insisted on a bath for Shannon, and she'd even gotten her hair washed and a comb through it, which after the last few days was no small job. Though the day was waning, her hair still dried quickly in the Arizona heat.

She was wearing one of Kai's pretty dresses, white with beautifully stitched decorations around the neck and hem using all the colors in the rainbow. Part Mexican, part Navajo, all beautiful. Shannon felt nearly human now that she'd bathed the last of the blood out of her hair and shed her filthy, tattered gingham blouse and sweat-stained riding skirt. Mrs. Kinlichee had even washed those clothes out—after Shannon had discreetly removed the contents of her hidden pocket of course.

Kai Kinlichee was even determined to remove the worst of the bloodstains and mend the rips. She was a very sweet lady with a spine of pure iron when it came to having this wedding.

All clean and sweet smelling, fed and given plenty of water to drink, Shannon now had the energy to stop this madness.

Gabe walked over to her as soon as she stepped outside. He was cleaned up, too. And ready to escort her.

To the wedding.

Their wedding.

Her wedding.

To a man she'd known for two days.

They probably had thirty seconds to think of a way out.

"We can just refuse, point-blank refuse to get married." Gabe sounded so reasonable, but this wasn't a situation that called for a lot of reason. It seemed better to think in terms of desperation.

Shannon caught him by the wrist and took all her need to strangle someone out on his arm. "I already tried that if you'll remember."

"Yes, I remember." Gabe narrowed his eyes at her. "You're the one, I believe, who said 'nothing much' happened. Nothing *much*? Which means a little something. Nice work. Just the very thing to reassure the parson."

"Well, did you want me to lie to a man of the cloth?"

"No, but you could have kept your mouth shut."

Shannon narrowed her eyes at Gabe. He didn't seem all that upset about the wedding, honestly.

"And you're the one who said we slept together." He jabbed a finger at her chest.

"I did not."

"Oh yes, you did. And then," Gabe-the-Calm went on, "you tried to hire Doba to come along on the trip you planned to take with me—the two of us—traveling *on* together, completely destroying the story I told about me finding you and returning you to civilization. It sounded like we'd been on the trail together for days."

"We had been."

"Like we were on a journey we'd planned long in advance, and the only trouble we had on the trail was losing some of our hired hands. It sounded like I was accompanying you on your treasure hunt from the beginning."

"I never said that."

"Well, you offered Doba a job right smack-dab in front of Parson Ford."

She went back to throttling his arm. "I said that before I realized the man is a fanatic."

"I don't think that's fair. He's a man of God. Besides, I think the parson would have let us off if Hosteen What's-His-Name—"

"Tsosi." Shannon wished she could forget the man's name. And his wife Hozho. Cranky people, the Tsosis.

"The way they see it, they found two unmarried people virtually living together right under their noses."

"Living together?" Shannon gasped. "That's only true if the whole state of Arizona counts as a house."

"I guess the parson counts it." Gabe shrugged. He remained oddly calm, which gave Shannon pause.

"But we can't get married." Shannon wanted to throw herself into Gabe's strong arms and demand he think of a way to prevent... being thrown into his strong arms.

"Shannon, I've thought long and hard about this."

"It's been less than an hour."

"And I've decided we *should* get married."

"What?" Shannon let go of his arm and grabbed the collar of his shirt. She was going to strangle something more fragile this time.

"I've reached an age where I need to take a wife. I'd like to go along on this adventure with you, but it really isn't a good idea to proceed without being married."

"Why not?"

"Why do you think?" He sounded upset for the first time.

"I have no idea."

Gabe made a little growling noise in his chest. "I'll show you why not."

He tore her hands off his collar and pulled them around his neck. Then he slid his arms around her waist, yanked her against him, and swooped down to kiss her.

Far too much time passed before Gabe straightened away from her, smiled, then once again leaned down and stole another kiss, just plain stole it like it was her treasure map all over again—and he was a whole band of outlaws.

"That's why." He spoke against her lips, and a very warm shiver raced up and down her backbone. "I've been wanting to do that all day."

"You have done it."

"Not nearly as often as I wanted to. And that definitely counts as improper. And by the way, the whole idea of improper is when men and women spend long stretches together alone, the woman with her arms wrapped tight around the man's waist—well, a man can get real improper thoughts in his head. And I might as well admit it. I did."

"You did?" Shannon didn't mean to whisper, but her voice wasn't working quite right.

"Oh yes, I did."

"I did, too."

Gabe kissed her again. "So now I think it's right. I think you're the prettiest woman I've ever seen, and I like holding you in my arms, and my ma was always after me to pick a woman and settle down. She thought it was the way life was meant to be. So, I've decided to marry you."

"We don't know each other, Gabe." Shannon meant to yell that. Instead, she just sounded like she was begging him to talk her into it. Which. . .maybe. . .she was.

"Well, we can spend the next fifty years fixing that. Let's go. And since I'm drifting anyway, we'll drift along hunting for your treasure. When we give up on that—"

"You mean when we find it."

"Okay." Gabe smiled and slid one finger across her chin dimple, then cupped her face with his hand. "I own a ranch in Wyoming. We'll go up there and live, run some cattle, raise us a herd of brown-eyed babies. What do you say, huh?" He slid his arm back around her waist and kissed her again.

Shannon didn't say yes. But then she was very busy kissing Gabe, which many very reasonable men could take to mean yes.

The kiss ended when Gabe butted his head into hers.

"Ouch." Gabe looked over Shannon's shoulder just as Parson Ford slapped him again. It was no friendly pat on the back.

"Enough of this. Now, my foolish children, we will have the wedding."

Gabe turned and looked into her eyes until it seemed as if he'd entered her mind and maybe her heart. "Yes, Shannon, it's time for the wedding. Let's go. Then we'll have us a wedding night, and tomorrow we'll go on our way, wherever you want. Isn't that your wish?"

Getting butted in the head served to clear Shannon's thinking a bit, and she remembered something very important. "Uh, I think I'd better tell you all something before we proceed with the wedding."

"What's that?" Gabe looked at her, really cheerful, the big dope.

"It changes nothing." The parson looked as if he could pour brimstone on her head with a single burning look. And was eager to prove it.

"It really does change things. And I'll admit I've been a bit... distracted."

"Distracted by the attentions of Mr. Lasley?" Kai Kinlichee

came up beside her and smiled like this was the romance of the century.

Shannon supposed there was some truth in her being distracted by Gabe. But it wasn't the *biggest* truth. "No, distracted by having my life threatened and being left stranded in the wilderness, almost falling off a cliff and being hung from a noose."

"What?" Doba asked. The man seemed interested in hearing a good story.

"Time for talk later," Parson Ford interrupted.

"Who hung you?" Kai asked.

Shannon jabbed a thumb at Gabe, and Kai frowned. "And still you want to marry him?"

"The thing I need to tell you is I'm engaged to be married." Shannon swallowed and forced herself, in the pursuit of honesty, to add, "Nearly."

Poor Bucky. She'd forgotten.

"Yes, I'm well aware of that," Parson Ford said. "Though it's a short engagement—around an hour long—you are definitely engaged."

The parson pulled a small Bible out of his large pocket, and it as good as fell open to the place the man wanted. Or so Shannon assumed because the parson didn't flip a single page. How many marriages had the man forced on people in his life?

"No, not to Gabe. I'm actually promised to someone. Back in St. Louis. I really can't wed anyone else. Bucky is expecting me to come home and marry him."

"Bucky is destined to be disappointed." The parson ran his finger down the page and looked ready to commence.

"Engaged?" Gabe's goofy good cheer melted like ice in the Arizona desert. "You're engaged to another man? Then why did you kiss me?"

And that was a truly fair question. Shannon turned to face Gabe. He deserved an explanation certainly, the truth. Just because

Bucky had completely slipped her mind until this moment didn't mean he wasn't her intended.

For one thing, it was the only way her mother would ever welcome her back to St. Louis. "We are. . .are. . .*promised* to each other. Not engaged."

"Then it doesn't signify." The parson went back to looking for his place on the page. "Engaged wouldn't signify either, after you've spent the night with this man."

"It signifies to me." Gabe frowned, glanced at her lips—which seemed somewhat swollen from his kiss—then frowned even more.

"Yes, it definitely is important, and the truth is, Gabe, I *have* made promises to another man." She looked at his stern and clearly disappointed face and almost wished she'd never mentioned Bucky. But her childhood friend deserved better than that. And Shannon *had* planned on marrying him. Someday.

When she'd broken her father's code. And followed her father's map. And found her father's gold. And restored her father's good name. And maybe written a book about her adventures, dedicated to her father. And led an expedition to the golden city to do the research her father had planned.

But after *that*, she'd definitely expected to marry Buckstone Chatillon Shaw. In fact, she'd been looking forward to it, after a fashion. Bucky was a nice man, after all. True, she'd never kissed him, unlike Gabe. "So, you can see it would be a betrayal of a previously made promise to marry someone else. I can't do it."

"You can and will." Parson Ford glared at her.

She wasn't an obedient woman by nature. Being the only child of two older parents had given her unusual freedom growing up. No doubt that freedom is what had led her into the wilderness, left her stranded in a mountaintop cave, and led to this moment when it seemed like a good idea to marry a stranger. She decided then and there that her own babies were going to follow a lot of strict rules. "I can't and won't."

Hosteen Tsosi and his dependably cranky wife, Hozho, came up beside the parson. "We cannot allow a woman of low character to stay here with us. Think of the bad influence to our children. If there is no wedding, she must be cast out of the village."

Shannon looked past the old codger and saw sheep being herded up to a watering hole across the lush green valley. Several children ran behind them, and one young woman who did not count as a child, who seemed to have eyes for Gabe.

Shannon had a wild need to marry Gabe quickly. Which she stifled.

"Your reputation is in ruins if you don't go forward with this marriage." Parson Ford looked at Doba.

"Shannon," Gabe's voice drew Shannon's gaze away from their surroundings.

"I'm sorry, Gabe. I never should have. . ." Shannon glanced at the parson and Doba. Kai and the Tsosis.

Hosteen made the parson look all soft and sweet by comparison.

Shannon decided not to mention all the things she shouldn't have done with Gabe.

"So, you're really going to marry some other man?" Gabe sounded hurt. And he had a right to be hurt. She had certainly not acted the part of an engaged woman.

"I can't marry you when he's waiting for me, Gabe. It wouldn't be honorable."

Gabe's eyes narrowed, and Shannon suspected he didn't think her kissing him was all that honorable. Then his expression hardened, and all the hurt was gone. Which most likely meant all his softer feelings for her were gone, too.

Gabe stepped a good solid pace away from Shannon then reached for her arm and turned her to face Parson Ford. "Let me say one thing to you, Parson."

"Nothing changes what must be done." The parson certainly had a way with words.

"Understand this." Gabe jabbed a finger right at the parson's nose. "Shannon Dysart is an honorable woman, and I am an honorable man. No sin passed between us in the hours we spent together. And that time together could *not* have been avoided. I found her in dire straits in the desert. Yesterday afternoon, when I found her, she was in no condition to travel for long hours over a hard trail. We will not apologize for being together or allow you to call our time together sin."

Shannon's heart swelled at Gabe's strong defense of her. She didn't deserve it. She tried to imagine Bucky saying such a thing. Then she tried to imagine what Bucky would say about the time she'd spent with Gabe. She needed to include the truth of all that had passed between them.

"I saw the way you just kissed her, son." The parson sounded kind but unrelenting. "If nothing happened between you, then why do you hold each other as if *everything* has happened between you?"

"You're right that circumstances led us to feel some bit of. . . affection for each other." Gabe's expression turned fierce. He leaned forward.

Shannon was surprised and a bit disconcerted to see the parson back up a half step.

"But we were in a perilous situation. If we clung to each other, *innocently* clung to each other for support, I will not have you calling her a sinful woman." Gabe gave Shannon a hard look then faced the parson, his shoulders square, his chin lifted in defiance. "I will not marry a woman who is promised to another man. If you forbid our presence in your village, so be it."

Which meant they were being cast out. Shannon had never been cast out of anywhere before. It reminded her of the devil being cast out of heaven somehow. It pinched.

"Shannon," Gabe's voice was cold, "we need to go."

Then to Parson Ford and the Tsosis he said in a voice that cut like a knife, "We will have to ride on to another place. That will require us spending yet *more* time alone together, and *again* that is improper, but it can't be helped since the *good people* of Doba's family have judged us to be unworthy of them. But if our travel together is a sin, it is on your heads, because you've forced us to make this choice." He faced down all three men who'd pushed this marriage on them.

Finally, Doba said, "No harm is done by you staying here another night."

"I disagree, Doba." Hosteen taking that position was no surprise.

"You've made that clear, Hosteen, but I make the decisions here."

The old man's brown, weathered face bent into its deeply etched scowl. His wife's expression was a perfect match for her husband's.

"But your time together is finished." Doba turned to Gabe. "You will separate immediately. Miss Dysart, go along with my wife."

Shannon almost left, but instead she looked at the older Navajo man who had been so harsh. "I understand that you want to hold your family to the highest standards, sir. I do. I am a woman of faith, as is Gabe. . .except for the part about being a woman, but I digress. Please at least try to believe that we have not sinned."

Parson Ford said quietly, "I fear you have most assuredly sinned in your heart, Miss Dysart."

Shannon had no response to that, because she suspected the parson might be right. "We will leave immediately in the morning."

To Gabe, she added, "Whatever town is closest is fine for you to leave me. I will hope for a place to wire home, and I will have funds forwarded to me to hire more help and continue my journey retracing my father's steps. We will have time to speak of it more tomorrow, but you saved my life, Gabe. I—I have been so overset these last days. I believe the trauma of the rescue and my gratitude—well, they—I—truly did forget all about Bucky for an unfortunately long time. I ask for your forgiveness, sir." She rested her hand on Gabe's forearm and looked at him, now cold and hurt. "Once you offered to go on my treasure hunt with me."

"Treasure hunt?" Hosteen's black eyes opened and gleamed with interest.

"Yes." Shannon turned to the man. "I have a map to a. . .a lost city. We are planning—"

"Lost city?" Doba smiled. "I know this land. There are no lost cities."

"It's hidden. I've got a map that leads into the canyon to the west. I believe I can find it."

Turning to Shannon, the old man said, "You speak of needing help to find this lost city, in the belly of the canyon?"

"Yes, that's right.

"No city down there," Hozho said with complete assurance. "The Supai have a village far to the south. It is in no way lost."

"I trust my father. I plan to see where his map leads."

Gabe heard the chill in her voice. She wasn't about to forgive the old couple.

"And you plan to spend your own money to hire someone to take you down there?" Hozho asked.

"Yes, I have to get to a town large enough to have money sent. All I had was stolen from me before Gabe came to my rescue."

"My wife grew up in the belly of the canyon." Hosteen turned to his wife. "If they need to hire someone to take them down there, who better than you?"

"And we can leave tonight." Hozho caught both her nearly white braids in her hands as if her hair was threatening to stand on end. "Remove their presence from our village."

Gabe couldn't decide if the couple was motivated by greed or piety, or maybe the old lady was homesick.

"I believe I'll ride along, Kai," Doba told his wife, "if you can handle things for a week or two."

Gabe didn't see greed in Doba's eyes, just a desire for adventure. Of course Shannon had been very careful not to say the word *gold.*

"Go with my blessing." Kai smiled like a wife of many years who was used to her husband's occasional wandering.

"And I haven't been to see my flock in the Supai village for years," Parson Ford said. "I hate horses. A necessary evil for traveling place to place, but a journey like that, into the canyon..." The parson shuddered. "I've shirked for too long. If you're going that way, I'll accompany you." He cast a look of loathing at a horse tied nearby. His expression didn't suit a man of the cloth.

Gabe looked at Shannon. She asked," Do I have to hire all of you?"

Everyone but Parson Ford nodded.

"Well, okay."

"Let's gather supplies for the trip," Hozho said. "We need to be on the trail before the sun sets."

Ten

They didn't make it out of the settlement.

Somehow the hunt for the lost city calmed everyone down, and Gabe and Shannon were allowed to stay the night at the settlement. Probably because no one else could get packed up quickly enough. They were well on the trail before the sun rose the next morning, however.

"There's the turnoff." Hozho was leading, and she took off south.

Gabe took the left fork right behind her.

"Come back here!" Shannon shouted, and Gabe turned around and gave her a look of pure pity. Like she was an idiot and a burden and a brake dragging the whole expedition to a halt.

Well that was just too bad. It was her expedition. She'd be a burden and a brake if she wanted to.

She glared at the man who had saved her life. Something she deeply valued.

Gabe had bought her a horse from Doba.

Shannon was very appreciative.

He had also insisted on paying Mrs. Kinlichee for the washing and mending she'd done.

Grateful didn't begin to describe her feelings.

She knew she was now in the company of a nice group of people who were good Christians, if a bit cranky, and who knew the land was a precious gift, and they wouldn't be here if not for Gabe's strong defense.

She was much obliged.

Honestly, he was such a generous man, things ought to be perfect.

They weren't.

"We can make the shade of that stand of trees by midday." Gabe pointed at a barely visible dot a long way in the wrong direction.

The man was bossy, and there was no denying it.

Shannon's pinto snorted, wanting to follow Gabe. The metallic clink of the bridle and the horse's tossing head stirred Gabe's chestnut, but he brought his horse under control with an ease Shannon admired. She'd felt a lot safer with her arms wrapped around his waist.

She looked at the sun straight overhead. "There are plenty of trees for shade here. Let's take a break now."

"We can get a lot more miles behind us before we stop." Gabe had been a short-tempered nag all morning. And beyond snapping at her, he'd barely spoken a word.

She badly missed the kind man who'd saved her life. She even missed the snarly man who'd ridden double with her yesterday morning. Especially now that she knew he'd been grumpy because he liked her arms around him.

She suspected his problem now was that she'd angered him by not mentioning Bucky until after she'd kissed him several times. He no doubt had her pegged as a woman of low character.

"I'd much appreciate a break from this ride." The parson had shown a real bent for whining, which struck Shannon as strange.

The man owned the rudest, runtiest mustang Shannon had ever seen. She couldn't decide if the testy little horse was really as badly behaved as the parson said or if the parson was the cause of the horse's misbehavior.

Why did a man serve the Lord in the American West when he didn't like to ride? Yes, it definitely struck Shannon as strange, but she had enough to contend with. She didn't bother worrying about the parson's or his horse's persnickety nature, whichever the case might be.

Doba, who brought up the rear, said, "Let's rest and eat some of that food my wife sent."

"At last." The parson almost fell off his horse. His foot stuck in the stirrup, and he only saved himself because he kept an iron grip on the saddle horn. Almost as if he was used to nearly falling and prepared for the worst.

Shannon dismounted and stalked off toward a stand of scrub pines.

Gabe yelled after her, "Where are you going?"

Turning back to him, she hesitated. "Uh. . .I just need a moment of privacy."

Gabe flinched as if she'd jabbed him with a hat pin.

Satisfied she'd shut him up, she stalked behind the trees and fetched her map, careful to study it, decide her next direction, then conceal it in her skirt pocket—not the hidden one. She wanted to be able to get to it later. This is how she'd conducted herself on the earlier leg of her journey, and of course that had led to disaster. But then, she still had her map, didn't she?

Studying it, she saw that Hozho was leading them in the direction she wanted to go. No need to take over leading this expedition quite yet. Somehow she thought being in charge of this group wasn't going to be easy.

When she returned to the group, a few more of them had scattered.

Doba was tending to his horse.

Gabe had his back to where Shannon had left, but he stood there, almost like a sentry, guarding her. He was not happy with her, but still he protected her.

In a moment of what she decided to think of as wisdom, she stepped up to Gabe and confided in him. Only him. "I got my map."

"Wait a minute." Gabe's eyes narrowed, but he whispered, too. "I thought you said those outlaws took your map."

"How'd you think I was going to lead us to the city of gold?"

Gabe shrugged. "Gotta admit I wondered about that. But you definitely told me your maps were stolen."

Should she show it to Gabe? Her eyes slid to the others. Not trusting anyone was deeply ingrained. "They took *some* of them."

She glanced again at Hosteen and Hohzo Tsosi, talking quietly a few yards away as they unpacked a saddlebag stuffed with food. They'd changed very quickly from wanting Shannon cast out as a sinner to coming along. She hadn't told them about the gold, but had they somehow found out what she searched for? She was going to their ancestral home. That might explain their interest, a simple desire to go home for a visit, maybe even a wish to protect their home from a scheming woman.

She decided not to tell exactly how she'd tricked her attackers. And she'd resume hiding her maps, careful to never let anyone see her hidden pocket.

"But there were more?" Considering he had been pretty much ignoring her ever since she'd mentioned that idiot she'd promised to marry, poor Bucky, Gabe leaned very close now, being secretive right along with her. She wondered if he too distrusted their traveling companions.

"Yes, I'm sure the folks who stole it think it's the one. They searched me thoroughly and left me to die. It's not likely they planned to come back and search me again. But if one group of people was willing to kill for gold, another group could be, too. I'd prefer to keep the map to myself."

Opening his mouth, Gabe hesitated then finally said, "I'm used to trusting people, and I judge these folks as pretty trustworthy."

"Still, I'm afraid they'll chang their tune if they hear about the lost city of gold. Hohzo especially seems eager to hate me."

"She's harmless, just an old woman with firm ideas of right and wrong. That's not such a bad thing."

Shannon arched an eyebrow. "I got real tired of it when she was trying to throw me out of her village. I noticed no one said *you* had to go."

"Things are a little different for men."

Shannon snorted. It was the only response she thought necessary.

"It's not right. It's just the way things are."

"Well, I'm very certain the good Lord doesn't have a different set of rules for men and women."

"I'm sure you're right. While we're talking about men. . ." Gabe leaned close enough that she could feel his warm breath on her face. Based on the flash of anger in his midnight eyes, he might be breathing fire—her very own personal dragon. "Why don't you tell me more about *Bucky*."

Shannon didn't step back, but most likely only through sheer stupidity. "Not much more to tell."

"You're going to marry him, and you can't think of one single, little, teeny, tiny thing to say about the man?"

Truth be told, there wasn't much to say about Bucky. Their parents wanted them to marry. Promises had been made. Mostly unspoken but clearly understood. And she'd never minded— much. Bucky was a pleasant enough sort, a lifelong friend. No mouth that breathed fire or eyes that threatened to burn her to the ground; no oversized moustache that tempted her to smooth it. No kisses. At all. Ever. But a nice enough man.

Into the silence, Gabe asked, "Is he named after a horse?"

Drawing in a slow breath to keep from laughing, she said, "I'm not going to dignify that question with an answer."

There, that sounded good. The truth—that Bucky was named after the Buckstones, his mother's mother's family, because they owned a nice chunk of a railroad, and naming him after the family helped him to be remembered generously in an inheritance—didn't make the man sound all that tough. And out here, people respected tough.

"And what about you, Gabriel? Did your mother name you after an angel?" She prepared to run as she spoke in an overly cute voice. "My angelic little baby, Gabriel."

She wasn't prepared for Gabe to smile. Honestly, it was hard to torment the man back, when he was so often very nice.

"My ma gave us all Bible names. Considering my poor brothers—especially Canaan, Darius, Ephraim—I got off lucky with Gabe.

"*C, D, E. . . G*? What happened to *F*?"

There are seven of us. Abraham, Bartholomew, Canaan, Darius, Ephraim, Felix, and Gabriel."

"Seven?" Shannon smiled at the thought of seven rambunctious little boys all with black eyes and dark hair. "That's wonderful to have a big family."

Gabe shrugged, "Spent a lot of time wrangling with each other, but it was fun I reckon."

"Is there really a Felix in the Bible?" Shannon considered herself well read, and she'd certainly been a faithful churchgoer, but she'd never heard of a Felix.

A quick smile bent Gabe's moustache up at the corners. "There is indeed. Not a nice character according to my brother, who made a point of tracking that down. I think my ma was regretting she'd started the whole alphabetical Bible name thing by the time she had her fourth son. The names got a little hostile. I mean, come on, she could have named Darius David. What would be wrong with Elijah? Lots of Elijahs running around in the hills. But no. She's gotta pick Ephraim. She said once when she was nagging at us for—"

Gabe's eyes lost focus, and Shannon knew he was remembering something that he enjoyed. He looked into the distance and stroked his moustache for a moment. "I think it was the time Bart kicked a hole in the back wall of our cabin during a wrestling match. Then he didn't want to admit what he'd done, so he covered the hole up by moving a quilt rack in front of it. Ma *didn't* notice for a few days, the weather being mild and the hole being small. But then a skunk moved in and had a litter of kits under Ma's bed. I think that's when she told us all that she had some real nice girl names picked out and it wouldn't have broken her heart to use a few of 'em."

His smile was one of fondness. "Ma was one of a kind. She was tough as could be but the finest Christian woman I've ever known. She could bake up a ham that was so tasty a grown man might be tempted to cry while he was chewing. And she claimed she could cut out a pair of overalls in any size just by looking at us and whacking away with her scissors on the fabric. No pattern, no measuring. Made the best oatmeal cookies I've ever tasted. Played the piano like a dream. We didn't have much in that old cabin, but somehow Ma had a piano, and she could make music I think brought a smile to Jesus' face."

"That sounds nice." Shannon tried to picture her mother cutting out a pair of overalls, with or without a pattern. The image was impossible to conjure. Her mother had a cook, so baking cookies was out. They had a lovely and very expensive pianoforte in their music room, and Mother had occasionally played a bit of Mozart, but not well, and Mother liked doing everything well or not at all.

"Time for a meal," Doba called out. "Then we need to be off."

Gabe shook his head. "I let him tend all the horses. I should've

117

helped." Looking back at Shannon, he said, "You never did tell me much about Bucky." The moustache was definitely turned down on the corners now. "You shouldn't oughta be kissing a man if you're promised to someone else. It's not right to the man you're promised to. And it's not right to me."

Shannon couldn't meet his eyes. Honest eyes. Black and deep and wise and honorable. "I know, Gabe. I was so upset and so grateful."

"So you throw yourself at every man who does you a good turn? My ma had a name for women who did such things and warned all her sons against 'em."

The pinch of Gabe's contempt—well, it hurt. And she had it coming. "Saving my life is more than doing me a good turn, Gabe. I was so—"

"Upset, yep, you said."

It took all her courage, but she lifted her chin. Gabe had a right to his anger, and she had a responsibility to let him tell her how wrong she'd been. She needed to apologize for her actions and opened her mouth to do so, though with no idea how to explain that the very existence of Bucky had fled her mind before and after their kissing. And certainly during.

"I think I feel sorry for your intended if this kind of thing is what he can expect from you." Gabe reached up and tugged on the brim of his hat, pulling it low over his eyes. He turned and walked over to the others, leaving Shannon nearly gasping with shame.

Worst of it was he was right. Bucky deserved better.

Poor sweet Bucky. She wondered if he'd gotten her telegraph, the one Gabe had asked that mule skinner to send. He'd be worried sick.

Eleven

Bucky rose from the velvet cushions of the couch in the Chatillon Car.

His mother had named the train car. She never missed a chance to gloat about their relation to the important and wealthy St. Louis Chatillons. Though his father's Shaw relatives were possibly even wealthier and more influential.

He looked out at a collection of ramshackle, one-story buildings and a board sidewalk. Dust everywhere. A wagon or two. Horses tied at hitching posts, standing with their heads down.

He wondered at the stories he'd heard of Louis Chatillon's longing for the West. That Chatillon blood flowed in Bucky's veins, but as he watched a tumbleweed roll down the middle of a mostly empty street, he suspected that fur-trapping blood was really diluted.

As he stepped down on the streets of whatever town this was, a man raced up to him with an out-thrust piece of paper. "You're Mr. Buckstone Shaw?" The man had on a white shirt and black vest. Black bands around his upper sleeves and a distinctive hat made it clear the man worked in the telegraph office.

"Yes." Bucky saw others from the train, nearly all men, straggling into a bedraggled diner and felt only relief that he'd brought along an icebox full of food and his own cook.

"Telegraph for you, Mr. Shaw, sir." The man spoke through a moustache so bushy his mouth didn't appear to move. "It came through an hour ago with instructions that it be delivered as soon as the train pulled in."

Looking around the dusty town, Bucky was surprised they had a telegraph. It was a very different world out in the West. Quite rugged. He felt that bit of Chatillon blood pulse somewhat, though not enough to risk eating in that wretched restaurant.

Several men scurried around unloading mail and filling the water car from an overhead tank. Steam chuffed out of the engine as it growled and chugged without moving.

Bucky took the paper, and his first impression was that it was very long for a telegraph. His second was that his already completely upside-down life had just gotten far more complicated. He pictured Shannon's dark eyes, beautiful, thick dark hair, and perfectly cleft chin. Her straight little nose always buried in some fusty old papers of her father's. He tried to make himself believe she was worth it. It didn't matter anyway. Simple human decency demanded he go save her. His third was more primal. Someone had tried to kill Shannon. She needed him, and he'd go save her. Then he'd drag her home by her hair and marry her and make sure she never wandered off again.

"What's she doing in Flagstaff—and where is Arizona Territory? Are we in it yet?"

"Excuse me, sir?" The telegrapher jumped and wrung his hands.

Bucky wondered what exactly his mother had done to engender this level of nerves in the telegraph operator. Money had no doubt changed hands. "I need to get my train car detached and put on the tracks heading to"—Bucky referred to the wire—"the Arizona Territory. I need to get to Flagstaff."

Bucky looked at the telegraph operator, who looked back, a baffled expression on his face. "There ain't no tracks to Flagstaff, sir. I've got to get back to the telegraph office. I'm not supposed to leave my station." The man as good as ran away.

With no clue how to proceed, Bucky went into the decrepit train station restaurant.

Approaching the engineer, who was eating what might be a steak, Bucky controlled a shudder and, though he found it humiliating to ask directions, said, "How do I get to the tracks heading to Arizona? I need to get my car attached to a train heading for Flagstaff."

The engineer, in his black suit, soaked with sweat, chewed as he looked at Bucky. "There ain't no other tracks in town, mister."

Mulling the problem, Bucky realized he might have to wait to change directions in a somewhat bigger town. "When is the next town where I can reroute my car?"

"These are the only train tracks until the end of the line." The engineer turned to the man beside him.

The coal man no doubt, judging by the man's face being blackened with soot, added, "Best you can do is take a stagecoach south. You can hook up with the train in Albuquerque. That'll take you into Flagstaff."

"Stage just went through yesterday," a woman called from an open door that appeared to lead to a kitchen. She came out with a pot of coffee and began pouring. "Won't be another one through for a week."

"Then how do I get there from here?"

The room fell silent. Finally, one man said, "Ride a horse, how else? Gotta go about three days south."

"He can make it in two if he pushes hard, and he'd better. No good water along the way." The woman continued pouring coffee.

"Two to the train, then another two or three to Flag."

Raising his letter, Bucky said, "My fiancée is in terrible trouble. We last heard from her in Durango, but now we've gotten a wire from Flagstaff, and she's in danger somewhere in the wilderness north of there. I need to get to her as quickly as possible. And I've got four men traveling with me to act as guides and to help me track Shannon."

"What's a fiancée?" the coal man asked around a mouthful of meat.

Bucky opened his mouth to explain.

"You've got good horseflesh in the cattle cars." The engineer went back to sawing his steak."

"I got a brother hunting work," the coffee pourer said. "He's been all over New Mexico and Arizona Territory. He'd be obliged for a few days' work. He'd even go with you to hunt down your *fency* in the wilderness."

"Fi-an-cée," Bucky spoke all three syllables carefully. "The woman I'm engaged to." Not quite engaged, but Bucky didn't have time for unimportant details.

"Havin' a hard time keepin' track of your woman, greenhorn?"

Bucky wasn't sure who said that, but he was sure about half the restaurant laughed. It was embarrassing, but since it was true, he didn't bother getting into an argument. "Since the day I met her." Bucky shook his head, and the restaurant laughed again, but he didn't let it pinch because there was a definite note of sympathy.

"I'll go get my men. Can someone here unload my horses and saddles?" Bucky knew how to ride a horse well. He spent most mornings riding in the park near his home. The men his mother had hired seemed to be competent sorts.

The engineer sighed and gave his mostly devoured steak a mournful look. "I'll get 'em for you, Mr. Shaw."

The man was so agreeable, considering his reluctance, Bucky wondered about his mother and money again. Bucky had a bad feeling he was going somewhere no amount of his family's money could penetrate. "And can we find your brother, ma'am, so I can get going? I can see you're busy, but it's urgent we move quickly."

"Gracie," Coffee Pourer shouted at the top of her lungs toward the kitchen, "go get Willard moving. I found him a job."

"I'm goin', Ma." Bucky heard a door slam.

He went back outside and reread the telegraph. Men had tried to kill Shannon? She'd been rescued and taken to a settlement of friendly Navajo Indians north of Flagstaff?

Bucky's blood turned ice cold even in the heat. All that was Chatillon in him woke up and prepared to fight.

He saw the engineer come out and head for the train car that held his horses.

He raced for the train to tell his men their plans had changed. And to tell his cook he was now apparently going to have much less work to do. Reaching his car, he yelled, "We're heading south on horseback."

The cook poked his head out of the tiny kitchen area of the car. "On horseback, Mr. Bucky?"

With narrow eyes, Bucky glared at the cook. "Call me Buck. And you're staying here."

The cook heaved a sigh of relief.

"Go find the men and tell them to get packed up fast." Bucky—now Buck Shaw, a much better name for an adult man, especially in the West—packed the minimal amount of supplies, took what food would transport, then went to help load the horses.

His men, who stayed in sleeper cars with the regular folks, there not being room for them in Buck's private car, were with him before he'd gotten his own horse saddled. They seemed eager for action.

"We're all ready, Mr. Shaw," the oldest of the four men said.

"Call me Buck."

The men nodded, and they swung onto horseback just as a

man who proved to be Willard rode up. Their trail guide. On his say-so, they added a lot of water to their supplies and let their horses drink deeply before they set out. They were on the trail south before the train had pulled out of the station.

Buck's worry built with each passing mile as he prayed he'd get to Shannon in time to protect her. He decided then and there he'd marry her as soon as he caught up with her. With or without her permission.

It was the Wild West. It was a man's world out here. He fully intended to take control of his willful woman once and for all.

They bedded down near a red rock wall just as the sun set. Doba built a fire of scrub brush that was soon crackling and warm. They made a quick camp meal of jerked meat, hardtack, and coffee and were soon rolled up in their sleeping bags.

"Father!" The whisper was sharp and anxious.

It woke Gabe from a sound sleep. "Who's there?"

A voice shushed him.

"It's Ahway, my son." Doba's voice was so low Gabe could barely hear it.

"What are—?"

Gabe practically threw himself across the camp to slap his hand over Shannon's mouth. "Quiet."

From behind his hand, she said, "Gabe, I—"

"Shh."

He heard Doba speaking with someone but couldn't understand the words. Then Doba's voice rose enough to be heard. "Quickly." Doba's voice was an urgent hiss. "Pack up. Bad men."

Gabe heard a horse, off a ways, restless, tossing its head and sending a metallic click in the night air.

Doba left the fire burning.

Gabe didn't douse it. Firelight and the scent of wood smoke

carried a long way in the thin air of the high desert. The wind was blowing from the east, too, the direction the rider approached from. Gabe heard a second sound that made him sure there was more than one rider, and they were definitely coming this way. They had only minutes to clear out.

Emmy appeared out of the dark so suddenly Gabe almost went for his gun. The girl grabbed both saddles then vanished back into the night, toward where Gabe picketed his horses. With quick, efficient motions, Gabe helped break camp. By the time they were done, Emmy had all the animals in their leather and stood with a boy close to her age, Emmy's brother, Marcus, who held the reins on all their mounts, and Ahway.

Parson Ford strode to his horse, and Gabe noticed Ahway hand the reins to Emmy. Then Ahway and Marcus helped the parson mount up without a ruckus.

Gabe caught Shannon's hand and dragged her to her brown and white pinto.

Tossing her up in the saddle, he strapped on the bedrolls and saddlebags, then caught her reins and mounted his own horse. The Hosteens went first. Doba followed and the parson. Gabe looked at Emmy, who made a gesture that Gabe should fall in line. Quietly he led Shannon away.

Once they'd left the shelter of the fire and rock, the wind cut through Gabe's clothes. It had to be worse for Shannon. He wished he'd kept a blanket unrolled to wrap around her. She had no heavy coat. He should have thought of that at the Kinlichee homestead.

Shannon's horse emerged from the sheltered area, and she gasped audibly from the cold.

"Shhh." He whipped his head around in the darkness and waited until she nodded. He felt merciless, but silence was their only protection against a bullet until they put some rocks between them and their visitors. Doba led, and Gabe was acutely aware of every boulder they passed that added something solid between themselves and Doba's "bad men."

Without the glow of the fire, the whole world went pitch black. Gabe's eyes adjusted quickly, and he looked back to see Shannon, washed blue in the moonlight, riding behind him. Emmy, Marcus, and Ahway rode single file, with Ahway bringing up the rear. Gabe wanted to ask Doba a thousand questions, but now wasn't the time.

They'd gotten out, but maybe Doba had misread things. Maybe whoever was out there in the dark would ride up to camp and call out nice and proper. Maybe they could go back to the warmth of their fire.

Gunfire split the night.

"What's he doing in Flagstaff?" Abe looked at the telegraph, scowling.

Tyra jerked it out of his hand. She saw Abe's annoyance, but she had to read the wire because she saw more than annoyance. She saw fear.

Reading quickly, she said, "Gabe ran into trouble. He mentions someone named Doba Kinlichee?"

She looked up at her pa. "Is that Indian? Gabe could be in serious trouble, but he doesn't go into any details."

Abe stood beside Madeline and his children—two of them more man than boy, all lined up for the excitement of receiving a telegraph. That didn't happen every day. "Last time I got a telegraph, it was from Gabe, too. He told me our ma had died."

Tyra drew in a long, unsteady breath. "It sounds like he needs help, Abe. Flagstaff isn't that far." She looked over her shoulder at her father. Over sixty years old now. Definitely stoved up some. Too many battered falls from horses he was breaking. Too many kicks from testy longhorns. But a strong man still. And a man determined to have Abraham Lasley's brother for his son.

"I think we oughta ride up there and bring him back." Pa turned to Abe, frowning. "I got enough men to run my place for a few weeks. "I can go if you're tied down with the ranch."

"Obliged, Lucas." Abe looked at Madeline again. "I've got to go help, Gabe, honey. Will you be all right?"

The boys frowned. The two older ones were nearly Abraham's height these days and did the work of men. They didn't run as big a place as the Rocking M, but they had a few hands.

"We'll be okay, Pa," Abe's oldest son, Adam, said. "You go see to Uncle Gabe."

"I can send a man or two over every day to take up the slack, Abe. Gabe don't know me. If he's got trouble riding with him, he might not know who to trust."

"I'm going, Pa." Tyra braced herself for trouble. Pa let her work hard alongside the men. She stood there in a riding skirt, wearing a six-gun, a Stetson on her head where a bonnet ought to be, and proudly dressed this way right smack-dab in town where people could see her. Pa didn't object to it. But there were limits.

"Yep, I think you oughta go, Ty. Might as well carry on with you and Gabe gettin' hitched."

Tyra couldn't agree more.

"We can pack up a horse with supplies and head out." Abe had that grim expression on his face.

Tyra had seen it many times when Abe talked about his little brother. But Tyra was the youngest, too. Her mother had died when she was little, and she'd grown up running wild. She was no fragile flower of a young maiden.

Tyra kicked constantly against being treated as if she were still a kid. Gabe was a tough man who knew how to work hard, despite what Abe said. She was going to hunt Gabe down, marry him, and spend the rest of her life proving youngest brothers and sisters could manage their lives just fine.

"Take care of your brother, Abe. We'll be fine." Madeline was as competent and calm as any frontier woman. "Boys, let's go fill our list and head home. We got chores." She headed for the general store with her four children—Adam, Benjamin, Caleb, and David.

Abe waved them off and watched them walk away. He muttered, "I hope we have a girl when we get to *F*."

"What?" Tyra didn't quite understand what that meant.

Abe gave her a worried look. "If your name was Frankincense, but everyone called you Frank. . .if you were a boy, I mean. . .you wouldn't hate your father for it would you? Girls aren't quite as likely to hate their fathers as boys, do you think?"

"Are you sure you want to go, Abe?" Tyra would have checked Abe's forehead for a fever if she was a little closer. "Pa and I can find him."

"Never mind. Let's hit the trail."

They had a packhorse and spare mounts so they could make good time. They had a long ride ahead of them, but a horse, with saddles switched often so they could run without a rider, could cover a hundred miles a day. They'd make Flagstaff fast, find out where Gabe was heading, and save the poor boy.

Tyra caught herself. She'd been affected by Abraham's "little brother" talk. Gabe wasn't a *poor boy*. He wasn't going to need to be rescued. He could handle things himself. But they'd show up, and he'd see she was all grown up and came with a fancy ranch—one of the biggest in the area—and he'd come along quietly, counting himself lucky.

For just a second, it pinched that the ranch might be a bigger lure than the wife. Jutting her chin out, she refused to let it bother her. Gabe would figure out just how lucky he was soon enough. She'd spend her life making sure he knew how good things could be.

Gabe jerked his revolver from his holster and looked back, but he couldn't see anything. The bullet that had fired sounded like it was aimed upward.

"Throw down your guns!" A shout from out of the darkness on the east side of the camp sounded as deadly as the gunfire.

Wherever they were hiding, the hombres couldn't see into the shadowed area behind the fire and didn't yet realize the camp was empty.

Only silence met the order to disarm.

"The next bullet's coming right into your camp."

All the night animals had gone silent. Not a bug chirped, not an owl so much as fluttered its wings. Every creature, and Gabe included himself, held its breath, waiting.

"She's gone!" A dark shape silhouetted itself against the firelight. While one man had threatened and shot from cover, another had slipped into camp in the dark to get the drop on. . . whoever it was they were after.

Outlaws, varmints. They made Gabe killing mad.

Others broke from a stand of trees not that far away from where they'd camped.

"I see four of 'em." Gabe muttered.

"No, five." Doba sounded positive.

Gabe felt more than saw Shannon kick her horse. "Five?"

"Let's move," Hosteen said. He turned his horse and vanished into the night.

"Walk. Running is too noisy." Doba went after Hosteen.

Shannon's pinto surged forward as if to follow, but Gabe subdued it with a rigid grip on the reins. He didn't want Shannon out of his grasp. And he didn't want her to lose control of the horse because it would run, especially if there was more gunfire. Pounding hooves would lead that gang straight to them.

He pulled Shannon close so she rode on his right-hand side, putting his body at least somewhat between her and the outlaws, shielding her. Once she was alongside him, her hand settled on his, and for a second he thought she meant to wrest the reins away and run.

Instead, she gripped his hand tightly and drew his eyes to hers. "Thank you." The words were softer than the gusting of the wind, but he heard them. More than that, he *felt* her gratitude.

Gabe wanted to tell her not to be grateful. If it had been up to him, they'd still be back there, shot to ribbons.

He remembered the clinking of the approaching horses and wondered, hoped, he'd have noticed. But Doba's son and the Crenshaws had gotten there ahead of those back-shooters. Gabe thanked God for that.

He concentrated on the fading squabbling voices from their camp. At least one of them was female.

He couldn't let Shannon give him any credit. "They must have seen our fire and ridden in. If the kids hadn't come, we'd be dead or trapped."

She turned to look back with such a hard twist he grabbed her arm to keep her on the saddle. "You said there were four people, right?"

"Yes, but Doba's right. There were five."

"Are you sure?"

"I'm sure as can be in the pitch dark from a distance. Why?"

"Just—nothing."

"Shannon, why? You're not telling me something."

Doba picked up the pace, but still they walked for the sake of quiet. Shannon's silence was in perfect harmony with the night.

There was not time to stop and shake the words loose that she was obviously holding in. But even on the move, under the cover of that wicked attack, he could definitely talk to her. "I want to know right now, Shannon Dysart, what you meant by—"

The shouting from behind them stopped.

Gabe quit talking just as fast.

Silence reigned in the night, broken only by the moan of the increasingly frigid wind. The trail Hosteen followed descended and twisted. A stony, tree-studded wall rose on their right; the ground fell away on their left.

Emmy, Marcus, and Ahway came up closer, and Doba dropped back on a trail barely wide enough for two to ride abreast. They all listened intently.

At last Doba whispered, "They'll be coming."

The trail circled an outcropping of rock. In front of them, the path was more rock than dirt. If they picked up speed, their hoof-beats would practically shout for the outlaws to come after them.

Winding around a clump of pine, the trail began to descend and twist until it reached lower ground. Gabe hoped the outlaws didn't know what direction to ride. He fought down the urge to turn and fight. His second reaction was to race at top speed away from whoever had attacked them. But using iron control, he did neither.

The trail steadily rose then dropped again. Gabe judged that they'd put at least two miles between them and the site where they'd camped. More importantly, they'd put a mountain between them. The Hosteens knew this land very well. No sound would travel that far. And few outlaws would go haring off in the night, possibly in the wrong direction.

If they were following, they'd need to abandon silence anyway, so a few words wouldn't hurt a thing.

"Hosteen," Gabe still spoke barely above a whisper, "do you know the trail ahead well enough to ride faster? They won't hear us from this distance."

"We'll pick up the pace for a while," Hozho answered. Gabe realized the old woman was actually in the lead. He could barely make out vague shapes at this distance.

She'd said she'd grown up in the canyon, so maybe she knew this land better than any of the others. Hozho kicked her horse into a trot.

Gabe stared at Shannon, not sure whether to trust her off his lead. "I haven't forgotten you know something about that attack, but we don't have time to talk about it now. Let's move out."

She jerked her chin in agreement, and her dark eyes, black in the night, shined with intelligence and calm in the moonlight. It satisfied him. With a quick flip of his wrist, Gabe pulled the reins into place and gave Shannon control of her horse. He kicked his chestnut into a lope, and Shannon's pinto followed down a trail that seemed bright and obvious as a highway.

Would those outlaws follow? And if so, how soon?

Hozho rode as hard as the night would allow, and the pace suited Gabe. He felt as if the moon laid a clear path before them, or maybe a torch was held by the guiding hand of God. He listened with every ounce of concentration for pursuit.

No rider was skilled enough to see tracks on rocky ground in the black of night. Not even the moonlight would be enough. He hoped hard they'd have the whole night to put distance between themselves and danger. And though this was a clear trail, it forked off in several spots, and those outlaws would have to be pure lucky to pick the right one to follow.

As they rode, Gabe had plenty of time to wonder what Shannon was keeping from him. Plenty of time to imagine the worst.

"They're gone!" Lurene nearly dropped her Colt revolver when she thrust it in her pocket. The coat she wore had pockets big enough, but she wasn't used to guns. She'd made her ill-gotten gains in a much less violent way back in St. Louis.

But she'd enjoyed pulling the trigger as Cutter had told her to do. Just point like the gun was a finger and fire. She was looking forward to doing it again. And right now she was mad enough. She wouldn't have minded if the Dysart woman had been right in her line of fire.

"They heard us coming."

Lurene looked at Ginger, who was jerking on the reins of her poor horse even now. "You're too rough with that animal. You made too much noise. It warned them, and they got away." She kicked a glowing chunk of wood still in the fire and watched it bounce off the red rock wall and explode red cinders into the air.

"Watch out." Cutter gave her a deadly glare before he stepped into the space between the fire and the wall.

Lurene felt a shiver of fear and pleasure when Cutter turned those threatening eyes on her. She thought about pulling him aside and asking him point blank if he'd like to thin out their gang. There was no need for five of them to trail after Shannon Dysart and whoever had rescued her. Two, she and Cutter, would be plenty.

Cutter had needed a respectable woman when he'd gotten the job to guide Shannon. He'd come to her, told her he'd always thought she'd clean up good. Hating the life and how it was getting harder every year to compete with the new girls, she'd let him lure her with his talk of gold until she could almost taste the rich food and fine wines that a woman could buy with a city full of the yellow wealth. He'd arranged for her to have the right letters of recommendation. Then he'd assembled the rest of the crew, and they'd hired on for a trip into the Wild West.

She'd always figured this trip came down to her and Cutter. Cutter had the skills from time he'd spent in the West. She had the brains. She fully intended to thin the herd when it came time to split the gold, but she was enough afraid of Cutter to hesitate. Until they'd made their play and left Shannon in that cave, she'd never seen any signs of much intelligence in the rest of the crew. But now Randy had her worried. She and Cutter ought to get rid of them and soon.

The icicle-hard heart she felt beating in her chest told her that getting them out of the way was the surest route to her never having to endure the groping hands of a strange man again. She could put up with it for Cutter, because she needed his fast gun and the strength of his back, but no one else. Her jaw firmed as she swore in her soul that she'd find a way never to go back to that life.

Cutter crouched and studied the ground. "They haven't been gone long. They definitely spread out their bedrolls here."

"Let's get after 'em." Ginger yanked on her horse's reins as she tried to mount up, and the horse whickered in protest and turned in a circle, trying to follow where he was led. Ginger's hair caught the glow of the scattered fire, and it reflected red on her crooked teeth until they nearly looked like fangs dripping with blood.

Lurene thought Ginger looked like someone who'd been loosed by the devil himself.

"Stand still, you stupid brute." Ginger smacked her horse, and it fought her, tossing its head, making the bridle jingle.

"Which way?" Cutter rose to his full height and looked across the dying fire at Ginger. He spoke loud enough to get her to stop fighting with her horse.

"I dunno." Ginger looked left and right. "You tell me. That's your part of this job, tracking."

"Well, I *dunno* either." Emphasizing the word, Cutter clearly called Ginger stupid. A quick flash of a mocking smile told Lurene that Randy got it, too. She didn't even bother to look at Darrel.

"How can you not know?" Ginger clearly missed the insult.

"It's night, that's how. There are ten directions they could have gone, most of 'em over rock. I expect I can pick up their trail in the daylight, but there's no way to see a rock barely scraped by a horseshoe in the pitch dark."

The scowl on Ginger's face seemed to call Cutter stupid. Lurene wished Cutter would shut the fool's mouth permanently.

Instead, he shook his head. "Let's not sleep in here. Smart spot to camp, out of the wind. It was picked by a man who knows his way around out here. Same kinda man who might come sneaking back and unload his gun into our hides."

"We shoulda gone in and questioned those folks at the waterhole." Darrel went to his horse and swung up. "Them Navajos."

"Navajos aren't much for talking." Cutter shook his head.

"Well, we coulda *made* 'em tell us who she was with." Darrel formed a fist as if he had a throat crushed in his hand. "They'd've told us everything before I was done."

"No sense having a bunch of folks see us, maybe be able to tell a marshal about it. Shannon Dysart is a woman lots of people will ask about if she never comes back to St. Louis. No one thinks much of a person going missing in the West, but no sense having our faces known to people in case someone comes looking."

Darrel growled in the dark, as if he were a wolf on the hunt. "Then we shoulda asked our questions, gotten our answers, and then shut those folks up for good. There weren't that many of 'em."

"They're Navajo. A peace-loving people mostly, unless they get pushed too hard," Cutter said. "I've been in this country before, and the folks that live here won't put up with much pushing. Even if we killed 'em all, and that wouldn't be as easy as you make it sound, they've got friends. We might bring a whole tribe of tough fighters down on our heads. Better to skirt around their hogans and not let 'em see we're anywhere in the country. They wouldn't've told us more'n we learned from riding wide of the spring and reading sign."

Lurene mounted. "Where do we camp, Lobo?"

Cutter swung into the saddle and set out without responding. Lurene followed because she didn't have much choice. And because of all of them, Cutter was the one who had the best sense in the wilderness.

Missing Shannon Dysart tonight stung. It felt like defeat, as if she were eating desert dust instead of being served on plates of gold.

Lurene wasn't settling for dirt when she could have that precious yellow metal in her hands. She didn't care who she had to kill.

Twelve

In the gray light of dawn, Gabe looked back just in time to see Shannon's head nod forward. She slid sideways in her sleep, and he moved quickly to catch her before she fell to the ground.

She woke up when he dragged her onto his lap. Blinking her pretty brown eyes, she gave him a smile so sweet Gabe did his best to forget Bucky. Did a fair job of it, too, which no doubt meant he was a complete idiot.

A realization that honestly came as no surprise. Not after two whole days of acquaintance with Shannon Dysart.

No, he'd figured out his own stupidity a few hours into this mess. That'd been about the time he'd finally gotten her down from that cave and she'd thrown herself into his arms and he'd felt that warm, grateful handful of woman and thought about how much his ma always wanted him married.

"How'd I get into your arms?" Shannon's voice was husky with sleep. Her cheeks were pink, partly from too much sun, but Gabe saw the memory of the affection they'd shared in her eyes.

He decided he liked himself better when he was stupid. He

lightly touched that intriguing dimple in her chin, barely realizing he'd done it. He already had habits when it came to touching Shannon that were probably bad. "You fell asleep and I caught you. I'm sorry we've had to push so hard all night. But we had to get away from those folks. And we can't stop riding now and rest up. Now, tell me what made you so jumpy last night?"

"You mean besides a group of gunmen shooting at our camp?"

"Yep, I mean besides that. You know what I mean."

"I do. I think I know who it was." Shannon ran one finger across his moustache. "Those people who attacked us, Gabe—they must be the ones who left me stranded."

"Why would they come after you? They wanted your map. They got it."

"They didn't get it. I told you that."

"Yes, but they think they got it." Gabe shook his head. "No, there are plenty of outlaws in this country. No reason to believe that bunch was the same one that attacked you."

"There were five of them." Her hand slid down and clamped on his shirt front.

Glancing at her tight grip, Gabe wondered how terrified she really was. She'd held up okay through the long night. "We saw five, but we don't know for sure how many there were."

"There's another reason it might be them."

"Those folks rode off and left you for dead. They got what they wanted, and they'd have no reason to think you're wandering around. And even if you were, you've got nothing they want."

"Well, I suppose what happened is they went back." Shannon's grip tightened, and Gabe had to decide soon just how badly he needed to breathe.

"To save you?" Gabe doubted it very much. "You think they had a change of heart and decided to rescue you; then they got mad when you weren't there and decided they wanted you dead after all?"

Gabe noticed Doba, riding in front of Parson Ford and trailing the Tsosis and Ahway from the rear, trailing Emmy and Marcus, riding closer, listening to every word. What exactly had brought the warning from the Kinlichee settlement? There'd been no time to talk as they rode.

"No, I think they must have figured it out somehow. Lurene, the one who was the friendliest to me, she must have seen that what I gave them wasn't all I had."

Grinding his teeth together, Gabe asked, "Did she know enough about your map to figure it out this fast?"

"All things considered—since they attacked our camp last night. . ." There was an extended silence. "I'd say yes."

Gabe scowled. "I'd say definitely yes." Gabe would have objected to being strangled if he didn't have more important things to worry about.

"I suppose she watched more closely than I realized." Shannon lifted her chin to look Gabe in the eye. Then she brought her other hand to his shirt and shook him. "I never left the maps lying around, and I was very careful about hiding them. No one saw that I have a hidden pocket."

"You do?" Gabe's eyes skimmed her body. "Where?"

"Sewn inside my skirt."

Gabe's skin heated up a little when he thought about her producing that map from such a personal hiding place.

"She definitely talked with me about the maps. Once she got on the trail, she must have tried to follow it and realized I'd kept back a few important pages."

"A few important pages." Gabe scrubbed his hand over his face. "So you're saying those cutthroats who left you to die slowly in the wilderness are now on our trail."

Shannon shrugged. "Who else?"

"And they think"—Gabe rested one hand over both of hers and did his best to open up some breathing space—"we have the

139

only map to a city built out of gold."

"Gold?" Doba sneered.

Gabe knew people like the Navajo, who eked out a living in this hard land, considered a quest for gold foolishness. Gabe tended to agree with them.

Parson Ford fought with his unruly horse and tried to guide it back to join the talk. It balked, but it was clearly tired and eventually came toward them.

"We *do* have the only map."

Groaning, Gabe scrubbed his face as if he could wash Shannon and her map right out of his life. He knew good and well it wasn't that easy. "So while we ride farther and farther from a town with a lawman and folks who'd back us against outlaws, those people, who picked up our trail mighty fast, which means at least one of 'em is a first-rate tracker, are coming to take that map."

"Yes."

Gabe shifted so he could grab Shannon's wrists and jerk them off his neck. And it wasn't because he wanted to breathe. It was because he wanted to shake some sense into her. "And they are willing to take it by force at the point of a gun."

Shannon didn't seem to notice she'd been strangling him, and she didn't seem to care he'd made her stop. She clearly had bigger worries. "It would seem so."

"The same ones who left you to die slowly, trapped in a cave a hundred feet off the ground."

Nodding, Shannon didn't even bother to pretend he was wrong.

"Which makes them the worst kind of yellow-bellied, murderous varmints."

Shannon looked up from where she'd been staring straight at the second button on his shirt. "We need to go faster."

"I agree. We need to give up on the gold and head for the nearest town as quick as we can."

"We need to follow the trail I've mapped out." She looked

over her shoulder at Doba. "What direction have we been riding through the night?"

"My people live that way." Hozho pointed to the southwest.

"And they're the ones I need to visit. They're part of my mission field." Parson Ford's mustang tossed its head and kicked, bouncing the poor pastor around until Doba caught the horse and calmed it.

Gabe jerked her around to keep her attention on him until he could force her to admit this was pure stupidity. "Salt Lake City is a few days' hard ride to the north, but that's okay. It's on my way home." Gabe smiled, but there was no humor in it. "I'll get you on a train back to beloved-though-forgotten *Bucky* and go on home myself. I can go visit my brother some other time. I've had enough wandering."

"Doba, can you tell us how to get to the Grand Canyon?" Shannon looked away again.

"Once we're in Utah," Gabe went on, "we can—"

"We've been riding," Doba answered Shannon over Gabe's words, "toward the canyon all night."

"In Salt Lake," Gabe continued, "we'll report those outlaws."

"Put her down. It's not proper for you to be holding her in your arms in such a way." Parson Ford was a lot more willing to ignore the proprieties when he was trying not to get bucked off his horse.

Shannon sat upright in Gabe's lap. "We've been going the right direction? That's wonderful."

"It's terrible, because straight west, where you want to go, is a dead end." Gabe didn't need Shannon to listen. They were doing things his way whether she paid attention or not. "That's why I went along with this direction for the last few hours, to lose those polecats following us. They'll never suspect we went west. Why would they? There's nothing there but a canyon that's completely impassible. So, we'll head north now for Utah and find a U.S.

marshal and report this."

"And I and my family will hide off the trail until we're sure the outlaws have chosen a different route and then go home." Doba was talking to Shannon, no doubt explaining things to her.

Good, saved Gabe the time.

The rest of them were on horseback while they squabbled, pretty much in a circle by now, with Gabe holding Shannon in the middle of it.

Hozho dismounted and caught the reins from Gabe, then pulled Shannon's pinto around. "Get back on your horse."

Gabe would like to go to Salt Lake as directly as possible, but it was a rugged land. "So, which is the best trail, Doba?"

"Yes, how do we get there most quickly?" Shannon asked.

Doba pointed in the direction they'd just come. "My home is the closest safety, directly east of here."

"We're going west," Shannon insisted.

"I mean the trail north," Gabe spoke at the same time.

"Put her down right now." Hozho jabbed Gabe in the leg with a finger as pointy as an Indian warrior's tomahawk.

All four of them fell silent. Gabe glared at Shannon, who got a look of stubbornness in her eyes that Gabe was already starting to recognize.

Emmy suddenly appeared out of the dusk. Gabe realized the young woman hadn't ridden up when Ahway did.

"I set a false trail." Emmy looked smug. "The outlaws are heading south miles back."

"You left Emmy behind to lay a trail?" Gabe shook his head. All this talk of what was proper and they'd as good as abandoned a young girl to a gang of cutthroats.

"Emmy is the best." Marcus slapped his sister on the back.

"Better than any of us." Ahway smiled as if his friend's skills were a source of great pride.

Doba nodded. "Good. We go home now." He wheeled his

horse to the east toward home.

"We're going north, Doba." Gabe turned to the youngsters. "Thank you for warning us. You saved our lives."

"Bad men think they are sneaky." Ahway said with a smug smile. "We smelled them, heard them, and saw them. We watched as they circled our home. They are as sneaky as a stampeding herd of buffalo."

Smiling, Gabe said again, "Thank you."

"Doba, I have to go west." Shannon's eyes glinted with pure stubbornness.

"We know the way west," Hosteen said.

"You get on your own horse, Miss Dysart," Parson Ford growled.

Gabe's smile faded fast as he looked in Hosteen's calm eyes. Shannon was going north whether she wanted to or not.

But Gabe could see that the Tsosis really did know a way down into that canyon. Shannon's map might not show it, but Hosteen knew the way. Gabe was very sorry to hear that.

Shannon gave Hosteen a very bright smile, considering the man and his wife nearly had Shannon-the-Sinner cast out in the wilderness yesterday. "Thank you for your help."

"We're not going into that canyon." Gabe plunked Shannon back onto her horse then caught her reins.

Hozho sniffed. "About time."

She exchanged an arched look with Parson Ford who said, "Long past time."

Gabe sincerely hoped he didn't have to lead her horse all the way to Salt Lake City with her thrown over the saddle.

"You said you'd go, Gabe."

And how did I know she was going to say that?

Thirteen

Yes, I said I'd go, but that's before I knew we had killers on our trail. Emmy led those folks who were following us astray. But her tricks will only work for a while. If they found you after they left you stranded so far behind, then they're good trackers. They'll realize the false trail ends and be back."

"Once we get to that secret trail and get down in the canyon, we'll be safe."

"We'll *never* be safe as long as we're in the area."

"They won't find us. Doba, you said your home was close and a safe place, but we don't want to bring those folks to your family." Gabe saw Doba hesitate.

"You want to ride all the way to Wyoming to get away from a band of cutthroats." Shannon jerked on her reins and gave Gabe a dark look when he wouldn't let go. "But you *know* the canyon is the closest protection with the exception of Doba's settlement."

"It is a wild land," Doba interrupted.

"The river isn't for passage," Hozho said. "No boats. Few trails. Stretches where water is scarce. Very steep ride down that edge.

144

Nothing in the canyon is safe or easy."

"Once down there, we'll find that city of gold." Shannon smiled at Hozho, who wasn't a woman who inspired smiling, so it was all fake.

"There is a village down there, but those people, they keep to themselves." Hozho shook her head. "They would not have spoken to your father."

"He said there was a city."

"No one could live down there, Shannon. Not from what I've heard."

"There is at least one village. One part of Father's notes mentions two. But I couldn't tell if they were just various camps set up by the same tribe or several different tribes. Are they Navajo?"

Gabe looked at Hozho. "Is that true? There are Navajo Indians living down there?"

"Not Navajo. They are not of the *Dineh*," Doba said.

"Dineh?" Gabe furrowed his brow and wished everyone spoke English only.

"Yes, Dineh, the People," Doba went on. "The true name of my people. Navajo is a white word."

"*Pai*, some call them *Supai*." Hozho nodded. "I am from the *Yavapai*. My people live in many small villages scattered around. This land with its scarce food and water does not support large groups."

"Those people will protect us." Shannon reached out and snagged Gabe's arm.

It annoyed him how much he liked her touching him. And how much it made him want her happy. And how much it made him hate Bucky, who didn't deserve to be hated one bit. Gabe arched a brow at Hozho.

She shrugged. "The Supai are not warriors."

"My father's writings were a little vague. He talked more about the village than the people. But he found his way. They must have been helpful to him. I think they'll treat us well."

"You think?" Gabe wondered if she ever listened to herself talk. "You don't know?"

"No, I don't know."

"Well, finally, we've found something Miss Shannon Dysart doesn't know."

Shannon sniffed and turned up her little nose as if Gabe smelled bad. "I am going to find that trail with or without you. I'll just go on with whoever does want to go." She turned to Hozho. "Will you take me?"

Gabe tugged on his arm, and since Shannon was still hanging on to him, it drew her attention. "I agreed to go before I knew killers wanted a map from you that will lead them to a city of gold."

A smile broke over Shannon's face, and her hand tightened on his arm. "So you finally believe me? You agree that the map leads to a treasure? That's so sweet. I'm so delighted. You're wonderful, Gabe."

"No, I don't believe you."

Her smile vanished and her brows slammed down. "You're nothing but a stubborn old goat."

"I don't believe it." Gabe lifted his eyes to heaven and prayed for patience. "But those people chasing after you clearly do. And that's why we have to get out of here."

"We have to stay." She tugged on his sleeve.

Gabe twisted his arm loose and caught her by the wrist. "We're going north."

"If you won't go west with me, I'll go on alone." Shannon tilted her snooty nose even higher.

Ahway and Emmy were clearly taking mental notes to tell stories of Gabe's humiliation. It was all too much.

Gabe lost his temper. *"You are going to mind me, woman!"*

Shannon froze, fear on her face, her hand white-knuckled on his sleeve.

He hated to do it, but a man had to set his foot down.

Her eyes went bright, and he thought she was going to explode, yell at him, unleash pure rage. One tear spilled, cutting down to wash a clean track in her dirty face.

With a gasp, all the men jerked back from her.

Hozho, on the ground, reached up and patted Shannon's leg and glared at Gabe.

"I'll go with you." Emmy dismounted and strode to Shannon's side, her arms crossed, her brow lowered for battle. "I'm better on a trail than Gabe is anyway."

"What are you doing?" Gabe asked Shannon in horror. He'd never been around women much. In fact, except for his ma, almost none. Oh, he'd been around Annette some, and Elijah Walker's mother. But on serious thought, he'd have to stick with almost none. He'd never seen Ma cry. She was the best kind of woman there was, so if his ma didn't do it, then no woman should do it.

"I'm—I'm trying to convince you to help me." Another tear ran down, then a third.

"Stop crying!" Gabe shouted then regretted it immediately when she cried harder.

"I think it is best if I and my children return to my family. And I have to take Emmy back. Parson Crenshaw wouldn't allow her to go so far without her family."

"I'd be fine, Mr. Kinlichee." Emmy gave him that bright smile.

"I am more than sure you would, Emmy. It is a fact that you would be a great help. But no. You must go back with me."

"But Gabe"—Doba turned to Gabe and caved like a snow-laden mountain overhang in an avalanche—"it wouldn't hurt for you to ride down in the canyon a little ways."

The traitor.

"No, please, Mr. Kinlichee, let me go."

"No, and don't try crying either."

Emmy sniffled.

"Your mama and papa would kill me if I let you go alone, and my Kai will kill me if I don't come back with her sons. Do you want me dead, Emmy? Answer me that."

Emmy rolled her eyes but quit asking to go. Gabe thought she quit crying a little too easily, too.

Unlike Shannon.

Gabe studied on Doba's words and demeanor. Emmy seemed to be going to obey him. But maybe that was only because he *was* her father's friend and was acting as if he were her father. And of course it might also mean that Emmy believed her mother and father might be terribly worried. So Doba was getting his way, but he wasn't exactly in charge of his life either.

Gabe realized at that very moment that he had no idea how to handle women. . .well, not women. Woman. Just one. It wasn't his job to make Emmy mind, and he doubted he'd ever be around many others. In fact, he seriously considered taking a vow about just that right there on the spot. And considering Shannon had a man waiting for her, he probably wouldn't be around her much longer either. So why bother trying to learn anything?

"We will go with you, Shannon. Let your friend abandon you. We'll be fine." Hozho proved there was another woman he couldn't handle, and he didn't see Hosteen arguing with his wife.

He braced himself for Parson Ford and Ahway and Marcus to start getting after him. And maybe the parson's horse would give Gabe a swift kick while he was down.

"Okay, we'll go." He couldn't remember right at that moment why they shouldn't go. No one would follow them. Probably.

The weather was nice.

He'd sold his cattle to Elijah Walker, planning to start up a new herd when he returned to his ranch. Which could be as long from now as necessary. He hadn't homesteaded—he'd bought the ranch outright—so he didn't have to live there to prove up.

The trip in the canyon would be fine. In fact, it'd be fun.

Shannon swiped the tears, her lower lip quivering. "You're just saying that to stop me from crying."

"Uh. . .yep, why else would I agree to do such a blamed, fool thing?"

Doba slapped him on the arm hard enough to leave a bruise.

The tears started right up again. "But I want you to come because you *want* to come, not because I *cried*." Shannon buried her face in both hands, her shoulders shuddering under the tears.

Doba hit him harder just as Gabe opened his mouth.

Looking sideways, Gabe shook his head and mouthed silently, "What?"

"I think it's a good idea to go. I have to go home. I have the children's safety to consider. But you can go."

Shannon's shoulders stopped shaking quite so hard, and she looked up at Gabe, who got the very solid feeling that there was a right way and a wrong way to act, but he'd be switched if he could guess what it was.

Since Doba's words had ended the tears, Gabe decided to go along with him. "Uh. . .well. . .yep, okay. . .let's go. And. . .uh. . . I have no need to see my brother or head home to Wyoming."

The sun rose in Shannon's eyes. "Really?"

Gabe knew he'd guessed right. "Really. I'd decided to go down there, but those folks chasing you, well, I. . .I. . ." Gabe felt himself stepping into quicksand, so he trod carefully. "I let my worry for your safety change my mind about what I wanted to do anyway."

A smile bloomed on Shannon's face.

Gabe heaved a sigh of relief. "So now I believe it'll be safe, so let's go on down."

"You're sure you want to?"

Of course he wasn't sure. Was the woman crazy?

"Yep, I want to go bad." Gabe was learning.

"Hozho, you know the way down, or does Shannon need to get

her map?" His hand darted out for fear she'd reach for her skirt.

"I know one way down, and I can lead you to the village in the canyon. It's the only village I know of, so it must be the way your father went, too." Hozho smiled.

"You in or out, Parson?" For some reason Gabe wanted the parson to go along real bad. He felt like it was him against Shannon and Hozho. Hosteen evened it up, but it was still half women and half men. And Hosteen might not be that much help, what with his being partial to his wife and all. Gabe could use another man on this journey.

"I'll ride along. As I said, the Yavapai are part of the people I serve. I'm overdue to go down in that canyon." The parson shuddered a bit. "Terrible ride on horseback. Might be best to walk down."

Gabe had to wonder how rugged that canyon really was. Of course the parson seemed to hate his horse, so Gabe decided not to judge the trip just based on the man's attitude.

Doba pulled on his reins and turned to head east. "Farewell then. Stop at our settlement when next you pass this way." Doba and his sons rode off as if they were being chased by wolves. Or maybe by one crying woman.

Emmy looked at them, pure envy almost eating her alive. Then with a frustrated grunt that was way more kid than woman, she turned to follow Doba.

Going down in that canyon with those outlaws on their trail went against Gabe's common sense, but Shannon was getting her way. He'd have complained, except he was afraid she'd start crying again. And he'd rather be chased by killers and swallowed up by a canyon than let that happen.

He smiled as bright as day. "Let's go find the canyon."

"We lost 'em." Cutter hunkered down to study the dusty trail.

They'd been going slower and slower until the frustration

was driving Lurene mad.

Now Cutter was on foot, leading his horse, crouching to study the trail every few steps.

Lurene had no choice but to inch along. When she got too impatient, she'd silently chant, *John Jacob Astor, John Jacob Astor, John Jacob Astor.*

After a while she put a tune to it and added the jingling of gold coins—not the ones they'd found in the Dysart woman's saddlebag, but the ones they'd earn once they had her in their grasp.

Because it was daydream or go mad, she conjured up a saloon. Yes, she'd own a saloon when they got their money. A classy one. Go to San Francisco and open up her own place. First class. Good liquor. A roulette wheel—she'd seen one in St. Louis once, and she'd hire a piano player and dress in red velvet.

She was actually starting to design the dress and pick out costumes for the card sharps she'd hire—and not having that much fun doing it—before Cutter moved again.

"This is the way they had to come." Cutter rose and looked forward, scowling. "It's about a five-day trip that goes to the southern rim of the canyon. There are known waterholes. There's no way across the canyon straight west. You have to go around. To the north is desert. It's a mean trip, a'course south ain't no easy stroll through a park. To the west, a dead end. To the east, they'd've run into us.

"You're sure this is their only choice?" Randy had gotten more and more smug and sarcastic as the day wore on.

Cutter turned on Randy, his temper shorter as the hot, dry day stretched. "You want to take over tracking?"

Fighting to keep a leash on her own temper, Lurene stepped in before a fight broke out. "What do we do? Keep pushing? Hope we find a sign? Just because you don't see one doesn't mean they didn't come this way. Rocky ground. Wind blowing across what few places would show tracks. If they had to go this way, then they must have."

Lurene looked back at a green area still visible a mile back. They'd filled their canteens and taken a break in the shade for a couple of hours. She hadn't minded getting out of the worst heat of the day, but there was still plenty of heat left.

"I'm not wrong." Cutter kicked at the heavy dirt in this sheltered spot. "This trail is narrow. There's no wind. Anyone heading this way would have to pass in this sandy soil, and they'd've left tracks. Even if they tried wiping them out, I could tell. Nope, we lost 'em. I think we're gonna need to go back. I saw where they left the trail to turn south. I know they started this direction, but somewhere they turned off. We've got to go back."

Lurene noticed the sun lowering in the sky. Another day wasted.

"Ready to forget all about that city of gold?" Randy sneered.

Cutter looked up. He made no sound, but Lurene felt as if they had a cornered wildcat in their group. He was furious, hot, frustrated, and tired of this. And they were completely dependent on him. Lurene thought of just riding away. Strike out for California. This trail would take them there.

John Jacob Astor, John Jacob Astor, John Jacob Astor. "It's not about a city of gold anymore, and you know it. It's about the woman having a stack of gold coins in her pack and plenty more where that came from."

Randy turned on her. "Maybe, but I don't know much about kidnapping. The more I think of it, the more I don't see how it's gonna work."

Randy's smug question got her stubbornness up. "Go on west if you want. You don't want to stick your neck out to get your hands on a woman who's wandering around out here defenseless. Kin to one of the richest families in the country. You go if you want. But that city woman tricked me when she switched those maps. I'm not inclined to forget it."

"Maybe she didn't figure she owed you much, what with Cutter threatening to throw her off that cliff and Ginger knocking her down and leaving her bleeding."

"She figured wrong then." Lurene reined her horse roughly, for one short second hating the heat and the stinking animal.

Then she remembered her life back in St. Louis. Plenty of heat there, and the stinking animals were all the woman-hungry men she'd had to endure. An almost maniacal desperation not to return to that life stiffened her resolve. "I think she owes me plenty, and I mean to make her pay."

Turning, she headed to the green behind her. "I'm going to keep tracking her then make her look back fondly on the day she was left to die in a sky-high cave."

Fourteen

Wait a minute!" Shannon pulled her map out of her pocket. "We need to keep heading straight west here."

"Trail bends south. That's the way into the canyon." Hozho pulled her horse up, turned, and rode back even with Hosteen. The two of them seemed part of the land. Their weathered faces, their clothing worn and faded until it was more the color of the stone than whatever it had once been.

"No, I recognize that buttress of rock." Shannon pointed. "That one right there. My father's map says to go to the north side of it."

Gabe came up beside her and looked at her map.

She had to fight the urge not to keep it out where he could see. All her instincts told her to hide it from everyone, even Gabe. But she forced herself to trust him and pointed to the line of numbers and shapes.

"How do you figure that says go north of that rock."

Shannon looked up. "It's in code. Here." She pulled the paper out from underneath the one she studied. Two years of work, but she'd figured it out. "My father substituted numbers and characters for words. It was a version of a game he played with me when I was young. This is far more complicated, but I broke his code." She pulled the map out and pointed to a shape that, to Gabe, looked like a cross between a star and a dung beetle and a cinnamon roll. "This mark here definitely refers to that oddly shaped red rock."

Hozho shook her head. "No trail that way into the canyon. My people live two days journey to the southwest. To the northwest you have to go much farther. You said he met Indians. The Pai are the only ones who live down there."

"That's another thing. You said Pai or Yavapai. I was sure my father's code referred to Hopi. If I'm right, then there must be others living down there."

"No, none." Hozho didn't hesitate a second.

"None that you know of, Hozho. There might be other groups down there. You say it's rugged—how can you be sure of who all lives in the canyon? Have you or your people been all through it? Are they a large enough group to have been sure no others dwell in the bottom of the canyon?

The parson came up behind Gabe. "My motive for going was to visit members of my flock, and those folks live to the southwest."

"If you've never gone the way I want to go," Shannon said, "maybe you've missed members of your flock."

Shannon kept her spine rock solid. She would not be swayed. She had to obey this map, and unless she handled this exactly right, she was going to lose the Tsosis and Parson Ford. And she couldn't go on alone with Gabe. . .assuming he stuck with her. Could she do it alone?

She didn't think so. Maybe she needed to return to a city. Flagstaff was many miles in the wrong direction, but they'd have a telegraph. She could get a bank to send a wire east and confirm that she had money and arrange the funds to be sent, then write bank drafts and finance a new trip. She'd get money, hire people loyal to her. . .like. . .Lurene and Lobo Cutter. With a tired sigh, she knew her judgment wasn't the best. She'd probably be better off alone.

"Well, I have to follow my map. I'm sorry. If you feel you must go to the south, I regret that, but my whole expedition is for the purpose of following my father's map, and he says there's a trail into the canyon farther north. Of course my promises to pay you end now if you abandon me."

She took a deep breath and faced Gabe. "You can't go on with me if the others leave. If I could have a share of the food, I'll go on alone."

"Are you crazy?" Gabe exploded. "You can't be on your own out here!"

"I certainly don't want to be." Shannon fell silent, her eyes flicking between Gabe and the others, praying they'd stick with her.

Gabe stared into her eyes and must have figured she meant what she said because he turned to the others. "When I set out on this trip, agreed to go along with her, I figured her map would lead her nowhere, so I'd ride along, mop her tears when she was forced to give up, and then get her to safety." Gabe smiled at her in the least friendly way imaginable, like she was a child being humored, and he wasn't even trying to pretend anything else.

Her fist clenched, and she satisfied her anger by picturing herself slugging him right in the nose.

"So, how long will it take to ride to the edge where this trail doesn't exist?" Gabe arched one brow at the group.

Hozho scowled. "Not long. We should be nearly there by tonight. The canyon is much closer to us if we go straight west. The southwest route would take another day or two. We can follow your map." She gave Shannon a very clear "you're stupid" look.

It wasn't the first time Shannon thought about just how rich her family was and how much she didn't like being treated like this. All that money had, she was now realizing, smoothed the path of her life pretty well.

Of course she'd always gone her own way, much to her mother's dismay. Shannon tried endlessly to be included in her father's studies as a way to earn a place in his life. Her mother really hated that.

But her mother was obsessed with the family's status in society. She rarely let a conversation go by without working in the words, "The Astor branch of my family. . ." or "The Campbell side of my family. . . ."

Well, Shannon's family tree had more than one set of roots. She considered herself more Dysart than Astor or Campbell or Fontaine—her mother's maiden name. And her mother's tenuous connection to the Astors hadn't translated into any great business sense on Shannon's part, but it had led to plenty of money. Even Mother's snooty Campbell relatives went back to a fur trader who made his fortune trapping in the Rocky Mountains. A tough man.

St. Louis was purely civilized these days, but it wasn't that long ago that it had been the far edge of the wilderness. There was still a rawness to the town that helped Shannon find people who would go west with her without much trouble.

Although, considering the "left to die alone" situation, she should have taken more trouble. She decided now wasn't the time to demand respect. If she could get them to ride along with her with a sneer on their faces, she'd take it. Then she'd find her city of gold and make them all admit she was right all along. She liked that plan fine. "So you'll go?"

Hosteen shrugged. "I can find water on the northwest trail. We won't die." Which wasn't exactly eagerness, but Hosteen sounded resigned.

"Fine, then we'll go that way." Hozho had a look like a

depressed hound dog. "No point in not following her map. If her map doesn't lead to the Pai village, then it's a long way to visit a village with people in it we don't know. I've got no family there." She shook her head.

Shannon ignored that pessimistic shaking head and grabbed hold of those words, because if the elderly woman didn't accompany them, she'd have to go on alone for propriety's sake or go back. "Parson, will you come?"

"Of course. Maybe there are more people this direction." His voice said clearly that he doubted it. "If there are, I'll bring them the good news of Jesus Christ."

"All right, Shannon, we go to the north of that big rock right there." Gabe seemed demoralized but willing to hang on for the rest of the ride.

Beggers and choosers came to Shannon's mind. She wouldn't demand a good attitude.

"We're not riding on tonight, Tyra." Abe raised his voice to be heard over the squeal of the incoming train that was braking only a few yards away.

She was enraged, so it was her distinct pleasure to yell right back at her brother-in-law. "You're getting to be an old man. Your brother might be fighting for his *life,* and all you can do is hunt for a comfortable bed."

It was pitch dark. They'd pushed so hard since they'd left home that both them and their horses had been worn to the nub. They'd been in town for a couple of hours, but Abe and Pa had spent that time working hard hunting down any information they could find about the telegraph Abe had received. Tyra had been left idle to fidget and fret about the delay. Pa had found the mule skinner who'd sent the wire, just back in Flagstaff from another trip packing supplies.

Abe's look was so dismissive that Tyra wanted to strangle him. She'd have to strangle her father, too, unfortunately, because Pa said they wouldn't push on tonight. "The mule skinner gave me directions for the settlement where he met Gabe. It's a half day's ride from here, and not much water along the way; and what's there is hard to find. We aren't going riding through a rugged land like that in the dark when we're this tired and our horses are spent."

The train shrieked to a halt, and a blast of steam blew out of the side.

Tyra refused to admit she was exhausted, too. "Reckon old folks like you and Pa need to rest your weary bones from time to time."

Pa had led the horses to a watering trough, so he wasn't there to growl at Tyra, which was probably why she had the nerve to be so rude.

Abe chuckled and refused to engage in the fight she was spoiling for. "Let's go see if the hotel has a meal they can rustle up, baby sister."

If Tyra managed to drag Gabe to the altar, Abe'd be her brother twice over. She liked that real fine because she liked Abe a whole lot better than her own bossy big brothers.

Pa stood across the street from the hotel near the tracks. He was dickering with the livery owner about the cost of feeding and bedding down the horses.

"I'll go see if they've got rooms. Best hurry before any folks get off the train in case the hotel fills up." Abe went up a step to the board sidewalk and entered the hotel.

A man in a black suit jumped off the train and set a box on the ground for a step. People began straggling off. The first to appear were men, one after the other until six of them were heading for the hotel. The group had a determined look, no stretching or casual talk between them. They were filthy, sooty, and sweat-stained, but they were well dressed.

Abe came back outside. His eyes narrowed as he passed the men, studying them, taking their measure. Then he reached Tyra's side.

Pa came up on her other side a bit fast as if he'd rushed to her side before those men got to her.

"I rented two rooms," Abe told her and Pa.

"Why not three?" Tyra asked.

The six men all trooped past her in single file, walking behind her father's back. Tyra noticed the last of the men, his shoulders slumped, his clothes travel-stained, walked as if his feet weighed a hundred pounds each. As he drew even with her, he looked up, directly over Pa's shoulder.

Their eyes met. In the dim light cast from the hotel window, she couldn't make out the color, but she wanted to look closer. For some reason it seemed really important that she know if they were blue or brown. The whole world seemed to slow down. His eyes on her. Her eyes on him. The screen door on the hotel had a hollow, distant sound.

Tyra could smell the dusty streets and the coal from the train. There was food in the hotel. All her senses were unusually acute. At the same time, the world seemed distant and vague.

He kept walking and staring at her as he moved by.

"We won't need but one bed," Abe spoke.

That jolted Tyra out of whatever strange slow-moving world she'd been in. She felt herself blush to think that Abe had said the word *bed* right in front of this man.

The man's eyes narrowed. He walked smack into the step that led up to the hotel door and fell over on his face.

The man in front had opened the hotel door. The others helped the fallen man regain his feet. He glanced back and was close enough to the hotel lights that she could see his eyes were blue. Bright, beautiful blue. And his cheeks were bright red. He was blushing just like she was.

She smiled.

"You all right, boss?" One of the men clapped him on the back.

He looked away and glared at the man who'd spoken to him. "Call me Buck." The man brushed the helping hands away, slapped at the knees of his black broadcloth pants as if they weren't so filthy there was no saving them at this point, then looked right into Tyra's eyes. His eyes fell shut as if his embarrassment had just doubled. He turned and must have opened his eyes again because he managed the steps just fine as he entered the hotel.

The door snapped shut, and the world seemed to come back to her father and Abe planning her life and talking of beds as if she were an infant. They headed into the hotel just as the man with the blue eyes and blushing face said to the hotel manager, "We got a telegraph from my fiancée telling me to find a man named Doba Kinlichee."

"What?" Tyra charged the man and grabbed his arm. "What's your business with Doba Kinlichee?"

He turned and she saw, up close, the man looked as tired as she, her pa, and Abe did. Bloodshot eyes. Bristly beard stubble. He smelled to high heaven, too. As she was sure she did. But his eyes flashed with smarts, and he had the squarest jaw and the straightest nose she'd ever seen.

He stared at her for much too long. Then his eyes rose and went past her. "You're looking for the Kinlichee fellow?"

"Yes," Tyra said.

"We are," her pa said.

Buck responded to her pa. "I got a telegraph saying my. . .my. . ." He stumbled over the next words, glanced at Tyra, then said, "A young lady named Shannon Dysart was in danger, and she was staying at a settlement north of Flagstaff. She said the place was owned by a man named Doba Kinlichee."

My what? Tyra wondered.

Abe came up beside Tyra on the left. "We're heading out there

161

tomorrow. I'm Abe Lasley." He extended his hand. "My brother, Gabe, said there was trouble. He mentioned someone tried to kill a young woman and, well, he didn't say a lot, but I didn't like the sound of it. We decided to ride up here and help him get shut of whatever trouble was doggin' him and get him back home."

Pa appeared on Tyra's right. A glance told her he was taking the young man's measure and Buck was coming up short.

His clothes weren't right for the West. They weren't wrong, just too new, despite the stains. His Stetson was bent wrong. Most cowpokes broke theirs in with living, tugs and twists that shaped a hat until it shaded the eyes and protected the backs of their necks from the sun and rain. His broadcloth pants were pure black, not faded one bit. His boots, well, Tyra knew boots, and these were expensive ones, but they had barely a scuff on them.

He wore no six-gun, and she saw dried blood on his hands, right where hands would bleed if a man without calluses rode long and hard on horseback. He had a black vest on and a white shirt that had turned almost pure brown with dirt. And the real reason she knew he was a city boy—he didn't wear any of this comfortably. Somehow it seemed as if he had on a costume. Which meant her pa was right now pegging him for a greenhorn, and there was nothing Pa enjoyed more than tormenting a city boy who was trying to find his way in the West.

Tyra had an almost uncontrollable urge to protect the man. She could size up a man, too, and though he might have a soft city look about him, his eyes were clear and direct. Nothing sly or dishonest about him. "You can ride out there with us." Tyra felt Pa's hand land heavy on her shoulder and wished she'd kept her mouth shut. But it was too late now.

My what? she wondered again.

"I'm Tyra Morgan." She extended her hand, feeling a bit foolish because she didn't shake hands often.

The man reached up and shook with such ease she knew even

more he was used to city ways. "Buck Shaw." He held her hand just a second too long then released her and turned to her father, his hand still out. "I would be grateful for any information you could give me about Shannon."

Buck Shaw. Sounded western. Sounded tough. Maybe he'd toughen up to match his name with just a little help.

"I'm Lucas Morgan." Pa shook, possibly squeezing a bit too hard, but Buck didn't flinch. "Gabe didn't say a name, just called her a young woman." Then Pa looked at the hotelier. "Any chance you've still got some food in the kitchen? Even a loaf of bread, some cold meat. We could make our own sandwiches."

"Got plenty left from supper. I'll bring something out. Come in the dining room and sit a spell while I get you fixed up." The man rounded the counter and hurried through double swinging doors that must lead into the dining room.

"We can sort this out, young fella. If your Shannon is with Gabe, then she's in good hands. But we aim to find Gabe and fetch him home." Pa looked at the men surrounding Mr. Shaw. "Looks like you brought some help with you."

The men all nodded, quiet men that Tyra couldn't quite judge.

"Good to meet you, Mr. Morgan. I'll be grateful for any information you could share about Shannon's whereabouts. And if she's with your brother"—Buck turned to Abe—"from the sound of your telegraph, it sounds like he's watching out for her. We'd like to join up with you and help with the hunt for both of them."

"So who is Shannon, and how'd she end up with Gabe?" Tyra asked, dying of curiosity. Dying to ask, *My what?*

"This is men talk, Ty." Pa never took his hand off Tyra's shoulder as he guided her through the doors. "You sit there and keep quiet." They were just a step ahead of everyone else, but Pa wasn't one to care if he was overheard when he had an opinion to give or an order to be issued.

The dining room was nice, full of rectangular tables of various sizes. Pa aimed toward a big one that would seat eight if they pulled it out from the wall, which Pa did. The nine of them crowded around.

Pa urged her into a chair near the wall and took the one to her left so no one could sit by her. Abe sat around the corner at the foot of the table so she had someone on each side, as if she were under guard.

Buck Shaw sat straight across from her. He had none of the wrinkles around his eyes a man got squinting into the sun for his whole life.

She wondered why he'd come here and just what this Shannon Dysart was to him. Not a sister, because they had different names—unlikely a woman wandering the West alone would be married. But family maybe. He'd said, "My. . ." then changed to "a young woman."

Tyra was left mulling just exactly, *My what?*

Fifteen

That's the rock formation." Shannon jabbed a finger at the oddly shaped outcropping. It had a pile of stones at its base that could not have occurred naturally.

The world seemed to stop past that odd-shaped parapet and the small pyramid of fist-sized rocks as Shannon rode toward it. The rocks had been scattered and toppled a bit, but they were still a clear stack, and they didn't belong there. No place for them to have fallen from. "My father said he left a cairn of stones just like that." She spurred her horse, its shadow cast long in front of her with the rising sun at her back.

"Cairn?" Gabe asked. "What's 'at mean?"

"Uh, stack."

"Why didn't he just say stack then? Why didn't he just—" Gabe sucked in a breath that sounded like part of the wind.

The world fell away at Shannon's feet, and she jerked back on the reins so hard her horse reared and fought the bit. A gasp escaped even as her throat swelled shut. She swung down off her horse, only distantly noticing the others coming up beside her and

165

Gabe. From each, a gasp to match hers and Gabe's was the only sound. . .save the wind.

She wondered if every person who ever rode up to this place made exactly the same sound. Very possible because there were no words sufficient to express it.

She was only distantly aware of her companions dismounting in complete silence, absorbing the beauty of the canyon that opened before them. Time crept by, but there would never be enough time to absorb something this magnificent.

"The Grand Canyon," Hozho spoke quietly, reverently. Her voice was too small to truly invade the silence.

More time elapsed as they stood, five in a row, their horses behind them. They breathed in the extravagant splendor, the impossible depth and breadth of what lay before them.

Finally, the vastness of it forced Shannon to speak, though it felt like sacrilege. "How can we ever find anything down there?"

"There's nothing to find, Shannon." Gabe, on her right, reached over and took her hand. "Surely you can see that this is a wild place. Too rugged. Who would go down there? There's no city to be found. And who would build a city of gold in there? Gold would be a pale insult in the midst of that."

She heard pity in his voice. That broke through what was a blissful moment. She had to almost physically tear her eyes away from the depths and rock sculptures, the towers and the layers of color: reds, browns, grays, whites, and blues. Impossibly majestic.

"Don't you see, Gabe?" Their eyes met. "Of course it's down there. This city *has* to be remote. It *has* to be hidden or it would have been found by now."

"You have to give it up, Shannon." His words weren't so much bossy as they were a plea to her.

She remembered his arms around her. Remembered how close they'd come to being married.

Remembered Bucky.

"If you want to walk on streets of gold, you're going to need to do it in the next life. God has a different kind of treasure for you to seek on earth. Treasures of love and forgiveness and faithfulness. Treasures of marriage and family and home."

"If I was one of those bishops looking for a place to hide and protect sacred objects"—she looked back at the terrifying wildness, the staggering beauty—"I would know the moment I saw this canyon that I'd found the perfect place."

Gabe shook his head. "I see no trail. This can't be where your father's map leads."

"Give me a few more minutes to look at that"—her hand swept wide to encompass what lay before them—"then I'll find the place where we can descend."

He nodded but didn't speak. He clearly doubted her, but she could see that he would stick. He had committed to this search, although with the snippy notion that he was on a fool's errand and his main job would be to dry her tears. He had no hope of finding what Shannon knew her father had discovered. It hurt that he doubted her. But along with the hurt was pleasure that he was willing to help.

She thought of her father. Her thoughts were too much with him, she knew. Her mother had so many times begged Shannon to let go of Delmer Dysart's obsession and get on with a more conventional life. It was right now, as they stood on the edge of eternity, that she finally, truly saw why she was out here.

She'd been rejected by her father all her life, coming in a poor second to his work.

At the sight of this Grand Canyon, she felt that maybe her father had picked something worthy over his daughter. If his work had meaning—if it had profound historical value—then maybe it was all right that he'd had no time for her.

As she looked down into the canyon, she understood how a person could become obsessed with something this magnificent to the detriment of his wife and child. But somehow that didn't comfort her one bit.

She had to admit that she'd come in second to a wonderful thing, but nothing should be more wonderful than love, than a child. Just as Gabe said, the treasure is marriage and family and home. However worthy this effort, she was still unimportant in her father's eyes.

She finally grasped the truth, and it was a terrible thing. She almost told Gabe they could go. There was nothing for her to prove anymore. But she didn't say the words that would set her on a path to a calm, peaceful life in St. Louis.

And not because of her father or treasure or pride. She stayed silent because the canyon called to her.

"I want to go down there." She turned to Gabe. "Don't you? How can you not want to descend into that wild land?" And while she became part of this canyon, she would do her best, whether she found a city of gold or not, to let go of her last questions about her father and his poor love.

"Get your map out." Gabe drew in a deep breath as if he could absorb that view into his lungs. "Let's see if we can find a way down."

Shannon looked at him, grateful for his generous willingness to stay with her. She was surprised to see a smile. "You're looking forward to it. You want to go down there."

"I find that I do indeed." Gabe looked to the others. "I firmly believe that we'll find no gold, but I would love to climb down there if Shannon can show us the way. Are we ready?"

"Yes," Hosteen said in reverent tones. "If we can find a path, we'll go."

Hozho nodded, still silent.

Shannon was amazed at the Tsosis's fascination with the canyon and the parson's rapt wonder. Parson Ford didn't even comment about how long and hard the ride was bound to be.

Shannon approached the cairn, praying silently that her

translation of her father's notes had been true. They'd led her here, hadn't they? She reached the stones, knelt, and began removing the stack.

Gabe was on his knees beside her helping without her needing to ask.

It took only minutes to uncover a ragged cloth. Years old.

Carefully Shannon unfolded the packet to find oilcloth inside. The oilcloth gave way to papers. More of Father's code, but Shannon knew what she was looking for now, and she smiled. "There is a way down." She studied the cryptic images and numbers, the mathematical equations and scientific abbreviations. It all made sense. "There." She pointed to a spot not that far from them, an impossible spot to Shannon's eyes. But whatever Professor Delmar Dysart's failings as a father, he'd been a brilliant historian and scientist.

Gabe walked to the spot and looked over the edge. He turned back, his face pulled into lines of doubt. "Maybe, if we're very careful. We can tie ropes. We can—"

"My father said a horse can make it down." Shannon looked again and couldn't doubt what she read. "He says there's a herd of wild mustangs that go over the rim there. That's how he found the trail. And his own horse went right down after them."

She saw Gabe's throat move as he swallowed hard.

"Down that. . .trail?" the parson squeaked. "On horseback?"

Shannon knew how he felt. And she liked her horse.

"What do you think, Hosteen?" Gabe asked.

The elderly Indian shrugged. "These are mountain- and desert-bred animals. They can go where a wild mustang goes." He turned to Shannon. "We'll trust our animals. If they'll step off that ledge, they'll be following a scent and a trail we can't see. If they refuse to go down, we'll accept that and find a place to fence them in with some grass and climb down."

There was no point arguing with what was eminently

sensible. "Agreed." She stood, her father's map in her hands. She'd told no one, but what she'd had in her possession up until she'd moved those stones had only brought her this far. If the map hadn't been there, they'd have had to turn back. Her father had talked to her, told her things, and she'd written it all down word for word. But all his notes and encoded maps had led her here and no farther.

Eager to go on, she let the view catch her once again. It was impossibly lovely. Impossible period. Nothing so grand could exist. The canyon seemed to be a place of miracles. The kind of place that was vast enough and miraculous enough to lure a group of priests into its depths then enfold them, surround those noble men and keep their golden secret for seven hundred years.

Finally shaking off the grip the stunning view had on her, she swung up onto her horse.

"I'll go first." Hozho headed for the rim. "My horse is as surefooted as a mountain goat."

The elderly woman walked straight for the invisible trail, riding strictly on the word of a man the world considered delusional. And she went over and sank quickly out of sight. A sigh halfway between wonder and panic escaped Shannon's lips as Hosteen went next and vanished after his wife.

Parson Ford didn't move. He looked to the heavens, and his lips moved in obvious prayer. When he finished, he and Gabe both turned to her.

"You're next, Shannon. Then the parson."

"No, I'll go." The parson's throat worked as he forced himself to swallow. "Putting it off will only make it worse."

Gabe smiled. "Fine. Then Shannon. I'll bring up the rear."

With trembling hands, the parson guided his horse after Hosteen, and the horse went willingly.

Gabe met Shannon's eyes and gestured to the canyon rim. "Give your pinto her head."

Her mare went as calmly as if she walked off the edge of the world every day.

Majesty.

It was the only word that came close to doing the canyon justice, but it didn't begin to go far enough. Gabe wouldn't have turned back for anything. If Shannon suddenly came to her senses and saw the futility of this treasure hunt, he'd still take the ride.

He'd never had anything touch his soul like this except for God. Gabe went over the edge and knew God was part of this, which made the canyon a holy place. A place of majesty.

There were sounds. His horse's bridle jingled. Soft thuds of slow-moving hooves. The wind brushed across the vastness, humming, singing. But all of it was too small. The tiny sounds somehow just drew attention to the hush. Nothing was big enough to overcome the extravagant majesty and immense silence of the canyon.

Hozho fearlessly descended. Hosteen stayed right on her tail.

The path wrenched Gabe's stomach, but he never for a moment considered not following it. His chestnut picked toeholds Gabe never would have called a trail.

Shannon just ahead of him never moved, sitting rigidly on her mare's back. She looked as if she was terrified to make a wrong move and upset her horse's balance. Not an irrational fear at all.

They were a row of ants crawling down, down, down. Their presence was a violation of this place, as if they were ripping aside the veil of the holy of holies. This descent into the canyon called for humility and prayer.

Gabe felt small, insignificant, and closer to God than he ever had. He had a strong sense that God approved of a man realizing there was a lot that was greater than he was. He hoped God was with them on this journey, because they had never needed holy protection more.

The worst of the descent ended, though the trail was a terror. Vivid red rock was laid out like stair steps—only much less regular and far narrower. No one ever would have thought of this as a way into the canyon, and he suspected that included Professor Dysart if he hadn't seen a band of mustangs go down here.

The drop was fast, hundreds of feet every few minutes. And so much farther to go. Gabe said a quiet prayer of thanks for his horse. He hated the thought of climbing down this rock wall on foot.

The view drew him from his fretting. The countless towers of red stone erupting out of the ground. The rising sun casting shadows into the deep that made parts of the canyon seem bottomless. Maybe they were. Everything striped as if layer after layer of rock, each a different kind and color, had piled up or worn away or both.

Minutes stretched to hours, and still they went down and down and down. All of them remained silent, the soft clop of hooves and the gusting of the wind seemed more a part of the quiet than an intrusion into it. They all trusted their horses to pick out a trail.

Gabe noticed that Shannon never consulted her new map. Maybe she was afraid unfolding paper would knock her horse off a cliff. There was nowhere to leave this trail anyway. It would serve no purpose to look at the map.

When Gabe thought of ascending this on their way out, his stomach quailed so violently he turned to let the view draw him in again. A golden eagle soared past, screaming in the wind, playing on the currents. Gabe felt as if he were part of the flight, part of the sky.

He saw God in these terrifying, staggering cliffs in a way he never had before. And he felt closer to his heavenly Father in a new and blessed way until every step his horse took was a kind of worship.

The canyon wall curved out and then back, in constant tortuous switchbacks. As Gabe rounded the rock wall, it was so steep he could have reached straight out with his right hand and brushed the rock. That kept his attention until he was all the way around the latest buttress of stone, and then he was stunned into a deeper kind of silence as the river appeared far, far below.

The bright blue of the Colorado River twisted like the grand-daddy of all rattlesnakes in the far depths of the canyon. The sun had risen now, and it cast the river in a vivid blue that made the red rock even brighter. The vibrant colors, the impossible rock formations—all of it kept Gabe's mind firmly off this mad slide into the belly of the earth.

A slightly less treacherous stretch of the trail opened up before them. A grassy slope crept around boulders.

"Hoof prints." The parson looked over his shoulder at Gabe and pointed to the ground.

Gabe had noticed, too. The trail was clearly worn and obviously well used by what must be a herd of wild horses. Amazing.

"That's a deer track," Hosteen said, pointing to the side of the trail. "I wondered if we'd find food. If there are deer, there will be smaller game, too. We'll be fine."

The cliff overhead jutted out so far it turned nearly to a cave. Suddenly Hozho stopped and stared at the rock wall beside her. The trail wasn't wide enough for even two of them to stand abreast, but they closed the gap between them, Hozho, Hosteen, Parson Ford, Shannon, and Gabe, as Hozho pointed at the wall.

"There have been people here before us." Hozho looked over her shoulder at Shannon. "Maybe your priests did come this way."

Gabe was close enough now to see pictures on the wall. Definitely man-made. One image might have been a lizard of some kind. It was such a primitive picture he couldn't tell. He

173

could identify a stick figure of a man. They sat on horseback and stared, and Gabe had the wild notion to stay down here forever, exploring these depths, maybe finding people here living in a city of gold. Just because they'd been lost for seven hundred years didn't mean they were dead. "Can whoever drew this still be down here?" Gabe asked.

"Very old," Hozho said. "But maybe there *are* people down here." She pointed at an odd broken line. "This is a symbol favored by my people."

They stared again. Gabe was barely aware of the passing of time. His senses needed to absorb it all.

"Look at this, Gabe, everyone." Shannon's excited voice pulled him out of almost dreamlike pleasure at the canyon and the way it stretched miles and miles, until it seemed endless.

He turned to see Shannon with her papers out. The ones she'd pulled out of that pile of stones stacked at the rim of the canyon.

"My father says we're to turn off rather than go all the way to the river." Shannon pointed at a pure white outcropping of rock ahead, jarring in the midst of red and gray. "He said we'll see a white rock formation that looks like a twenty-foot-tall seashell."

Gabe hadn't seen a lot of seashells in his life, but Shannon held out her papers and there, sketched in a fine hand, was a picture that could only be the fan-shaped rock they now approached.

"The river isn't that much farther," Hozho said. "The wild horses went on down, but there is a second trail in the direction your father's map points. We need to go water the horses before we begin walking along the side of the canyon wall. The trail to the river is clear at this point, and the edges of the riverbank are low. We might not find water so easily later."

"There must be a spring feeding this grass." Gabe looked at the little oasis of life in this stony place.

"We can search here if you want," Hozho said. "But it will take time. Faster to go to the river for water, then come back and follow the new trail.

They headed on down, but when they got low enough, they found a drop-off to the river that was insurmountable. But their own horses, given their heads, walked around boulders taller than a man on horseback and found a spring filling a little pond no bigger than a water trough that spilled into the river in a beautiful fall. The horses drank their fill as did the people. They ate a quick lunch. The parson grumbled when Shannon eagerly urged everyone to move, but he followed everyone else and mounted up. They headed back to the shell stone.

"How far are we going?" Gabe asked.

"I can't tell from what notes Father has left." Shannon looked at the white stone. "He only gives landmarks, places to turn, not distances."

"And he says in that note, clearly, that he found a city of gold down here?" Gabe began to think he might well be on the trail of treasure. The professor's notes so far had proven true.

"He says the treasure is here. It's all very terse and in code. He wrote the word 'Cibola' clearly, though. He's seen it with his own eyes."

"Cibola?" Hozho had turned her horse to follow Shannon's trail but paused at Shannon's words. "What is Cibola?"

"Coronado was an explorer who followed a man, a Pueblo Indian some say, who swore he lived in a city of gold. He called that city Quivera. Coronado never found that city, but others said the Indian purposefully led Coronado astray. His people feared the Spanish and wanted Coronado far away. More exploration took place in this area, but nothing was ever found. There was a legend about seven cities of gold. Some called them the Seven Cities of Cibola. The story came to my father of a second city, Cibola, that was near the Pueblo's land, where people drank from golden cups, wore emeralds and diamonds, and walked on streets paved with gold."

Gabe's pulse picked up. Common sense told him it was all a fable. But he couldn't pretend it wasn't enticing to think he might well be on his way to an ancient city of gold. Standing in this canyon made a man start to think outlandish things were possible.

"Pueblos are simple people," Hosteen said. "Apaches are warriors, but Pueblos, like the Navajo and the Yavapai, don't want wealth or power or war. Their desire is to live in peace. They build simple homes using the rocks and trees and adobe that surround them. If a mighty army of priests came here bearing gold, they might well use it as metal, to make cups and plates, but why pave the streets with it?"

"The Bible speaks of streets of gold, Shannon," Parson Ford spoke quietly. "Surely you can see that this is a legend. A legend that has been twisted through the years until it's grown into something larger than life. You speak of heaven on earth."

Shannon looked from one to the other, finally resting her eyes on Gabe.

"We're going with you, Shannon." He'd almost been forced to marry her, and he'd been willing, more than willing. Shannon had put a stop to that, not him. Still, he didn't want to crush her dreams. "But if we find something less than your city of Cibola, if we find ruins like those cliff dwellings where I found you or a village of Indians in hogans like at Doba's settlement, we've still spent our time walking through one of the most majestic places I've ever seen. Don't let it break your heart if we find a different kind of treasure than what you're searching for."

"My father spent his last breaths telling me of his discovery." Her chin tilted upward slightly, defiant fire blazing in her brown eyes. "He wanted me to follow his maps and share his discovery with the world. He wanted me to pick up his quest and go forward with it. Why would he spend his last moments of life telling me a lie?"

Because he was dying and sick and half crazy? Because he was obsessed? Because he cared more for his name and reputation than he did for his daughter?

Gabe couldn't bear to say any of that out loud. "Let's go."

They set out on a trail that was narrow and twisting, going down, then back up, then down again. There were treacherous talus slides from when the edges of the canyon had crumbled in avalanches. Huge boulders blocked the trail and could barely be circled.

They trusted their horses, though Gabe had to bite back the desire to dismount and lead the animals through the worst of it. Every time they came on a grassy stretch, Gabe remembered it in case they had came to an obstacle the horses couldn't get past and had to retrace their steps to a place they could picket their horses then go on by foot.

To walk among these layers of colored stone, the depths and the towers, the swift waters of the Colorado, to be buffeted by the wind and hear the screams of the eagles overhead, Gabe didn't mind this treasure hunt, but he thought he'd already found the treasure. This place was the treasure. He didn't need to find bishops and gold to convince him of that.

No words were sufficient.

One word was close.

Majesty.

Sixteen

❦

et down." Cutter jerked Lurene by the shoulder, and the rest of their group followed as he pulled Lurene to the desert floor.

Cutter was the one who had insisted they water their horses and fill their canteens then get away from the watering hole. Leading the way, he'd found a place shaded by rocks. They were just finishing their noon meal of hardtack and jerked beef when he hissed his orders.

Cutter rolled onto his belly to look through a scrub mesquite that blocked them from their desert pond. Lurene imitated his movements.

All five of them lay silent, watchful. Lurene heard the slide of metal on leather and looked to see Cutter with his gun out, aimed and ready as an older man, a young woman, and two younger boys rode up to the pond and dismounted.

"Navajo," Cutter whispered.

Lurene nodded and got her six-shooter out of her pocket.

"I don't see why we couldn't go to the canyon." The young woman swung off her horse with a grace Lurene envied.

The boys nearly had a man's height but still had the gangly movements of youth.

The old man rode so comfortably in his saddle he seemed to be nearly one with the horse. "We need to get back to the settlement, Emmy. Get the horses watered, and let's move on. Your parents will wonder where we've gotten ourselves to." The older man smiled in a lighthearted way, as if he didn't have a care in the world.

Lurene shook her head, wondering how someone could live in such a harsh land and ever smile. What was there to be happy about? Then she thought of her own life back in St. Louis and wondered why she wasn't thrilled to be out here in the heat and sand, with only the scorpions to try and harm her.

Her ma had sold her when she was ten. And until she'd left St. Louis, that same evil man had still owned her. She'd been fighting all her life to escape, and with Cutter she'd finally made it. And yet here she lay hot and angry. Jealous of a young girl's grace. Bitter about an old man's ease in the wilderness. Greedy for Shannon Dysart's wealth.

She should have been happy, no matter the discomfort.

But maybe her misery had nothing to do with that house and the red dresses she wore and the men she entertained. Maybe it was just her, deep inside, a twisted soul and ugly mind that she'd carry with her wherever she went and however she lived.

She'd always blamed her mother for the life she'd been forced into. And she'd blamed men for what she suffered at their hands. But had she ended up exactly where she belonged? Was the evil in her dragging her down to the level that matched? If she believed that, she might turn her revolver on herself.

Shaking her head to drive away the ugly thoughts, she turned to gold and ransom, treasure in any form as long as there was plenty of it. Believing those things would save her was the only thing that kept her sane.

"I have always wanted to see the Grand Canyon." The woman worked as she spoke. She had a quick grin, too. She was dark haired and deeply tanned, but Lurene saw freckles on her arms and caught a glimpse of bright blue eyes. One of the boys had lighter hair. The others were some kind of Indians. Cutter had said that village was Navajo.

The woman's complaints were good natured as if she had no expectation of getting her way but enjoyed the squabble.

"Never seen no one go straight west of here, Pa," the dark-skinned boy said. "Reckon they'll get to the edge of the canyon and just turn around and come back."

"Then we'll have company again, son." The older Navajo finished drinking at about the same time his horse did. He swung up onto the Indian pony and headed away from the desert spring. "Let's go. The sheep will be missing you, Emmy."

The young woman yelled in mock anger but climbed onto her horse, as did the young men. The four rode off at a brisk trot.

Cutter stood, his eyes riveted on the receding form of the riders.

"Shoulda grabbed 'em," Ginger said. "We could've made 'em lead us to the Dysart woman then killed all of 'em."

Cutter turned on Ginger so abruptly she backed up two steps. "We don't want the Navajo on the warpath against us, so shut your stupid mouth. Fools don't survive in the West."

Lurene's throat went dry as she waited for Cutter to pull his gun and close Ginger's stupid mouth forever. She didn't care about Ginger, but she didn't want Cutter to start shooting anyone who bothered him. In case her turn came.

Ginger nodded. "Right, of course not. I just thought we could—"

"Don't say it. Mount up. I heard enough to know which way to go, so let's ride." Cutter swung into his saddle and spurred his horse up the trail the Navajos had just come down, straight west.

180

Lurene had heard of the Grand Canyon but had no wish to see a big hole in the ground. She fell in behind Cutter and did her best not to say anything stupid.

Gabe woke up in the pitch dark, but he knew he'd slept a long time and it was near dawn. There was a barely visible lighter gray hue in the east that revealed the jagged lip of the canyon. The moon had set, and the night was alive with blazing stars.

The canyon wall looked so high overhead, blocking the view to the east, that Gabe wondered how late in the day dawn would come to this side of the canyon. Likely they'd walk in shadows until midday. Which might spare them if the day got warm.

A coyote howled and an owl screeched. The canyon echoed the sounds until Gabe couldn't begin to know if the animals were close by or miles and miles away.

He pushed back his blanket in the chill of the morning and stood, staring into the black, wondering at God's almighty hand to create something such as this. He stepped away silently from the campsite, letting the others sleep a few minutes longer.

As he put distance between him and the camp, his eyes adjusted to the night. He saw a flat rock, waist high, a few yards away, and sitting on it—it had to be Shannon, her slender figure looked like a statue silhouetted black against the slightly lighter shade of black that made up the night. She had one knee drawn up, her arms wrapped around it, and she stared upward toward the west at the beautiful predawn sky.

He walked to her, and she turned, aware of his approach. He sat down beside the woman who'd come real close to being his wife.

"The sun is going to hit that side of the canyon long before it comes down here. I want to look at day while I sit in the night." She smiled. They looked at each other then turned to watch the first ray of light shine across to hit the west side of the canyon rim.

Down here in the belly of this goliath hole in the ground, it was still pitch dark.

After a few moments passed, Gabe could finally stop looking at the beautiful blaze of orange and pink and turned to Shannon. "So, we found our way down here. Does your father's map guide us all the way to Cibola? Or was it. . .uh. . .Quivera?"

"He says Cibola. But I'm not sure if he just named it after the legend or what exactly."

"He didn't say whether there'll be folks living there, did he?"

"No, I can't tell that from his notes."

"But he says it's gold? A whole city full of it?"

"His exact words were treasure. But that's what treasure is, right?" Her voice sounded uncertain, and she turned to watch the light creep an inch at a time down the west canyon wall.

Gabe noticed the flat top of one of the stone towers gleamed as the sunlight brushed against it. Gabe rested one hand on her shoulder, and she turned back to him. "So, tell me about this man you're promised to."

"You asked that before."

"And you didn't answer. Is this Bucky really your intended?"

Silence stretched between them. Gabe's hand slid down her arm until he held her hand, but he waited. In this quiet world, neither of them could pretend she hadn't heard the question.

"I think—" she faltered.

Gabe didn't prod her, but he threaded his fingers between hers and held her hand so their palms touched fully.

"I think that when I get home, I'm going to have to tell Bucky that I'm not so sure about marrying him." She turned away from the view and looked at Gabe.

Something flared in Gabe's eyes. "And why is that?" He lifted their hands and, one by one, kissed her fingers where they lay woven between his.

"Bucky and I. . .we. . .we are old friends."

"Just friends?"

"We grew up together. Our mothers are friends even more than we are. They are both very proud of their roots in St. Louis. Lots of influence, lots of wealth."

"Treasure?" He felt Shannon shudder delicately as he kissed the back of her hand.

"No—I mean. . .not treasure like a city of gold."

"Was your father one of them? Was he a rich, important man?"

"No, he was a scholar. He was a genius, and I believe my mother loved that about him."

"So it was a happy marriage, despite your father spending years searching for the cities of gold?"

"It wasn't a happy marriage in the end." A soft gasp broke Shannon's voice when Gabe turned her hand and kissed her wrist right on the pulse. "Whatever brought them together didn't survive. She and my father were so different from each other."

Gabe thought of how different he was from Shannon.

"That's why my mother wants me to marry Bucky. We come from the same world."

"So your father went searching for treasure and abandoned his wife and child?" Gabe asked softly, hoping he could get the truth without hurting her badly. "Did he do that hoping to make your mother proud, hoping to become rich enough, important enough to find his way into her world and make his marriage a happy one?"

"No, that wasn't why."

Gabe slid his hand around hers so he could lift her wrist fully to his lips and kiss her pulse. Searching for that beating life, searching for what he'd found when Shannon had kissed him before. "I think it was." He abandoned her wrist and, still holding her right hand in his left, slid his other hand around her neck and pulled her close for a kiss.

Long moments later, he pulled away just a breath. "So if you're not going to marry Bucky, then why don't you think about staying out in the West? Why don't you think about striking out on your own, making your own life away from your mother's wealthy friends and your father's professional reputation?"

It wasn't a proposal of marriage. Gabe wasn't quite ready for that. But if he could find a way for her to stay out here, spend some time with her, maybe that would come.

"I have to tell him personally. I won't break my promise to him in some letter or telegraph. I—"

Gabe cut off her words by kissing her more deeply, deciding to distract her since he didn't want to hear what she had to say anyway. "We could go together, tell him together."

"No!" Shannon jerked away.

That cleared Gabe's head instantly, and the closeness he felt to her was replaced with irritation. "Why not? I'm not afraid of anyone named Bucky."

"It's not Bucky. It's my mother."

"What about her?"

In the silence, Gabe noticed that the sun had risen higher. He wondered how long he'd spent kissing her. It hadn't felt long, not nearly long enough, but the light was creeping lower on the far canyon wall and catching the towers that jutted upward from the canyon floor, reflecting light so Gabe could see her clearly now, though they still sat in shadows. They'd moved far enough from the camp that he couldn't tell if the rest of their group had stirred. Most likely they had. It was time to get back.

"If I did stay out west, my mother would never forgive me, Gabe. I've always seen this. . .this quest I'm on as a way of finishing the unfinished business of my father. Then I've intended to go home and be the daughter my mother wished for. If we don't find Cibola, I'll have failed my father, and if I don't go home and marry Bucky, my mother will never forgive me."

"So, you'd pick that life over a chance for a life with me? Is that right?" Gabe thought of what she said, and he thought of how she'd kissed him. The two didn't match, and he decided he'd believe the one that suited him.

He let go of her hand and slid his arm around her waist. He lowered his head and claimed the kiss in the way he truly wanted to. Her response meant more than words. Her arms slipped around his neck, and he was only distantly aware of pulling her onto his lap.

"Gabe! Shannon!" The parson's voice jabbed Gabe like a red-hot branding iron.

Shannon jumped sideways and toppled backward. Gabe grabbed her before she fell off the rock they sat on. Good thing they weren't on the edge of a cliff or she'd have plunged right over.

She rubbed on her lips and then clamped both hands in her lap. Between falling and being saved, somehow she was still on his lap. Her chin quivered. She looked up at Gabe. Their eyes locked.

The parson hollered again.

"You go on back," she whispered. "I'll come in, in a few minutes, from a different direction."

"We don't need to sneak around." Gabe touched the lovely little dent in her chin, which led his eyes to look at her lips. "I refuse to pretend like I'm ashamed of my actions."

Which she most certainly should be if she had no interest in staying with him.

"If we show up together, with your lips shiny and swollen and my hair rumpled. . ." He could still feel her fingers sinking deep into his hair. He noticed hers was out of its braid. Then he looked down and saw the leather thong she used to tie it back, twisted in his fingers.

She followed his gaze and snatched her hair tie away from him. "What? If we show up. . .what?"

"The parson's gonna go right back to that shotgun wedding he almost carried out a few days ago. Is that what you want?"

Gabe looked at her.

She refused to look back. Instead, with unsteady hands, she braided her hair and tied it together at the ends.

"Is it, Shannon? Are you going to waste your life on your ma's society and your pa's treasure hunt? Or are you gonna be a big, grown-up girl and live the life you want?"

Her chin came up. "Meaning staying here with you is the life I want? We don't know each other well enough for me to make a decision like that."

Hozho called this time, coming their way.

Gabe eased her off his lap to stand on her own two feet. Then he slid off the rock and landed so close to her she stepped back, but he grabbed her before she could put any space between them. "I know you, Shannon. I know exactly what's going on in your mixed-up head. You're searching for a treasure you don't even want. You're living your life for your pa and ma and maybe Bucky. Everyone but for God and for yourself."

"Well, you may think you've got me all figured out, but I don't know you, Gabe. I'm not so foolish as to think I know a man I've only met a few days ago."

"Then I suggest you keep your kisses to yourself from now on, Miss Dysart. Because your behavior with a man who's a *stranger* to you is nothing short of sinful." Gabe turned before he said something even more stupid, though what could be more stupid than calling a woman sinful and warning her that he very much wanted to kiss again but that she'd better keep her kisses to herself?

He stalked off in a direction that would bring him into the camp from the east, while Shannon could approach from the south. Behaving just exactly like a sneak, like a man who was ashamed of his actions.

He'd put a couple of big rocks between himself and that maddening woman when he heard Hozho say, "There you are. Why didn't you answer me when I called?"

"Just enjoying the sunrise. I'm sorry I was slow to call out."

The two voices faded as they headed for camp. Gabe kept walking until he'd gotten his temper under control. When he calmed down, he remembered how Shannon felt in his arms, and it was either stay mad or fall completely in love with her.

He found to his dismay that he might be capable of doing both.

"They went into the *Grand Canyon?*" Abe's hands came up as if he was going for the Navajo man's throat.

Pa grabbed him. Tyra was one beat slower, but she had Abe's other arm.

"*Why?* What fool notion made my baby brother ride into the Grand Canyon?"

The smiling Navajo, who called himself Doba, had quite a tale to tell, and he seemed to fear nothing, not even a whipcord-lean, heavily muscled rancher with a bad temper and a clenched fist.

Doba Kinlichee kept talking fearlessly as he told his story of midnight riders, gunfire, cave dwellings, treacherous canyons, and lost cities. A confident man, and Tyra had to admire it.

"A map sent her to the west of the trail when anyone else would have told you to go south," Doba went on. "I'll point you in that direction. You'll probably meet them coming back. There's no way into the canyon in that direction."

"Sure there is." A man, tanned until he was brown and so skinny he looked like skin draped over bone, stood from the watering hole.

Tyra hadn't paid him much mind. Mr. Kinlichee had come out to meet them, and he'd had enough to say to keep her attention riveted right on him.

"You know a way into the canyon, Hance?"

"Yep, been scouting it for a while now. I found me a trail, I did, right down off the edge of the world. Hard one to get along on. Steep, my oh my, it's shore enough steep. But it can be done. Only trail on the whole east side of the canyon that goes to the bottom. The next one is all the way south at the Supai village. And I'm the only one who knows about it." Hance wore a fringed buckskin jacket and a floppy brimmed hat. He had a beard and moustache as wild as this country and eyes sharper than a rattlesnake.

Tyra took his measure and believed what he was saying.

"And is there truly a city down in the canyon?" Doba asked.

"An old one, abandoned. I can lead you to it." The man's brow furrowed and his sharp eyes got a little shifty. "For a price."

Abe relaxed enough, so Tyra dared to release him.

"I'd be glad to hire you to guide us to this abandoned city," Buck said as he came up beside her, his arms crossed.

Kinlichee interrupted the business arrangements. "You oughta know, there were varmints on their trail. Bad men. We laid a false trail, so hopefully they'll ride all the way to the canyon where it goes down by the Supai village. Most folks don't know of any way into the canyon straight west."

"Including me." The Navajo man scowled at the man who offered to guide them. "Why haven't you told me of your trail into the canyon?"

Hance shrugged, his eyes wily. "Found a way down is all. Man's got a right to make some money off his hard work. If someone wants to go down there on my trail, they can pay for the privilege."

"How much?" Buck asked.

Buck was no cowpoke. But this was about money, and suddenly Tyra could see that the city man did know a few things. Like how to make a deal.

Hance named a price that nearly closed Tyra's throat.

Buck made a counteroffer.

She glared at him. He was dickering over Shannon Dysart's *life*, and that was his right, but he was also trying to save money on *Gabe's* and that made her mad.

Then Hance came down a few dollars and Buck came up. They'd worked it all out before Tyra could glare a hole in Buck Shaw.

"We're in a hurry. Can we leave now?" Buck's question was smooth. His gaze was calm, almost lighthearted. It was the right way to handle Hance. Nothing like Tyra's chosen method, similar to Abe's with Kinlichee—go for the man's throat until he helped them.

"Yep, reckon we might as well get on our way." Hance turned toward his horse and ambled over. Before he'd turned away, Tyra saw the gleam in his eyes. The man was thrilled with the deal he'd made. She suspected, though the man was greedy, he wasn't evil. Just a businessman who'd made the best deal of his life.

"Good." Buck still sounded smooth. "We can get a few hours down the trail before sunset." He swung up onto his horse smoothly enough.

There was no denying that Buck rode a beauty of a mare, a thoroughbred, sleek and tall with strong muscles. The horse was pure black except for a white blaze on her face and four white socks. She'd make a fantastic colt teamed with the stallion her pa had back on the ranch.

The horses ridden by his men were excellent horseflesh, too. The horses of a rich man. And from the sound of some of the talk, they all belonged to Buck. They'd moved tirelessly all day, too. So even though they looked pampered, they were well exercised. Buck showed good sense in taking these horses on this journey.

But they were heading into rugged land. The kind of land better suited to a tough, little mountain-bred mustang. Tyra hoped the thoroughbreds came through.

The horses were watered and ready to go, and they had a good supply of food still from Flagstaff, so they headed out.

As they left the little settlement, Buck rode up beside Tyra.

"Tell me more about Gabe. Is Shannon in good hands?"

"For a man who's worried about his woman, you drove a real hard bargain with Hance." Tyra tried to glare at him, but truth was he'd handled Hance real well.

"I've known men like Captain John Hance before." Buck smiled. "He wouldn't have respected me if I hadn't bartered with him."

Tyra knew men like that, too. "He got the best of you, you know. You're paying him about twice what this trip is worth."

"That's because I *didn't* drive a hard bargain over Shannon." Buck looked ahead. Hance was well in the lead. "I talked with Doba a bit more about those men on their trail. He told me they left Shannon to die about a day's ride to the east of here. Your friend Gabe found her and brought her into Doba's settlement. He said she convinced a few people to follow her to the Grand Canyon. She had a map that leads to a city of gold. Doba doesn't believe a word of it, and neither do I, but the important thing seems to be that Shannon believes it. She's been working over her father's notes for a long time to the exclusion of everything else." There was a touch of something sad in his voice.

"Including you?"

The man smiled, and Tyra had a very hard time not looking at his shining blue eyes and his amazingly white teeth. "Sure, including me. But that's just Shannon. I understand how important her father was to her."

"Are you in love with her?" Flinching, Tyra wished someone would come and gag her. She hadn't meant to ask that.

"Shannon is—" Buck fumbled for an answer. "I—I don't know."

Hance picked up the pace, and they began trotting toward the setting sun.

"You said she was your friend." Tyra's horse was comfortable on the easy trail, and she gave all her attention to Buck. He was a good-looking man, no denying it. Shame his hands were bleeding where he should have had calluses, and he was sunburned when he should have been darkly tanned. Shame, real shame.

It occurred to Shannon that they had the same coloring. Dark hair, blue eyes. If he hadn't been such a greenhorn, they'd have been a good match. She shook her head to dislodge that ridiculous thought.

"Shannon and I grew up together. Our main connection is our mothers. Both of us spent a good part of our childhoods hiding from them." Buck smiled again, but his words didn't strike Tyra as particularly funny. "And, since they visited each other almost daily, Shannon and I often had the opportunity to hide from them together."

"Hide from them? How? Where?"

"We both lived in big mansions in St. Louis, just a few doors from each other."

"Mansions, really?" Tyra thought of the cabin she shared with her pa. It was big, but there'd been a lot of them.

"Oh, sure." Buck shrugged and looked a little sheepish. "We were raised on how important our families are. I am a Shaw. My mother is a Chatillon. Shannon is a Fontaine and even more importantly an Astor."

"Never heard of none of those families."

That earned her a smile from Buck. "I'm glad to hear it."

She added, "I thought her name was Dysart."

"It is, but her mother wasn't overly fond of her father and tended to ignore that part of the family, even though obviously Shannon is half Dysart and the connection to the Astors is distant."

"But Shannon is living her whole life to follow in her father's footsteps. Her ma might not like the Dysarts, but Shannon seems to."

Buck nodded. His mind seemed distant.

"Why didn't you come out here with Shannon?" Tyra wanted

to figure out just what the connection was between Buck and Shannon. She wanted it something fierce. She saw no spark in Buck's eyes when he talked of her, no romance. But Buck's presence here said more clearly than words that Shannon was important to him.

"She didn't ask me. And I thought it was a stupid idea. I've had things really comfortable back home. The notion of coming west was appalling."

"What is it you do back east that's more important than taking care of your friend?"

"Do?" Buck furrowed his brow as if the word made no sense. "Yes?"

"Uh, do?" Buck stumbled over the question and fell silent.

"A job?"

"Job?"

"Yes, a job. That thing people have so they make money, so they can eat and keep a roof over their heads."

She might have imagined it because he was sunburned, but she thought there was a faint flush to his cheeks, like he had the grace to be embarrassed for not recognizing the word *job*. It wasn't as if she'd started speaking Navajo. "My pa is a rancher. I help him on the range, and my ma is dead, so I do a lot of the work inside. I cook and clean, haul water, and garden. Do you drive a wagon? Run some store back in the city? Help run the railroad? What?"

"I don't have a job. I have money from my family, enough to live on."

Tyra's opinion of him sank to the sandy desert floor. "Doesn't that get boring? I mean, what passes your day when you wake up in the morning? Surely you don't just sit around the house all day, waiting for bedtime."

"No, I keep busy with. . .things."

"And Shannon, too? Does she have so much money she doesn't need to work or get married to get by?"

"If anything, Shannon's family is wealthier than mine. Of course she doesn't have a job, and she doesn't need a husband to support her."

Tyra was unable to stop a snort of disdain. "Well, no wonder she's running around out here in the wilderness. She was probably half crazy from all that time hanging heavy on her hands."

Buck was silent for a while. Finally he said, "You know, you might be right. Honestly, in some ways, that's how I ended up here, too."

"And you said your family money came at least partly from a fur trader?"

Buck nodded. "Since I've headed west, I've enjoyed thinking I can feel a bit of Henri Chatillon's blood in my veins. We talk a lot about heritage, our roots, how important our families are."

"You and Shannon?"

"No, well, some I guess, but more my parents, my mother, and her friends. I think since I've been out here, away from that talk, I've started to realize I want more for myself than rich, powerful *ancestors*. I think there is a little Henri Chatillon in me."

Tyra shook her head. "Never heard of the guy."

"He was a fur trapper."

"So you said." Tyra nodded. "Out here?"

"In the Rockies. I think he traveled all over. Don't think I've ever heard of where exactly he trapped. Just the Rocky Mountains."

"That covers a lot of territory. The tail end of the Rockies reaches all the way south to Mexico. Though some folks say different names for the mountains, different ranges, to me it all seems part and parcel of the same big old bunch of mountains. We could be riding straight along your grandpa's trail right now."

"He's not my grandfather. He's more distant than that, a cousin a few generations back. But he's part of me." Buck sat more erect in the saddle. Tyra heard a ring of iron in his voice that hadn't been there before.

"Tell me about him. The name isn't familiar, but maybe some of the stories will be good'uns."

Buck told a winding story about his mountain man kin. She thought, from his tone of affection, maybe there *was* some of the guy's blood flowing in the city boy's veins. The city boy with so much money he thought the word *job* was some foreign language.

Seventeen

Shannon's day started out with dreamlike beauty and ended up being a nightmare.

Yesterday when she'd set eyes on the canyon, she'd been awestruck. Plain and simple. Every word she said was faint praise, every thought, ever flight of poetic language, all so pale and insufficient.

She would have told anyone in the world that she could never stare long enough, never get close enough to the beauty.

One day later, she was heartily sick of it.

They were riding along the east wall so they had shade until about noon, though the heat was stifling. She'd ridden in a daze of confused pleasure after Gabe's warm kisses and quiet strength. The lure of him was wonderful, added to the surrounding beauty, and yes, Shannon's morning had been a walk in paradise.

Then the sun rose high enough to slip over the canyon rim, and the whole world became an oven that burned every ounce of poetry and romance clean out of her heart, mind, and soul.

The trail they'd set out on this morning had nowhere to stop, nowhere to rest, nowhere to graze the horses or refill canteens. Shannon sipped carefully, drinking only enough of the tepid, sulfuric-scented water to wet her throat.

The horses' hooves ground steadily against rock until it was sand scraping on Shannon's ears. The group ate jerked meat, and there was plenty, so they wouldn't starve. So great, they'd live a long, miserable life unless the oven managed to cook them to death.

Water was nowhere to be found though. With no end to this trail, she worried about having enough to keep the horses going.

They were virtually crawling along the canyon wall. A layer of rock, barely wide enough for the horses, formed a terrace that stretched ahead of them as far as they could see—which wasn't far. The vista out into the canyon was undeniably spectacular. The striped colonnades glowed red and white and blue. But the view didn't give them a respite from the heat nor a drink of water. The terrace followed the rattlesnake curves of the canyon. They jutted out then curved in. They climbed in places then dropped.

And if that had been the only problem, she might have been fine. But every few hundred yards or so the trail was cut by talus slides, a crumbled stretch that reminded Shannon of the way those ledges at the cliff dwellings had broken off under her feet. The sure-footed horses picked their way across slopes Shannon would never have attempted.

Her throat went dry every time they had to face another obstacle, which made the water shortage even more punishing.

There was no talk. They were strung out too far to make that practical, though occasionally Hozho, in the lead, would shout a warning or instructions as she neared another death-defying spot. Hosteen followed her. Then Shannon. The parson came next, and Shannon could hear the steady grumbling the man did at his horse. Gabe brought up the rear.

Hozho and Hosteen were calm. They moved as if they were

part of this land, as if they needed no water, felt no heat. They left the work to their animals and never shifted or wiped at sweating brows. It gave Shannon a notion of how differently they'd lived, how much a part of this hard land they and their people were.

Shannon pulled her map out often, more to distract herself from the thirst, the burning of the sun, and her fear. But as the day wore on and the heat baked into her bones, she grew dull and stupid and quit caring what lay ahead. She'd been following all day; she'd continue to follow. It took no effort on her part.

Studying her map for what had to be the tenth time, inspired more by boredom than need, she barely noticed when her horse suddenly stepped onto a talus slide, already crossed by two horses.

The rocks gave. She wasn't even holding the reins.

The horse slid, screamed in fear, and then leaped forward. Shannon tumbled backward, and the pinto left her behind.

She landed hard. The terrible drop she knew lay below her drove her to claw and scramble. A scream hurt her ears. She only distantly realized it was her own.

Fighting to hang on, the rocks skittered away. A stone slammed into her face. She slid, belly down. Dug in with her toes and knees. An agonizing jerk on her arm stopped her. With a sickening swoop, she seemed to take flight.

Then she landed with a dull thud flat on her back. Swinging her hands, hunting for something to grab hold of, the pain felt like a knife rammed to the hilt in her shoulder.

She was no longer falling. She was stabbed, pinned like a bug to the canyon wall, her back and arm in agony.

Blinking, it took a second for her vision to clear. She could see Gabe kneeling beside her. The parson was past Gabe's shoulder holding the reins of two horses.

"She's all right," Gabe yelled.

Craning her neck, Shannon saw the Tsosis across the treacherous trail with her horse firmly in hand. When she moved her head, the whole left side of her body caught fire. She instantly stopped moving.

The pinto had made it across the slide without a scratch. She was tempted to side with the parson in his constant grumbling about horses.

"What happened?" Her voice grated, her words were slurred. The fall was only dizzying, vague images distorted by terror and pain. How had she kept from plunging to the bottom of that cliff?

Gabe reached for her, touched her gently on the forehead, and pulled his hand back.

She saw blood.

"You fell."

"Off the cliff?" Shannon thought of the wicked ledge they'd been on. "How...how am I still alive? How am I up here with you?"

"You didn't fall to the bottom. You just fell off your horse, and before you went over, or just as you did, I lassoed you."

"Around my tough belly again?" He'd saved her twice now. Him and his trusty rope. Tears burned in her eyes, but she didn't let them fall. Being dehydrated no doubt helped.

Gabe smiled. "I got an arm this time."

Following the line of his gaze, she saw that he was loosening a noose around her wrist. And then the pain came fully alive. Shannon's vision twisted. "My arm. I—I think it's broken."

Gabe quit moving the rope. "It must have been too much. I yanked so hard." His eyes, black with regret, suddenly turned calm and steady. She remembered he'd been in the cavalry. He was a strong man who'd faced trouble many times.

That steadiness helped her to stave off panic at the thought of a broken arm, so far from medical help.

Gabe looked across the talus slope. "Can you get back across here, Hozho? Her arm may be broken. You've done some doctoring, right?"

Shannon wasn't sure how Gabe knew that. Then she thought

of that trail. "No! They can't come across that slide. They can't!" Shannon gritted her teeth to turn, wave Hozho back, only to find the elderly woman already at her side.

"No need to fret, *ah-tad*. I'll set the bone." Hozho knelt beside Shannon on her left.

"S–set the bone? Doctors set bones." Shannon had never had a broken bone, but she'd been to the doctor a few times. Her mother was related to one of the most respected doctors in St. Louis.

Gabe was on his knees on her right. Shannon saw the parson, his lips moving as if in prayer, his eyes solemn, standing behind Gabe.

"We think there is a way to lower ground ahead." Hozho brushed Shannon's hair back off her forehead. "Hosteen will take the horses and find grass for them, then come back."

"We can't cross that."

"Shhh, ah-tad."

"I don't know why I brought you all here. Why did I think this was important?"

"Hold here." Hozho spoke with little more than a grunt to Gabe. She rested steady hands on Shannon then pulled away and let Gabe's hands replace hers.

"Hold where?" Shannon asked.

Gabe was suddenly all she could see. His face filled her vision, her world. She saw terrible regret in his eyes.

Hozho's fingers moved expertly, straightening Shannon's elbow.

White-hot pain arched Shannon's body until her back came off the ground.

Before she could get up, run, scream, Gabe had her firmly back on the rocky ground. "I'm sorry, Shannon," Gabe whispered. "It will hurt, but we have to keep you still."

The traitor wasn't going to help her escape from Hozho's

torture. Shannon's jaw firmed, and she did her best to lie still when every impulse she possessed told her to flee.

When the elderly woman touched Shannon's shoulder, the pain glowed like a fireplace poker. Pinned to the stone ground by Gabe, recoiling from it was beyond Shannon's control.

"Don't let her move."

Gabe's hands became iron bands. She didn't fight him; it was too painful.

"Not broken," Hozho said with grim satisfaction. "Her arm has been pulled out of the shoulder joint. We can fix."

Hozho pushed Gabe back firmly then was in front of Shannon's eyes. "It will hurt to push the joint back in place, but I've done this before. You will be fine. Much quicker to heal than a broken bone. But it will hurt terribly for just a few seconds."

Since Shannon was hurting quite terribly right now, that didn't worry her all that much. She looked into ancient eyes. Hozho seemed full of wisdom.

For the first time, Shannon realized that the elderly woman had been right to try and force Shannon to marry Gabe. She'd been right to insist that such a situation couldn't be allowed to continue. But Shannon had thought she knew better and found a way out.

Found a way to avoid marrying the nicest man she'd ever met. A man who'd lassoed her twice to save her life.

"Thank you, Hozho."

"You may not thank me in a few minutes when I'm hurting you. But it has to be done, ah-tad."

"What is that?" Shannon needed to focus on something besides her arm. "Ah-tad."

"It means girl." Hozho took Shannon's wrist and lifted slowly, steadily.

Every movement caused Shannon's shoulder more pain. "No, wait. I'm not ready."

"Look at me, Shannon." Gabe's warm voice drew her attention. In that awful heat of the canyon, her arm suffering until she could imagine the torments of the devil, his voice might save her life just as his lariat had.

A deep moan that might have been the wind sweeping between the colonnades and canyons and river, or might have come from her, was the only response.

Then came a brutal attack. Hozho jerked on Shannon's arm. A dull snap near her left ear, and Shannon's shoulder went from blazing with pain to merely hurting like mad.

A scream cut through the canyon. That scream, Shannon's own, echoed back to her over and over, as if the pain had a life of its own and would forever be a part of this majestic, terrible gouge sliced into the belly of the earth.

Call the canyon grand, because it was, certainly. But call it a killer, too.

Shannon opened her eyes to see mercy and guilt on Gabe's face. Then the world narrowed until she looked through a tunnel, only Gabe's face, only his eyes, only darkness. The pain in her shoulder followed her into unconsciousness.

It was irrational.

He recognized that. So he controlled it. But Gabe really needed to punch somebody.

Watching Shannon scream and faint from pain while he held her down made him fighting mad.

He looked up at Hozho. No, probably not an elderly woman.

He looked down at Shannon. Well, that was just stupid.

He heard the parson praying quietly over Gabe's shoulder while he wrestled with his horse. Not right to hit a man of God. Not right at all.

Hosteen was long gone with three of the horses. Not that

Hosteen had done a thing wrong.

Gabe had a strange impulse to punch himself in the face. He was the only one left, and he really needed to punch somebody.

In the time it took to rule out the potential victims, he gained control of his furious need to pound his fists into someone's face. Then he looked back at Shannon. Her cheek was bleeding, scraped against the rocks as she fell. There were bits of sand embedded there. Her skin was burned red by the sun. Little blisters on her lips told the story of how much that was going to hurt later. Her shoulder was probably going to help distract her from the sunburn. Her hair was snarled, and it looked like it was half full of gravel.

Yep, looking for a city of gold had been a little slice of genius.

Blaming Shannon suited him, but he'd come along, hadn't he? Not that she'd given him much choice, but honestly, he'd wanted to come down here.

It's a beautiful place.

Gabe could clearly remember thinking it and saying it.

Let's go on down.

Yep, he'd been willing, eager even.

I would love to climb down there if Shannon can show us the way.

He'd said those very words out loud. He was an idiot, and he went back to wanting to punch himself.

"We will put a sling on her arm now, before she wakes up." Hozho brought Gabe's thoughts back to practical things.

"I have the horses picketed." Hosteen called from the far side of the talus slide. "I found a trail down to get water. Not far. Do you need me over there?"

"Yes, see to the horse," Hozho said to her husband as she eyed Shannon's arm. "I need more time to see to Miss Shannon. We will finish with her and come after you on foot. Help the parson cross that slope."

"Parson," Hozho continued being in charge.

Gabe was busy mentally battering himself.

The parson was all tied up with prayers and his wretched horsemanship skills. Someone needed to give some orders. "Yes?" The parson pulled his attention away from his skittish horse.

Gabe could see clear as day that the parson was making his mustang nervous. The little animal seemed like a well-trained critter whenever the parson was not around.

"Get the horses to water."

"Me? I can't make these beasts behave. I can't figure out why no one comes up with a better way to get around than on horseback. I lived in Michigan for a while near my brother's family. Had a bicycle." The parson shook his head. "I loved that bicycle, but you can't ride a bicycle around in the desert. God called me out here loud and clear, but still, the horse situation is—"

"You ride, Parson." Hosteen was across the slide. "I'll lead the horses. We'll get across fine."

"I'll walk." The parson might be a man with plenty of faith in God, but he put little faith in his horse. Gabe knew of no verse in the Good Book that said he had to.

Parson Ford grabbed his reins while Hosteen took Gabe's horse, and the two men left, crossing the ugly stretch of trail without incident. In fact, as Gabe watched them cross, even that nasty slide looked solid. How had Shannon's horse managed to knock a stone loose?

"Help me, Gabe. Before she wakes up." Hozho pulled him back to the task at hand. She took a shawl off her own shoulders and fashioned it into a sling. "Hold her arm against her body."

Positioning the arm, Hozho made short work of getting it tied down. She finished just as Shannon's eyes flickered open.

Relieved, Gabe leaned forward. "We've got your arm set. It's not broken."

Licking her blistered lips, Shannon said, "Hurts."

"Your shoulder was wrenched from the socket." He wasn't

sure how much she'd realized from before. "Putting it back in hurt, but it should heal much more quickly than a break."

Gabe looked at Hozho. "Did you keep a canteen? She needs water."

Hozho had more common sense than Gabe. He'd let the parson and Hosteen lead the horses away without keeping any water. Hozho had hers at hand.

Gabe slid one hand behind Shannon's neck and eased her forward, holding his breath, knowing every movement caused more pain.

She clenched her jaw to hold back any sounds.

He hated it. At the same time he was grateful she was being brave. He raised the water to her lips.

She took a quick sip and pushed with her one working hand. "That's plenty."

"Drink all you want." Gabe raised the canteen again. "Hosteen found a place to camp just ahead. There's plenty of water, so we don't need to ration it."

Shannon's hand trembled as she grabbed at the canteen again and gulped the water.

"No, not so fast. You'll get the collywobbles." Gabe pulled the canteen away.

A flicker of a smile twitched at the corners of Shannon's poor blistered lips. She nodded. "Help—help me up. I think I'm ready to go now."

"You look ready to pass out." Gabe took a second to coil up his lasso and hang it from his belt. Considering that he'd saved Shannon's life twice now with the thing, he decided he'd just wear it like a part of his clothes from now on. He gathered her gently in his arms and rose to his feet, bearing her weight as if it were nothing. Cradling her against his chest, he was vigilant in his care of her arm and still knew he hurt her.

"I can walk."

Nodding, Gabe said to Hozho. "Lead out."

Shannon didn't protest being carried. Gabe suspected she intended to, but she just hadn't gathered the strength yet.

Gabe followed, careful to set each foot exactly where Hozho had set hers. They'd crossed so many of these slides he'd gotten in the habit of thinking they were solid. They mostly were. He reached the other side without mishap and looked down to see Shannon had closed her eyes. "We're across."

She blinked her eyes open and gave him a wan smile. "Thanks."

Her left arm was the one injured. He held her so her right side pressed against his chest. Her right arm slid around his neck, and as he shifted his grip on her a bit, for just a second or two. . .or ten, her face was raised so close to his that he could hardly avoid a kiss.

So he didn't. Avoid it. "I'd better watch where I'm walking."

"You can put me down." Her fingers tangled in the hair that brushed the collar of his shirt in back. Like she was combing snarls out of it for him. Helpful little thing.

"Just let me carry you for a few more minutes. Shannon?" He kissed her again, and she really wasn't all that close to him. He had to stretch. No problem. "I think. . .maybe. . .you're not going to marry Bucky Shaw."

Their eyes met.

Held.

Held.

This time she kissed him. "I think maybe you're ri—"

"Down here!" The parson drew their attention.

The trail they were on kept crawling and twisting along the edge of the canyon as it had all day, but another trail beaten by years of deer, wild mustang—who knew what else was down in this canyon—led down to a green stretch. The horses were already grazing.

Shannon's eyes landed on that green, and she twisted in Gabe's arms to study it. "This is the place."

Gabe didn't think there was a city of gold around here, and they'd been talking about who she *wasn't* going to marry, which might lead a man to consider that she had someone else in mind, and there was a parson and two witnesses right there, so, "The place for what?"

Shannon pointed to a gap were the river twisted away and a massive stone wall blocked them from approaching it. There was a gap in that stone wall. "The place my father marked on his map. The place we'll find Cibola."

Yes, she could point to it, but it was across a vast sweep of rugged land. "It's a long way, Shannon."

"Let's go right now."

"We can. It *looks* close, but I'll bet it'll be days of riding. You've got to take it easy and let your arm heal."

"No, I can ride." Shannon used her right arm and Gabe's neck to pull herself more upright. With her left hand, she reached for Gabe's shirt for balance and gasped in pain. The color leeched from her face.

"Lay still!" He stopped walking, afraid to take even one more step when she was in such agony.

Her eyelids dropped shut, though there was still such tension in her that he knew she hadn't fainted. Pain etched lines into her face. She didn't move, just eased the air in and out between clenched teeth with a quiet hiss, as if hanging on until it eased.

At last her eyes flickered open. "We're going to have to wait awhile. You're right."

"Can I walk? Will that hurt too badly? We can get you a drink, settle you on your bedroll."

"I—I think it will be okay if I keep my arm still."

Gabe's jaw was so tight he thought he might break off a few teeth. Carefully, he took a step, then another. She bore it well, and he walked, as gently as possible, down the trail to the grassy meadow where Hozho was building a fire.

The parson had a bedroll out. Hosteen was walking away with a rifle.

"He saw signs of game." Hozho looked at them through a curling column of wood smoke. "He's hoping to get fresh meat for supper."

"Lay her down over here, Gabe." The parson stepped back, serious, calm, wise. Gabe was surrounded by calm, serious, wise people. He included himself in that number. Honestly, all of them but Shannon.

Oh, she was serious enough. . .unless he counted that she was looking for a fairy tale. But she was dead serious about it. Calm enough when she wasn't crying or slavering over that stupid map or fainting or escaping death by the skin of her teeth.

Wise? Not even close.

That wasn't to say she wasn't smart enough. The woman could probably add and subtract and even multiply like nobody's business. She poured over her pa's strange notes constantly so she could clearly read. And her pa was a professor. Gabe was sure the woman was plenty book smart.

But Gabe's pa had occasionally used the phrase "educated idiot," and Gabe had to give serious consideration to the possibility that he might be holding one in his arms right now.

He was, in fact, planning to marry one without delay. Because no matter how much credit he gave her for her obvious intelligence, he couldn't credit her with being wise.

So why were they all following the orders of the headstrong miss who shouldn't have been out here to begin with?

Gabe hated it that the truth might come down simply to the word *gold*. Though they all denied it, it might be that they were all out here because of a sinful hunger for earthly treasure. If so, then not a one of them was wise or serious or calm.

And that meant they were on a quest that God wouldn't honor. And God might start dishonoring them right back. Maybe He'd start telling them they were in the wrong by letting one of them fall off a horse. . .

"Set her down over here, Gabe." The parson was on his knees spreading Shannon's bedroll behind a massive pile of rock that would shade her from the broiling heat of the day.

Hosteen was picketing the horses on grass. Their muzzles still dripped with the water they'd so clearly relished. Hozho was busy digging in her pack.

As Gabe knelt with Shannon still in his arms, he realized how completely he didn't want to let her go. . .and knew he was gone.

He kept his attention riveted on her to notice if a move on his part caused her a single jarring moment. He gently settled her on the blanket.

Her jaw was a tight line; her lips and eyes clamped shut as she bore her pain in silence.

He hadn't hurt her, at least no more than simple breathing hurt her, but it wasn't enough. He needed to do more.

He tore his eyes away from her and was confronted with the majestic canyon. He leaned back on his heels and saw the colonnades, the terraces of every color, the rushing waters of the Colorado River. He thought of the talus slides and the treacherous terrace trails. The long, broiling day in the sun with little water. This was a place of staggering beauty and deadly danger. The bottom of the Grand Canyon was a merciless place to be against the will of God.

He looked from the windswept glory around him and saw a wounded woman. The pretty little loco weed had opened her eyes and twisted around to look at that gap she'd identified. It looked close. If they could travel as the crow flies, they could get there in a few hours. But Gabe was getting to know this canyon. And he was no crow. They'd be days tramping to that gap, twisting and turning on ledges that clung to the side of the canyon just like today. Plenty of chances to die between now and then.

Shannon would heal well, heal fast. But she'd had almost miraculous good fortune. God's way of telling them to go back? Or go on?

Whether God had intervened in Shannon's fall or not, Gabe got the message loud and clear that they were in danger. But while Gabe had been hearing God, Shannon heard gold. From the fascinated gleam in her eyes, he was just as sure that Shannon hadn't changed her mind one bit about her search for treasure down here in the savage belly of the earth.

Gabe was really starting to hate this canyon.

Eighteen

Buck was really starting to hate Captain Hance.

"An' then I got to the rim of the canyon and the fog was so thick, I just walked straight off the edge of the canyon and walked across on the fog."

Captain Hance had been telling stories ever since they'd set out. Unfortunately, the trail was wide enough they could all hear him just fine. And the man was setting a blistering pace—with real blisters. Thanks to the blazing sun.

He leaned close to Tyra and said, "I could really go for some fog about now."

She swatted his arm with the back of her hand and smiled.

"But the fog started to burn off when I was about halfway across. I started running, but it got thinner and my feet started sinkin' into the clouds, and I got to one of the towers in the canyon and—"

Buck had read about the towers in the canyon. Colonnades, he'd heard them called. He'd seen a painting or two and a few photographs, but it all sounded outlandish to him. Deep canyon.

Big deal. He'd seen a deep canyon before. It was as outlandish as walking across fog.

"So there I was, trapped on that tower, and the sky turned clear and stayed clear. I had no water or food. Figured I didn't need it just goin' for a walk like I was. And blazin' hot on that thing. I felt like I was being roasted over a fire. And not a lick of shade of course. I thought about tryin' to climb down. Just then—"

Buck kept his horse back a few paces. In addition to being full of stories only a madman would believe, Hance smelled none too good. He'd also told a story about how he'd come to be known as Captain Hance. But it was so full of tall tales and pure outright lies, Buck settled on believing the man had made the military title up. Who out there was going to challenge him? The miniature horses who lived in the canyon? The ghosts who haunted this Indian village they were going to? The sturdy fog?

"I'd been there so long I started to think my beard might be long enough to lasso the side of the canyon, and I could swing myself across."

Looking sideways at Tyra, Buck arched one brow. Tyra smiled.

"But, before it came to that, a thin fog rolled in. Normally I'd've never made it across on those wisps. A man needs a thick fog if'n he's gonna walk on it. But I'd lost fifty pounds while I was up there, so gaunt I was nigh unto a shadow."

They both dropped back just a bit. Not far. They'd learned early on there was no real escape from Hance. The man just talked louder if someone lagged.

"Well, I had to risk it or starve, so I stepped out, and sure enough, the fog held me up. I'll tell you the pure truth. I ran like a man with a pack of wolves on his trail, afraid that fog would lift."

When they were back enough paces, but not too many, Buck leaned over and spoke very quietly. "I know just how the captain feels. Every time he starts a new story, I feel like a man with a pack of wolves on my trail. But I've got no choice but to stay right here."

Tyra stifled a laugh, and they dropped back a bit farther. She whispered, "He's going to get us there fast. Doba told me the man knows exactly where Gabe must have been heading. Hance swears he knows the only trail off the east rim. We may have to listen to some tall tales, but it'll be worth it."

They'd been at it all day, and who knew how long it would be until they reached their destination. Mr. Kinlichee admitted to not knowing much about the canyon in this direction. And Doba seemed to be a man who at least acted like an expert on any subject, so Buck feared the information for this trail was scarce. Yes, finding Captain Hance as a guide was a godsend. Even if it was going to make Buck lose his mind.

"Thar she is." Hance picked up the pace as if he was excited to be home. The most desolate home imaginable.

Buck couldn't really see what Hance was so excited about. Rugged ground, cactus, sand, rocks—he'd seen enough of those to last a lifetime. Hance stopped then Tyra's father and brother-in-law, who'd ridden alongside Hance.

And then Buck came up beside Abe Lasley and saw the canyon. And was stunned into stillness.

Tyra gasped, her voice swept away by the scudding wind.

They stared. The towers, some pointed, some level, the lines and layers of color. Buck's eyes followed the nearest colonnade down to see the depths shrouded by fog. The white did look thick enough to walk on. How far down did it go? The towers seemed to grow out of the clouds as if they weren't attached to the ground, instead floating in the sky.

Time stood still. Buck knew they held in place for a long time, but it had no meaning because there was no number of hours sufficient to see it all and absorb it all.

"Let's git on down." Hance cackled with laughter like an old hen.

It violated a sacred moment.

"Not yet." Lucas Morgan said it clearly as an order, and even Hance held his silence then. For a while.

"We'll lose the light afore we git to the bottom of the trail if'n we don't go now."

"We need to look just a little longer," Tyra whispered. Like her gasp earlier, her words seemed to be caught and tossed away, lost in the vastness.

Buck didn't think he could move. Then he suddenly wanted to go down, be a part of that city built on the clouds. He'd studied the Pilgrims in school and remembered John Winthrop's immortal words about America being a shining city on a hill. Surely there could be no greater city, no greater shining light than this place.

Even as Buck knew what he looked upon was stone—there was no sign that it was a true building inhabited by either God or man—he wanted to enter the canyon, be part of it, just as his faith gave him assurance he'd enter into heaven when God called him home.

"It could really be true." He tore his gaze away from the staggering beauty and looked at his companions. "A city might well be lost in the depths of this place. Shannon could be right." His Shannon, whom he'd indulged and patronized and mainly considered spoiled and a bit loony but with a good heart, could be on the trail to a city of gold.

"They is a trail." Hance laughed again. "I tole you so. I seen it, and I'll take you there or my name ain't Captain John Hance."

His words broke the spell, and the group began talking at once.

"Let's go, Captain Hance," Buck said. "Lead the way."

Hance's response to that was to put two fingers in his mouth and let out an ear-piercing whistle that made the horses jump and mill around. Buck had his hands full keeping control.

Once his mount settled down, he glared at Hance. "Why'd you do that?"

Two Indians appeared from around a rock.

Buck braced himself for an attack. Had Hance brought them out here to be robbed and killed?

Hance swung down from his horse and handed the reins to the first brave who approached him. The men wore little clothing. Their hair was contained in black braids. Each man had two hanging down his chest. One of them wore a Stetson that looked like a horse had trampled over it. The other was bare-headed and carried a tomahawk in the belt of what could only be described as a loincloth. At least that's all that the clothing covered.

"Hance, what's going on here?" Tyra's father demanded.

With a glance over his shoulder, Hance must have figured out they were all suspicious because he started laughing. That went on until the man coughed. Then his throat must've tripped over his laughing and coughing because for a while, Buck wondered if the man would choke to death. At last he got control of himself, and with eyes gleaming with tears of laughter he said, "You didn't think we could ride a horse down there did'ja?"

Buck looked back at their horses, pack horses loaded with supplies and water. His four hired men were each leading a pack horse, and the men were right now looking at the Indians and the canyon suspiciously. If the horses weren't going, either the supplies got left behind or—

"Let's get these horses unloaded. My Yavapai friends'll tend 'em for us while we're gone." Hance turned to a leather pack on his horse, pulled it loose, and strapped it on his back. "We'll have to carry the supples."

Buck exchanged a doubtful look with Tyra. Lucas looked at the Indians calmly helping Hance and shrugged. "Let's get unpacked."

With a resigned sigh and another look over the edge of the world, Buck swung down and pulled his saddlebags off his horse, trying to think what he could use for a pack. There were bags on the pack horses. He'd rig one of those to—

"Buck." One of the men his mother had hired interrupted his planning.

"Yes?" These men were tough. Mother had chosen well. And they'd finally stopped calling him Boss or Bucky.

"The boys and I have talked it over, and we're not going down into that canyon on foot. Fool idea."

Buck was startled. He'd never considered this. "You're abandoning me?"

The man shrugged. Buck noticed then that they'd been working some, but none of them had fashioned a pack for himself. They'd kept busy unloading supplies. In fact, they'd unloaded all of them, which Buck now realized was a bad sign. It left them free to ride away on unloaded horses without being accused of stealing supplies or leaving Buck to starve.

"We aren't climbing down a cliff, and we don't want to hand our horses over to a pack of savages."

"They seem like decent men." Buck glanced doubtfully at the Indians.

One of his men snorted. "Without horses, we'll starve or die of thirst trying to walk back to that Navajo settlement, and even then we'd have a long way to go to Flagstaff and the closest train."

"We could walk back without starving," Buck said hopefully.

"And all that won't get a chance to go wrong if we go down into that canyon. The canyon looks to us like a killer, and once down there you want to find whatever it is you're looking for and get back up here alive. Then we worry about walking out."

"None of that will happen if the Indians bring our horses back."

Another sound of sheer doubt.

The spokesman for the group shook his head. "No one can pay a man enough money for his life."

The Indian men Hance had summoned had been fairly

civilized. He'd called them Yavapai, which meant absolutely nothing to Buck. Doba Kinlichee had been Navajo. Buck was sure of that. But these men were obviously acquainted with Hance, and he trusted them. So, unless Hance was in cahoots with them. . . "They seem honest to me."

That rude snort again. It was starting to irritate Buck.

"We wouldn't leave you alone, Boss, but you've got enough help. We'll make sure folks know you came out here. If you turn up missing, they'll know where to start looking."

Buck thought of the canyon he was planning to climb down to find Shannon, a needle in a haystack if ever there was one. He could only hope that the city Hance claimed he knew of was the same place Shannon was heading. His deserting men wouldn't be a lot of help to a search party.

Buck nodded. What other choice did he have?

The men mounted up and rode away.

Tyra came up beside him. "Where are they going?"

Buck explained what was going on.

"Small groups do better down there anyway. Better they should head back." Hance kept making his pack larger while he talked.

The men leaving barely stopped them in their packing. Buck was learning that western men and women didn't spend a whole lot of time fussing about things they could do nothing about.

Tyra came and helped him fill a satchel then used leather strips to hang it on his back. "That's all you've got room for." Tyra looked at all they were leaving behind.

It twisted Buck's stomach. "How far are we going down into that pit?"

"Fill your canteens," Hance shouted. "Water's what you'll need most."

"Does that mean water is hard to find? The Colorado River is down there somewhere." Buck picked up two full canteens. Then he saw a few more things and decided he could take one more armload of supplies.

"Can't carry no more'n that." Hance shook his head at the sight of Buck with his pack loaded and his arms full. "You're gonna need your hands free when we go crawlin' down the side of a cliff."

That image sent Buck's stomach dancing.

"What do I leave behind?"

He shouldn't have asked. Hance was all too willing to help, and it was humiliating to see what the old man considered a necessity. Buck had very different ideas, but he let the man pick and choose what was to be left behind. He couldn't stand to think of how they were going to survive down there with little more than water, guns, and bedrolls. Back in St. Louis, they had running water in the house. He could turn a nozzle and get a tub full of hot water.

Home. He really missed it.

The Indian braves began leading the horses away, and Buck wondered if they'd ever see the animals again. It was a long, long walk back to St. Louis.

His eyes fell closed on a heartfelt prayer. If Hance was luring them into that canyon for nefarious purposes, they were going to need a merciful God more than ever.

Hance took off, and they followed like brainless sheep.

After Hance, Tyra's father fell into line.

Abe Lasley next. Abe would've gone first if he'd had half a chance. The big brother.

Buck had a flash of sympathy for Gabe being the youngest. Abe and Gabe. Tyra had said there were seven brothers. Buck wondered what the others were named—Babe, Cabe, Dabe, Fabe, and Habe?

Shaking his head, Buck let Tyra go next. Then with one envious glance back at the trail his men had taken back to Flagstaff, he followed.

When he took his first step over the rim, he felt like he'd gone over the edge of the world.

Lurene stalked back and forth and back and forth trying to figure out how to get over the edge of the cliff. She fumed, ready to explode from Cutter's slow pace. They'd trailed the Navajos easily enough, right up to the edge of the canyon. Then they'd stopped dead. There was no way forward.

"They must have gone on to the north or south." She slapped her gloves in her hand and paced, and slapped and fumed. They'd been here two hours and nothing had changed.

"I see no sign of it. It looked to me like they just walked straight off the edge of that cliff." Cutter ran one of his beefy hands over the beard he'd grown since they started this. He'd been clean cut when he was charming the Dysart woman into hiring them. But he'd quit shaving and bathing from the minute they'd headed west. All of them had. But on Cutter it was worse somehow. He'd gone from a civilized man to a savage.

Lurene had always respected him, and fear was part of that respect. But lately, in the heat and the slow travel and Ginger's constant harping, fear had gained strength while Lurene's respect had worn thin.

The Lloyd brothers had found shade by a tumble of rocks, and Ginger sat with them. Randy appeared to be asleep. His head was tipped back, the brim of his Stetson pulled low. Darrel sat with his knees pulled up, chewing on a strip of beef jerky. Ginger was stabbing at the sandy ground.

Lurene was sick of her constant movements. The woman wasn't even still in her sleep. The sun burned down on Lurene until she thought her brains might be baking.

"Let's take a break, Cutter. We've got to decide what to do."

Muttering short, crude words, Cutter rose from a crouch

and stalked toward the group in the shade. With the sun moving lower in the west, the rock's shade stretched enough that Lurene and Cutter could sit down facing the other three.

"Do we give up or keep hunting?" Lurene could taste the defeat. She hated it. The harder it was to catch up to that woman the more she was determined to do it. Shannon Dysart was a weakling, a woman who should have been lost and alone. Finding her should have been as easy as running after a baby on its hands and knees.

The silence was thick, a solid wall. It reminded Lurene of that monstrous canyon. A canyon so deep she wondered if they went into the depths of it, would it lead them straight to the devil?

"I'm sicka' this heat." Ginger of course spoke first. Her face was burned bright red, blistered, and peeling in spots. The dirt on her face was streaked with sweat and smeared into mud. Her hair was pulled back into a knot at the base of her skull, but curls escaped in all directions. "Let's forget the Dysart woman and get outta here."

Lurene had asked a serious question, but Ginger couldn't bother to give serious thought to it. She just reacted to whatever she felt in the moment.

All Lurene could think of was the way she'd made her money back in St. Louis. Her skin crawled to think of going back. Lurene knew she was a hard woman. She'd had to get hard to survive. But at that moment the hardest part of her heart and soul turned to pure stone. She couldn't go back. She wouldn't! She'd steal and kill, and certainly kidnap, so she could keep the groping hands of men away.

"Those tracks," Cutter said, "tell me the Dysart woman is down in that godforsaken canyon. If we want her, we've got to find a way down."

"Just give it up. Let's go somewhere and get out of this blasted heat." Ginger swiped at her brow and added to the filth on her face.

"There is no way down I can see." Cutter looked at Lurene. He was asking her to give up. Ride on and forget this whole crazy scheme.

Sin had never made Lurene rich, and she'd engaged in plenty of it. But not on this scale. This was big-time sin, because before this was over, Shannon Dysart would be dead and several if not all of her partners would be, too. "Remember she's an *Astor*. She's rich. As sin. We ride on and we're heading for nothing."

"We've got a lot more than nothing," Ginger sneered. "We've got a hundred dollars each. I can use that to have a mighty good time."

Lurene glared at Ginger, who held the gaze for a couple of seconds, then started to squirm and scooted just an inch closer to Darrel. They'd teamed up, Lurene realized. And if Ginger was with Darrel, then the Lloyds and Ginger were all together. Three against two. Lurene caught herself. She was figuring Cutter was on her side. A woman did well not to count on any man. She sure hoped she didn't have to bet her life on Cutter siding with her over the others.

"What are we going to do then? Jump off the edge?" Ginger poked the ground with her stick and threw it down. It bounced and hit Lurene.

Lurene's temper ignited like a torch set to dynamite. She grabbed the stick and threw it right in Ginger's face.

With a growl that'd do justice to a wildcat, Ginger came up on her knees. She reached for the stick, which had bounced closer to Lurene.

"Cool off." Lurene slapped the stick aside.

"How'm I supposed to cool off in this place?" Ginger's hand closed over a rock.

Lurene had her colt revolver in her pocket. She braced herself to go for it. She wasn't having a fistfight with this nasty woman. She'd shoot her and be done with it.

Lurene felt the Lloyd brothers come to full alert. Cutter moved, putting himself in a better position to settle trouble without getting hurt himself. It could be a bloodbath if they all opened. Or it could be quick if she just shot Ginger dead and no one cared enough to protest.

Lurene's hands clenched as she thought of her pistol. The heat and her temper and frustration made her killing mad.

Ginger's fingers clutched the stone.

Thunder cracked across the sky. The noise disrupted a perfect chance for Lurene to get rid of one of her oversupply of partners. The most useless one of the bunch.

"Rain?" Ginger let go of the stone and looked up. "I wish it would rain."

"Not rain." Cutter wheeled toward the edge of the canyon. "Quiet."

The thunder echoed. It bounced off the canyon walls that stretched and stretched as far as Lurene's eyes could see. What in the world was making that sound? Not rain? An earthquake? Lurene had heard of those.

A horse appeared over the edge of the canyon. Impossible. It came right up over the edge of a deadly drop. The animal was small, stunted maybe because it looked like a full-grown horse rather than a colt.

Another appeared and another. Brown horses, pintos, reds, roans. Black and white and buckskin. All undersized, all climbing a wall that no horse could climb.

The five of them were frozen by those galloping horses. Then they were gone. Two dozen horses at least in that herd. They galloped straight north and rounded some sagebrush and rock and vanished.

If dust hadn't hung in the air, Lurene wouldn't have believed she'd seen it.

"That's a trail to the bottom of this canyon." Cutter headed

221

for his horse, tied off to the side—and a good thing they were tied tight.

Lurene looked at the nervous mounts, eager to run off with their wild friends.

"A trail a horse can handle."

Lurene was only a step behind Cutter. By the time she was on horseback, the Lloyds and Ginger were untying their mounts.

Cutter rode toward the edge of the trail. Lurene shuddered as he approached the spot where those horses had come up. He went over the edge.

She half expected to hear the sound of his body falling, the horse screaming. But nothing. This was a trail, impossible. She could almost smell the gold in that pit or she'd never have gone after Cutter.

Lurene smiled for the first time all day. They were back on the trail of the Dysart woman and a city full of gold.

Luck was with her, that was for sure. That gold was as good as hers, whether it came from a city down there or from a wealthy family back east. If she did this all exactly right, it might come from both.

And when she was rich enough, she could make her own rules for herself. She could be clean and free to do as she pleased.

No man would ever put his hands on her again.

Nineteen

I'm up to the ride." Shannon's need to head for that gap—the one clearly marked on her father's map, the one she just needed to step through to find gold and prove her father right and restore him to respectability, *that* one—gnawed at her until she started to rise from her bedroll, only to be stopped by the pain. She managed to sit upright, but that was as far as she was going without help.

"More rest, girl." Hozho roasted rabbits in their fire. Hosteen had brought in several, enough for a feast. She also stirred a small pot that steamed and smelled of herbs and grass. Some potion to help Shannon's arm feel better.

It was still early in the day. The sun hadn't risen enough, and they sat in the relative cool of the shadows.

All Shannon could do was chafe at the delay. A delay caused by her. "Just get me on that horse. We can get there today. It hurts, but it will loosen up once I'm on horseback."

"Stop whining." Gabe carried all the canteens in one hand, hanging from their leather straps. They'd all been drinking water steadily, all last evening and ever since they'd gotten up. Trying to

223

get fluid in their parched throats. Stock up, get ahead in case the next stretch of this trail was as long and dry as the last.

"I'm not whining!" Flinching, Shannon definitely heard a whine in her voice. Disgusting.

Gabe handed all the canteens but one to Hozho.

Hozho wrapped a cloth around a tin coffee cup and poured the liquid out of her little pot into it, then handed that to Gabe. "Get her to drink this. All of it." Hozho shot Shannon a bossy sort of look.

Shannon was getting really tired of being pushed around by the people who were supposed to be working for her.

Emptying some leaves out of her little pot with a crack of metal on rock, Hozho then reached for the canteen and poured water into her pot to make coffee.

"Drink it all." Gabe gave Shannon the tin cup, careful to keep the cloth around it so it wouldn't burn her hands. "And when you're finished, drink more water. You oughta be mighty wrung out after yesterday. The crying alone should've dried you to the bone."

"What is this stuff?" Shannon ignored Gabe's remark about her tears and stared suspiciously into the cup.

"It brings down swelling, keeps a fever from setting in. It will help." Hozho gestured with the canteen she'd just emptied then stood from where she knelt by the fire.

"I will get more water." She headed down the trail Gabe had just come up. She left three filled canteens on the ground and only carried one, so the woman was just going to the river to get away from Shannon. And her whining.

Snatching the canteen with her right hand, Shannon did her best to control a shudder of pain. Everything hurt if she moved— her head, her legs. Even breathing hurt. How could one stupid shoulder hurt all over her whole body?

"We're going to rest for a day." Gabe lowered himself to the ground beside her and drew in the scent of the rabbit, which helped Shannon remember she was starving for that sizzling meat. They'd had enough food, but it hadn't begun to taste good. The smell of the meat was now driving her crazy.

Shannon reached for the lid of her canteen with her left hand by reflex. Even stopping instantly, with an arm tied to her body by the sling, the pain almost knocked her out. Her vision turned black around the edges. She blinked her eyes open to see Gabe leaning over her with her cup in his hand.

"Shannon. Shannon, talk to me." Gabe knelt beside her, easing her to the ground, so worried, so careful about her arm. Kindness radiating out of the dark of his eyes.

It made her throat ache with unshed tears.

"I know you're eager to get on with the trip, but you can't ride, sweetheart. I'm sorry. But please be careful."

A hiss of pain slipped through her lips before she gathered her control enough to speak. "I know. I'll quit. . .whining." It stung to say that.

Gabe smiled. "My big brothers always accused me of whining."

"Seven of them, right?"

"There are seven of us in all." Gabe slid his fingers between the tightly fastened sling and her arm. "It's pretty tight. I don't want it too tight, but tight enough. Does it hurt?"

"Compared to what?" Shannon spoke through clenched teeth.

Gabe brushed his hand over her hair.

"So six brothers then, all older, and they always told you that you were whining. Bet you didn't like that."

"I hated it. I suspect it made me run to my ma crying a thousand times."

"Whiner," Shannon said sarcastically. She was proud of herself for achieving sarcasm. It took about everything she had to appear that clearheaded. She swallowed as she looked at Gabe's gentle eyes. She'd like to hunt his mean big brothers down and give them a thrashing.

Gabe's eyes went to her throat, and he said, "Here, let's get you a drink of this medicine."

He must have noticed her swallowing. She decided to let him think it was thirst. He eased one strong arm under her shoulders, from the right, so careful of the injured left side. He shifted with agonizing slowness until he'd slid behind her. He raised his knees and leaned her back against his chest to give her a resting place. Then he guided the medicine to her lips and she sipped.

"Ugh, what is that?" She turned her head aside.

Gabe followed her with the cup. "Drink it all. You heard her. You don't want Hozho mad at you, do you?"

"It tastes awful, bitter. Why isn't Hozho worried about me being mad at her?"

Gabe laughed. "Because she's scary and you're not."

True.

"It's warm but not too hot anymore." Gabe moved the cup so he could touch the tin. "Drink it down now. Be a good girl."

Shannon felt free to roll her eyes to heaven, since Gabe was behind her and couldn't see. "Just help me drink the stupid stuff."

"Swallow fast and it'll be over."

Shannon gulped and gulped the hot liquid. She shuddered the whole time and, for a second, thought she might toss it right back out of her not-so-tough belly.

"Collywobbles again?"

"Oh yes. Can I have a drink of water, please?"

Gabe set the cup aside and picked up the canteen. Uncapping it, he moved again and got one hand on the nape of her neck while the other raised the canteen to her lips.

It tasted heavenly.

Gabe let her drink a few seconds then lowered the canteen.

"Icy cold water." Shannon swallowed deeply, trying to suck enough water in to fill her belly and her skin and her burning eyes. "Where did you find it?"

"There's a spring right down by the river, pouring out of a fissure in the rocks in a little waterfall. The water is as cold as melting snow. I don't know where they found any melting snow in Arizona in the summer, but it sure is cold, even if it don't make any sense." Gabe raised the canteen. "Another drink?"

Shannon nodded, careful not to move her head one inch more than necessary, because it hurt her shoulder. "Yes, please." She drank, then rested, then drank some more.

Gabe attended her so carefully. When a dribble of water ran down her chin, he noticed and followed the path of that rivulet in a way that made Shannon very aware of his strong arms around her.

"Thank you so much. For the water and for helping me." Shannon's eyes would have filled with tears if she'd had any water in her to spare. Maybe after this long drink worked its way through to her eyeballs. . . "I owe you my life. Again. You've saved me twice now."

"Whatever we find in that canyon, Shannon, you know that your pa found something important." Gabe lifted the canteen past her shoulder.

She very carefully shifted around so she could see him. Her eyes followed when he touched his lips. She was strangely aware that her lips had just touched that canteen in the exact same place.

He had one knee resting on a shading boulder, and she leaned against it, grateful for the cushion from this stony world.

He drank deeply then recapped and set the canteen aside. "You know that just finding a trail down here was a big accomplishment, don't you?"

He pulled a handkerchief from his hip pocket and dabbed at her chin, pausing at that silly dimple she'd inherited from her father. Gabe seemed to like it, and so Shannon decided she liked it, too.

"Do you really think so?" She caught his hand where it touched her face. "Do you think after all his talk of a Cibola and Quivera, after all his rantings and the way he died, he'll be able to rest in peace?"

Gabe's eyes had rested on her chin, or somewhere very close to it. Now his gaze lifted until he met her eyes. "I think you know that the Bible doesn't talk much about such a thing."

Her brow furrowed, and the movement hurt her burned skin. "What do you mean? Rest in peace—people talk about it all the time."

"Well, yes, sure, but they don't mean that someone in this life can fix things after you're dead and somehow give you a happier afterlife. What happens after death is between a man and God. And the choices a man makes about faith come before he dies. Your work can establish a good reputation for your pa. And maybe that'll give *you* some peace of mind. Maybe it'll help your ma feel some pride in her husband. But your pa, well, he's at God's side now—if he was a believer—and busy being in heaven. Whatever you do back here becomes between *you* and God. Your pa has no part in it."

"So you're saying I'm wasting my time?" Shannon's hand tightened on his.

"No, I don't mean that. There's no harm in helping your pa be remembered well. It just doesn't make much difference to him. Just to you."

"You talk more about God than a lot of men, Gabe. Were you always a man of faith?"

"Reckon I am. My ma"—Gabe's worried eyes softened with affection—"well, you couldn't be her son and not be raised right. I embraced her faith from an early age, making it my own. She was a mighty warrior for the Lord."

"Your ma?" For some reason that made her smile. "You think of your mother as a warrior?"

Gabe nodded and his smile stretched from ear to ear. "I wish you could've met her. Elva Lasley was the smartest, toughest, sweetest Christian lady who ever lived."

Shannon knew she was looking at a man who loved his mother. It hit her hard. Did she love her mother? Did Bucky love his? They were such distant creatures. Yes, Shannon knew, she did love her mother. But she didn't know her, didn't like her. It was a sad kind of love. "She taught you words like *collywobbles* and *shimmy*."

"She did indeed. She taught us everything. There wasn't a school close by, so she taught me to read and cipher. And she taught all of us real good."

Gabe's smile was so full of affection, Shannon began to wish someday the thought of her would bring such a smile to him or to her children. And she didn't even consider correcting Gabe's grammar.

"But mostly, you should've heard her play the piano. She could make you feel what she was *feeling* when she played her hymns. All that talent, and she lived out most of her life in a little cabin, crowded to the rafters with boys. We had a piano in there, though. Pa got it for her long before I was born. She always said a home without a piano was a sad place. She wanted it more than a roof over her head, and Pa had found a way. We lived a far piece from any church. Ma would play hymns of a Sunday morning. She played every day, but on Sunday we'd all sit around her and sing. Pa would read from the Bible, his preaching and Ma's piano and all us boys singing at the top of our lungs." Gabe laughed. "It's a wonder we didn't tear off the roof with our Sunday service. But it was fun."

With a trembling hand, Shannon reached up and touched Gabe's smile. She wanted to be closer to it. Closer to him. "I wish I'd had a chance to know her, Gabe. It sounds like you had a happy childhood."

"Reckon it was as much fun as a boy dares to have, running wild in the woods hunting and fishing and playing with my big brothers. We had to work, too. Work hard to feed all of us. There were chores aplenty, and Ma and Pa both were almost as quick with a switch as they were with a hug. The good Lord knows I got my share of both. But we all worked together, and we had us a lot of fun." Gabe was looking into the distance—into the past.

He came back to her and looked down, moved his chin so her hand rubbed on the stubble of his jaw. "How about you, Shannon. One child alone. Did you have fun? Did you have music, a church to attend? Was your pa's studying and mapmaking something you enjoyed while you were growing up?"

"My family isn't like yours, Gabe. Home wasn't a place for play or music or worship."

"Aren't you a believer?"

"We were prominent members of a large church in our neighborhood. We attended faithfully."

"I like a church service if I'm ever near enough to attend one."

"Ours was very formal. My mother certainly didn't play the piano. She isn't. . .I'm not. . .close to her. She's not a person to give hugs or sing along with." Her mother didn't even bother with a switch. "I had a nursemaid when I was young, a governess and tutors in later years. I attended a young lady's academy day school during my teens to learn comportment and etiquette."

With a furrowed brow, Gabe said, "Comportment and etiquette, what's that?"

"I suppose it's—it's—well—my mother's version of colly-wobbles and shimmy. The language of the people I lived among."

With a shrug at her nonanswer, Gabe said, "You need another drink?"

"Yes, please. The water tastes good."

Gabe raised her up again with such gentleness it brought tears to Shannon's eyes.

With a sigh, Gabe said, "You must have enough water if you've got it to spare for tears." He helped her drink deeply.

When she was done, he reached across her to set the canteen down, and that brought him very close. Once the canteen was set aside, he seemed to notice just how close. He studied her tear-filled eyes for a length of time that Shannon lost track of, then lowered his head to kiss her.

When Gabe pulled away, he studied her closely. "Remember me saying you should keep your kisses to yourself if you didn't intend to stay here with me?"

Shannon thought maybe she did remember something like that. "Yes."

"I'm taking this to mean you're thinking of staying."

And she was. Very seriously. Thinking. About staying.

No, that wasn't exactly true, because she was really only thinking of one thing.

She used her good hand to pulled Gabe's head down and start the kiss all on her own.

"How long have we been going down?" Tyra stood beside Buck as they watched Hance drop down on his backside on a ledge, roll over on his stomach, and scoot backward over a cliff. Again.

She mopped her forehead with a bandana and wished she could shed her long-sleeved shirt and switch her riding skirt for something lightweight like calico. Those Yavapai were dressed about right for the area with their loincloths. She wondered what their women wore. The mental image was more than a little shocking.

"I'm starting to hate this canyon." Buck ran his thumb along the straps that tied his bedroll and pack onto his shoulders.

Tyra knew just how he felt. "But the view. . . Can you imagine anything so beautiful?"

Buck shook his head as Tyra's father sat down where their guide had been. "Captain Hance said about eight or ten hours to get to the bottom. It's well past noon."

Tyra looked up at the blazing sun. "I miss the morning. I promise tomorrow I'll appreciate the shade."

"If we survive until morning." Buck didn't sound like he was having one bit of fun, though she did catch him looking across the canyon on occasion, as if transfixed by the beauty. She'd done it plenty herself.

She went next down the cliff. It wasn't that far, and it wasn't a sheer drop. She could worm her way down, carrying her heavy pack with no damage, but it was a slow way to roast to death, spread out on rocks under that relentless sun. It gave her some sympathy for the rabbits they had snared and planned to roast for supper tonight.

She waited for Buck to come down, and they walked side by side on a briefly wider stretch of trail that rattlesnaked its way up and down, side to side, mean and hot and—if they weren't careful—deadly. But whatever kind of loco Hance was, the man knew his trail.

It was a tough route, but she didn't see an easier way. She could tell Hance had done this many times before. They'd been lucky to find him.

He'd never stopped talking the whole way down. Usually they were far enough back to ignore him. And the man didn't seem to care. She wondered if he talked this way when he was alone.

"And I first found the canyon because I got caught in a buffalo stampede."

Tyra and Buck exchanged a glance but didn't comment. It didn't help. Nothing stopped the man.

"Well, I was on a flat stretch a' land with nowhere to hide as far as the eye could see. And I knew that the one place no one wants to be is in front of a buffalo stampede."

Tyra and Buck slowed a bit more.

"Then I spotted one skinny stick of a tree between me and

that stampede, and I ran fast and climbed that tree just before those buffalo hit."

The trail ahead seemed clear, and Tyra estimated that she had up to five minutes before she'd face another chance of falling to her death. "Are you really going to marry the woman we're searching for?" Tyra liked it when Buck turned his blue eyes on hers. They... sort of sparkled. They were a bright blue with glittering stripes of lighter color separating the blue into what seemed nearly jewels.

He smiled, and she admired his white teeth. "I've been thinking about life back home. It's a sight easier than the West."

They rounded a curve in the trail and saw a tower ahead of them that defied description; it was so dazzling in its height and the layers of color. Beyond that lay another one and another and another. Stone of all colors, dotted with bushes and bristly trees. Surely the most beautiful, rugged place.

"But there's nothing like this back there," Buck continued. "Nothing. It's a hard land, but it's worth it. To me it's worth it."

"Well, I knew that tree was going over, and if you think it's bad to be in front of a buffalo stampede, well, let me tell you it's even worse being *under* a buffalo stampede. So I saw the biggest, meanest buffalo bull coming toward me, and I knew it was jump or die, so I—"

Tyra moved a bit closer to Buck. "My pa's ranch is twenty thousand acres. We've got good water and grassland, but there are places..." She looked at that colonnade. "Well, nothing like that, but the land is beautiful. Powerful. A hard land. Challenging. It pulls at you until it's part of you, or maybe until you're part of it. You're closer to God on the land. The seasons, the rain, the heat, birth and death—it's a good life."

"I like what this place makes me feel." Buck tore his eyes from the colonnade. Then those eyes rounded to her and got just as stuck. The voice droning on with its tall tales faded as the rest of their traveling companions rounded a curve and vanished.

"And what is that?" Tyra liked what she was feeling, too, though she was hard put to describe it.

"I think *challenged* is a good word. It's asking me to be strong, to work hard, to test myself against the land and the sun and the water and the cliffs. I'm doing it, too—passing the test. Life isn't very challenging where I come from. I think. . ." His voice faded, and he shook his head.

"What?" Tyra reached out and touched his arm without really planning to. This was important. She leaned closer to encourage him. . .and to see his eyes just a little better.

"I think I could be a better man if I stayed out here." Buck's eyes seemed closer. "I think I'm up to that challenge. I'd like to have a chance to prove that I could manage without all the safety of my comfortable home and the cushion of money. You know I've never worked a day in my life?"

Tyra couldn't quite imagine it. "Never?"

A gust of wind brought Hance's voice to them. "I dug my fingers into the shaggy hair of that buffalo, and I hung on, and the bull took me for a ride that lasted two weeks. . . ." Hance's voice faded.

"I've studied." Buck shrugged. "Schoolwork. But not real labor, not even a job sitting at a desk. Why would I when I was born with more money than I'll ever need?"

Why indeed?

"But out here, I can see that no man ought to live that way. No man can take real pride in himself if he's never faced something hard and come out, win or lose, knowing he did his best. Knowing he endured." Buck was looking through her into the past or the future or his dreams—she didn't know what.

"I know climbing down into this canyon doesn't really qualify as enduring. Not when we've got lots of supplies and a trail guide, but it's the most satisfying accomplishment of my life. I like it."

His eyes focused on her. "I like you, Tyra Morgan. You make

me feel almost as much as this canyon."

"Then to stay alive"—Hance seemed to be shouting his story now, probably feeling sorry for anyone who dared to miss a syllable—"I started in eating that buffalo from the top down while I rode on his back. The bull finally collapsed right on the edge of this here canyon."

Tyra probably shouldn't be honored to be compared to a hole in the ground, but this was the grandpappy of all holes. "Really?"

"I feel more for you in the few days since we've met than I ever have for Shannon."

She opened her mouth to say. . .she wasn't sure what.

His lips cut off whatever she'd been going to say. And just as well, because this was a much better idea than talking. She slid her arms around his waist and ran into his huge pack. Pulling back, she smiled at him and moved her arms so they surrounded his neck.

Buck was more determined. He found a way to hook his hand around her waist and draw her close, deepening the kiss.

"Tyra! Buck! Where are you?"

With a guilty jerk, Tyra whispered, "Pa!" She turned to look down the trail, and there was no one, but the voice wasn't that far away and coming nearer. She looked back at Buck. "We'd better go"

"Yep." Nodding, Buck sneaked in one more quick kiss. Or two. "But this isn't over, Tyra."

His quick glance at her lips told her just exactly what he meant by "this."

"In fact, pretty lady, it's just begun."

Tyra's knees felt far too weak to continue trekking down a canyon wall.

"Tyra, Buck, are you all right?" Pa's shout had taken on an edge of worry.

There wasn't much choice but to make her legs work. She

stepped away.

Buck caught her arm and reeled her back for one last kiss. "Okay, now you can go."

She smiled and he laughed, his eyes flashing hot and blue like the heart of a flame.

Tyra walked quickly toward her pa while she considered all the reasons the Grand Canyon was about the grandest place she'd ever been.

Twenty

───────────❦───────────

We'll move out tomorrow morning." Hozho took the cup of bitter liquid.

"It's horrible to drink, but it really does make me feel better." Shannon shuddered at the aftertaste then sighed with relief that the medicine was gone.

The elderly woman adjusted the sling and ran one work-calloused hand through Shannon's hair. "It will be painful but bearable, I think, and you want to go, don't you?"

Hozho's gruff tenderness was more than Shannon had ever gotten from her mother. Realizing that sad bit of truth hurt worse than her shoulder. She wanted to get this done now. Finish with the quest, go back and deal with Mother and Bucky, then maybe, just maybe, see if she had a future with Gabe.

Hozho pulled the blanket up to cover Shannon, tucking her in for the night like a child.

"Why is it so cold at night and so hot during the day?"

"Just the way of the desert, especially the high desert."

"This is high?" Shannon asked. "We've been walking downhill for days."

In the bright moonlight, Shannon saw a smile curl Hozho's lips and all her deep wrinkles fall into unnatural lines. The woman wasn't much for smiling. "Get some sleep, ah-tad. Tomorrow, maybe we'll get to your lost city."

"Aren't the rest of you going to sleep yet?" Shannon shifted under the cover, and the pain nearly tricked a gasp out of her, but she was doing her best to be stalwart in the hopes they'd let her ride tomorrow.

A snap of worry in Hozho's black eyes told Shannon the elderly woman wasn't fooled. Hozho gave her cheek a rough caress. "Gabe is within your sight. The parson will be back soon. Hosteen and I must check our snares tonight then take them down. We don't leave them behind to take an animal's life when we aren't there to accept the gift of food. If we wait until morning, we'll be getting a late start."

Shannon saw the parson's horse try to bite him in the arm. The parson started snarling.

"Let me picket him for you." Gabe hurried to take the black mustang toward the others to graze. "You want to fill the canteens?"

The parson, who'd been muttering dire threats against his not-so-trusty steed, perked up, grabbed the canteens stacked near the fire, and whistled a hymn as he walked away on the moonlit path.

"I won't be gone long." Hozho pushed away from Shannon.

"Thank you." Shannon caught her calloused hand. She could have thanked this lady, who had been so hostile to her at first, for one hundred things. "Hozho, I want you to know that—"

Silence reigned for a moment.

"My mother knows every rule there is for polite manners and proper behavior. She dresses beautifully and. . .and comports herself perfectly."

"What is comport?" Hozho asked.

Shannon shrugged. The pain in her shoulder made her regret that. "She knew all sorts of rules of good manners, but she didn't know how to be kind, Hozho. She didn't know how to care for anyone but herself. When I say thank you, it's not enough. But I just want you to know I mean it sincerely. I am so thankful for your care, your kindness, the food you and Hosteen find for us. Your wisdom about this land. And that you stayed with me when it made more sense to leave. Thank you."

No smile this time, as if Hozho had used them all up for the day. "You're a good girl, Shannon. Loco, but with a good heart. I hope we find this city you search for, but if it's treasure you want, you need to search for it in your heart, in your soul."

"I just want to finish this. Then I'm going to stop living my life for my father and mother and start living it for myself."

"True treasure is inside your heart—it's a soul that is at peace with God. So live this life for God, ah-tad. Not for your parents or yourself. Streets of gold are for the next life."

"I know." Nodding, Shannon wondered if Hozho was wishing they could get out of here, go back up to the rim, and leave this beautiful, dangerous place behind. Well, they would, but not tonight. She felt her chin firm with determination; some might call it stubbornness. But she'd learned to be stubborn in the last two years as everyone she knew, most especially her mother, pressured her to give up this quest.

Just one more day and they'd find what Shannon's father had found. Then everything would be fine and in good order. Just one more day.

Hozho looked at her, concerned and a bit amused, and seemed to understand what Shannon was thinking. With a shake of her head, Hozho said, "Good night, ah-tad."

Hosteen and Hozho left the camp.

He'd heard what passed between Shannon and Hozho. Heard Shannon's determination. It chafed at Gabe, but he hadn't expected different. He suspected Hozho hadn't either. But it had been worth a try.

He finished caring for the horses and came to her side. "Think you're ready to move tomorrow, then?" Gabe dropped to his knees on Shannon's left, by her wounded arm.

"It's better. I'm not saying it's healed up, but it's much less painful. I can travel tomorrow."

"Listen, we've got a couple of minutes before the parson comes back."

Shannon shifted just slightly, careful of her arm, to focus on him.

"Some things passed between us this morning, Shannon. Things that make me wonder. . .that is. . .hope. . .that you might not be. . .what I mean is. . ."

"I don't feel like I've known you long enough to decide about the future, Gabe."

His heart sank.

"But I have known you long enough to know I don't have a future with Bucky."

Then it soared.

"I wouldn't feel what I do for you if there was anything real behind the understanding I have with him." Shannon swallowed hard. "I don't even know if he'll be that upset when I break things off."

She said *when*, not *if*. Gabe hoped the parson went about his water work real slowly.

"But my mother, well. . . I know you think my father was a madman."

"Not really." Not completely mad. A little maybe.

"But he was the nice one of my parents. You're going to have to meet my mother."

It was Gabe's turn to swallow. "That's fine. I'd like that."

"No, I can promise you *won't*. And she won't like it either. She'll turn up her snobbish little nose at you and tell you you're not worthy of me. She'll insult you and take every shot she can straight at your pride."

"I'm from a decent, hardworking family. We were hardscrabble back in Tennessee, but we took care of ourselves and had a roof over our heads we'd built with our own hands." Not his hands precisely. He'd been too young, but still— "And my brothers are spread all over the country. A couple still live in Tennessee with nice farms. A couple ranch in New Mexico and Texas. One's in California and—"

"I know they're good men, Gabe." Shannon reached across her body with her right hand and rested it on his forearm. "I know you're a good man. And in America anyone willing to work hard and be honest can make a living, and you'd take good care of...of...well..."

"A wife?" Gabe supplied with a grin.

Shannon shrugged then winced in pain. "And even if you did have money trouble, I've inherited a tidy fortune from both of my grandmothers and I have a—"

"A fortune? Really?" Gabe bristled at that. "I don't need your inheritance to take care of you, Shannon. I own a nice ranch in Wyoming. We'll go back and get things straightened out with Bucky then let your ma have her say. Then I'll give you all the time you want to decide if we finally know each other well enough to get married. But I think you get to know a lot about a person when you go through hard times with them."

"But it's only been a few days. We can't—"

He cut her off. "But these haven't been normal days. It's been life and death. I've seen you terrified, furious. I've seen you fighting for your life and laughing and in prayer. I've seen your determination and intelligence." He didn't mention common sense, and for a good reason, but he figured he had enough for both of them. "I think days like these last few reveal what a person is really like inside. How they'll hold up over the years."

Gabe's temper rose as he thought about what she was saying, that he'd kiss her and walk away. That she'd kiss him while she was promised to another man. "If we treated each other *honorably*, we would have a good life together."

He shut up before his temper snapped and he said something he'd regret. Did he think that he could *yell* her into caring about him? Maybe he had a few gaps in his common sense, too.

He thought of his ma, how he'd abandoned her. His friendship with Annette and how he could have built something with her, too, maybe. He could have made up for his negligence of his mother by taking care of Annette. And now here was his chance again to stick by a woman. Would he fail her? Would he lose her to another man? Here she lay, hurt. True, he'd saved her, but he hadn't kept her from getting hurt to begin with.

"You didn't even let me finish about my mother, Gabe. She'll insult you until you are furious, and then she'll start on me. She'll remind me of my responsibility to my name and my birthright. She'll make me feel guilty, and she'll tear down my father, and the worst part is—"

"There's a worse still?" Gabe admitted he was getting a little nervous.

"The worst part is she'll do it all without raising her voice. She'll do it with cold, precise cuts that slash at your feelings. Tiny little cuts you can't defend yourself against, some of them you won't even feel, slice your feelings. But in the end, she'll leave both of us bleeding to death inside. She's a master at the chilly social insult."

"Would it be different—better—if we showed up. . ." Gabe hesitated to say it. He knew she wasn't ready. "Already married?"

Shannon fell silent. The gaze between them was steady, solid. Gabe liked it more than he could imagine. His fingers itched to reach for her, settle things right now. Call the parson back. If only she'd see sense. They could finish this treasure hunt as a married couple. Then, when she was so disappointed, he'd be there to dry her tears, just as he planned. But he could comfort her day and night. Kiss away her disappointment in a way that would give her something to move on toward—a future, a ranch. Children.

"Maybe."

Gabe reached for her.

"Maybe that might be the best way."

He slid one hand to caress her cheek.

She smiled. "Let's ask the parson to—"

The sharp metallic click of a gun being cocked stopped her words.

Gabe straightened away from Shannon. He had no gun. No way to fight that noise coming from straight behind. He braced himself for the slam of a bullet into his back.

"Don't move, not one inch."

Shannon gasped, and a glance at her told Gabe she recognized the voice.

He heard movement behind him and tried to figure out which way to dive, how to protect Shannon. He realized as he knelt there he'd failed. Just as he'd failed his ma, he was now going to die and leave Shannon to her fate. How many times did he have to fail?

Something slammed into the right side of his head.

He toppled to the left, only distantly aware of landing hard against the rocky ground. From a distance he heard a woman's voice he didn't recognize, just as the dark night faded suddenly to pitch black.

"Now you're going to help us, Miss Dysart."

"Lurene!" Shannon couldn't believe her eyes. "Why did you come after me?"

"You know exactly why." Lurene crouched beside Gabe's still body.

Shannon saw a trickle of blood from his temple where Lurene had smashed the butt of her gun.

"You didn't give us the right map. I'm here to get it, and you're going to take us where we want to go, or I'm going to kill your friend here." She pressed her revolver to Gabe's head.

"Anything, just please don't hurt him." Shannon didn't even consider trying to bargain with these villains. They'd left her for dead and laughed about it. Murder was not beyond them.

She saw movement, and her eyes focused on Cutter, his gun trained on her. The Lloyd brothers stood to one side, a pace behind Cutter, Ginger to Cutter's other side. All of them greedy and evil, with a thirst for gold riding with them.

"Get the papers, and we ride." Lurene rose and stepped back.

The gun hadn't been fired. Once Shannon left with them, Hozho could tend Gabe. The only one in danger because of Shannon's quest was herself. Except a blow to the head could kill. So Gabe might well be dying even now.

"Darrel, saddle the horses for our two friends here."

"Two?" Shannon tore her gaze away from Gabe.

"I see the way you look at him. We're taking him along. Any time we need your cooperation, we point a gun at him." Lurene moved her pistol toward Gabe's still form.

The Lloyd brothers hurried to where the horses grazed, grabbing saddles as they passed.

"Any time you give us trouble, I'll aim my gun at your man. As long as you work with us, he stays alive."

The parson's horse was the closest, and they began saddling him.

Shannon dreaded riding the cranky mustang.

"Let's move fast before the others come back." Cutter started saddling another horse.

"We know there are more of you." Lurene's eyes flashed in the firelight. "But we'll take the map and you and this hombre here and leave them behind. Do you intend to behave, Miss Dysart?" Lurene addressed her formally, but with such a sneer Shannon's throat went dry.

"I'll cooperate." Shannon groaned in pain as she pushed back her blankets. "But I fell earlier. I'm hurt. Can't you just take the maps and go? I'll slow you down."

"You lied to us last time about the maps. We're not letting that happen again. Let's go."

With rough shoves that nearly buckled Shannon's knees, Lurene herded her to the closest horse, the fiery black mustang. She held her arm tight to her body, hoping the sling would support it enough not to reinjure the shoulder.

The Lloyds led the other horse up and slung Gabe over the saddle. Cutter must have realized Shannon couldn't mount by herself because he caught her by the waist and boosted her up.

"Have you got the maps?" Lurene swung her gun toward Gabe. "*All* the maps?"

"Yes, I'm carrying them in my pocket. I have everything." Which was true. There wasn't much left. Just directions to that gap.

Shannon had much respect for Hosteen and Hozho in the wilderness, but she'd seen nothing to think they were capable of taking on five vicious outlaws. And they had no way to go for help.

"Which way, Miss Dysart, ma'am?"

Lurene's mockery of respect didn't even bother Shannon. She had too much at stake to be upset by words. She began praying, hoping they'd be spared a terrible end, and if they weren't, she reached out for God and asked for forgiveness. Setting her soul right. It might be a good idea since it looked very much as if she'd soon be walking on streets of gold in heaven.

"To the left, we take that shelf right there." The moon and stars lit up the canyon nearly like day, washing every bit of color out of the world and leaving it with a blue-black tint. Deep shadows were everywhere.

"Lead the way." Lurene gestured with her gun. "And we'll have your hero back here in case you make a break for it."

Setting out, Shannon thought of how she'd fallen in the bright light of day. Every step on this narrow terrace was dangerous. She prayed that God would guide her steps and protect Gabe and forgive her for setting things in motion that had led to this madness.

Gabe came awake in a shaking, shimmying world. His stomach swirled with collywobbles. He didn't move. He didn't remember what had happened, but he sensed danger, and that didn't make him a genius.

The throbbing in his head told him he'd been hurt. He slit his eyes open and saw. . .the underbelly of a saddled horse. He was hanging upside down. Doing his best not to visibly move, he looked side to side and saw riders ahead of him and behind him. Testing his hands, he found them free, drooping down nearly to the ground, but he felt ropes that must mean he was tied to the saddle. He was being carried.

Had he been hurt and, rather than let him heal, his stubborn little Shannon had strapped him down and headed on to her treasure?

That seemed rude. Not something Shannon would do. Usually.

A quick peek again told him the rider ahead was a man he didn't know. Hard to see from this angle, but the man had broad shoulders and a tied-down gun on his left, which meant the man was either left-handed or he wore two guns. A gunman might do that.

Behind him rode a woman with hair the color of fire. No, this wasn't his group. These people. . .they had to be the ones who'd stranded Shannon to begin with. Cruel, murderous thieves.

He was still muddled, and his head was in agony. The world swooped every time he turned his head. Since he wasn't up to fighting and didn't know what he was up against anyway, he decided to play at being unconscious for now and wait for a chance. A chance to fight, to get his hands on someone's gun. To grab Shannon and shoot his way out to. . .where? He didn't even know the way out of this place.

Did they have the Tsosis and Parson Ford, or had they grabbed him and Shannon and run? Was Shannon hurt, too? He couldn't see past the riders behind and ahead. He thought of her arm and how much this would hurt and wanted to get his hands on a gun and punish these lousy coyotes.

With a sudden sickening throb of his head, Gabe felt the world spin, and he knew he wasn't going to have to fake unconsciousness.

He awoke again when rough hands dragged him off his horse. He struck the ground with his shoulder and rolled to his back, remaining limp.

"Don't hurt him!"

Shannon's voice. She was alive! He felt someone land almost on top of him, heard the soft moan of pain and knew it was hers, being shoved around with her arm still so sore. "Gabe, are you all right? Gabe, please speak to me." A trembling hand brushed his cheek.

It might have been wiser to continue to fake being knocked cold. It might give him an opening, but Shannon sounded near panic, and she'd faced everything else so bravely, he had to give her this assurance. "I'm awake." He opened his eyes and looked into her milk-white face.

Pain had etched lines around her mouth and eyes. She lay half on top of him, her arm cradled to her stomach, still in a sling.

"Gabe, oh Gabe, I'm so sorry."

"You said you needed a break. Take it and get back here."

Gabe's eyes swung from Shannon to a woman, young, dark haired, evil. The hardness of that woman's eyes told Gabe they could easily die before this was over. He scanned the area, saw five people in all. Two younger men, a redheaded woman, and an older man who looked strong as an ox, cool as ice, and mean as a rattler.

So, they hadn't brought the Tsosis or Parson Ford. But had they just grabbed Gabe and Shannon and run, or were they left dead on the trail?

These people were surviving down in the canyon, so he didn't underestimate their toughness, which meant they knew he and Shannon weren't alone. Still, he wasn't going to ask any questions that might alert this group to the others.

"Gabe, are you all right?"

A set of hands grabbed Shannon, and Gabe looked up at a sharp-eyed young man. There was greed in the way he reached for Shannon, and Gabe had to use steely self-control to keep from lunging at the man. Surely the greed was for gold, not to harm her. Because there was no doubt in Gabe's mind who these people were and why they'd taken Shannon.

The dark-haired woman stepped close to him and crouched low, bringing her gun to Gabe's temple. "She won't run, Randy. She knows we'll kill her partner here if she does, don't you, Miss Dysart?"

Gabe hated that he was being used as a tool to torment Shannon. It made him a weakling, nothing but a stick to beat her with.

"I'm not leaving him. I told you I'd take you to where the map leads." Shannon jammed her one healthy arm on her waist. "We'd all be right here if you hadn't attacked me to begin with. We'd all be heading to the same place at almost the same time. If we really find a city of gold, it will be a treasure beyond what any of us can count. There will be plenty of it for everyone to be wealthy.

There's no need to keep threatening him or shoving me around."

"Get going." Randy stepped closer. "Lurene's got your man covered, but if you're hoping the folks we left behind are stupid enough to come after you, give that up. If they come, it'll be better for them if they *don't* catch us, so think hard before you slow us down."

"I'll hurry." She turned, and a gasp of pain had her grab at her left arm and support it as she left the small grassy area where they'd stopped.

Lurene lifted the gun away from Gabe's head, rose, and stepped away.

He heard the trickling sound of water and turned to see a spring. "Can I have some water before we go on?"

"Help yourself." She kept the gun trained on him, cold amusement in her eyes, almost as if she wanted him to try something reckless and give her an excuse to pull the trigger.

He tried to sit up and almost fell flat. His head pounded as if a herd of longhorns were stampeding through his brain. His stomach jumped and swooped. Collywobbles. His arms and legs were numb, probably because his blood flow was all mixed up thanks to his hanging over that saddle for so long.

Deciding he wasn't up to walking, he crawled to the spring. Wouldn't hurt these folks to underestimate him. And maybe it wasn't underestimating. Maybe he'd've fallen on his face if he'd've tried to stand.

He drank. The first splash of water ran cold all down his gullet into his belly. For a bit, he was afraid he might lose the water back up onto the ground. He fought the sickness. When his belly settled, he drank again. Bathing his face, he found a lump the size of one of Ma's spring turnips on his skull, just above his right ear. He remembered hearing that gun cock from behind and expecting to die.

As the stampede in his head slowed a mite, he drank more and felt steadier. Not steady enough to take on five armed outlaws, but steady enough to think.

He had a knife in his boot. It wasn't much. He flexed the muscles in his leg and shifted a bit and felt the hilt tucked in his boot, so they hadn't taken it. This was no time to try and use it, with him and Shannon both hurt and with no direction to run.

Gabe said a prayer, and he felt more keenly than ever the absence of his big brothers. This crew would have a war on their hands if all seven Lasley brothers bought into this fight.

But of course they weren't there. Gabe had done his best to strike out on his own. He'd spent a lot of years trying to live down being the youngest, proving himself to brothers who loved him just like he was, no proof required. And he'd left the friendships he'd made in Wyoming, too, still trying to prove something. Though that wasn't the only reason he'd left. He admitted that in Wyoming, he'd had feelings that weren't honorable for a married woman.

And now he'd met a woman who could make him forget Annette, and he might fail her like he'd failed his ma. Somehow Gabe's whole life seemed as if it had led to this moment. Him, injured and useless. A woman counting on him who should have known better. Gabe wondered where he'd gone astray from God's plan that had led him to such a place of worthlessness.

He drank again just as Shannon came back. Their eyes met, but Gabe knew the outlaws were paying close attention.

"Let's move on." The dark-haired woman seemed to be giving orders, but the older man didn't seem like the type to take them.

Gabe tucked that away and wondered if he could play the outlaws one against the other.

Maybe. But not now. It wasn't time to fight now. It was time to think and plan and pray.

Twenty~One

So, Buck, did you have any idea your Miss Dysart was out of her mind when you knew her back east?" Tyra glared at Buck before she slid down another death-defying cliff.

Tyra didn't like Shannon, and that was a fact. It was, also, Buck decided, a very good sign.

They'd camped on this trail overnight, and Hance had promised they'd reach their goal in the midmorning hours of the next day.

Buck bit back a smile. "There were several indications." He watched Tyra go over the edge and had a little bit of trouble remembering exactly what Shannon looked like. Pretty bad considering they'd been good friends for their entire lives and she'd only been gone on this journey of hers about a month.

He could probably conjure up her face, honestly, but he just couldn't be bothered to try, not when pretty, fiery, sassy Tyra Morgan was right there in front of him. He wondered if he'd make a good rancher. Then he decided if he didn't, he'd hire a foreman and stay in the ranch house with Tyra and the children.

His mind swooped around thinking about that for a while, and he had to banish the thought of Tyra and babies before he fell completely off the cliff.

He slid down, mostly under control, then smiled at Tyra—who stood there glowering at him, but waiting, too. He wondered if she realized just how faithfully she always waited for him. And how pretty that little worry line was across her forehead.

She didn't want him to fall off a cliff. She cared.

So did he.

It might be a little soon to speak to her father, but it wasn't too soon to speak to her.

"So, Tyra, when we get out of this canyon. . ." He reached forward and caught her hand. They'd been bringing up the rear for most of this journey and if her pa or Abe Lasley noticed, Buck couldn't tell it.

"Yes?" She smiled. An encouraging sign.

"Do you think—"

"That's it!" Captain Hance pointed to a grassy stretch that spread out wide and pretty. A soft spot in a hard land.

Abe Lasley, whose brother was right now supposed to be lining up to marry Buck's woman, yelled, "Let's go! We should find Gabe in there."

Buck decided then and there he hated Abe Lasley.

Tyra dropped his hand quickly as if afraid her father would catch them.

Why would that be so bad? Buck bristled a little while he considered that. Tyra shouldn't be kissing him if she wasn't willing to hold his hand right out in front of her father. And she had most certainly kissed him all right. Repeatedly. She was in full cooperation.

Trudging onward with his huge pack on his back, Buck again brought up the rear so he was the last to see the whole of this meadow. "Where's the city of gold?" It was pretty clearly not there.

"Not a huge surprise, really," Tyra said. "But where's Gabe?"

And that was the real question, because if they weren't here—

"I ain't gonna be able to take you to no other cities down here," Captain Hance said. " 'Cuz they ain't none. This is the only city."

"What city?" Buck had to ask, since the meadow was pretty clearly lacking anything even vaguely resembling a city, golden or not.

"It'll be a hike, but I'll show you." Hance waved his arm to encourage them to follow him.

"Ghost city," Tyra whispered to Buck.

Buck smiled, and Tyra flashed a grin that made his heart beat fast.

Hance began talking again. "Word was that a huge flood came through here and cut out this canyon with a single swoop. The Havasupai have a legend about it."

"Of course they have," Buck murmured to Tyra, who swallowed a giggle.

"The world began with two gods and no people. Tochapa was the god of goodness and Hokomata was the god of evil. Tochapa had a daughter named Pu-keh-eh. His plan was for Pu-keh-eh to be the mother of life in the world. Hokomata decided to prevent this by sending a great flood."

"There's no way to get him to round a big rock out here." Buck was sorely tempted to catch Tyra's hand and hang on. But it was too open for that. Her father was going to notice right away.

"Tochapa stepped in to save his daughter by knocking down a great tree and hollowing it out. He put Pu-keh-eh in the hollow, and she survived the flood. When the floodwaters went down, rivers were created and one of them cut down and down into the earth until it created the Grand Canyon."

"So what were you going to say about when we get out of the canyon?" Tyra whispered.

Buck saw the shine in her eyes, and he had a good idea what

she *hoped* he'd say—and she was very much interested.

"Then, as the legend goes, Pu-keh-eh came out of her log boat and gave birth to two children, who being perfect could marry."

The word *marry* jolted Buck out of his little whispered conversation with Tyra.

"A brother and sister got married?" Buck asked.

Hance glared at him as if he'd stomped right on his toes, instead of asking about the fable. "They began the race of the Havasupai."

Buck had heard that word before. He was sure of it.

"And Tochapa told them to stay forever in the bottom of the canyon where the earth was good and the water pure. Tochapa promised there would be plenty for all."

"Who was Tochapa again?" Buck asked only Tyra this, afraid Hance would answer by starting his story over.

"The god of goodness."

Smiling, Tyra said, "The flood—that sounds like the Bible."

"This is where the first people lived, and they spread far and wide. Some of them left the canyon, but the righteous stayed here." With a gesture almost as grand as the canyon, Hance pointed to a bluff a mile or more across the sweeping basin. "I found their homes up there. It's a beauty of a spot. Good defense."

Defense against whom? Buck tilted his head a little to take it in. No gold, but someone had lived down here, all the way down here. Why would anyone come into the belly of the earth like this? What sort of people were so bold?

Hance jammed his fists on his hips and strutted forward, cocky as a rooster. "I've counted me fifty rooms or more. Fifty houses, I mean. Some of the houses, you kin make out several rooms."

"Who built them?" Buck studied the bluff, excited to climb up the steep edges and see for himself. It was hard to judge the size from down here. Could there have been a town up there? He'd been in plenty of towns on his train ride west that didn't have fifty buildings.

"I done tol' you the legend already." Hance sounded disgusted.

"But that's. . .that's. . .Noah and the ark."

"Yep, I reckon these folks have their own names for God, but it sounds mighty like the story of Noah, don't it?"

Buck wasn't sure what to think. Everyone knew Noah and his ark were somewhere around Bethlehem, where Jesus was born. But who could say how this canyon had been formed? He'd seen a lot of rivers. He lived on the Mississippi. And he'd seen bluffs pushed up along the flood plains in many places. He'd gone down the river to New Orleans, and he'd traveled on a ship to New York and gone a ways up the Hudson. He'd seen a lot of things. But he'd never seen anything close to this for grandeur. Believing God had carved this with the Great Flood made as much sense as anything.

Buck decided he liked the idea.

Tochapa? God? Did the names a simple, faithful people gave to their stories make them less about God? Buck wasn't sure, but he liked the idea that God had made Himself known all over the world. The flood was worldwide after all. So, of course there would be a story. He'd let smarter people than him decide about it, but he liked the idea. Having these legends could help people, when they heard about Jesus, accept Him more easily. And no doubt God understood that better than anyone.

"So, if there ever was a city of gold, the gold is long gone." Tyra pulled her gloves off, tucked them in her hip pocket, and looked. . .calm. Like gold didn't hold much interest to her.

Another idea Buck decided he liked.

"So then where's Gabe?" Tyra asked.

And that was something Buck didn't like at all. "Maybe we got here ahead of him."

"No." Hance shook his head. "If he was ahead of us on the

trail, he'd be here. And if he didn't find this trail, we'd've met him heading back east. This is the onliest way down the canyon the whole stretch."

"That you know of," Tyra's father said.

"I know this whole canyon." Hance glowered, clearly insulted.

"No one," Abe said, squaring off against the crotchety guide, "could ever know this whole canyon. If you told me you'd been exploring it for fifty years, maybe I'd believe you. How long did you say you've been here?"

The man was ancient in his quirkiness but not that old in years. His jaw turned stubborn and his eyes flashed fire. "Long enough."

"No, *not* long enough to know the whole canyon. There could be another way down."

"You don't wanna take my word for what's in this canyon?" Hance puffed up with outrage.

Buck wondered if he might start spewing lava out of his ears until he carved another gully out of the canyon.

"Get by without me then." Hance stormed off, fists clenched.

"Hey! Don't you want to stay and earn your money? I haven't even paid you yet."

The grumpy response made Buck wince. Hance vanished around a curve.

He looked at Tyra. "Can we get out of here? Did you pay enough attention to the way we came down?"

"Sure." Tyra shrugged.

Buck thought of all the drops they'd climbed down. Could they climb back up? Especially if they weren't in exactly the right spot?

"I was watchin' my trail," Lucas said gruffly.

Even a person skilled in the wilderness could get really lost in this place.

"We'll make it fine." Abe turned to the meadow.

Buck was surrounded by confidence, but he couldn't even pretend it would be easy to retrace the twisting, turning trail they'd come down.

"I wonder when my baby brother will come limping in here." Abe started unloading the pack on his back.

"I'll set up camp." Lucas dropped his pack and pulled on the ropes that bound it together. "I saw deer sign if you wanna go hunting, Abe. I think there might be some fish in that creek over there." He pointed to a low spot where Buck hadn't, until now, noticed water.

"There's a lot to learn about the West, isn't there?" he asked Tyra, feeling stupid and weary and worried.

Smiling so her white teeth showed in her darkly tanned face, she said, "I reckon. Let's help Abe set up so he can do some fishing. Maybe we can have fresh fish with our midday meal. While he handles that, I'd like to scout around, see if there's anything on that bluff that looks like there'd once been gold in this place." Her brows arched. "Or even a city."

"How much farther?" Ginger gulped deeply from her canteen.

Shannon wanted to dive at the woman before all the water was gone. "I don't know." Shannon had no canteen, and she'd been allowed a sip of water twice today. And she wasn't exactly seeing a lot of groundwater to replenish their supplies while Ginger guzzled. But of course she didn't dive. Too many guns. But the heat was a killing thing. How long could they go on like this, even if the water held out?

"I thought you had a map." Ginger took another deep drink. "What good are you if you don't know nothin'?"

"It's hard to tell about distance down here. We're heading for that green stretch right there." Shannon's left arm had settled down to a dull ache that barely penetrated her other miseries, like hunger and constant thirst and the sun bouncing off every rock in a stifling heat. Shannon was starting to understand how a biscuit felt in the oven. And she'd really like a biscuit about now.

They stretched out single file. Ginger rode in front of Shannon, Lurene ahead of that, Cutter in the lead. Randy Lloyd was behind her, then Gabe, then Darrel. The trail crawled along the side of the canyon, up and down, narrow and sometimes wide. But never a sign of water or grass.

Shannon's horse walked with its head drooped down. And these outlaws hadn't given her a bite to eat since they'd taken her last night, and now the day was waning. She'd beg if she had to, but not yet. For now she just added her growling stomach to her other aches and pains and kept moving. Food was the least of her troubles.

To Shannon's surprise, Parson Ford's fiery black mustang was a well-behaved horse, spirited but not nervous. The parson must really bring out the worst in the little animal.

Gabe had spent most of the night and an hour or so after sunrise unconscious. He was riding now, his hands tied to his pommel, his horse being led by Randy.

Lurene hadn't even threatened to kill Gabe in hours. They were too tired, too hot. It wasn't worth the effort to work up a temper, especially when Shannon was guiding them straight to where they wanted to go.

The day wore on and the shadows crept across the canyon floor toward them. Shannon watched those shadows stretch as if they were the saving hand of God, bringing a respite from the heat of this dreadful day. They curved around a canyon and downward, and the shadows of the west wall swallowed them.

On they went down, now in near dusk. And suddenly a glimpse of green, still gleaming in the sunlight, appeared ahead of them. Her father had made detailed notes of the rock formations, and Shannon knew there could be no mistake.

Shannon's horse suddenly raised its head, and its ears perked forward. Shannon heard it before she saw it. Water. A creek flowed ahead, and grass lined the rocky edges of it. This creek was very possibly the one her father had noted in the map she'd found hidden at the rim of the canyon. She'd handed all of it over to Lurene, but Shannon had read it over and over. She had every word memorized. The creek cut into a narrow canyon, and beyond that was an *X* and the end of this trail.

"This creek—we need to follow it!" Shannon had a glimmer of excitement, despite the day and their terrible circumstances. She'd found the canyon that edged the creek, leading to the grassy basin her father had marked on the map. Surely this was where they'd find his treasure.

And then what? Would Lurene shoot her and Gabe down like dogs? Shannon with her arm in a sling, Gabe tied to his saddle?

All this work to restore her father's name, and even if she found what she sought, the word would never get out. If anything, her father's reputation would be tarnished further because his delusions had led to Shannon's vanishing, never to be seen again. They'd lay that on her father's head, and her mother would be the first to blame him.

Shannon wondered if her mother would even grieve or just be annoyed that her plans to marry Shannon into a dynasty were thwarted.

Lurene turned to look at Shannon, greed glittering in the woman's eyes.

Swallowing hard with a throat as dry as cactus, Shannon waited, wondering if Lurene might decide she no longer needed any help.

The greed in Lurene's eyes was about more than gold. It was a hunger to hurt someone. Shannon wondered what life Lurene had led that brought her to such an ugly desire.

"We'll stop for the night. The horses need a good drink, and so do we." Cutter rode up to the water and dismounted. He seemed spiritless. As if the heat had baked away all his energy.

Shannon felt the same, but that look of evil in Lurene's eyes forced her to keep alert, thinking of a way to escape.

The whole group had the same idleness about them. The water was their only focus. It was due to this that Shannon ended up beside Gabe. Not asking for permission, she untied his hands. He had to drink, too. He swung down off his horse, and his knees collapsed as he landed.

"Hey, leave him tied up," Cutter ordered, but there was no fire behind it.

"He can't hurt you. He can barely stand." Shannon crouched beside him, steadying him to keep him from falling forward onto his face.

His horse almost stepped on them as it made its way to the water. Shannon's mustang had waited, ground-tied where she left it, but when Gabe's horse went on, the mustang went, too. It flickered through Shannon's mind that the parson had a very gentle, well-trained horse. Why was he so grumpy about the poor animal?

"Let her take care of him. Why should we have to?" Ginger snipped as she rode her horse eagerly to the water's edge.

The Lloyds were right behind her, too thirsty to bother standing guard, let alone help.

"Let's get you some water." Shannon slid an arm around his waist with no idea how she'd get such a large man to his feet. His head was tipped forward as if he bordered on unconsciousness.

As soon as the Lloyds were well past, Gabe whispered, "I'm not that bad off." He tilted his head up just slightly so she could see the bright clarity of his eyes. "My hands are numb from being tied up all day. I need to get some feeling back into them. There's a knife in my boot, but I'm not sure I can hang on to it. I'm going to stay wobbly, hope they don't think I can do them any harm, which I probably can't right now. But let's drink slow, put off the time they tie me back up." Gabe worked his fingers, opening and closing them, trying to get the feeling back into them.

"You quit talking over there." Shannon turned to see Lurene drop to her knees beside where her horse drank from the stream. Though she'd shouted, she had the same careless attitude as the others. The water was too powerful a draw.

"He can't stand. Someone help me." Shannon did her best to sound pathetic. These outlaws seemed happiest when someone was hurting.

"You want him to have a drink, you figure out how to get him over here." Lurene cupped the cold, clear water in her hands and drank deeply.

Shannon's throat convulsed at the sight, sound, and smell of the rushing creek. "I'm going to help you up. Lean hard on me."

Gabe nodded. "Aim a little upstream of them. I'll stagger a little. Hopefully they'll think we had no choice in where we get our drink."

"Have you got a plan to get us out of here?" Shannon's heart began to pound with excitement.

"No."

That calmed her down.

"But I just want to be ready if a chance comes. I was in the cavalry for most of ten years. I'm not afraid of a fight. And Shannon"—Gabe looked at her, his dark eyes gleaming with regret—"they're almost surely going to—" His voice faltered.

"Kill us?" She knew that's what he didn't want to say.

"Yes. Get me up. That young one, he's watching."

Shannon wasn't sure how Gabe knew that. He didn't seem to be looking around. Pulling Gabe's arm around her neck, she was barely able to get to her feet, so heavily did Gabe lean. But not too heavily. Just enough to make it look really good.

"What's the matter with him?" Lurene asked. "He's been awake, riding all day."

"I don't know." Shannon took a few steps. "He's probably dizzy from the blow to his head."

Gabe stumbled and pulled Shannon sideways from the group. They made their way to the creek with a good amount of space between them and their captors. Shannon lowered Gabe to his knees. He bent to drink and wash his face, and Shannon did the same. She didn't have to pretend desperate thirst.

Shannon watched Gabe work his hands under the water, open and close them, massage them briskly while he appeared to be washing. She did her best to block everyone's view of him so they wouldn't realize just how alert he was.

Gabe drank deeply and sluiced water over his head and neck. Only because she was watching him so closely did she notice him reach for his boot, slip a slim knife out, and tuck it up his sleeve. "Maybe I can get my hands loose if they tie me up again."

"This narrow canyon leads to the place my father marked. Whatever we find up there, gold or not, they won't need me any longer. If they're going to kill us, we'll find out soon."

"What are you two talking about?" Lurene stood from where she'd leaned against a boulder, next to the creek. Her strength was obviously renewed by the rest.

"I'm just asking how he is, if I can do anything to help him."

The horses left the creek and began cropping the grass along the canyon.

"Let's move on. We can get through this canyon before full dark and maybe spend the night sleeping in a city of gold." Lurene's harsh laugh had a ring of madness to it.

Shannon held out no hope that she would survive this.

"No, too far." Cutter went to his horse and began stripping the leather. "We camp for the night and start early tomorrow."

Lurene looked as if she wanted to fight, force Cutter to move on, but the man started setting up camp. The dusk deepened, and finally Lurene growled and stalked toward her horse to unpack it.

"And then, we might just take Shannon back home and see if her family thinks she's worth paying to keep alive." Randy Lloyd stood, looking alert and suspicious. There'd be no taking him by surprise.

"My family? What do they have to do with this?"

Randy turned to catch the horses and led Shannon's and Gabe's to them. "Take care of your own horses. We can talk about ransom later."

A wild look at Gabe told Shannon he was as dumbfounded as she was. Shannon took the reins to both horses.

Randy left to deal with his own.

Gabe leaned close and touched Shannon's cheek with one finger. "That's good. It means they don't intend to kill you."

He kissed her quickly then turned away and staggered to his feet, the knife securely hidden. He got to his horse and nearly fell while uncinching the saddle. All a sham—Shannon hoped.

Shannon went to the sweet mustang and got to work. Ransom? What in the world? Did they plan to take her all the way back to St. Louis? Or did they plan to kill her and trick her mother into paying? One thing she knew, if these outlaws could find a way to make it easy on themselves, they would.

She determined then and there, she'd make it hard.

Twenty~Two

The sun rose straight overhead, and the day turned boiling hot. Just like all the rest of the days they'd spent on this fool's mission. Buck had a notion to find Shannon and turn her over his knee. Except if it wasn't for her obsession with this expedition, he'd never have met Tyra.

Buck hadn't gone all the way to the bluff yesterday. Setting up camp had been slow work.

"They should be back with the fish any minute. Get out of the way so I can get a fire going." Tyra swatted Buck on the shoulder.

He grinned at her. "I don't know much about building a fire, Miss Morgan, but I can learn. Just you watch me."

The smile she flashed him made Buck want to laugh out loud. He felt free in this place, with this woman, in a way he never had before. He took the few steps that separated him from Tyra and pulled her to her feet, away from the fire. "Just leave that alone. Listen to me, Tyra. Do you think—"

The soft whicker of a horse had him turning away from Tyra toward the mouth of the canyon that led into this place. "Maybe

Hance came back. We don't want him to catch me kissing you."

Tyra laughed softly. "Better Captain Hance than my pa."

Buck laughed, then the laugh died as a group of riders appeared through the narrow mouth of the canyon. How had they gotten horses down here when Hance hadn't been able to, and was that— "Shannon?" He took two uncertain steps toward her. "Shannon, you're here?"

"Buck! No, get out."

"Stay where you are." A bullet struck the ground inches in front of Buck. He jumped backward and sideways to put himself in front of Tyra.

An older man riding behind Shannon aimed. "Don't move again, or I'll shoot." The man cocked his gun, serious as a hanging. "Hands up where I can see them."

Buck looked over his shoulder to exchange a look with Tyra then faced the group approaching him. He raised his hands slowly, not wanting to startle anyone.

Shannon, now that he looked closer, was filthy. Trail worn of course—who wouldn't be? But her face was badly burned. Her hands trembled. One arm was in a sling. Tears filled her eyes. A man beside her had his hands tied to his pommel. Behind them rode the gunman, two women, and two other men.

"What's going on here?" Buck asked.

A dark-haired woman riding a length back between Shannon and the bound man said scornfully, "Miss Dysart here is leading us to a city of gold. It's supposed to be in this meadow, so where is it?"

Shannon shook her head. "We need to look. The basin is huge. There are hills it could be behind, bluffs it could be on top of. It's here. My father's map is clear that the city he was searching for is in this basin."

The city? Buck's stomach sank. That stupid city of gold was going to get them all killed. Who were these people, and how had they gotten their hands on Shannon?

"We're traveling down here to—to meet Shannon." The surprise had been too much. Buck now wished he hadn't let on that he knew Shannon, but there were still secrets to be kept.

Was there anything here to give away four people? They'd unpacked and spread things around enough that he didn't think it was obvious, though there were more supplies here than two people could possibly carry. They hadn't laid out any bedrolls, which would have given away that there were four people.

Lucas Morgan and Abe Lasley were tough western men. They'd be careful after hearing that shot. Buck just had to keep Shannon and Tyra alive until help could come or a chance showed itself to get free.

Considering Tyra was a lot more at home in the West than Buck or Shannon, he knew he wouldn't have to do it himself. Shannon's saddle partner looked as if he'd been hurt, so was that Gabe? Was that who Abe Lasley was looking for? It had to be.

"Can we get down?" Shannon asked. Her eyes burned into Buck's, and all he saw was regret. She blamed herself for the danger they were all in.

Good choice. Buck blamed her, too.

But she looked so tired and subdued, not his intrepid Shannon at all. It did no good to assign blame.

Later, when they were safe, he might have a few choice words for his lunatic friend.

Without waiting for permission, Shannon swung down using only her right hand. Her knees gave out, and Buck started forward.

"Stay back!" The dark-haired woman had her gun aimed straight at Buck's chest.

He hesitated and Shannon steadied herself.

"I'm fine, Bucky." Shannon rested her face against the saddle of her sturdy little black horse, her hands clinging to the pommel.

From behind his back he heard Tyra whisper, "Bucky?" then

give a very quiet snort. Tyra sounded like she was holding up pretty well if she had time to laugh at him.

Shannon drew in a slow breath, and her shoulders squared. Buck caught himself doing the same.

The others dismounted, all but the one tied to his saddle. Shannon slowly released her grip and turned to walk unsteadily to the man who must be Abe Lasley's brother.

Though Shannon's captors watched her, they let her untie Gabe. He seemed to slump sideways, and Shannon helped ease him to the ground, favoring her injured left arm. Upright, but with wobbly legs, she guided him to the fire Tyra had gotten crackling. A large boulder acted as a backrest for Gabe. Shannon mostly collapsed beside him.

"I don't see a city of gold around here anywhere." The dark-haired woman licked her lips as if the word *gold* had a taste to it. She crossed her arms as she looked across the expanse of the meadow.

Buck knew he had to react to that. The only person who could ignore it was someone who already knew the story. "City of gold? Down here? Where?" He looked around, hoping he had a bit of acting skill. He'd acted interested in all the things his mother talked about. *That* took some acting.

"We're just exploring the canyon." He didn't have to do much pretending to be cautious of these folks and their drawn guns. "We just got here. But there are bluffs and rock outcroppings big enough to hide a city, I suppose."

Buck thought of that Indian village Hance had spoken of. Could that be what Professor Dysart had found? The man had always been fascinated by history. It was possible he'd found ruins and considered them a treasure. But where did the gold come in? Buck had seen a lot of Shannon's notes. He occasionally had tried to get involved with the biggest passion of her life, to find a way to be included.

"Look folks, we didn't come down here mining or treasure hunting. We're not going to fight with you over any gold. We were getting ready to eat. We packed a lot of supplies down here." He felt more than saw Tyra go tense, afraid he'd mention her pa and Abe. "My—my *wife* and I were—well. . ."

Buck saw Shannon's brows arch at the word *wife*. Then the surprise was replaced by confusion and a quick glance at all their supplies. She was figuring it out. She knew he wasn't married, and she knew Buck wasn't down here alone with a young woman.

He hoped that she followed his thinking that he wasn't about to reveal that there were other people with them. "I'd heard Shannon talk about this place, and we wanted to do some wandering. We came down here, not really knowing if we'd find Shannon of course, but—but—"

"Join us for a meal." Tyra came to his side and took his hand in hers, adding to the tale of marriage. "Then go along with Shannon on her treasure hunt. We won't get in your way."

"I'm really glad you're down here." Lurene crouched across the fire from Gabe and Shannon. Her eyes slid from them to Buck.

"Why's that?" Tyra edged closer to Buck.

"Because we've been getting her cooperation by threatening to kill her friend."

Buck swallowed hard and looked at Gabe who had pulled his knees up. From this angle, Buck could tell he was working his fingers, no doubt numb from the rope. On this ride with Tyra, Abe, and Lucas, Buck had heard enough about Gabe, former cavalry officer, Wyoming rancher, to know he was a tough man. Probably not as beaten down as he appeared. Smart to encourage these villains to underestimate him.

"Trouble with killing him is once he's dead, how do we get her cooperation then?" Lurene leveled her gun straight at Tyra. "But if you know her, then we've got some spare prisoners. Might be a good idea to prove we mean business by shooting one of you right now."

For one heart-stopping moment, Buck thought the woman was going to do it. He braced himself to throw Tyra to the ground and block the bullet with his own body.

A harsh laugh erupted from the redheaded woman with the group. "Spare prisoners. And with plenty of food. Who'd've thought we'd find that down in this godforsaken place?"

Not godforsaken, Buck thought. Just the opposite. God was here. All the way down here. It settled his terror at the thought of that gun firing, bullets striking Tyra and ending forever her fiery spirit and flashing smile.

Keeping her gun level, Lurene said, "You, what's your name?"

"Tyra."

Buck heard the control in Tyra's voice. He suspected she was thinking hard right then. She was no shrinking maiden who got a fit of the vapors in the face of trouble. She was a tough woman, a good one to have in a fight. Probably had a better grasp of this mess than he did.

With grim humor, he thought that Tyra and Gabe would make a much better match than Tyra and him. Too bad.

"Let's scout around this place," Lurene barked at the others with her.

"Can't we eat first?" Ginger gave a longing look at all the packs. "We've been living on beef jerky and water for days."

"Take a quick look in the packs then, but only while the horses drink. And take any weapons you find."

Ginger, one of the younger men, and the older one began searching.

"A rasher of bacon, Lurene." Ginger held up a cloth-wrapped object. "Let's eat before we start hiking around."

"We're not going to sit around lazy while there might be gold close at hand." Lurene looked as if she'd cut Ginger's throat with little provocation. "Randy, you come over here and keep a gun on these four."

Randy was the youngest of the group. Buck wondered how a man, just a barely grown boy, ended up so far out in the wilderness, living by his gun. The gun stayed level, the aim true as he took over.

"Get over by that boulder so we can keep you covered." Randy gestured with the gun as casually as if it were an extension of his body. "And keep your mouths shut."

Buck held tight to Tyra's hand as he walked over to Shannon and sat down so Gabe was between them, Tyra on the end.

Randy's eyes dared them to speak a single word.

Buck noticed Tyra tilt the brim of her hat down as if to shade her eyes more fully from the sun. But the gesture made no sense since the sun had lowered past the rim of the canyon. Tyra had just signaled someone. Someone like her father or maybe Abe. Or both.

Buck was very careful not to react, but he braced himself for whatever came next.

Help had arrived if they could just figure out how best to make use of it.

Gabe was so happy to see his big brother he almost smiled. A grin wasn't the weak, wounded image he hoped to give to Lurene and her gang, so he suppressed it, but honestly, he was getting a little tired of acting like a weakling. He thought Abe might have a few remarks to make about that.

They had a fighting chance now. Gabe had also seen another man with Abe. Both of them had very carefully shown themselves. Tyra had reacted to let them know she saw them, and so had Gabe. He didn't think Bucky and Shannon had noticed, but that didn't matter. Neither of them was going to be much help when the fighting started.

"Let's go." Lurene took two long strides for her horse and

paused. "We've got seven horses and nine people." She glared at all of them as if deciding who to kill. "Randy, you stay here with that one." Lurene jerked her head toward Gabe. "Better to have 'em split up anyway."

Gabe's fingers were mostly working again. He knew because they were on fire. Working them, he went through in his head, over and over, how he'd strike. The knife. It was all he had. And he had a lot of people to protect. Bucky. . .what kind of stupid name was that for a man? And what in blazes was he doing in the bottom of the Grand Canyon? He'd popped up out of the ground like some stupid gopher.

Randy's eyes went cold. "I'm not staying behind while you find gold and maybe never come back for me."

It wasn't so bad Bucky was here. Convenient even. As soon as Gabe bested these outlaws, with his brother's help, he could have Shannon break things off with Bucky, and Gabe could hunt up Parson Ford and have him marry them then take her straight for Wyoming. After he had a nice visit with Abe of course. Shannon could write her snooty mother a letter explaining the situation.

Lurene jabbed a finger at the canyon they'd just threaded through. "That's the only way in and out. Where are we going to go except right past you?"

"How do I know that's the only way out?" Randy sounded cool.

Gabe would have preferred a hothead. He hoped his brother didn't underestimate any of these outlaws.

The woman Bucky had called his wife caught Gabe's attention when she pulled her hat off and slapped it on her leg. The movement was casual, something anyone might do. But it struck Gabe as deliberate. Who was she anyway? Abe was here. He'd have gotten Gabe's telegraph and come hunting to help. Maybe Abe had met Bucky and the girl on the trail somehow and dragged them along.

Bucky was clearly a greenhorn. The woman, however, looked comfortable in her western clothes in a way Shannon didn't. So maybe she was with Abe. But she was way too young for Abe's wife; Gabe had met her years ago. And too old to be one of Abe's children, not to mention his brother had only sons. Gabe shook off all these secondary matters as he mulled his choices.

Lurene turned on Randy. "You think I know my way *around* down here? I don't know of any other way back to the top of this pit but right out the canyon we came in through."

"But if you found another way out and had your hands on the gold, you'd risk it." Randy wasn't pleading or whining. He was telling the straight truth as he saw it, and it was a shame, because Gabe didn't blame Randy one bit for not agreeing to stay behind.

"With a city of gold," Lurene sneered. "What pocket am I going to stuff that into?"

If they left Randy and Gabe behind alone, he'd take care of Randy, team up with Abe, and be after Shannon and the rest in a couple of minutes.

"You'd go off in a second if you thought it would give you a bigger share of the gold."

And that, Gabe knew, was the bare truth. Lurene had a hunger in her eyes for gold that she couldn't hide. He suspected she intended to thin everyone out she could when it came time to split up any money and gold.

A few tense seconds passed.

"Who stays?" Lurene asked.

"I'm going," Darrel said. "I trust my brother to look after my share of anything you find, but I don't trust my brother alone with any of you. I'm going along to watch his back."

Honor among thieves. Gabe had never particularly believed that old saw, and nothing there was changing his mind.

Gabe really hoped it was Ginger. He thought she looked like the weakest link, and he could relieve her of her weapon hopefully without shooting. He'd been in a few battles in the cavalry, and he'd done some killing. He could do it again. But he was sorry he had the memory to live with. And he'd never so much as been in a fight that involved a woman. He didn't want any new memories to haunt him.

"We're all going," the older man said. "I don't trust none of you enough to leave you behind because I'd have to turn my back on you. The horses are worn thin, so leave 'em behind and go afoot."

"We're gonna hike this whole basin, Cutter?" Darrel asked.

Cutter. Gabe had all their names now. As far as he could tell, these weren't known desperados. Shannon had brought them west with her. But at least Cutter seemed comfortable in the West. He might have changed his name ten times.

"No, we're not gonna hike the whole basin. If I were setting up a city in this place"—Cutter jabbed his finger at a bluff a mile or so away—"I'd put it right there."

It was a likely spot. Had a good overlook to the canyon entrance for defensive purposes. Water flowed near to hand. It was a bluff with steep walls, hard for anyone to launch a sneak attack. Raised land to keep them above a flood. Woodland nearby that would make for good hunting. Yes, a likely place.

"Unless you've got more on those maps of yours." Lurene aimed her gun straight at Shannon's chest. It always came back to Shannon.

"No, my father's maps led me to this canyon. That's where he stopped. This is where he said he'd found his treasure."

Gabe looked at the bluff with the flat crown. He couldn't see what lay on top of it. He wondered whether they really were on the verge of discovering an ancient city of gold.

"If we skirt the basin, we can get out of the heat." Gabe tried to look wobbly. Between that and the brutal power of the afternoon sun, maybe he could lead them into the woods. The woods where his brother even now lay in wait.

Lurene gave a jerk of her head that meant she was hot enough to go along with Gabe's request. "You first, Miss Dysart." Lurene had her gun aimed straight at Shannon.

They headed for the woods. Getting that sun off of Gabe's head really did help. His brain started working as they threaded through the trees. Shannon was in the lead with Lurene. Ginger walked along with Darrel next to her. The two seemed connected, a twosome within the gang. Then Buck followed with Tyra at his side.

Randy was next, then Gabe, with Cutter at his back. Gabe would rather have had anyone else. But if Abe started picking people off from the back of this line, having Cutter go down first would be for the best.

Gabe saw Tyra whisper a few words to Buck, and the sudden tension in Buck's shoulders told Gabe the citified man now knew rescue was at hand. He clearly was not married to Tyra. They'd never have ridden down here alone together if they weren't married, but it made sense that the man with Abe was some kin of Tyra's to make things proper. But why'd they bring a woman along on this trip in the first place? To cook maybe?

The woods were thicker than Gabe had dared to hope. They walked into a grove that lined the basin all the way to the bluff. The very place Gabe had seen Abe. Gabe moved slower and slower, putting space between him and Randy. Cutter didn't shove at his shoulders, which told Gabe the man was tired and had relaxed his usual razor-sharp vigil. But the shade was helping them all revive.

It must have helped Lurene, because she stopped and grabbed Shannon's arm, turning her to face everyone. "Get up here. Stay close." A wide spot in the trail let them all walk to where she waited for them.

With a sinking stomach, Gabe knew his brother couldn't attack them when they were bunched together. Yes, he and the other prisoners would help, and they had a fair chance of winning this fight, but blood would be shed. Not all of it outlaw blood. And Lurene was strung tight as piano wire, and she had the look of someone who had a hunger to kill. Gabe was sorely afraid Shannon would die first.

As they walked up, Lurene held her ground until they were a tight knot. "We've got five guns on four prisoners," Lurene said. "I want to make dead sure you're all aware of that. If there's any trouble, I unload my gun into Miss Dysart here first."

Lurene seemed to enjoy the snide way she called Shannon Miss Dysart. A reminder, Gabe imagined, that Shannon had originally hired her, and now Lurene was the one in charge.

But if there was no gold on top of that bluff, which Gabe suspected there wasn't, he wondered if the woman would ever realize that she'd have been a lot better off just doing honest work, taking the pay Shannon had offered her, and then going on to another honest job.

"Darrel, you're for Bucky here."

Darrel nodded.

"Call me Buck."

Gabe mentally rolled his eyes, though he had to admit Buck was a better name.

"I'll take the girl." Ginger looked at Tyra with cold eyes.

"I'll keep my eye on Gabe here," Cutter offered.

Lurene jerked her chin in cold satisfaction. "Randy, we've got a spare. You just keep your eyes open and help whoever might need it."

"Done." Randy smirked, clearly knowing he'd been assigned the job of nothing.

Lurene turned to Shannon. "A city of gold, dead ahead, right?"

Shannon's lips trembled. "My father was searching for a city of gold, Lurene, but when he talked of what he found, he used the word *treasure*. You saw those ruins in the cliffs. Father called that a treasure, too, and had it marked on the map. I hope that this second location is the real city of gold. I've been hoping that those cliff dwellings were the place the priests first settled with their gold, then they moved on and found a place where they could hide their city better, down here. But we have to prepare ourselves for a different kind of treasure."

Shannon's gaze lifted to Gabe's. He saw in her eyes that she'd finally figured it out. She'd realized that this dream of hers was a tale of heaven. Streets paved with gold. But she hadn't been able to give up on such a place existing here on earth.

Her jaw firmed as she looked directly into his eyes. "I dragged you, Gabe." Then her eyes took in the rest, all of them, even the outlaws. "I dragged all of you off the edge of the world, into this beautiful valley, and we've found nothing. And I finally understand."

Gabe would love one minute alone with her. To hold her and tell her he was glad he'd come, all but this last part. "I wasn't searching for gold, Shannon, but I'm glad I came." A smile quirked his lips. "All except for the guns of course."

"Shut up and let's get moving." Lurene jabbed her revolver into Shannon's side.

Flinching from the pain, Shannon said, "Yes, we'll go, but I just want all of you to know I finally understand. I've given up years of my life to find this fabled city, and now that we're close to the last place it could be, I realize I don't even want it."

"Well, I do." Lurene licked her lips as if she could taste the gold.

"God was wise to promise paradise after death as a blessing for faith during this life. What good will a city of gold do any of us?"

"It will let me live as I choose."

"What life do you hate so much that you're driven to kill to escape it?" Shannon asked the woman.

"A life like none you've ever known." Lurene cocked her

gun and lifted it to press against Shannon's temple. "And I am willing to risk death to escape. The only reason you're still alive, now that we're here, is because of the chance of ransom." Then that ugly gun swung from Shannon and stopped, aimed at Tyra, then moved on to Bucky, then on until it was dead centered on Gabe's heart. "And the only reason they're still alive is because you're cooperating. As soon as you try something I don't like, one of them dies."

Lurene's smile made a shiver of fear crawl up Gabe's back, and he wondered for the first time if Lurene wasn't completely sane. She was crazy for gold, but could she be just plain crazy? Her smile told him yes.

"I'm going to cooperate," Shannon said quickly. "But if there's no gold up there, my friends here will not be harmed. You'll need me to write notes or something to prove to my mother you've kidnapped me. You can't force me to write a thing, and I won't if any of them get hurt."

Lurene's smile faded. "As for that, we'll just see, won't we? If I kill one of them, will you really get stubborn and let them all die? Or will you do anything to save the last two of them?"

"I don't need money," Shannon said.

"Lucky you."

"And I'm not interested in fame like my father was."

Lurene shrugged.

"My father cared about that, but now that he's dead, restoring his reputation wouldn't touch him in any way."

"My father's dead, too, and good riddance."

Gabe heard only pain and hate in Lurene's voice.

"My mother, well, arrogance and superiority have been bred into her very bones, and that has only been nourished by her overindulged life. She may well give you money to save me, but I can't do anything to make her care about me."

"My mother started selling me to men when I was still a

child." Lurene's cold voice didn't conceal the pain. "Tell me again how bad your mother is?"

"I turned my back on Bucky, in St. Louis, then Gabe here in Arizona Territory."

Gabe looked at Bucky and Bucky looked back, his brows arched in surprise.

"And all for gold I neither need nor want." Shannon's expression was so serene it lifted Gabe's heart regardless of their circumstances.

"It's very possible," she went on, "I'll be walking those streets of gold in heaven before I'm done with all of this madness." Looking squarely at Gabe, she said, "I believe you called this a fool's errand."

"I did."

"Well, you were right, and Bucky"—she turned to him—"you used similar words a few times. I just want to tell you that, whether we find it or not, I'm sorry. I've finally realized that, but much too late." She turned to face the butte ahead. "Let's go see what's up there." Her quiet talk, the peace in her voice, had taken the edge off all of them.

With a single tug on Shannon's arm, Lurene took the lead. Ginger and Darrel walked behind Lurene. The rest of them stretched out. Buck and Tyra walked in single file followed by Randy, Gabe, and Cutter. There wasn't a real trail here in the forest, but the trees were close together, and though Lurene kept right to Shannon's side, the rest of them walked one by one. It was easier.

Gabe realized Tyra was lagging, just as he was, stringing out their little parade.

The trail curved ahead, and a clump of heavy underbrush blocked Gabe's sight of Shannon and Lurene. His nerves itched having her out of view. Then Ginger and Darrel vanished, then Buck rounded the trail, next Tyra, then Randy.

A dull thud from right behind Gabe told him his brother had arrived. He glanced back and smiled.

"You take the one in front of you," Abe whispered so quietly it was barely more than a soft hiss in the breeze.

Abe and an older man dragged the big man off the trail. Within seconds the older man reappeared wearing Cutter's shirt and vest. The old man wasn't as broad as Cutter but the same height, and with his hat pulled low, someone would have to look close to notice the switch. Abe vanished.

The brood of Lasley brothers had grown up making a game out of ghosting around in the woods. Abe was always the best at it. Abe's friend was real good, too, and of course Cutter wasn't going to make any noise.

With no one at his back, Gabe could handle Randy, but he had to do it quietly. He hurried to close the distance.

It was time to put an end to this.

Twenty~Three

---✿---

Pa was here.

Tyra bit back a smile and focused on the couple in front of Buck, leaving Randy to the men. She waited until she heard a dull thud and a groan of pain that was cut off instantly, then glanced back to see Abe falling into line wearing Randy's Stetson. She looked quickly away before she could smile. Two down, three to go.

Picking up speed, she reached Buck's side, her eyes sharp on Ginger, Darrel, and Lurene. Lurene was the only one with her gun out. The others had relaxed, leaving Lurene's threats to hold their prisoners in line.

Swallowing, Tyra brushed her hand against Buck's. His eyes seemed to burn into Shannon. Which made Tyra a little annoyed. Had seeing his old friend reminded him of why he wanted to marry her? Well, too bad. She was keeping him.

She bumped his hand again and again, but he kept looking straight ahead. So she punched him in the side. That got his attention. He clutched his belly and glared at her. She caught his arm and kept him moving forward. She jerked her head back, and he glanced behind. Tyra looked, too, and saw Abe give him a little salute.

Buck turned forward and, propelled by Tyra, they closed the gap between themselves and the redheaded woman and her boyfriend. The men behind them closed the gap, too.

Something, maybe just the sound of footsteps closer, drew a look from the redhead. Those beady eyes went past Tyra and Buck. She felt more than saw Abe shift a bit, using Tyra's body to block a clear view of him.

Tyra held her breath, afraid Cinnamon or Ginger or Red Pepper, whoever, would notice they'd changed the makeup of the outlaws, but the woman wasn't really checking for details. She just bounced a look off the men trailing and went back to eyes forward.

Breathing again, Tyra moved closer, kept a tight grip on Buck—much as she liked him, she really hoped he'd let her pa and Abe handle this—and prayed that a bend in the path they trod would take Lurene out of sight for just a few seconds. Then they'd dispense with Darrel and Nutmeg and turn their attention to Lurene. They'd have to move fast. No one could masquerade as the redhead.

A huge boulder ahead took Lurene off to one side. Tyra held her breath as hands on her shoulders that she was pretty sure were Abe's guided her to one side. Buck was also eased aside just as Lurene vanished ahead.

The Lasley brothers leaped forward and grappled with the pair. Tyra jumped forward, snatched Ginger's gun from its holster, and gave her a sound whack on the head with the butt. Her pa silenced the man in the same ruthless fashion. The two were tied up as fast as any new calf at branding time and dragged off the trail in silence. The men all rushed forward as silently as possible but knew they had seconds to finish this—overpower

Lurene before she realized all her cohorts had been dispatched.

They rounded the boulder to find Lurene standing with her arm around Shannon's neck about twenty paces past the big rock. "Stop, all of you, right where you are." Lurene looked at them, studying Pa and Abe, realizing she was badly outnumbered.

"Give up, Lurene. Your gang's all been taken care of."

"No, go get 'em. Let 'em loose. Do it now or she dies."

"They're dead." That was pa talking, and Tyra shivered a bit when he said it because it sounded true. Mean and true even though Tyra knew it wasn't.

"There's no getting them, Lurene. It's you out here alone with us." Gabe stepped forward. "All of us. You can't kill us all."

"Yes, I can. I've got six bullets, and there are six of you."

"We're all armed." Tyra noticed Gabe had a gun. It was just a little annoying that her pa hadn't given her one. "We're not going to stand here while you unload your gun. You'll die if you start firing. You'll kill, and then you'll die. None of that has to happen. Let Shannon go and give up."

"No!" Lurene's hand trembled.

Tyra's breath caught at the thought of that shaky hand on the trigger.

"You've got no choice." Gabe's voice rang with authority. He took two steps forward.

Lurene took two back. "I won't go back." Lurene sounded crazed. Her hand tightened on Shannon's neck. "And if you killed Cutter and the others, then you'll kill me."

Shannon fought against Lurene's grip. "Please, I can't— can't—breathe."

"Stop fighting me, or I start shooting. I'll start with your man, too."

Shannon quit struggling. Tyra saw her fight to take each breath.

"Lurene, what are you going to do if you kill us all?" Gabe

asked. "Can you even get out of this canyon by yourself? Can you find the way back to the rim? What good does a city of gold do if you're trapped down here with it? It's worthless."

"I can find my way out." Lurene's eyes shifted like those of a cornered rat. "And when I do, that gold will save me."

Gabe shook his head. "Gold can't do that."

Suddenly a look of such rage crossed Lurene's face that Tyra braced herself for flying lead.

"You have my word we won't harm you." Gabe took another step forward, his hands raised. "We'll even go on to the city. If there's gold there, we can. . .can give you a brick or two of it, as much as you want. We can help you get it out of here. You can live the rest of your life on that gold and never go back to your old life."

"No one gives gold away, and why settle for a brick of it when I can have a whole city full?" Lurene suddenly released her hold on Shannon's neck and grabbed her hair. She pulled backward, glancing to see where she was headed, but only for an instant each time, bringing her attention back to the onlookers too quickly to give anyone an opening to stop her.

"Lurene, wait!" Gabe took a step toward her, now past the edge of the boulder that would provide shelter if Lurene opened fire. Tyra wanted to yell at him to come back, but she knew Gabe wouldn't have listened.

"Stay back or I'll kill her." Lurene sounded near panic, crazy enough to kill for sure.

Gabe froze in place. Tyra had heard so much about what a kid Gabe was. The baby of the family. A whiner. She didn't see a bit of that in him. He'd been in the cavalry and had been promoted to officer over the years. A leader of men. Someone who made hard decisions fast. He took charge here as naturally as if he'd been doing it all his life.

She remembered that she'd intended to marry him and knew

he'd be a better choice for her than Buck. No, it was *Bucky*. What a name. A city man. Not a good match for her at all. What had she been thinking to let herself get so wrapped up in a man who was so wrong for her? It pinched to admit it, but Bucky belonged with Shannon, and neither of them belonged out here.

"Maybe it'd be too long a chance to kill six armed people with six bullets, but I can sure as certain kill one." Lurene pulled Shannon back slowly, steadily, with an occasional look behind her. A cautious woman, but terrified and sick with gold fever.

Lurene passed a clump of underbrush then rounded a tree. She took two more steps and disappeared from view.

Gabe surged forward, everyone else right behind him running to keep Lurene in sight.

When they got around that tree, Lurene was gone.

Lurene dragged Shannon behind a clump of aspen trees. A chasm opened in front of them. They went over the edge.

Lurene's arm stayed clamped to Shannon's neck, cutting off any sound. The slope was rocky but slanted enough that they didn't fall so much as slide. They quit sliding in time for Shannon to look up and hear running footsteps rush by twenty feet overhead.

Shannon tried to scream. Lurene's arm tightened on her neck until Shannon's vision began to go dark.

Lurene pulled the sling off Shannon's arm with rough jerks. It hurt, but the arm was healing. Shannon needed her arm to be free anyway.

Lurene used Hozho's old shawl to gag Shannon before she could gather her wits together sufficiently to call for help. The footsteps of her rescuers faded, racing past.

"You haven't forgotten I promised to kill a few of those folks, have you?" Lurene hissed in Shannon's ear. "You leave that gag in place or I'll tie your arms. We'll follow along the bottom of this cut. It leads in the right direction."

Lurene stood, her gun aimed with trembling hands, and Shannon got to her feet.

Nearly sagging with despair, Shannon stumbled forward. She had no idea where Gabe and the others had gone.

What in the world was Bucky doing down here? It was too strange to consider, so Shannon turned her thoughts from it. She worked her arm carefully, stretching the elbow that hadn't moved much in days. It hurt, but Shannon could use it.

Goaded by the gun, Shannon picked up speed. There were heavy trees at the top of the cut and a lot of underbrush down here. An occasional thin spot in the trees showed the butte they headed for. Shannon tried to remember if there'd been open space between the trees and the butte. Surely they'd have to get out in the open to climb the steep hillside. Shannon and Lurene would reveal themselves, and Gabe would come for her.

The crevasse shallowed as they moved. A trickle of water gushed out of a crack and formed a small stream. They rushed along beside the flowing water, Lurene never missing a chance to shove. She hit Shannon's sore shoulder, and Shannon was soon nearly running to keep Lurene from inflicting more pain.

The gentle water was joined by another spring, then another. The rivulet became a fast-moving creek. Shannon listened frantically for a sign of Gabe or any one of the crowd of strangers Bucky had brought along. With a disgruntled huff, Shannon thought of how all of them had managed to get themselves free while leaving her in Lurene's clutches.

The little ditch they moved along was soon only shoulder high. Though the trees still lined it, Shannon took frequent glances through the underbrush to try and catch sight of her rescuers. They'd vanished. Finally, the twisting ditch revealed the butte right in front of them. Shannon reached the base, and as they came up from what was left of the crevasse, Shannon nearly fell into a gaping black hole in the ground down which the stream cascaded.

She skidded. Lurene shoved her forward. Shannon's feet slipped on rock made slick by the running water. She slid straight for the pit yawning at her feet.

"Where did they go?" Gabe slammed the side of his fist into a tree trunk and whirled around to look at the five people who were fanned out behind him.

Bucky might not have a brain in his head, but the rest of them shaped up to be tough. And they'd all been fooled.

"We have to go back." Tyra turned to look in the direction they'd come. "We moved too fast and missed where they veered off."

Gabe had figured out who she was. Tyra was only a child when he'd been visiting before, but she'd grown into a beautiful woman. The business of her being married to Bucky was all a lie.

They'd nearly reached the base of the bluff. Gabe, along with the rest of them—except Bucky—searched for a trail. "They couldn't have just vanished."

"Lurene couldn't have gotten to the top yet." Abe studied the broad scope of what lay before them. The trees stopped at the base of the butte, all except a few, slender, gnarled pines that clung to the sides of the sheer slope. The land seemed wide open. "And we'd see them if they were climbing."

"I don't know." Lucas Morgan's eyes were sharp, savvy. Gabe remembered him. Abe's father-in-law. Lucas Morgan had knowing eyes. He'd been in this rugged country longer than any of them. "The ground can look smooth and hide a lot. There are cuts in the side of that thing, maybe caves in it. We're just guessing that Lurene'll take Shannon to the top."

"I don't think she's sane enough to wait." Bucky stared up that steep hill. "That woman can only see the gold."

"Should we go up there and wait?" Tyra asked. "That's where they're heading, even if they picked a route we don't see. Let's go up and lie in wait for them."

"No, they have to be in these woods." Gabe shook his head. "We can't just climb up there and sit around resting and hope Lurene brings Shannon up unharmed."

"I think we should scout our trail." Abe looked at the woods.

Lucas scowled. "We need to walk along the base of this butte. If we're sure they're headed this way, we can lie in wait and catch Lurene when she's busy hanging on to Shannon while she climbs that butte."

They all stared at each other.

"Well, we can't just stand here talking." Bucky swung his arms wide in exasperation. "Since everybody's got an idea, let's split up."

Gabe didn't like it. "I'd like to face her with all of us."

"We had her outnumbered before and it didn't stop her," Bucky snarled. He looked ready to explode.

Gabe knew how he felt. No answer was the best. Lurene wasn't rational, and under those circumstances, she could do anything. No possible way Lurene had climbed up here. Gabe had set a slow but steady pace, searching for tracks, but they'd come straight here. Finally, Gabe looked between Lucas and Gabe. Then Gabe jerked his chin, deciding for all of them to. . .do what Bucky suggested. "Abe, you're the best tracker. You go back to where we lost her and find out what happened."

Abe didn't even pause for one second to taunt Gabe about giving orders to a big brother. He nodded and rushed toward the trees.

"Scout the base of this hill, Lucas. See if there's a place they could have gone up that would give them cover."

Lucas rushed toward the bluff and was gone before Gabe thought to tell him to take Bucky or Tyra or both. So, since he didn't want to leave Tyra alone, though she seemed savvy, and leaving Bucky was like staking a baby out on a hill of fire ants, he decided they'd come with him.

"Bucky, you and Tyra. . ."

"The name's Buck, all right?"

Gabe really wanted to shut Bucky's mouth with a fist, but that might not be all that fair. For one thing, Gabe was about halfway to a raving lunatic with worry about Shannon. And for another, a man had a right to name himself. "Fine, *Buck*, you and Tyra come with me. I'm going to the top of that bluff." He jabbed his finger straight at the place where all this would either turn into a discovery the likes of which the world had never seen—a lost city of gold—or end in blazing gunfire, blood, and death.

The worst part was it might end with both.

Buck strode straight for the steep sides of the butte.

"But we're not going up right here."

Buck stopped and turned, glaring. "Why not?"

"Because, greenhorn, I want to get to the far side and come up from that direction so we don't pop up there right in the line of Lurene's gun."

"Are you done giving orders? Can we go?" The tense corners of Buck's curled-down mouth told Gabe he needed to move.

"Yes, let's go."

They set a fast pace around the butte, though Shannon had to be afraid. But it was the best way to get up there without dying and getting Shannon killed in the process.

Gabe led, but Buck kept up. As they moved along, Buck drew even and the two of them eyed each other.

"So, you and Shannon seem close." Buck glared.

Gabe didn't blame him. Then Tyra came up so that Buck was between them. Looking past the city boy, he said, "I remember meeting you before. You were still a kid."

Tyra managed a smile, but she was just as worried as any of them.

"You've sure turned into a pretty woman, Tyra. What happened that you got stuck coming along with your pa and Abe?"

The smile softened, and Tyra met his eyes for a long second. Then her tanned cheeks pinked up and her eyes went shy and dropped to her toes, even as she kept walking. An embarrassed little shrug was her only answer.

Gabe remembered more about the little girl. She had a sassy mouth and was always underfoot. She'd given him a few dreamy looks that had made him real nervous. By the end of his visit, he'd started keeping solid space between him and his brother's pretty little sister-in-law. And Gabe knew why she'd come. And he also knew she was a lot better fit for him than Shannon Dysart.

A grunt of disgust that didn't even pretend to be polite escaped from Buck's throat. What in the world did that mean? Why would Buck come halfway across the country hunting for Shannon and now care if Gabe had any ideas about Tyra?

The city boy seemed to think he could stake a claim on all the women in this whole canyon.

Clawing at the ground, Shannon lost her footing and landed hard on her back. She grabbed at a bush as she went over the ledge of the black hole.

For one sickening moment she dangled. One of her feet kicked the side of the chasm, and the noise echoed and echoed forever. The water poured over her hands. Her grip was precarious. Her shoulder protested. Then one foot caught on a ledge of rock no wider than her thumb. But it was solid. She shifted her grip then boosted herself up and rolled onto the ground, safe.

From flat on her back, she looked up at Lurene and saw the woman smirk. She hadn't jumped in to help. She'd never lowered her gun.

Shannon hadn't made a sound thanks to the gag Lurene

had knotted over her mouth. Now she wanted to launch herself straight at her captor, but her shoulder hurt badly enough she didn't. She wondered if her knees would give out if she did attack.

Looking back at the cave, Shannon saw it spread wider. A crack on the ground that reached for twenty feet along the foundation of the butte. Shannon listened to the water rain down into that crack. She couldn't hear it land below, as if the hole reached all the way into the heart of the earth. She halfway expected steam heat to come pouring back out when the water hit the blazing hot core where the devil made his home.

Lurene dragged Shannon to her feet and gave her a little shove toward the black hole.

"Deep," Lurene whispered into Shannon's ear. "A bottomless pit." A rough laugh sent a chill of fear crawling up Shannon's spine.

"Maybe I'll just throw you into it. You say that city of gold is up there?" Lurene pointed with her gun. "Why do I need you anymore?"

Gagged, Shannon could only listen and pray Lurene would decide she might still need Shannon's help.

"I'll save it for later, huh?" Lurene pulled Shannon roughly away from the hole. "Let's climb."

They moved on past the pit until Shannon saw the place she knew they'd climb. She was in trouble. The cut they'd been walking along went all the way up the butte. It was steep and it'd be a scramble to get to the top, but they'd be able to do it in this narrow slit without anyone seeing them. And when they got to the top, there'd be no city of gold. Shannon had admitted that to herself now.

Bishops. Ships full of gold. Quivera. Cibola. The bottom of the Grand Canyon.

It was all outlandish. All a myth. And she'd given it two years of her life. Worse yet, her father had given it all of his. Even more devastating, she'd brought deadly danger to her friends—all for a myth.

"We're here," Lurene spoke into Shannon's ear. "We go up this hill and we find my gold or you die."

Shannon thought Lurene's voice sounded barely sane. If the woman would remember there was another chance at wealth—ransom—maybe she wouldn't just reach the summit and, when no gold was there, start shooting.

Lurene shoved Shannon hard enough to knock her to her hands and knees. "Start climbing and keep quiet."

The rocks scraped Shannon's knees and the palms of her hands. Her shoulder was aching until Shannon didn't know when it might simply give out. The smell of her sweat seasoned with terror swamped her senses. The gag threatened to suffocate her if she didn't carefully draw breaths in through her nose.

Shannon went up about ten feet, glad she was crawling. The steep bank wouldn't allow for anything else. Another ten feet, and she took a quick glance back. Surely Lurene had to holster her gun. But that peek wasn't enough to see Lurene's hands. Shannon would throw herself backward. They'd fall. Shannon could fight for Lurene's gun. The climb up was steep but not too high, maybe a hundred feet. But a hundred feet was enough to kill. If Shannon waited much longer, the fall would be too much. Neither of them would live through it. Bracing herself to turn and dive at Lurene, a sudden blow to the head stopped her.

"I saw that look, and I know what you're thinking." Lurene caught a handful of Shannon's hair and wrenched her head back so far her neck bowed and Shannon could see Lurene, her eyes blazing with lunacy.

"You think you can fight me and win, rich girl?" Lurene jerked on Shannon's hair until she felt it ripping from her head. "I've been fighting all my life. Every day is a fight. Every man I've taken money from was a fight. Some nights just staying alive while they sweated over me was a fight."

The arch of her neck felt as if it would snap Shannon's spine. "I killed them all in my head, but never for real. I knew I'd die for it if I killed even the worst of them for real. But I have it in me, building up for years. I'd welcome the chance to kill you with my bare hands. If you attack me, I'll do it and love it. In case you think different, I'm doing just fine climbing with one hand and holding my gun in the other." Lurene shoved the muzzle of her gun at Shannon to prove it. "So you just keep climbing if you want to live."

The only trouble with that was this nightmare wasn't going to end any way except in death. Fighting Lurene now or after they found a pile of rocks instead of gold. The only difference between now and later was that it was later.

Shannon found she wanted to live. She wanted it enough to keep climbing. Keep hoping. Put off the fight to the death even another hour.

The gag kept Shannon from speaking. A warm trickle down Shannon's neck was heavier and warmer than sweat. Blood. A cut from that blow of Lurene's gun.

Shannon nodded, and Lurene shoved her away, releasing her.

Reaching ahead, Shannon began to climb again. Her knees hurt. Shannon felt a nail tear against the rocks she gripped. She felt a well of tears fill her eyes, but they didn't fall. Maybe it was too much effort.

A stretch in the bluff wall became so steep, Shannon felt as if she was mountain climbing instead of crawling up a slope. A grip overhead barely big enough for her fingertips caved, and Shannon slid backward amid a cloud of dust and falling rocks. Only the gag kept her from screaming.

Lurene blocked her and stopped the fall.

Shannon looked at the woman, exhausted now. Why had she bothered to save Shannon's life? Maybe her instincts, at their most basic, weren't murderous.

"Get going. Move."

Shannon noticed Lurene didn't have her gun out now, but it no longer mattered. They were too high. A fall now would kill them both.

Shannon doggedly turned and went on up. Her lungs filled with the gritty, dirty air kicked up by her fall, and she thought she might smother. As soon as she was ahead of Lurene, she surreptitiously moved her gag below her bottom lip, not so much to cry for help as simply to breathe. She continued upward until she finally reached the top of the butte, and with a final heave, Shannon rolled over the edge and sprawled on her back, gasping for breath.

Lurene appeared on the rim, eyeing Shannon. As soon as she gained the top of the bluff, she pulled her gun and sat up, panting and wiping sweat from her eyes. Shannon noticed the woman had a canteen.

"Water." Shannon didn't even have the energy to beg.

Lurene looked at the canteen and seemed surprised to see it slung over her neck and shoulder. She only had it because she'd been carrying it ever since they'd left camp.

A deep drink for herself first, then Lurene handed the water over. She gathered herself to stand and look across the flat top of the butte. Shannon realized this was the moment, but she put off looking. She finished a long drink, seeing no reason to deny herself the lukewarm liquid at this point. At last she lowered the canteen and turned to see. . .something.

"There's nothing." Lurene's head dropped until her chin rested on her chest. The total despair Shannon saw in the woman's eyes was wrenching. Then Lurene raised her gun, and that despair had a different feel to it. The feel of a woman with no hope and nothing to lose and a world of hate in her heart.

Shannon looked back at this place she'd come to, very likely the last thing she'd ever see in this life, and again saw— "No, there's something here." Shading her eyes with one hand, Shannon studied the line of rocks straight ahead. "Those weren't left there by nature. Someone was building up here."

"Rocks. They built with rocks not gold." Lurene's voice echoed her hopelessness.

"Look closer." Every thought of Lurene and her threats and her gun receded to nothing. "Yes, maybe they built with rocks, but maybe. . .maybe there was some gold, too."

Shannon's pulse quickened. "Maybe there are pots or bits of gold jewelry. Not a whole city, but my father said he found a treasure in this basin." Shannon saw Lurene leveling her gun and talked fast. Shannon refused to die when she might be this close to vindicating her father. In fact, the way she saw it, her father had already proven his theory. Gold or not, he'd found ancient ruins. He'd found history that needed to be studied and recorded. And that amounted to treasure.

"Please, just wait before you start shooting." Shannon started toward the nearest line of stones. If Lurene wanted to shoot, Shannon probably couldn't stop her, so she'd get closer, get a glimpse before she died. "I'd given up on my father. But maybe I was too quick. Maybe it's up here after all."

Striding forward, Shannon knew they'd found it. A city, at the very bottom of the earth. The stones, though crumbled, were clearly in a rectangle about the length and width of a modest home. There was even a spot with no stones where a door could have been.

"Is it ancient though?" Shannon asked herself. "Could there have been others here, Hozho's people, the Supai or Havasupai? Hozho had called them both."

"What are you talking about?" Lurene came up beside her, but Lurene was looking at the stone foundation, too.

"Hunt around. Maybe there's gold, Lurene. I promise you I'll let you have it. I just want to live to write about this. The gold is yours. We'll help you get out of here and find a safe place." Shannon couldn't really make that promise for Gabe or any of the others. But maybe Lurene, if she got a gold cup or plate, would see the sense of not having a murder charge against her. And maybe she'd realize getting out of this place was a big task for one woman alone. Maybe survival, with or without gold, would triumph over whatever demons tormented her.

Shannon stood and paced the length of the house. Around twenty feet long and half as wide. Looking off across the flat land, dotted with widely scattered scrub brush, Shannon saw another one. She rushed toward it, thinking to find a village. Before she'd gone past the next foundation, she saw a piece of curved rock that didn't look natural. Dropping to her knees, she saw a pattern on the rock, and carefully she brushed at it and uncovered a broken bowl. "Lurene, look at this! They did leave things behind."

Coming up beside Shannon, Lurene crouched beside her. "That's not gold."

Smiling despite the situation, Shannon said, "We've only been here a few minutes, and we've already found signs of houses and proof that they worked in pottery. They could have metal here, too. And these houses, they aren't like the hogans back at the Kinlichee settlement. These aren't Indian buildings. Well, I mean, they could be, but I think they're more similar to the cabins built by nonnative people. Like maybe, just maybe, a group of travelers from far away."

"The city of gold?" Lurene asked in wonder.

Looking at Lurene and seeing a decent bit of rationality, Shannon said, "It stands to reason that there was never a whole city built of gold. That's the kind of legend that grows and grows. But gold artifacts. Plates and chalices. Statues, jewelry, crosses, and other sacred objects. Those might be here. And if someone came all the way down here to hide, where else would they go? Where else would be safer than this?"

"It is surely the ends of the earth." Lurene reached for the pottery shard.

Shannon had to resist the urge to protect the precious artifact from Lurene, but Shannon let her take it. The woman was calmer, but it wouldn't take much to set her off in a rage.

Lurene stared at the broken bowl. It had a reddish color to it, with badly faded black stripes that were the attempt someone made to add a pretty touch to an everyday object. "Okay." Lurene's eyes slid back from the edge of madness, and she looked determined but rational. "Let's search some more. Let's see if there's any gold."

Shannon caught Lurene's arm, gently. She didn't want the woman to think it was an attack, but she needed her full attention. "I don't know what kind of life you had back in St. Louis. You've said enough for me to know it was bad, a life you hated and will go to any lengths never to return to, but what we've found here is important."

Lurene looked away from Shannon at the lines of stone, and Shannon saw skepticism.

"It is. This is an *expedition* if you'll remember. I started this to follow my father's maps and find his treasure."

"Treasure." Lurene looked at the pottery and made a sound of disgust and shoved the bowl back at Shannon.

Fumbling to hang on to the precious object, Shannon managed to get the bowl cradled in her hands without dropping or breaking it. "Yes, treasure. You were part of a scientific expedition that took us to the bottom of the Grand Canyon. You've done a lot of hard work to get here hoping to find vast wealth, but if you'll only see, this is a kind of wealth." Shannon held out the bowl.

"And I can let you help me get the story told about what we found. I can help you find honest work you'll like. I'm willing to help you find a better life. Please, the real treasure we've been searching for is knowledge, and you've got as much of it about this place as I do. You're a witness to a huge discovery. What you've seen and learned has value. Give a different life a chance, please."

"No, if I go back, I'm trapped."

"Then we won't go back. I can help you start a new life somewhere else. Anywhere else. No one needs to know how you've lived, what you got trapped into as a child. You can remake yourself. You can start a life that you're proud of, a life of honor and dignity. I swear I'll help you." Shannon wanted to tell Lurene that God would help her, too. But she hesitated. It would be too much. If the woman would just agree to try an honest life, begin making money, find a home where she was safe, then the Lord could come next.

Then Shannon knew she was doing it again. Making the same mistake she'd made before about treasure and streets of gold. She was thinking of Lurene laying up treasures on earth, as if that was the first step. But it wasn't. God was first. That's the only way for Lurene to truly change. "Lurene, you need to put your trust in God."

A scowl turned the corners of Lurene's lips down. "Why did I know you'd start preaching at me?"

"I'm not *preaching*, Lurene. I'm telling you what I've learned. I've spent the last two years of my life pursuing this treasure." Shannon swept her hand over the grassy flat. "I've ignored everything else in life. I've endangered good people."

She thought of the news that all of Lurene's companions were dead. "My actions led to the death of your friends."

"They aren't my friends," Lurene sneered.

Shannon wasn't sure if the lack of compassion in Lurene's attitude was good or bad. She wasn't grieving, but it was so cold, so heartless. Could someone as lost as Lurene find her way back to God and a decent life?

Of course, yes, but Shannon was sowing seeds on a soul as hard and stony as this canyon. "It's all been because of my obsession with finding a treasure here on earth, and I didn't even need the money."

Gabe had said it was for pride. He'd been right. Pride and a need to prove her father had loved something worthy.

"You might not need the money, but I do." Lurene rose to her feet and, her face a bitter mask, turned away.

"If there's gold here, you can have it. If there's not, team up with me and let's *both* of us find a better life, a life where we search for *real* treasure, the kind of life that leads to walking with Jesus in heaven."

Lurene turned back. She was listening, considering, but her doubts were plain.

"Just think about what I've said, please." Shannon got a quiet sense that if she pushed Lurene right now, she'd lose her forever. "Let's search this place."

Reluctantly, Lurene nodded.

Shannon turned back to the stone foundation before her. She dropped to her hands and knees inside the rectangle. There was no more pottery to be found there, so she began searching outside.

Lurene had gone to another spot, another home, and was searching just as diligently.

An area turned up shards. Digging with her bare hands as the sun pounded down on her back, Shannon wondered if she'd stumbled on a trash dump. She carefully laid the shards in a row.

Wiping away the sweat that poured off her forehead, she decided to take the bits of pottery back to St. Louis. In her imagination, she saw herself presenting them to the college professors who had mocked her father. She'd force them to see Professor Delmer Dysart as the visionary genius he was.

After all the searching, she admitted there was no gold. There never had been. This might not have been an Indian village. There may have been white settlers here at one time, even some of Coronado's explorers. But more likely hunters or trappers. They were a bold bunch.

A small squeak drew her attention to Lurene who had moved from one sight to the next, not poring over them like Shannon, lingering over shards of pottery.

Silently, Shannon prayed that Lurene would catch the pleasure of searching for history rather than gold. "Did you find something?"

"Look!" Lurene held up an object crusted with dirt, working over it, cleaning it with her bare hands. Her excitement was clear. Dirt and sweat streaked Lurene's face; her fingernails were caked with dirt. Her riding skirt had grass stains on the knees. She was a terrible mess, but the smile on her face gave Shannon hope.

Then the object caught a ray of the relentless sunlight. Shannon stood slowly, her eyes drawn to the object. As Lurene's hands worked over the dirty thing, Shannon saw a chain hanging from it.

Shannon walked toward Lurene. The world receded as Shannon approached. The gusting wind that cooled her sweat-soaked gingham blouse was the only sound in the world. The blazing sun's burning power gleamed off what looked, as Shannon approached, like a—a— "Is that a cross?"

Lurene jumped when Shannon got close.

"Stay back!" She'd forgotten the world just like Shannon had. Lurene whirled and stepped away, the object clutched to her chest.

"It's a cross. I see letters on it. Is it Spanish? No, Latin." Letters etched in a cross that looked like. . .solid gold? Shannon didn't care about the gold. Sunlight glinted rays of color off gemstones embedded in the necklace. "This is it. This is really it. Proof that they were here, the Spanish bishops."

"Stay back!" Lurene drew her gun. Shannon looked up to meet Lurene's eyes. Lurene looked crazed and frantic as she backed away.

So completely had Shannon been fixated on that golden cross, she hadn't seen Lurene.

"This is mine."

And hadn't Shannon promised just that? Hadn't she given

blithe permission to Lurene to keep any gold?

But now, Shannon saw the real thing and she wanted it. She wanted her hands on it. She wanted to feel the weight and study the jewels. And it should have been for the historical value, but it wasn't. It was greed. She was no better than Lurene. But this expedition was *hers*. Artifacts found on it were *hers*. Wealth and fame to be gained from it were *hers*.

"Come back here with that." Shannon was only distantly aware of the gun as she stalked toward Lurene and Lurene backed away. Shannon's eyes were locked on that cross. It was bigger than Lurene's hand, probably six inches tall and three or four wide. A golden chain spilled down between Lurene's fingers.

The gun cocked and lifted.

Shannon advanced, her desire for that gold stronger than her survival instincts.

Another gun cracked behind her.

She tore her eyes away from the cross and saw Gabe. He was most of the way across the butte. He must have climbed up the opposite side.

"Get back here, Shannon. She can't take us all."

Shannon looked again. On the flat mesa she saw Gabe standing erect, but Bucky's head appeared over the edge of the butte, and he rolled and scrambled to the nearest of the scattered rock foundations. They'd all be here soon.

Shannon hadn't even noticed Gabe climbing because she and Lurene could see nothing but gold. Gabe strode toward them, still out of range but closing the distance fast.

"Get away from her," Gabe shouted.

"I have to get that gold, Gabe. It's what I've been searching for all this time."

"No, you know gold isn't the answer to anything. I thought you said you'd finally figured out where your true treasure lies." Gabe's eyes were steady. Sensible. And they were only for her.

She tried. She fought all the uglier impulses that were tearing at her and tried to focus on what was really important. Life, friends, love, God. But the gold was like a siren song calling to her.

Bucky rose to his feet and started forward as another head appeared. Tyra.

Bucky looked past Shannon.

Shannon whirled around and saw Lurene racing for the brink of the butte. "Stop her!"

Shannon's grasp on reason returned as she realized the risk Lurene was taking. "No, stop! You'll fall."

Lurene reached the edge, near the crevasse they'd climbed up. Shannon remembered that stretch of sheer rock. Lurene didn't even look before she leaped.

"No!" Shannon raced after Lurene and skidded on her stomach, still in control enough not to jump over.

Lurene dangled by one hand five feet below, clinging to a scrub pine that grew on the steep incline.

Shannon saw the cross dangling from its chain on the same bush, but farther out. Lurene must have dropped it when she fell, but the cross had snagged and now hung there just beyond Lurene's reach. The cross wasn't important, not as important as a human life. "Grab my hand!"

"It's mine." Lurene didn't even look at Shannon. She reached for the cross, her voice cracking with anguish. "It will save me."

A root popped as the pine that held Lurene gave and then stopped. Rocks and dirt sifted loose with a clatter. Pebbles bounced down, down, down, and Shannon saw a handful of them bounce off the edges of the cave far below.

"No, Lurene. Look at me," Shannon shouted, demanding that Lurene turn her eyes back upward. "That necklace *will not save you*. Gold can't save anyone. Take my hand." A *whoosh* of liquid drew Shannon's eyes to the bottom of the butte again, and she saw the water pouring into the pit that had almost swallowed her whole only a short while before. That pit was right below them. With horror, Shannon remembered the sound of the water flowing into it as if it fell forever.

"Lurene, a fall from this height might be fatal, but survival is at least possible. But that hole in the ground is right below you. You'll never live through that fall. No golden necklace will help you if you're dead." Hadn't Shannon survived a fall from a cave? Nowhere near this far, but she'd slid more than fell, and she'd lived.

Shannon's stomach twisted to think of Lurene falling into that chasm. In this dangerous, wickedly beautiful land, Lurene might fall forever, for all eternity.

"Look at me, Lurene." Shannon scooted out farther, reaching. "Forget the gold. It's not worth your life. There's a pit down there. Remember that? If you fall into it, you'll die."

Lurene looked up at Shannon then back at the gold. Its chain tangled in the branch, the cross hanging down. Her hand reached, clawed for wealth. She inched farther out on the tree, and it curved down—the cross slipped farther yet. The chain clinked and slid until only one link hung from a narrow branch on the tree. "I can get it. I can reach it."

"No!" Shannon screamed, reaching down, down, down, scooting farther out until she was bracing her stomach—her tough belly—on the rim of the butte. "No, look at me."

The tree root gave another inch. Lurene jerked lower, and fear must have penetrated her obsession because she looked back at Shannon and, in an instant of clear thinking, turned her attention to survival. She reached up, her eyes now awash in fear but rational. Their fingertips touched. Shannon scooted forward again, too far out, but she had to risk it. She clasped Lurene's hand. Lurene looked at the pine tree, now hanging by only a few strong roots. Their grip held.

Then, as if she heard the song, Lurene looked back at the gold. "I can get it."

"You can't. You'll fall. The roots are giving way."

The call of wealth was louder. Lurene released Shannon's hand, and holding with one hand to the tree, she threw herself wildly toward the cross.

"Lurene, no!" Shannon made a desperate lunge for Lurene.

Lurene's grip gave. To the echoing sound of Lurene's screams, Shannon tumbled over the edge of the cliff.

Twenty~Four

———————✤———————

Screams fell away. The dull thud of a body striking stone became more distant and more awful.

"Shannon, no!" Gabe landed on the edge of the bluff and looked over the edge to see Shannon below him, dangling from a fragile, gnarled pine tree.

Lurene was far below, her plunging body landed with a horrible bone-crushing thud against a rocky cave opening. Her body bounced. He heard the ugly crack of her skull on stone. Then Lurene vanished into the depths of that gaping black maw.

Sickened, Gabe said, "Grab my hand, Shannon."

Pebbles popped as the pine tree pulled away from the cliff, dropping Shannon beyond Gabe's reach. Her strong arm clung to the branch. Her other arm was free; her sling hung around her neck. But she was still injured.

He'd thought it was *her* screaming, *her* falling. Gabe had felt as if his heart were torn from his chest and cast into the depths with her in those seconds. Gabe reached for the rope he'd hung from his belt after he'd lassoed Shannon last time.

Her shoulder? He hated this, but he was going to hurt her again. If only he could somehow get it around her tough little belly.

He opened a noose and dropped it down. "Thread your left arm through this then poke your head through."

"You've been on the verge of hanging me ever since we met." Shannon fumbled with the noose. Gabe saw her pain as she worked it over her arm.

The root gave again, and Shannon shrieked.

"Hurry."

She poked her head through the noose, and it looked for all the world like a hanging.

Gabe tightened the knot, not liking a bit the way it looked. It wasn't as good a hold as he needed at all, but he saw no way to make it better. "That tree won't hold much longer."

She looked up. "Ready."

Gabe was sickened to think of her dangling from the poorly placed noose. Worse yet, of her body slipping through it while he stayed safely above and watched her plummet into that pit, falling, dying. Fighting the collywobbles, he eased her weight off the pine tree a bit at a time to see how the knot held.

"When I get you lifted enough, let go of the tree and grab hold of the rope with your right hand. It's stronger. Then hang on tight while I lift you up. It'll spare your sore arm and hopefully keep the noose from strangling you." Gabe swallowed hard, keeping his eyes locked on hers, trying to connect with her and share his strength.

She looked away. "Gabe." Shannon seemed to be staring straight out over the basin.

He followed her gaze. "What?" Gabe prepared to lift her, praying it would work.

"If you just let me swing over there, I can get the necklace."

Necklace? Gabe looked farther out and saw what looked like an oversized cross dangling from a chain. Lurene had held it. He realized that now, but he'd been too busy trying to get to Shannon to really see what was in Lurene's hand. It was gold. Even from up here, Gabe knew instantly that this was what Shannon had been searching for.

"No. Forget it. We're getting you up from this cliff, and we'll worry about the necklace later."

"But it's proof, Gabe. It's proof that my father wasn't crazy. And it's gold, pure gold." Shannon reached with her wounded arm for that cross.

"Let it go and hang on to the rope."

"But it might fall in that pit. We need to get it now."

"Shannon! Hang on. The tree can't hold much longer. You need to have a grip on the rope."

With what looked like nearly superhuman effort, Shannon looked back at Gabe. The tree roots snapped. Shannon screamed and grabbed the rope with her right hand. The tree plummeted with the gold necklace twisting around it and vanished into the endless pit.

Pulling with every ounce of effort, his eyes never leaving her, Gabe saw Shannon take a solid hold on the rope. An instant later, she cleared the rim. Gabe grabbed her by the back of her shirt and dragged her over the ledge and fell backward. She landed on top of him with a *thud*. They lay gasping for breath for a few seconds, then Shannon wrapped her right arm around his neck and kissed him.

They were still kissing when someone cleared his throat. Loudly. Repeatedly.

Gabe opened his eyes to see Bucky. A man who was clean out of luck if he wanted to marry Gabe's woman.

Twenty~Five

Buck looked away from his woman kissing this stranger. He did his best, but he just couldn't envision Shannon as a rancher's wife.

Even seeing her out here in the wilderness, the image just wouldn't focus. She'd spent most of her life deciding between entertaining callers in the drawing room or the parlor, deciding whether to eat in the breakfast room, the casual dining room, or the formal dining room, or having a tray sent to her room.

Even while she'd plotted and planned her way to the underbelly of the world, she'd mostly done it on paper, writing and decoding and figuring. Shannon was going to die if she had to wash clothes by hand.

Buck had a feeling, though, that she wasn't going to let that stop her. He wondered if she could hire a housekeeper out west. Abe had said his brother was from Wyoming. Buck had only the vaguest notion where that even was. No drawing rooms there. Probably not one in the whole state. On the other hand, she'd be far from her mother, so maybe laundry by hand wasn't a bad tradeoff.

He looked at Tyra, who was frowning down at the man she'd intended to marry. He hoped she wasn't feeling too bad. She looked up at him and smiled. No, not too bad at all.

He moved over to put his arms around her waist just as her father came up and almost burned Buck all the way to the ground with a single glare. "Get your hands off my daughter."

Buck dropped his arm but not his smile. "Fine. For now."

Tyra gave him a lightweight punch in the arm. "Anybody got any ideas how we're gonna get home?"

With a tired sigh, Abe said, "Get up Gabe."

Gabe was standing up anyway. He helped Shannon to her feet, so mindful of her arm it caught in Buck's throat a bit. The man really was in love with Shannon. He had his work cut out for him.

"We've got our work cut out for us." Abe looked between the two couples then at Lucas Morgan. "We've got prisoners to fetch, a long trail out of here, and not much daylight left to figure it all out."

"Can we search the mesa for more gold artifacts before we do all that?" Shannon asked.

"No!" Five voices in unison absolutely refused.

Of course they spent the rest of the day up there hunting around.

Shannon bagged up a bunch of worthless bits of broken pottery. Buck didn't think the woman had much sense, but then she'd come a long way to leave empty-handed.

They barely got down to the bottom of the bluff before the sun set. They rounded up their prisoners, who'd gotten real tired of being bound hand and foot in the woods. Not that anyone cared much what they thought.

They were bedding down for the night just as an Indian couple came riding in. Buck braced himself for more trouble. Shannon ran forward and threw her arms around one of them as soon as they were on the ground. Buck realized it was an elderly woman, and between that and the hug, he decided this wasn't shooting trouble.

"How'd you get horses down here?" Buck asked. The barrage of words almost made him sorry he'd asked.

A third person with them dismounted, and his horse pranced sideways. The man's foot caught in the stirrup, and he fell over backward. The horse dragged him until Gabe rushed over and caught the reins.

"I hate horses."

Buck noticed a clerical collar.

Lucas helped the man to his feet while Tyra dusted him off and Gabe stripped the saddle. The horse stood quietly while Gabe worked.

The Indian couple was introduced, but the names were odd and Buck wasn't sure just how to pronounce them.

"And this is Parson Hank Ford." Shannon brushed a bit more dirt off the parson. "You know, I've been riding your black mustang ever since we were kidnapped."

"Terrible horse. I should have sold him years ago." Ford glared at the little black horse, which stood picketed a few dozen yards away, grazing with the other horses. As if the horse heard the parson talk about him, he raised his head, laid his ears back, and bared his teeth straight at the parson.

"He's as gentle and well behaved as any horse I've ever ridden, Parson. And I've never been in wild country like this before. And that horse you rode in on is mine. No trouble there either. I think you must be doing something to upset them."

"I am not!" The parson's demeanor really wasn't a good match for his white collar, but the Navajo folks seemed to accept and like him. So maybe he was just a lunatic on this one topic.

Gabe chose that moment to lead the horse past the parson. When it drew even, it jerked the reins loose from Gabe's hand and lunged at the parson and bit him.

"Get away from me!" The parson tugged on his arm. The horse's teeth stayed sunken into his sleeve.

There was a flurry of activity before Gabe got the parson free and led the horse away. The horse took a wild kick at the parson, which only missed because the parson was stumbling backward.

"The horses do seem to be a little unruly around you," Buck said.

"A few more years and there won't even be a horse left."

Everyone burst out laughing. Even the four prisoners, bound hand and foot, sitting by the fire.

"People have to get around, Parson." Gabe came back from picketing the parson's horse in time to catch the parson's comment. "Horses are the only way, unless you're gonna ride cowback."

Abe and Lucas laughed, and the parson's eyes narrowed.

"Maybe buffaloback, like Captain Hance," Abe said, which only made everyone laugh louder.

"I rode a bicycle back east. My whole family hates horses."

"Waste a' time hatin' horses." Lucas then looked between Tyra and Buck as if he had a better use for his time—hating the man his daughter wanted to marry.

"I got a nephew who thinks he can put a motor on a bicycle. A motor that will be run with a coal-oil engine. I'm really proud of him. Lots of people back east are working on that."

Buck knew that was true, but he doubted they'd ever come up with anything more dependable than a horse. "Like all of us will have our own personal trains? The streets are crowded now, Parson Ford."

The group laughed.

"Laying track right through the middle of the city—that'd take a lot of time and money." Shannon walked to Gabe's side and slid her arm around his waist. She'd been within his reach for all but a few seconds ever since he'd pulled her off that cliff.

"My nephew Henry will show all of you." The parson fumed. "You just wait and see. He's a bright boy. You watch for the name Henry Ford and just see if he doesn't build a carriage that runs without a horse. He'll be famous. You mark my words. But that doesn't get us out of the canyon. I'm not riding a horse if you found a way to walk."

"The man who guided us down here took us over a trail that'd make a mountain goat faint dead away," Buck said.

"Horseless carriage? Might as well fly around in the air like a bird." Gabe laughed and shook his head. "We'll figure out who's walking and who's riding in the morning. Until then, what would you think about performing a wedding ceremony, Parson Ford?"

A shout from the mouth of the canyon turned them all around again. Captain Hance came striding in. "Where'd all you folks come from? And where'd you get those horses?"

"Who's that?" Shannon asked.

Buck shook his head. "Long story."

Captain Hance started yelling, but by now Buck was so used to ignoring him, it didn't even distract him much.

Shannon looked between Buck and Gabe, and then her eyes settled on Buck. "Um. . .sorry, Bucky."

Shaking his head, Buck said, "I kinda figured it out when you were kissing him before. And call me Buck."

Shannon's brows arched.

"It's a terrible idea, kid," Abe said to his little brother.

"I'm not a kid, Abe." Gabe sounded just the littlest bit whiny. Then he went on in a much deeper tone of voice. "I quit being a kid about the time my cavalry troop had the first tussle with Apaches."

"What happened to your voice?" Shannon looked worried.

"Hush." Gabe pulled her close.

"She ain't gonna make you a good ranch wife, kid. You need to pick a woman who knows the West." Abe looked over at Tyra in a way that wasn't the least bit subtle.

Buck moved closer to her. He wasn't real familiar with the West, but he didn't think a brother could pick a wife for his brother.

Unless he was in the mood to beat on him until he said yes.

And the exact opposite might be true of vetoing a husband that a gritty western man didn't approve of.

Buck looked down to meet Tyra's eyes. She smiled, and Buck saw all he needed to see. "Why don't we make it a double wedding, Parson."

"What?" Lucas Morgan scowled and came over to drag his daughter away from Buck.

"I don't mind learning to be a rancher, Lucas. But I'll take some teaching. And if you don't like it, Tyra and I can go back to St. Louis and live there." He looked straight at Tyra's dancing, glowing eyes. "Can't we?"

"Oh yes, we can." She tugged at her father's grip, and the man must have been momentarily stunned because she got away and came back to wrap her arms around Buck's waist.

"You're getting married, too, Bucky?" Shannon asked.

He didn't see one speck of regret in her eyes, the brat. "I told you to call me Buck."

Shannon grinned. "Good idea."

They squabbled awhile, but in the end the parson performed a marriage ceremony in the heart of one of the most beautiful cathedrals on earth.

Abe was Gabe's best man. Then, because Buck was a little afraid to stand too close to his very disgruntled father-in-law, and honestly everyone else was either an outlaw or had already been in a ceremony, Buck had Hosteen Tsosi—whoever he was—stand up with him. With some relish, he imagined telling his mother a Navajo Indian had been the best man at his wedding. It'd about kill her.

They settled in for a night's sleep, about a third of their number tied up. Buck probably wouldn't have pushed his luck and tried to get his brand-new wife off by herself. But when Gabe dragged Shannon off with the announcement that he was going to set up his own camp and start his own fire, Buck got brave and went in the opposite direction with Tyra.

"It might be best to be a little bit away from your father anyway," Buck whispered to his pretty new wife as they walked away. "I'm not sure he didn't have plans to kill me in my sleep."

Tyra laughed and put her arm around his waist. She leaned her head against his shoulder, and Buck decided he was facing death and dismemberment on a ranch for the best possible reason. They rounded a clump of trees, and he said, "I love you."

She looked up. Dusk had settled over the canyon. The spot she'd chosen for them was in deep shadows. "I can't believe I went out for a ride with my pa and ended up at the bottom of the Grand Canyon married to a city boy." Her smiled widened, and he could see the gleam of her white teeth reflected by the light of the rising moon.

"And I can't believe I'll never have to listen to my mother nag me again, but I will probably spend the next few months being tortured by your father until I've learned enough about ranching that I'm no longer shaming him with every breath I take."

Tyra wrinkled her nose at him. "Dreamer, it'll probably take years."

"Really?" Buck's voice squeaked a little. He tried to control it, but the terror got in the way.

"Yep, and I love you, too. Just because my life took a crazy twist doesn't mean I'm not real happy about it. I am. I'm thrilled."

Buck leaned down and kissed that pretty smile. "I think you don't really know the meaning of the word *thrilled*, little lady."

And then he found out that until now, he hadn't known the meaning of thrilled either. But they discovered it together in the depths of the most beautiful place on earth.

Twenty~Six

So you'll come to Wyoming with me?" Gabe lit his fire from a piece of kindling he'd brought from the main camp and tried his best to erase the image of Lucas Morgan trying to burn him to death with his eyes while a city man married Tyra. Like that was Gabe's fault.

"Yes, if you'll come to St. Louis with me first and meet my mother."

Gabe was surprised how willing he was to follow her anywhere. "You act like those two are equal. How hard can it be to say hi to your ma?"

Shaking her head, she gave him a pitying look in the growing firelight. "Of course they're not equal. You've never met my mother. A Wyoming winter is nothing compared to the way she's going to blizzard down on you. . .on both of us. It's a good thing we got married out here. We can just present her with a *fait accompli*."

"A fate of what?"

"That means we got away with it."

"Oh, well, she might not want a ranch life for you, but she'll want you to be happy."

Shannon snorted.

"Uh. . .Shan, Wyoming is cold. You know that, right?"

"Sure, it's cold in St. Louis in the winter, too."

"I've been in St. Louis in the winter." It was Gabe's turn to snort, but he suppressed the impulse. "Stopped off there after I left home and spent a few weeks one January waiting to head west with my cavalry troop. The wind can get a little stiff, but it's not the same kind of cold."

"I'll be fine."

"And it snows. Oh, does it snow."

Shannon smiled. "I need to get my clothes and some furniture left to me by my grandmother, and I have an inheritance I'll need to take to Wyoming. We can take my family's train car to Ranger Bluffs."

"Uh no, we can't. There aren't any train tracks there."

Shannon looked taken aback. "Oh well, how do we haul my things then?" Gabe's stomach sank. His wife was in for some real surprises.

"I guess we can hire a mule skinner to freight it out there." Gabe tried to remember where the closest railhead was. Cheyenne for sure had one. Salt Lake City? Maybe they'd built a line a little closer since he'd left. Wherever the train came, it wasn't close and there was a lot of rugged ground to cover to get to Ranger Bluffs. "How much furniture do you have?"

"Oh, lots. My grandmother left everything to me. Enough to furnish the whole house comfortably." Shannon turned, looking alarmed.

Gabe remembered that she'd cried before. He braced himself to say whatever he needed to prevent that.

"Is your house already full of furniture?"

"No, I've never really lived in the place. I stayed there for a few weeks, right after I bought it, and then I got to wandering. No furniture." Since Gabe's house was one room, about fifteen feet square, he had no doubt that was true. There'd been a few things, but he was pretty sure they'd collapsed or been stolen by now.

"Good, because Grandma's mansion was three stories. We'll have plenty."

With a quiet sigh, he decided he'd have to add on a couple of rooms. "We'll work out all the details as we go along. What's important is that we love each other and want to spend our lives together."

Gabe pulled her into his arms, heartily tired of talking. He kissed her until she seemed to have given up planning out their lives. He lowered her to the bed they'd made beside the fire and forgot everything that could go wrong.

But he did have one worry. "I'm sorry we didn't find any more gold for you, Shannon." Gabe lay beside her, the fire flickering and crackling. The scent of wood smoke wafting around them.

He felt purely at home here. He fit in the wild country. He hoped his new wife did, too. "There are other buttes in this place. There could be other villages tucked away." It worried him, this strange affliction of his wife's for gold. "Are you really disappointed? We could hunt around here more."

Shannon shifted closer to him. "I've thought about it."

The night chilled, as it always did, after the brutal heat of the day. Which was reason enough for Gabe to pull Shannon closer.

Shannon nestled her head on Gabe's shoulder. "And I decided it's right that the gold is buried with Lurene. She was willing to die for it. It should be with her."

"Do you want me to try and climb down in that pit and look for the cross?" They'd looked down and couldn't see the bottom. Gabe had dropped a rock, and they'd heard it land—eventually. But the edges were jagged. Maybe the cross was hung up somewhere. Gabe decided they could try again to see where that hole in the ground went.

"I think we've spent enough time dangling from ropes." She rose up so she could see his eyes. "And honestly, Gabe, I'm a little bit surprised at you for offering."

Gabe blinked in surprise. "Why? I want you to be satisfied with what we've done down here."

"Why are you worried about me being satisfied?" She kissed him, and he almost forgot the point he needed to make.

"Well"—he kissed her back—"because. . ."

She wasn't even trying to talk this out.

"Uh. . . honest, Shannon, I don't think—" For a while he really didn't think. Not one bit. But then it came back to him what he was trying to say. "I don't think we'll be back. Anything you want done down here, we'd better do now."

Shannon slid her arms tightly around his neck. "Listen, cowboy, the only thing we need to do right now is be. . .married." She lowered her lips to his and blocked out the beautiful moonrise and the stunning sight of the Grand Canyon in starlight.

Gabe's last thought was to give his worries to God. They'd work everything out. After all, they had a lifetime to do it.

Then together they found the closest thing to paradise a man and woman could find before the day came for them to walk on streets of gold.

Discussion Questions

1. Have you ever been to the Grand Canyon? Discuss your impressions of it.

2. Have you ever seen or heard of Mesa Verdi? What do you think happened to the people who build those cliff houses?

3. Talk about the ancient history of America. With nothing written down, it is nearly all lost outside of archeological discoveries, and many conclusions may qualify as pure guesses. What do you think are some possible things that are lost in history?

4. Why do you think that North America prior to Colonization didn't progress—in the sense of building cities, using the wheel, working with iron, having a written language, etc.,—like other continents did?

5. Can you imagine what it must have been like for someone to enter the Grand Canyon without a map or a guide or a clue about what to expect? How would you have reacted to what you saw?

6. Did the book capture the awe, the wonder of people seeing the Grand Canyon for the first time?

7. Was Shannon really interested in her father's legacy? Or did she just fall into his obsession? How so?

8. Did Gabe's need to rescue a woman come from his feelings of failing his mother? Or was he just avoiding going back to his ranch or meeting his brothers?

9. Recently a man came forward and admitted he had a secret trail down into the Grand Canyon that he'd found years ago, so the idea that there could be many undiscovered ways down is supported by this. Did it seem outlandish that the wild mustangs could have a trail that no one recognized until they saw the horses running up it? Why?

10. Discuss the Seven Cities of Gold and why a fable like this evolved?

11. Did Shannon and Gabe need to go after that gold to find happiness? If Shannon had given up her dream, would it have always bothered her? Why?

12. What happens next? Bucky isn't a good match for Tyra and life as a rancher. Gabe is in for some surprises when Shannon's furniture shows up. What do you think the future holds for these couples?

ABOUT THE AUTHOR

MARY CONNEALY writes romantic comedy with cowboys. She is a Christy Award finalist and a Carol Award winner. She is the author of the Lassoed in Texas Trilogy, the Montana Marriage Trilogy, and the Sophie's Daughters Series.

Mary lives on a Nebraska ranch with her husband, Ivan, and has four grown daughters: Joslyn (married to Matt), Wendy, Shelly (married to Aaron), and Katy. And she is the grandmother of two beautiful grandchildren.

You can find her online at these sites: www.maryconnealy.com, www.mconnealy.blogspot.com, www.seekerville.blogspot.com, and www.petticoatsandpistols.com. Mary loves to hear from her readers. Write to her at mary@maryconnealy.com.